Mares, Foals & Ferraris

Recollections of a Farmer in the Sport of Kings

By A. Allan Juell

Cover art (Vanity Fair Print Co.) vanityfairprints.com
Dedication (Ashley Cunningham) seedesignstudio.com
Small horse inserts (Ron & Joe) ronandjoe.com
Hand iluustrations: (Dennis Haskett) dhaskett@yahoo.com

First published by Dog Ear Publishing
4010 W. 86th Street, Ste H
Indianapolis, IN 46268
www.dogearpublishing.net

ISBN: 978-145750-492-1

TABLE OF CONTENTS

ABOUT THE AUTHOR

A. ALLAN JUELL has been writing about horses and the…well, those folks that tend to hang around with large, hairy mammals for roughly thirty years. His work has appeared in periodicals such as the *Chronicle of the Horse, EQUUS, Western Horseman, Thoroughbred Times, Anvil Magazine* and the *Washington Thoroughbred*, the latter as a columnist, that work compromising the core material for this book. He also wrote for many regional and international publications, including the newspaper trade. He also managed to pick up a few obscure literary awards along the way, as well as copious amounts of 'enlightened' criticism. Why they published his junk is anybody's guess. Probably desperate for copy.

He spent about twenty-five years as a farrier and farm manager and about fifteen years as an itinerant journalist, wandering most of the world's habitable continents and questionable bars. He holds a degree in history (international affairs) and sometimes attempts to further confuse the world's problems at Histryonics.com., or offering completely useless equine advice at Horsetrionics.com. He currently resides somewhere in North America, but nobody is quite sure where. Homeland Security is looking into the matter.

"Mares, Foals & Ferraris" is a one-year compression of some thirty-odd years managing and breeding racehorses. He always preferred jumpers – Grand Prix horses. But a lot of people end up in certain places due to random physics, a strong desire to eat on a regular basis or simply getting off at the wrong bus stop. Einstein was working on this theory when he died. Too bad.

This book is meant to be fun – perhaps educational if you happen to be a horse. However, if you plan on reading specific chapters to your *own* horse, it will be necessary to buy two copies since a horse's eyes are on the side of his head, not the front. No, glasses won't help. It's an engineering problem. God decided that it would be a good idea if a horse could watch the road and *you* at the same time. Less accidents that way.

The book is considered fiction, but then again most fiction is little more than random truths circling the nucleus of imagination. The French refer to this exercise as a *roman á clef.*   Roughly translated, it is how one introduces one's mistress at a formal event. We'll let the lawyers figure out the details.

For *Denise*.

Who worked hard,
played hard,
& couldn't quite stay for the finish.
Who owned 257 pairs of shoes
& danced at least one dance
in every pair.

And

To *all* the children of the storms.

PREFACE

SOME KIDS NEED a connection *with animals. You can't pick your parents. You cannot undo the past. Some kids find more trust, more understanding in the animal kingdom. Please read between the lines in this tome. No finger is pointed, no animosity toward the adult world is intended. (Well, maybe a little.) A parent is a mere mortal and humans are simply what they are. Children remain the most fragile eco-system on Earth, primarily because at some point in their lives they will become the leaders and custodians of that very same Earth. I look back at a pivotal moment in my own life and perhaps a billion other lives as well. October 22, 1962. It was a Monday and it seemed quite likely that this particular week would never see Friday. I somehow think that both Kennedy and Khrushchev stepped back from the brink, looked to their children and grandchildren standing on the outskirts of the apocalypse and called it a day. That is the power and the frailty of a single child.*

While this book is meant to be fun, good bathroom material as they say, it is also an appeal for a kind of humanity that encompasses more than the immediacy of the moment, the ingrained lessons of the past, or the mounting anger that precipitates the first shots fired in any conflict – personal or political. The conduct of war, by any definition, by any measure, annihilates hope, the one constant for a sustainable future. Soldiers are not alone in the suffering and dying embodied in a point of view, some arbitrary line in the sand, or the always dichotomous verdict in the trial of right versus wrong. Other wars with unseen casualties litter the landscape of societies cloaked in the hard veil of contradiction — that myopic dance of the uninformed, unwilling and ultimately unknowing. Sure, the victims testify at these trials, but somewhere between the Bible and the back door, the testimony gets lost. Sanctuary is not always a cradle for the frightened and the weak. All too often it is the untended grave of an inconvenient truth.

"My Friend Flicka" doesn't live here. We do. As I put the finishing touches on this manuscript, this country of ours is once again immersed in

far-flung wars over issues and real estate that few of us understand, comprehend or can even find on a map. I guess the local cemetery has a few vacancies. National policy planners seem to suffer certain vacant moments of their own: a chronic disregard of history, and perhaps worse, a self-ordained hubris once reserved for long-dead, lesser gods. We, the empowered few, dictating to the many. History is littered with the bones of the arrogant and self-righteous. How will the present be remembered by the future, once we become the past?

More than anything, this book is about one of those children who gave up on humanity and chose a life with animals: supposedly stupid, soulless beasts that asked little, yet were seemingly willing to hand over their lives and sense of security in return. In this contemporary world of ours, most people do not know what it means to trust someone or something unconditionally, and in our continuing paradigm of random violence and ambivalent love, the lessons offered and painfully learned quite often become the sole inheritance of these 'children of the storms.'

About now, most readers may be wondering when the fun part begins. Patience isn't necessarily a human virtue, and in my case it took about fifty years to locate some. That, combined with the ability to finally realize that the Greeks were right: tragedy and comedy are merely two versions of the same story.

Throughout this book, I look at history and war as a greater parallel to the subtle and sometimes viperous interactions found in the most basic of human relationships – the family. In some ways I'm trying to justify an expensive education. The truth is probably closer to a selfish and personal need to intellectualize the opaque realms of emotion, a process that is doomed to a sad and ultimately disheartening defeat. Or maybe triumph. Victory echoed in the laughter found in an optimistic kind of cynicism. Because there really isn't much else left at the end except the punch line from a Godly or godless universe. I guess that is part of the appeal, and perhaps the advantage found in working with horses. They leaven the bread and don't really give a shit about the rest. They'll listen to a ten-minute tirade on some vague injustice and respond with, "Yeah great, where's dinner?"

The characters in this book are inventions, composites – in many cases, wishful thinking. The era was one of the toughest (are there easy ones?) in American history: Vietnam to the collapse of the Soviet Union and onward toward what appears to be a new, though still pretty convoluted world order. The irony, if it actually qualifies as one, is the continuity of war as the supporting actor in a singular and frequently complicated life – or simply a case of trying to stay alive long enough to define that life's worth. Begs the question of just how we really define civilization under the rather artificial guise of a social construct. Or better yet, as an evolutionary process that seems oddly doomed to orchestrate its own extinction. So given those rather bleak options, it would appear that we define civilized society on the rather schizophrenic examples offered up in the obtuse realms of human behavior. If that is really the case then maybe we need a new model, or perhaps a less sophisticated set of rules. Or we simply need to try harder at weighing the perceived value of our lofty expectations against the hard reality of a selfish world.

I was a late bloomer. Really late. I got my first job at thirteen and left for college when I was forty-one. The first few chapters make a somewhat lame attempt at explaining the delay. Yeah, a woman, a horse, a school bus, a lot more horses, another woman, a racetrack...a cat. And an accident. An end that turned out to be a beginning.

The pity-pot is this padded toilet seat you sit on like a dethroned monarch and claim either mental constipation or some problem with your fan club. You could eat a box of Ex-Lax, but then, that might ruin the comfort of denial. Puckering up is the only way to hold on to the throne, but nobody can pucker-up forever – and you still have that question concerning the thunderous lack of applause. So the only choice is to either pull up your pants or flush the son-of-a-bitch. I had a small bathroom. The Fat Lady wouldn't fit. You see, I'd always confused my various careers with my life, assuming quite illogically that I would somehow be missed when it was over. No one had explained to me that life charges an admission fee and it always comes due when you can least afford to pay it.

Choices always seem limited under those circumstances. While I don't necessarily believe in God, I do believe that most accidents aren't really accidents. Instead, they kind of remind me of football. A serious guy in a striped shirt throws a yellow handkerchief on the ground and explains to you that you need to take a look at your behavior. That, and a fifteen- yard hike in a direction you hadn't planned on going. Life doesn't always need God, but it sure needs referees.

I decided rather late in life to go to college. Actually, that wasn't a decision – more like a way to trade in my pity pot on something more productive. I still sat on it for a while longer, but it was disguised as a chair and I was able to comfortably hide my face behind a book. The resume of a washed-up farm manager with a bad limp hardly warranted a second interview, especially when the sum total of my marketable skills required the presence of a horse. Most HR departments balked at that stipulation, noting somewhat sardonically that my horse didn't appear to be a US citizen. Evidently in the newly discovered world of 'political correctness' and 'social sensitivity' in the workplace, they weren't allowed to ask him if he was a horse…only a citizen.

Even so, I convinced myself that there was a connection between a college education and intelligence — something potential employers were bound to notice even if most of my friends (or the horse) didn't. Since I was a pretty good writer, I became an English major, convinced that reading fourteen Dick Francis' novels in a row constituted a complete education. Well, maybe. To tell the truth, I was what is known in the college bizz as a major-flipper. After three semesters of Shakespeare (he was a woman, by the way), I gave up the hunt for literary purity and switched to…no, not veterinary medicine — history. Yeah, I bought one of those sweaters with the elbow patches and smoked a pipe. Never mind what was in it. What finally forced me to reconsider my educational goals was roughly a toss-up between Kenneth Patchen's "The Journal of Albion Moonlight" and a course in literary criticism. I tried to deconstruct Patchen's rather convoluted allegory on the folly of looking for decency (or directions) in the middle of a world war. This was a book I started reading in 1967 and quietly dropped off in a coffee shop about three decades later. That was my way of surrendering without too many witnesses. Besides, the only thing that English majors really do is create more English majors. Closest thing to an academic perpetual motion machine ever invented, whereas in the case of history, the topics were centered on real and dynamic human motivation: discovering the brilliance behind something like invading Russia in winter. Especially after another brilliant guy tried it a century before. Stuff like that. Beat the hell out of a Marxist critique of "The Wasteland."

My senior thesis involved Benito Mussolini. He seemed to remind me of my completely useless alter-ego, which I carried around in an oversized steamer trunk that I would happily open and share with anybody dumb enough to ask me two questions in a row. The trunk was full of disguises, facades, deflections and an assortment of masks, most of which were either angry or apparently over-medicated in some fashion. Around 1988, a horse named CJ, who actually had more unhappy issues than I did, smashed my grand steamer trunk at the very moment when I seemed to need it the most. The trunk went to the dump and me to the hospital. And nobody came to visit because nobody knew who I really was. Instead, they all went to the dump, vainly searching for the battered trunk and what mysteries it might reveal.

Since most of my life seemed centered around the pitfalls and prospects adherent to war, Benito seemed like a fascinating subject to investigate. I actually considered Hitler, but he seemed a little too close to home. Not frightening, but darkly predictable. I couldn't quite bring myself to explore the subtle nuance of one more sociopath:

"Okay then. We'll gas the Jews, retards and the Russians first."

"Sure boss. The guys want to know if they get overtime."

Sounded too familiar. Nonchalance scared the hell out of me. Still does.

I was intrigued by *fascism* since it was a rather incomplete political ideology, happy to proclaim what it wasn't without really explaining what it was. On some levels, Mussolini himself suffered from the chronic ailment of most revolutionary (or reactionary) figures in that forcing radical change is one thing, administering it quite another. A little like Ché Guevara trying to run a car wash. Radical thinking lacks that power of ignition when there's still cash in the till. I suppose my own revolutionary notions from the 1960's played a role in my choice of characters – no. I saw a photo of Mussolini kissing a horse. He had the heart of a romantic. Never figured Hitler would kiss a horse. Not the type. Plus I had a genealogy/political affiliation problem: it appeared that my mother's family had a few Nazis in the woodpile and father's relatives were Vikings. (No, not Minnesota – the other ones.) That probably explained both my politics and my general lack of moderation. Teachers claimed it had something to do with my attention span and too much sugar. I knew better.

Mussolini had his own unique fan club in the United States which included the likes of Andrew Carnegie, Henry Ford and yes, Franklin Roosevelt, folks who clearly witnessed the ravages (and certain advantages) of selective greed unleashed by a weak central government. What was the 'New Deal,' other than the federal government enforcing its veto power over the board of directors? And of course, it offered an alternative to communism, viewed by many Americans as a very unpleasant alternative to capitalism. Did I say many? Coming on the heels of the depression and the dust bowl, 'many' might be overstated. Socialism, communism and *fascism* did offer two rather appealing alternatives to capitalism's ingrained social schism: accountability and a perceived economic umbrella – a leaky one at best, but better than a sheriff's sale. The flip-side of all three systems, at least philo-sophically, is that they required a dictator. And we did have Roosevelt working on a fourth term.

My professor, who happened to be English, (which seemed terribly important to him at the time) was not impressed with my dissertation, or the fact that most of my footnotes were in Italian. I thought it was a nice liter-ary touch; he in turn accusing me of acting "too American for my own good." Snobbery aside, the final straw seemed to be the five paragraphs devoted to Benito's horse. Hell, they made a nice couple of sorts. Seemed to be the only time Mussolini smiled. He didn't look too happy later hang-ing upside down in Milan's central square with his girlfriend, but at least they didn't hang the horse. However, I'm pretty sure at some point they probably ate him. Oh, I got a C-, which is what a university does when they just want to get rid of you. It didn't help either that I was 44 years old. They wanted that student loan money back before I was eligible for Social Security. Oh. You might be wondering if the degree boosted my employ-ment prospects? Not really. I went from 'under qualified' to 'over quali-fied,' though a couple of people did show some lukewarm interest in my horse. So I returned to the life of an itinerant journalist. Basically, that's a homeless guy who writes high-brow graffiti on condemned buildings.

I did learn one thing from Mussolini's mixed up political non-system: that being the notion that I was probably a *fascist* farm manager. I mean, think about it. I was a quasi-dictator, I controlled the labor force, (a cat and a backhoe operator) and I seemed to have my hands all over the 'supply and demand' sector: hay, oats, manure and diesel fuel. Plus, my subjects were either too naturally rambunctious to form a quorum, or bound to the sacred oath of the Herd Lodge, which basically meant that in either case, it would take years for any of them to pick a leader. And if they did, well, as soon as the election was over, I'd just sell the winner.

Had to be a downside, but I wasn't seeing it just yet.

I was born in 1951. *Cold War, Korea – no cable TV. Really, no TV at all unless you considered our neighbor down the street. He had the only one on the block and mostly it was like staring at a washing machine on spin cycle. He'd fiddle with the rabbit ears for hours, never realizing that the attention span of an eight-year old boy is under ten seconds. I guess if they'd had Ritalin in those days I might have caught a couple of good Westerns. Instead, we'd wander down to the swamp (our favorite hang-out) and have a rock fight or something.*

I lived in a north Seattle neighborhood called Ridgecrest. It was a grimy, working class suburb of another suburb. The houses were all two-bedroom ramblers of no distinction. Our house sat on a corner, with two intersecting streets that lacked a stop sign. So every few days a couple of cars would make a bad assumption about the right-of-way law and end up all smashed to pieces in our side yard. Sometimes it was a little gory, but a lot more entertaining than opening a Kool-Aid stand.

As neighborhoods go, it was probably okay for a kid that spent most of his free time in the woods or the big swamp. A few blocks away we had an old movie theater that seemed to go broke a lot and an ice cream parlor that tolerated us on those frequent days when real customers were in short supply. Probably the biggest event in those early days was the construction of Interstate 5 – they ran it right through our swamp. I'm sure we protested loudly – mostly to each other, but nobody seemed to be listening anyway. Looking back, it seemed that the only thing the neighborhood really needed was a higher divorce rate and maybe a few more stop signs. Might have made the place a little less prone to a whole assortment of accidents and misunderstandings.

Most of the adult men on the block participated in the second big war – World War II. Those that didn't weren't likely to talk to those that did, and us kids always knew who was who by the tattoos. Or by the loud voices, the smell of alcohol or the arrival of the police. It didn't seem that anybody ever went to jail and that was probably because most of the cops had the same tattoos. So like old war buddies seem to do, they'd just stand around outside next to the patrol car, drinking beer and smoking a lot of cigarettes. I would just watch carefully through a crack in my bedroom curtains. When you're scared, it's a good idea to keep your eye on the source of all the excitement.

In school, we had nuclear war drills. They were a bit like earthquake drills, but much stupider. It was like, "Right, crawling under my desk is going to stop an A-Bomb." The worst part was getting the gum out of your hair. There's a lot of used gum under those desks. The girls would giggle a lot and us boys would make fake fart noises, which caused more giggling. That was because nobody could tell for sure where the fart came from. Only later, alone with a friend or two, did we talk about getting killed in a nuclear war. We'd seen dead animals on the road, but that seemed to be a different kind of dead. Ours needed to be more like television. When somebody died on television it was always at the end of the show, or off-camera in another room. And if it was re-run season, then they were alive again right after the commercial. Death was always an assumption unless it was lying in the street. Television made the whole thing seem pretty painless and a lot more appealing than the truth.

I think a lot of us kids lived in fear – irrational maybe, but also very real. We were indoctrinated into a world that assumed that nuclear war was survivable. Safeway sold fallout shelters – right next to the patio furniture and barbecues. Collective denial was at an all-time high. Neighbors were busy digging up their backyards and hoarding canned water. Psychiatrists were seeking out other psychiatrists in search of a cure for the pandemic of wishful thinking. There was this folksy rationality among normally clear thinking adults that made a kid want to break most of the kneecaps of the parental world. Suburbia was digging in for a minor inconvenience. After a couple of weeks, we'd sweep up the radioactive dust and have a block party. All the Reds would be dead and the President would light the national Christmas tree. Nobody asked about my nightmares.

During the Cuban Missile Crisis, a bunch of us (we called ourselves the Rat Gang) crawled into a large sewer pipe near the swamp. We figured we were toast. Typically, we brought the necessary supplies: model airplane collections, favorite yo-yo's, baseball mitts. One kid brought his dog, but it ran off anyway. I guess the dog hadn't read a newspaper lately. We were well trained: don't look at the flash, get ready for the shock wave, figure out where you are in relation to the twelve-mile radius, that silly piece of geographical nonsense that was supposed to separate the annihilated from the merely deep-fried. We sat in the pipe for over fifteen hours. Finally, we got hungry and decided to go home. The world didn't end after all. Too bad. I had to go to the dentist the next day. That was a tough call. World war versus having your molars drilled? Khrushchev or Novocain? History is not always fair. But I suppose somebody had to feed my dog.

I guess that's where it began. A dog that needed feeding whether the world cared or not. A world where parents espoused love but practiced *something else, where political ideology, prejudice and personal agendas overwhelmed the gentle faith we held – or tried to grasp in a world that had apparently lost its mind. Like I said, Flicka doesn't live here. I do. There is a lot of fun in this book, but concurrently, a lot of pain and growth. If you get at least three good laughs a chapter, my job is somewhat complete. Somewhat? I figure if you're hanging out in the bathroom having a good laugh, you probably won't have time to help wreck **our** dysfunctional little planet.*

INTRODUCTION

A BRIEF HISTORY OF THE HORSE

IN THE BEGINNING there was man. There was also a great deal of volcanic activity, quite a few unfriendly animals and far too much responsibility for a guy with a club and a few rocks. Take-out food was a Mastodon with an attitude. Male bonding consisted of who had the biggest club. This meant a lot of trees bit the dust in the ongoing quest for a weapon of mediocre destruction. Global warming has a lot to do with man's continuing need to wave around a big stick.

God got wind of this problem and ripped out a few ribs from the guy with the biggest chunk of lumber, thus creating woman. Most of us were pretty shocked. She looked and acted different. It wasn't so much that she had gained a couple of parts and lost another one, but that she had this organizing fetish. She swept out the cave, threw away the old animal parts and insisted that we not only dress for dinner, but that we actually cook it. The latter was rather shocking since we hadn't yet discovered fire. Sure, we had that volcanic thing, but making the leap to a family barbecue was a bit of a stretch. Then there was that insistence about brushing and flossing after meals. Normally, we would smear dirt on our faces and dance a little jig, celebrating the fact that *we* weren't the meal. Kind of like a trip to a bar to celebrate another 49ers loss. Meanwhile, these women creatures were busy building nests, intent on capturing something that they probably didn't want anyway. A little while later, sex was invented and the whole thing kind of got confused. Instead of running from boulder to boulder, fighting to the death with hairy things, we started worrying about the mortgage on the cave. Civilization was invented. Took the fun out of hunting and gathering.

Man continued down the evolutionary path, even if he wasn't real sure what that meant. On weekdays he created turmoil, famine, war, glory and conquest, returning home and claiming he'd been to a ball game. All this activity changed the landscape, rewrote history, created new ideologies that eventually led to the formation of the John Birch Society, the Nazi Party, the Mafia, Lyndon Johnson's cameo with the dog, the sinking of the Titanic, hippies, the A-bomb, cloning sheep and most importantly, the cable shopping network. It also led to draft beer, the Super Bowl, guys playing golf on the moon and the idea that a movie star could be President *and* conquer the Soviet Union by broadcasting around the clock re-runs of "Bonzo" on *Radio Free Europe* while happily re-writing a new sequel to "Star Wars" with the Joint Chiefs of Staff. The world was finally marginally democratic, in the sense that everybody was a little too worn out to marshal up the troops for one more mindless shooting spree. Fighting to the death was just too damn time consuming. *Law and Order* was on at nine, and well, frankly, men can't figure out how to run a VCR anyway, so world order was once again maintained through gender incompetence and the Nielson Ratings.

By man's side throughout this tumultuous history was...oh no, it is not who you think. It was his horse. Woman was a little busy perfecting the art of 'guess what I'm thinking now?' Besides, this is a book about horses, which are a hell of a lot less confusing than human relationships or foreign intrigue and, admittedly, a lot safer to write about. But don't count on that kind of restraint. Being male, I subscribe to that notion of "going where no man has gone..." Hell, we're going to go there anyway.

Unlike the dog with its tail-wagging, self-serving, groveling, drooling propensity to suck up to people, the horse <u>pretends</u> it likes us. It doesn't. Most horses, aside from the occasional free-thinker (a euphemism for intentional, well calculated stupidity), sincerely believe that their eating habits are really a statement about lifestyle: *Equus caballus* – 'a large unfriendly mammalian herbivore, known to be a casual browser.' Which really means fat, unemployed and disinterested, cruising the salad bar in search of free samples. They are also apolitical, which kind of complicates the riding madly into war thing. They pull the conscientious objector argument or sign-up with a mail-order ministry: *The Church of Latter-Day Alfalfa Eaters.*

On top of that, horses have the inherent problem associated with the prey versus predator equation. In the old days it was known as saber-tooth tiger denial, in that the tiger is really only a problem for the other guy — the guy that doesn't have a lot to say because a large cat just ate his lips. Which, given the tiger's over-engineered orthodontic accessories, begs the question: How did these cats eat anything bigger than a bug with those fangs? They were like a hairy walrus that couldn't swim. Probably explains the purpose of extinction. God was working on the woman thing, so the animal kingdom was getting all kinds of spare parts and screwed-up orders. Same deal as your luggage at the airport. Fourteen different employees with no clue as to what happened to your underwear and socks or why a wildebeest in a tuxedo happens to be piloting the plane.

Prehistoric horses misjudged the future potential of man. Sure, some horses ended up on the menu at the local eateries, no doubt the clumsy ones or the exceptionally gullible individuals that really thought that the *nice* guy down the street just needed his lawn mowed. A few barbecued horse steaks here or there allowed the rest of the equine community to fumble through life in the accustomed fashion: eat, sleep and pass gas. Similar to a slow day in the US Senate. Man, as a predator, was still in the 'inept' stage, normally only catching anything as big as a horse by accident. Most of the menu choices were of a different, non-labor intensive undertaking: lemmings falling off cliffs, fish learning to walk on land for the first time, mugging hyenas – that sort of thing. Probably a lot of experimental eating as well.

"Here Bob, try this."

"Ah geez! It tastes like a dirty foot!"

"It is."

Still, early man did ingrain a certain paranoia in horses about human intentions. It got stamped somewhere in their psyches, explaining why a horse in a two-acre field can't be caught. They don't see a ten-year old girl with a carrot — they see a knife and fork with a Neanderthal attached to it.

One day, everything changed. A bungling cave dweller fell off a rock and was lucky enough to land astride one of his favorite meals. Lacking anything suitable for dispatching this sudden windfall, the caveman simply held on tight and pointed the horse toward home. Arriving at his rock-strewn cave, all the other guys were pretty impressed. The women, well they could deal with a few fish guts in the kitchen sink, but a 900lb pissed-off horse would require some major remodeling. Still, they all pitched in and presented the great hunter with a fancy necklace made out of some-body else's teeth, unaware that two historic traditions had just been born: the horse show and the pot-luck dinner.

Quite naturally, they ate the last minute guest. And for the next six months or so they chewed on the bones. But the seed had been planted. An idea festered in the dark recesses of these early male *sapiens*. Why carry your food when it will walk home on its own? Female *sapiens* weren't quite as impressed. Three hundred pounds of leftovers and no refrigeration. Well, they could get a pair of slacks and an accessory or two from the carcass, but they'd still need some new earrings, maybe a nice belt and somehow they'd have to convince the men to dance with them, rather than each other. And to stop *them* from smearing blood on their faces. Not attractive.

Though a little rubbed on the cheeks isn't bad...

It took a few centuries to digest the magnitude of that thinking. Sure, chickens were kind of stupid and cows were a little slow, more suitable for stuffing into a *fondue* pot, but horses were pretty speedy if you could figure out how to drive one. A little like a *Fiat* with right-hand drive. Before long it became apparent that it was possible to gallop up to a neighbor, thump him on the head, raid his refrigerator and gallop off into the setting sun. Two more traditions: fast food and motorized warfare. All in the same afternoon! The horse was suddenly elevated to a new stature. No longer would man casually dine on the public transportation system. Horse was going to live in the house. Woman was going to have to accept man's new best friend...within a week, man invented the barn.

The horse made war really fun again. Before, it was this endless procession, trudging here and there, always too tired to fight anyone once you arrived. Especially if the motel didn't have room service. Start a cranky fire with wet wood, cook a few stale beans or one of the slaves, finally get to sleep about midnight and the manager forgets the wake-up call! The other army is standing around the battlefield tapping their feet, wondering what the hell is going on. You get to the meeting late, but the other army got bored and went off to pick a fight with somebody else.

What's the emperor going to think? There goes the year-end bonus, the mileage allowance, the frequent trudging miles, the dental policy, the paid vacation, the discount on the swords and other fighting type junk – the $500 deductible on the health policy, especially the part about pre-existing conditions, like that left arm you sort of lost last month in that disagreement with those Hun guys. If it had been something like a head, or a few major organs, then it would have been a moot issue – oh, the burial policy. A bunch of vultures in the unemployment line. Geez, nothing is simple.

The real conundrum in all this was that most horses didn't share man's primal slant on running and fighting. They were thinking about throwing the whole mess at an outside arbitrator. Maybe form a union and include all the horses. No more falling for this nonsense about the good horses and the bad horses or saving women from barbarians. Near as the horses could tell, everybody was a barbarian, including the women. And no matter which slob won, the food didn't get any better or the hours shorter. And the guys still expected a ride home.

Truth was, the majority of horses felt that the trade-off of being eaten versus working the whole day was not all it was cracked up to be. They all felt that thundering across the steppes for a mile or so was okay, but invading Greece on a hot afternoon was another matter entirely. Sweaty leather, a bunch of guys with spears – I mean really, for an animal that considered hard labor as little more than chewing stemmy grass, charging at a bunch of people that were disenchanted with the real-estate prices at home wasn't the best career choice. Nobody volunteers for the firing squad unless they're trying to get a good deal on used ammunition.

Things really didn't improve much with the passage of time. Man figured out that if you covered yourself with a couple of hundred pounds of scrap metal then you'd get to keep most of your limbs. He also thought it might be a good idea to armor-plate his new buddy, the horse. Somebody had to carry all this stuff. It also became obvious that the blacksmith needed to come along since nobody could get dressed or undressed without a forge and an anvil. This was especially important if everybody had a little too much coffee with breakfast. Wouldn't want to rust the undercarriage. Then there was the matter of spare parts: swords, maces, lances, horse shoes, axes, pretty flags, a couple of maidens, a few lookouts, (rear view mirrors hadn't been invented) paramedics and a meteorologist. That much metal and you better have a good weather report. Knights in shining armor? Forget it. No maiden in her right mind would go near this ironclad pair. The inside temperature of armor was about 105 degrees and deodorant was still just an amusing idea. They weren't knights, they were marauding gym socks. However, knighthood did cement one lasting truth: women and the Pentagon shop about the same. The real costs lie in the accessories.

Mankind's worst invention (no, not the lava lamp – the gun), pretty much put an end to the age of chivalry. Most of the tin-enamored group got popped with a chunk of lead, fell off their reluctant horses and drowned in a bog. Most of the alien landing sites documented around the world are where certain members of the Round Table made a final impression. Literally. King Arthur? Went trout fishing during a rain storm. Rotten luck.

Not wishing to get shot, a good many horses took up agricultural pursuits. The food was adequate, the hours reasonable and the opportunities to be lazy or mischievous, endless. Horses developed most of their bad habits during this period. Running off, rearing over backwards, raiding the cornfield, biting small children and farmers, losing shoes, trashing stalls – all the prerequisites necessary for a ten-year stint in maximum security. Even though no one knew it, the world was in the eye of a hurricane. That weird sort of calm that occurs before your girlfriend discovers the toilet seat up again. Plus, most of the organized world was plowed, and given that, inflation and unemployment were just around the corner. As Bill Clinton noted, bad behavior was okay as long as the interest rates stayed low and the Vice-president kept his mouth shut. Something had to change.

Along came this guy named Columbus, who had had a wild notion about the world being round instead of flat. Actually, he was caught up in a love triangle and had a few tax problems and needed to get the hell out of town. The local queen, Isabella, was kind of bored because her husband was spending too much time at *The Inquisition* or off fighting with France or England over God knows what. So, she peddles the Jag and the *Porsche*, buys Chris a few used boats and tells him to discover the 'New World' and put it on the market. She's figuring condos. The three ships are renamed the Nina Rodriguez, Pinta Lamarcos and the Suzy Maria. Columbus seduced women by naming ships after them. Must have been a good line since he was pretty close to owning his own navy. He doesn't leave a forwarding address.

Columbus bumped into Puerto Rico, but missed North America completely. Even so, these new discoveries had a potential for another hundred or so years of fighting. Once again, the horse found itself dodging bullets, pulling wagons across Nevada and being painted grotesquely by a group of warriors that had obviously never attended art school. The indignities did not end there. Horses were forced to sit outside saloons all day, run around The Little Big Horn, invade Mexico, cross the Delaware and rent cheap apartments at the OK Corral. People shooting up the place, even on the weekends! Then, there was Doc Holiday's breath, the Civil War, the Pony Express, the invention of veterinary medicine, which consisted of turpentine *douches* and smoking dead mice, and the biggest horror of all: blacksmiths. Strange sweaty guys with a foot fetish.

Along came the Industrial Revolution. *That led to mechanized warfare, which managed to kill millions of men of killable age and most of the horses that had the misfortune of ending up in Europe. While the first Great*

War did usher in the retirement of most horses as tools of conflict, it still didn't convince mankind that rocks and clubs had moved to a higher, more dignified plateau. We dug deeper in order to kill cheaper, faster and with less guilt. Efficiency. Attrition on the fast track. Boy, nothing like a high-altitude bomber. Open the doors, press a button. A bunch of very nasty crap rains down on some poor son-of-a-bitch trying to steal a loaf of bread. Or maybe a half-starved cart-horse pulling a dead weed out of a crack in the cement because he hasn't eaten in three days. And along comes mankind's newest form of malicious indifference – the cruise missile. They should paint little smiley-faces on them. They lumber along like a drunken condor, suddenly make a right turn and fly right through your bathroom window. With the right software, you could actually sit in your favorite overstuffed chair and watch <u>yourself</u> getting blown up. I guess it's how you do a murder/suicide all by yourself.

Unlike humans though, horses are gifted with a hideous stoicism. They'll step on a land mine, blow off one leg and simply stand there for hours, days – then, simply fall over dead. If war should ever erupt in your neighborhood, break all the mirrors first. They won't be needed later.

Why is it that weapons evolve faster than knowledge? Two million years for a dinosaur to become a bird, a mere century to annihilate the effort. Darwin never saw the inanimate coming.

War may have been bad, but given the horse's natural disgust for hard labor, recreation was even worse. The bullets didn't fly, but the expecta-tions did. Quite a few horses ran off to Nevada and Utah hoping to re-establish their proper niche in the food chain. The rest stayed around, surrendering to another round of human rituals. Horses were forced to be clean, polite, do dressage and jump over stupid obstacles that fell down anyway. Others found themselves carrying around people with pointy boots and oversized hats, chasing small cows around large pens for no apparent reason. The most unfortunate individuals were chosen to be race-horses, an occupation that reminded many horses of those hot days on the steppes: run, run, run; stand around all sweaty and then have your picture taken. A totally embarrassing concept. And of course, an equally unlucky bunch of humans end up in the same place: on a farm, up to our eyeballs in horses, trying to once again ascertain just who or what is in charge.

1.

TORN FAITH

A FEW OF us are forced, at least in the beginning, to ride horses by people who suffer the notion that children were put on Earth simply to fill another roll of film. At a young age, we are loaded into station wagons, driven to the outskirts of Seattle, Washington and placed on the back of Old Roan. Here we sit, wailing in youthful protest while parents and grandparents take our picture. We are positive that we will die, that the horse will eat our small bodies, or that somehow we will be forgotten and forced to spend the rest of our lives attached to the spinal column of a large, hairy animal. Then, quite suddenly, we discover the true value of the horse – its speed – and we gallop away, far from the clicking shutters, far from the angry voices. And for a brief, incredible moment, we are free!

My first cognitive memory was of the house catching on fire – twice in one night. Things didn't really improve after that. Some 'It' smoking in bed during cocktail hour. I suppose I could call them something else, but no matter how hard I tried, I was still faced with a contradiction.

At about age thirteen, I obtained my first gainful employment at a local pet shop. Since I had survived the end of the world, it seemed like I should get a job. From the earliest days of my childhood, I had shown an arguably abnormal interest in the day to day activities of the animal kingdom. This was quite contrary to the abnormal activities of the human kingdom, which held virtually no interest for me. I collected bees, small lizards whose tails tended to fall off and cupboard mice that were about to experience *rodenticide* at the hands of my mother, who didn't appreciate little brown torpedoes mixed in with her cornmeal. Actually she was probably deflecting some leftover hostility involving two divorces, three car accidents and the

appearance of my step-brother. At least that's what my eighth-grade counselor told me. I figured the counselor was working on her doctorate or
something since I had no idea what she was talking about. I still nodded
politely at the end of every sentence. I wanted to avoid the next step, which
involved a piece of lumber and the Vice-principal. Nodding politely didn't
work in his office.

I did know that when it came to mice that violated the cornmeal law,
mother preferred to dish out death with a glue trap. Which meant the only
possible escape was to leave a leg behind. I got pretty good at mouse ortho-
pedics. Amazing what you can do with a little cellophane tape and wooden
matchsticks. A couple actually healed up enough to be released, only to
show up later missing two legs. I finally solved the problem by smearing
Crisco on the glue traps. Didn't help. Mom moved on to neck snappers. I
had to close my clinic.

I finally moved up (or maybe down), to snakes and spiders, the latter
causing my older sister Dana to spend long hours breathing into a paper
bag. Boy, that was fun. Made up for all the times she beat up my friends.
Sis was a tomboy. She took Gloria Steinem a little too seriously. She probably would've burned her bra, but I'm not sure she even had one.

Still, I needed to have a job. Mom was a single mother, working two or
three jobs to keep us in canned ravioli and homemade TV dinners. She liked
to save the trays and make her own. She didn't seem to realize that you couldn't
freeze things like potato chips and cottage cheese. Tough times seemed to lead
to tough measures. That meant powdered milk, sugarless cereal and Kool-Aid
Popsicles compliments of some genius at Tupperware. The ice cream man only
got a sad wave and the Spudnut seller took us off his route. Cookies were inven-
toried daily, M & M's hourly. Every Friday we had liver. I guess we were either
Lutherans or just couldn't afford fish.

I was the oldest male, but I was also this skinny pathetic piece of worm
bait that every bully for ten-square miles would slap around. Sis straightened most of them out, including the evilest of the bunch – Kevin. He lost
two teeth and one of his fingers never quite worked right again. I had to
tone down my spider thing with her. Sis was like having the 101st Airborne
at my immediate disposal. Cute and deadly. I could walk down any street,
blink once, and the toughs would run for cover. Of course, she had a lot of
trouble getting a date. Going out with her seemed to most guys like buying a hand grenade with the pin missing. Still, I figured the job might
improve my menu choices and besides…

*...I had to suddenly switch to Marlboros. Used to be Lucky Strikes.
Stole them from the 'It' that kept catching the house on fire. He wandered
off to either jail or a different part of town.*

*I didn't smoke because of peer pressure though. That was because I
was the peer pressure. Funny how you go from social outcast to idol with
the addition of one bad habit. But there was also the economic reality of
nicotine-induced stardom. No 'It,' no Lucky Strikes. Marlboros were
already over fifty cents a pack. Toss in some Sen-Sen licorice mints to kill
the smell – this definitely required employment.*

So with the new job in hand I was able to purchase an aquarium.
Shortly thereafter I acquired two more. I also managed to drag home two
or three hamsters, a black-headed rat with arthritis and an oversized poodle
that had the misfortune of ending up a strawberry blond instead of a
brunette. It's a gum thing. Women call it color coordination. Dogs, well,
they don't even floss, much less worry about if their gums happen to be the
same color as their paws. In the dog show world, the color of the gums is
supposed to match the paws – sort of like the shoes and belt requirement
that women and the army are pretty strict about, but in this case the poodle
was more interested in eating grapefruit and chasing cars. Especially UPS
trucks. This dog had a thing about overnight deliveries. It was really sort
of pathetic, I mean like he was determined to sign for the package. I always
had this image of poodles: French, suave, into decent red wine or *cappuc-
cinos* – the only car I figured a poodle would chase would be a BMW. UPS
trucks had to be some kind of social rebellion. The principal told me that
was why I smoked cigarettes behind the gym. I was rebelling against conformity. Yeah, that was probably right, but it still didn't explain the dog.

Soon it became apparent to my employer that not only did he have a
great little worker, but also the best customer money could buy...or, in my
case, the best his money could buy. My paychecks had the usual deductions: Social Security, FICA (whatever the hell that is), the standard poodle deduction, two or three over-the-hill fish, a rat with his own 401K and
the two hamsters who appeared to have an offshore account in the Cayman
Islands. The bloody animals had a better portfolio than I did, but I guess it's
that animal age thing. You know, one dog year equals seven of ours. They
were definitely motivated. Especially the rat, who was in litigation with my

boss over 'repetitive stress' disability issues. Something about running around that stupid wheel all day.

While my mother thought it important for me to learn about the responsibilities associated with a job, she wasn't convinced that the best approach involved owning a zoo. Often, when I came home from work, she would be in the kitchen putting the final touches on a pot of macaroni and cheese (with Vienna sausages of course), intent upon intercepting me before I could get to the garage where I kept my conformity rebellion supplies and the growing menagerie.

"Andy!" she would yell, even though I tip-toed past the kitchen like a *Sioux* Indian. "Andy, come in here!"

"Yes, Mom."

"What's in the box?"

"What box?"

"That box! The one that's moving."

"Nothing."

Of course, when I said "nothing" it was Mom's invitation to personally confirm the existence of what I considered to be 'nothing,' a process that necessitated opening the box.

"Mom, maybe you better not..."

"What is it this time? A hamster, another one of those salmonella infested green turtles? A pony?"

"Mom..." Too late. Before I could finish my sentence, she peeled open the box, and with a bone-fracturing scream, threw most of the macaroni and cheese onto the ceiling light fixture. It would be a full five minutes before she continued. I was an expert on hyperventilation, but this appeared to be something like a collapsed lung – maybe two.

"No! Whatever it is, no!"

"It's just a tarantula, a little one. Nobody wanted him, so I thought..." This was not a time to play on her sympathy. Not that she had a lot anyway.

Mom's eyes narrowed to small beads, bright blue against her green skin, her lips quivering as she shaped the word like an out of water fish, "No."

Ernie & Maude

Sometime before Mom's last divorce and the next questionable liaison, I had a couple of buddies named Ernie and Maude. They weren't much really. Somebody's discards that lived in my backyard in homemade wire hutches. If it got too cold, then they came in my room. Never was sure which one was Maude and which was Ernie. Didn't seem to matter as long as they honored the celibacy rule.

One day the new 'It' decided that Ernie and Maude needed a new career. 'It' was a large fellow who could drink twelve cans of beer in a single afternoon. He thought that my sister and I might like to watch this career change in person. So we stood in the garage holding hands while 'It' stripped them of their fur coats, spilled their intestines on the floor and discarded their faces in a black plastic bag. Later, Ernie and Maude showed up on my plate next to the mashed potatoes and creamed corn. Odd, but I still couldn't figure out who was who.

Later that evening as I stood on a chair scrubbing the hardened cheese off the light bulbs, Mom informed me that capitalism could be learned from a good book and only the fish would get a residency permit. Since I was a mere thirteen, my options were somewhat limited. I thought about running away to some place where kids are free, like Colorado, but I just couldn't picture trying to get on a Greyhound bus with two aquariums, three hamsters, a black-headed rat that limped, a poodle and a tarantula. What would I tell the driver? "Big earthquake at the zoo, gotta get these animals to Colorado, step on it Mac!" Or, "FBI, I'm commandeering this vehicle!" No, Mom was right. The garage was full, and nobody was going to grant any credence to a thirteen-year old FBI agent carrying a bowl of fish. It was hopeless.

Naturally I was heartbroken, but as time passed I discovered a part of the animal kingdom that I had yet to thoroughly explore. Girls. Especially a fifteen-year old junior named Paulette who had a certain knack for making me forget about oversized poodles and hairy spiders.

Paulette was my personal image of what the *Goddess of Love* had in mind. No, let's be honest. She was barely cute, but pretty heavy on attributes. Long, curly brown hair, green eyes that could melt granite and a pair of legs molded for a short skirt. Plus, unlike my sister, she did appear to own a least one bra. I could see the strap thing pretty clearly. Paulette also had a reputation, confirmed by noontime conferences held in the boy's lavatory next to the gym. Here, in the tiled dormitory of awakening manhood, the seniors would confide their sexual prowess for the benefit of their junior classmates, most of who were staring intently into mirrors in some vain hope of making their acne disappear. Every so often, Paulette's name would come up in these conversations, invariably followed by a boastful claim of having "gone all the way (somewhere) with her." I wasn't sure where they had all gone with her, but, as I stared at my own pimpled image in the mirror, I hoped I could one day make that excursion myself.

By the time I almost graduated from high school I had most of the answers to my adolescent questions. I knew indeed where the entire male senior class had gone with Paulette, I knew exactly which stories a cop would never believe on a Friday night, and I had experienced at least 190 variations on the American cheeseburger. I had also learned how to throw up on command, what happens when you smoke dope next door to a Taco Bell, hence the value of the former, and of course, the shelf life of a Hostess Ding Dong. We had a lot of interaction with Hostess products. That very strange coconut covering could actually fit over your head. I could punch a couple of eye slits in it and have an edible facemask. Not sure why that seemed important at the time.

I planned on trying out college, exploring the moral decay of life as an adult, being rich beyond my wildest dreams by the time I turned twenty-two and becoming the proud owner of my own horse. The transition seemed perfectly plausible: poodle, tarantula, horse. Rich, decadent and heading into the sunset. By the time I reached that magical age of twenty-two, my goals were muddied in the dark waters of adulthood. I had completed certain portions of college, though most of my class choices didn't include any kind of cohesive goal. (I could have gotten a minor degree as a Shakespearean dog catcher.) I wasn't rich, though I had the equivalent of rich in debt. Banks, like schools found my math skills pretty questionable, which

I learned later to be a form of dyslexia. If only I had known! It was the perfect excuse for not trying. However, I had experienced that form of decadence which finds the wrong woman in the back seat of your car. That only left the last goal: owning a horse, which the not-so-truthful-woman's husband suggested I ride quickly toward Antarctica. Mexico seemed closer.

Five hundred dollars later I had a horse, a broken-down old western saddle and a rough idea of where Mexico might be. The horse's name was *Hombre*, which I was to learn, roughly translates from Spanish into something like "furry four-legged death." About five miles from my point of purchase, the warranty (or some substance normally administered to bad horses to make them reasonable) ran out. I was also in the midst of two or three rather sudden revelations: one concerned the scary fact that *Hombre* wasn't real broke to the idea of wearing a saddle, or wearing a saddle with a human attached. Who knows? Maybe it was a fashion thing. Secondly, my butt wasn't real broke to that thing either. Some unidentified crisis was going on in my underwear that felt like blood soaked ball bearings and resembled undercooked beef jerky. Lastly, we had a serious compass problem, which meant that we were actually heading north most of the time anyway, except of course, when the horse would run backwards and flip over in a ditch. That was south for sure.

I finally lost the last of my pride in front of a riding stable near an on-ramp to Interstate 90, in the foothills of the Cascade Mountains. Hardly mattered. Within ten hours, this horse would have run backwards into Canada anyway. The owner of the place, willing to sympathize with someone who obviously couldn't ride a horse (or for that matter find south), offered me a job that was definitely within my current capabilities: mucking stalls. In exchange for my labors, he promised to teach my horse the proper social graces and me how to read an airline schedule. In my sorry condition, it seemed like a reasonable deal. Besides, I needed a little time to figure out what was going on with my butt. My "O" rings were compromised.

After a few weeks, it dawned on me that my place of employment was far more than a simple boarding stable. In fact, it was an urbanized version of a dude ranch. Each weekend brought a new horde of would-be cowboys, disenchanted with city life and seeking some sort of embrace with the Wild West. These clients were always new, as our rental horses were so terrible that repeat business was rarely a problem. Actually, the only repeat business we ever got was a follow-up call from some unfortunate soul's attorney who had been impaled on a tree. I suppose that the boss would have spent an inordinate amount of time in court if it weren't for the fact that his only asset was that string of rental horses. Few lawyers were interested in that bunch.

My first experience with Thoroughbreds began with my introduction to the rental string. There were two in the herd, Special Moment and Torn Faith. (Okay, a Thoroughbred is what we typically refer to as a racehorse – you know, the Darley Arabian, a bunch of bluegrass and "My Old Kentucky Home?" Just think of a 1970 Camaro.) Special Moment, as one might assume, was special, or at least the boss's wife thought so. No one ever rode the horse except her. Admittedly, he was a pretty sharp looking horse, but unfortunately he also limped a lot. The story went that he had tripped over an irrigation pipe and left one of his knees all the lumpier for the encounter. Every week though, the boss's wife would saddle him up and trot him up and down the driveway for her husband's patient assessment of his condition. After a month of this ritual I couldn't help but ask when this altercation with the pipe had taken place.

"Six years ago this spring," he said with a sigh.

I didn't ask again.

Torn Faith was a different matter altogether. He was about fourteen years old and had raced on the bush tracks until he was eleven. The boss explained that bush track racing was the same as playing baseball in the minors – no matter how fast you ran or how well you pitched, the only people who ever applauded were close relatives.

Torn Faith looked like he had run a few too many races. He had lumps on his legs in all the wrong places, and it was more than obvious that his mind had snapped years ago – a rare horse that could weave and crib at the same time – two neurotic habits horses develop when they run around in circles for eleven or twelve years. Weaving is the art of rocking back and forth in a vain attempt to create some new scenery; cribbing, a process whereby the horse grabs a piece of the stall door in its mouth and belches in reverse. It's probably a guy thing. Torn Faith also had a set of bucked knees that made his front legs look like a 747 that couldn't quite suck up its landing gear. No beauty here, just random parts. A fossil somebody dug up that wasn't really dead yet. He also enjoyed biting people, but with all the wood-grabbing air-sucking activity the best he could do was a good gum job.

I spent hours watching the old horse drift off to sleep. The weaving would slowly stop, his eyes would narrow to small slits, his lower lip drooping lazily in a sort of Novocain-induced trance. Finally, his poor old knees would buckle, somersaulting the horse into the hay manger. The resounding crash would jerk Torn Faith awake and he would scramble to his feet, peering around the stall to see who had stolen his legs. The odd part was that he never seemed to figure it out. Every night he would bash his head on the hay manger and turn right around and do it again. Never thought brain damage could be habit forming.

I was curious as to why old Torn Faith merited a stall. At seventeen hands, he was too big, too ugly and too psychotic to ride. A little like a freak show at the circus, except nobody seemed to be selling tickets. Finally, one Saturday afternoon, the clouds were lifted on my inquiry. A shiny black *Porsche* pulled up to the barn. Out one door came a smiling young woman and out the other came her boyfriend, complete with alligator boots, shirt unbuttoned to the crotch and a pound of gold chain hanging around his neck. The only thing missing was a six-gun or a pair of Elton John's sunglasses. While I saddled an old Paint mare for the lady, Mr. Goldchains sauntered over to the boss and said, "Listen, I want a horse with spirit!"

The boss stuck another wad of chewing tobacco in his mouth, gave me a wink and said, "Go saddle up Torn Faith." I started to ask if he was sure he wanted Torn Faith, but decided that the look on his face didn't warrant another word.

Goldchains threw himself into the saddle, emitted some kind of Latin cheerleading song and dug those alligator boots into Torn Faith's side. Suddenly, there was nothing left but a cloud of dust and Torn Faith's ass heading over a distant hill. The boss, seeming quite pleased with himself, turned to me with a grin and said, "Put 'em down for two hours. It'll take 'em that long to get that son-of-a-bitch stopped." Ever since then, I've had a certain affection for Thoroughbreds.

2.

UNDER THE SPREADING CHESTNUT...TARPAULIN

FURRY FOUR-LEGGED DEATH wasn't a Thoroughbred, though I really didn't hold that against him. As resentments go, I already had a long list so resorting to name-calling over something like race, specie or navigational preferences seemed pretty pointless. What we had here was in Paul Newman's words, "a failure to communicate." Of course the failure was probably mine, as the boss was more than happy to tell anybody in the western hemisphere willing to listen.

"Son, you ever been around a horse in your life?"

"Just him."

"Just him, huh? You know what this jug head is?"

Had to be a trick question. "He's an Appaloosa. The guy said he'd…"

"Yeah, he'd grow spots when he sheds out. Heard it all before. What you have here is a common piece of $100 dirt and he's missing a shoe. And he's got white feet which is even worse." He handed me the horse and scribbled something on an old hay receipt. "Call Jack here and get this thing shod. Can't ride him with that torn up club he calls a foot."

So I was right back at the poodle-gums-damn paw thing only now it was a horse instead of a grapefruit eating dog. Next thing he'd be going after UPS trucks. I put Death up in his stall and called Jack. Four days and three hours later Jack showed up. $25 dollars later he replaced one shoe on a foot that looked more like a bad compound fracture. Pink Bondo completed the patch job. He said the rest of the shoes looked tight and he'd be back in about a month.

The next morning the other front shoe was missing. Now I had one pink foot and another compound fracture. This time it was five days, two hours and another $25 to have matching pink feet. Probably better than white on the scale of things. At this point I was beginning to formulate a few economic theories on the horseshoeing business. One involved the notion of diminishing returns, in that if *Hombre*/Death lost one more shoe it would make better sense to just get another horse. By now I knew not to fall for the missing spots story and to be sure the horse had some sense of direction or a drug test. The other thought had to do with how fast I had parted with fifty bucks. If I could learn how to shoe horses then wealth, stature and a Ford pick-up were just a matter of…how though?

One afternoon Jack showed up to fix somebody else's mess (that was kind of reassuring in a sneaky pathological sort of way) so I had a chance to quiz him a little on becoming a horseshoer myself.

"You don't want to do this."

"I don't know, why not?" The mess he was working on began to bleed profusely. Jack was damming the leak with sawdust. "Seems like a good business…is that supposed to…be, uh well, I'd like to learn how."

"You *really* don't want to do this." Jack seemed to be talking through his teeth, not his mouth.

By now the blood was working its way out the barn door where two of the boss's dogs were lapping it up, sawdust and all. Jack put a piece of iron in his forge and just kind of stared at the fire. "They got horseshoein' schools you know. There's one down in Olympia, but you won't learn a damn thing." He pulled the hot iron out of the forge, picked up the bloody foot and seared it, the smoke billowing over his head, some of it hanging like red fog in his hair. "That should do it," he continued. "Here, put this horse away. Tell the lady he hurt a tendon. Be okay in about a week. Uh, you can skip the blood part, okay?"

I put the horse away and returned to Jack's truck. He was just about packed up. "I still don't understand. Why wouldn't I want to do this?"

"Look, I've been doin' this for thirty years and all I've got is this truck, a bad back, these old tools and alimony I'm paying on two cases of bad judgment. Like I said, you don't want to do this. Go to college or try the army. See ya around."

Well, other than the alimony part, it seemed better than a pitchfork and a wrong-way horse. A few phone calls later I was able to get a spot in the next class. It was four-weeks long and they guaranteed I would be a real professional *farrier* – the technical term – in that short period of time. They had financial aid, a bunkhouse, and I could buy my tools as I went along.

I told the boss my plans and that I'd only be gone for about a month. I didn't want to burn any bridges on my mucking career. He seemed a bit hysterical over the news, but offered to keep *Hombre*/Death for me if he could use him in the rental string. Seemed kind of ludicrous on the surface until the clarification came forward.

"Torn Faith fell over again last night. Broke his damn neck. I could use that idiot of yours for a while. You'll owe some work when you get back. I'm tired of paying these shoen' bills. Why in the hell would you want to shoe horses? I thought your horse was a little light upstairs, but geez. I'd say 'good luck,' but I can't spare any right now."

So I was off to school. The first thing I learned was that the brochure for this school was more imagination than fact. The financial aid was handled by two guys named Leroy and Bub. It was based on Leroy's credit card balance and ran about 21% on normal days. Trouble was, Bub had run up a pretty good bar tab at The Lariat, a greasy watering hole down the road that also handled the graduation parties for the school. The bunkhouse was really some converted stalls that smelled like a chicken processing plant and the showers were outside. Kind of bad news since it was November. They had lots of tools which turned out be the ex-property of the last bunch of students, who I guessed had upgraded to fancier ones. Leroy explained that the instructor was in the hospital and a couple of guys from the last class would get us new guys started. Leroy said he felt I should take the day off and find some money.

This appeared to be one of those cases that most young men find distasteful. Groveling. It's right up there with being wrong and apologizing, which is probably about the same anyway. In these cases, the phone is always more prudent.

"Mom, this is Andy." Not surprise on the other end, something else.

"I'm in a hurry. What do you need now? Be careful with that!"

"Well, I've decided to go back to school. Found something I'm really interested in. Going to learn how to shoe horses. Be careful with what?"

"It's the movers, now what were you saying?"

The movers? "Tuition. I need to pay tuition."

"So how much is this going to cost me?"

"Five hundred." Short pause as opposed to a longer one.

"Tell you what, I'll send you a thousand. You'll need books and things. By the way, I just sold the house. I'm moving to Idaho."

"When were you planning on telling me about this?"

Seems she was on her way to divorce number three, which would even her up with car accidents. The guy was from Texas and his previous wife was evidently locked up somewhere due to mental problems. I got the check, but there wasn't a forwarding address. I guess that resolved most issues concerning a potential inheritance. Leroy seemed pleased, though we didn't see him for a few days.

Wednesday morning we started the class. There were about seventeen of us altogether.

Three were on parole, two were sent down from the Bureau of Indian Affairs, two appeared to be cowboys of some sort and three guys seemed to be in the pharmaceutical business. The rest of us just lied about why we wanted to shoe horses, all except this one curious soul who appeared to be a woman, although at about 240lbs or so, it seemed difficult to prove conclusively. She did seem a little enamored with the anvils, spending a good portion of the afternoon stroking the horn on the biggest one. Most of us shied away from her. The police stopped by later that day and arrested one guy, so we were down to sixteen.

There were two other fellows who stood outside the building for most of the day drinking something out of a paper bag and chain smoking hand-rolled cigarettes. They had long hair and wore green army fatigues, with eyes that darted wildly at small noises and rapid movements. I was thinking militant hippies, but one of the guys said they were sent down by the VA – coined locally as the Vietnam Administration, an organization known to operate like the Post Office on a Friday afternoon. We nicknamed them the Siamese Twins since they seemed to be bound together at the brain. Whenever they spoke it was in unison and they answered every question with another question. They'd only discuss the war in the third-person, as if it were a movie they starred in, but never watched. Mostly they answered everything with an all-inclusive, "Man, that's just puppy shit."

PTSD hadn't been invented yet, *though the whole class decided that we'd be happy to testify that it really exists whenever they actually got around to identifying war as a causative in anomalous behavior. I found these two guys oddly reassuring in what seemed like a morbid or perhaps desperate kind of affection. Certain noises – the backfire of a car, a news helicopter in the distance, those things would suddenly silence them. Their bodies would tighten at the sound, yet their eyes never sought out the source. Then laughter, almost hysterical; another swallow from the brown paper bag. I knew that feeling. It would come over me when I heard a beer can open, or when the door knob rattled in my darkened bedroom. The muffled noises that filtered into my private space, delivered overtly from a sad kind of distant privacy.*

I too, was among the drafted — in 1969. Same year I attended our non-graduation party from high school. Couldn't really stand one more achievement followed quickly by an elevator ride down the totem pole. This time it wasn't just peer digression, but a potentially fatal encounter with most of Indo-China. On the surface it seemed like simple cowardice – not necessarily a negative reaction to being killed in whatever scenario the imagination could produce, but something else. An awakening born of a subtle oppression that lived in the '50's, but was being swallowed by the energy of a new decade that seemed to embrace an ideal that recess should never end. Woodstock put other people's expectations on notice. The 1968 Democratic Convention, held in Chicago, was a declaration of a different kind of war for America. One that would be waged unarmed — on the battlefields of conscience. The great orchestra of America would play on, but one by one, the musicians were leaving the building. I had left myself about 1967, the result of smoking my first joint while listening to my sister's Frank Zappa album: "Absolutely Free." Can't quite remember if it was "Son of Suzy Creamcheese" or that arresting symphonic riot known as "Brown Shoes Don't Make It." Probably the latter, given the fact that I was never able to wear brown shoes after that day. Seemed sacrilegious or something.

1969 also marked the introduction of "The Great Human Egalitarian Though Slightly Obscene Body Lottery for Eighteen Year-Old Males Born in the USA." Winning was actually losing and the grand prize was an execution hosted by a mob of well-armed angry strangers. Yes, the draft went democratic – or so they said. Instead of poor white boys and poor boys of color going first, the poor white boys and the poor boys of color would compete for the coveted title of "Less Likely to Celebrate Another Birthday." I fell for it until I found out that my birthday was drawn in the 38th round. A recount seemed out of the question.

I was requested to report for a physical by the Selective Service the same summer that Jimi Hendrix re-wrote the National Anthem. During the 'pee in the cup' ceremony I noticed the fellow next to me was wearing black panties and a bra. One of his fingers looked vaguely familiar. I figured he was a shoe-in for some kind of deferment since the Army probably frowned on cross-dressing in combat. Funny how things work. He went to 'Nam' – I was excused by a cliché: flat feet. That only resulted in a 1-Y classification. Three more slightly scorched draft cards finally earned me the coveted 4-F. The only question more difficult than one's own potential cowardice is the question about who's left standing at the end and why. But then again, I already knew the terms and consequences of violence. So I suppose if the military taught me how to kill, then the only remaining question would center on who I might shoot first.

A short time later, during the dark madness of that non-graduation-off-to-war party at a place called Richmond Beach, I took a brief break from helping to empty a keg of beer and stepped in front of a train. Freight train as I recall. Seemed like the thing to do at the time. Never knew humans could bounce. Train engineers often bemoan the hideous thump they hear when they have struck someone on the tracks. They should try it from my side.

Bub started the day with a pep talk, explaining how we were going to be the last of the true independent businessmen (and business/other) and that there was great money to be made shoeing horses. He described our tools to us, most of which looked like a collection of broken can openers and also showed us the specimen legs that we'd work on first. They used to belong to real horses, but were currently residing in a freezer in our bunkhouse, along with the TV dinners that were included in our tuition. Around four o'clock, we all went down to The Lariat where Bub introduced us to a bit of school tradition – new students buy.

On Friday we started working on the frozen legs. We wrapped the bloody parts in burlap and tied a string to one end. The other end was tied to a post so we could hold the leg between *our* legs, which would sort of imitate real life conditions. Those of us with money had a heavy leather apron, those without, bloody jeans. Overall, it was pretty disgusting, though I assumed it was merely the price of education. The 240lb question mark seemed quite pleased to have something between her legs. There was a lot of whispered talk about what else might end up in the freezer.

We spent a good deal of time sharpening our tools. We were told the instructor was really critical about sharp tools (he was still missing) and if any of ours were dull, he'd break them. That sounded expensive, so I practiced sharpening pretty hard. Shortly thereafter, I had a new nickname: the bleeder. It was a good thing Mom sent extra money since I was going through a lot of Band-Aids. I never knew blood was so slippery.

By the second week, we were down to twelve students. Two just disappeared one afternoon shortly after they spotted a green sedan loitering in the parking lot. One of the cowboys beat up the other one and one fellow developed a really accelerated case of black lung disease after trying to start one of the coal forges. The forges had been constructed out of old swimming pool pumps and the medics figured that between the burning paint, the asbestos and the coal smoke, the guy should probably stay on oxygen for the rest of his life. All 240lbs of sexual indifference was hanging in there.

The instructor finally showed up one afternoon and talked for three hours straight about proper balance, all things being level, good angles and some diseases we were likely to run into in our work. Tetanus was pretty high on the list. His name was Carlos, but he didn't look Mexican. He was short though and overall he seemed pretty emaciated by normal standards. When he wasn't shoeing horses, he told us that he jockeyed at a local track. That explained his weight. Fortunately he didn't break any tools, because most of us were pretty broke by now. He seemed to take a real liking to one of the pharmaceutical guys, spending an extra hour with him on trimming techniques. I don't remember the guy buying any beer after that day.

On the third week it was announced that we were going to start making shoes out of pieces of steel bar. No live horses had showed up so we were still using the dead legs, most of which were being slowly consumed by maggots. Carlos explained that 'real' horseshoers made their own shoes, except for racehorses, which required expensive aluminum shoes made in France or somewhere. The key to making shoes was that the hind feet are shaped like a triangle and the fronts like a square. Most of mine ended up looking like a hubcap for a Buick. This wasn't lost on Carlos. "You might as well work on the track, you never will figure out what a normal hoof looks like." I thought that might be a compliment, but he didn't seem too sincere.

The last week some horses finally showed up. We had a spot next to the building with a tarpaulin nailed to the wall for cover. It was about a week until Christmas; that, coinciding with graduation, making the temperature outside about 14 degrees. No matter, we were ready to do some real shoeing.

There were three horses and all were caked with mud or manure or both. Two immediately pissed on our dirt floor, turning it into a kind of foamy mud with little steam vents next to each submerged leg. This made it a little hard to determine Carlos's interpretation of proper balance or maybe in this case, flotation. We got some shoes on the front feet of the first horse, but as soon as Harlan (the remaining cowboy) reached for a hind leg, the horse kicked him, apparently doing some serious damage to his right knee. Leroy was going to run him up to the hospital for an x-ray when the horse kicked one of the Indian students a little bit higher up the leg. Leroy decided to take him as well. I immediately went to work on the second horse, figuring the remaining 9 students (we lost the pharmaceutical guy due to a chronic nosebleed) could probably handle the situation. Not so. The horse tagged two more of them. They went off to the bar to reconsider their career options. It was down to this horse and all 240lbs of feminine persuasion. She reached down to grab a hind leg and when the horse went to kick her she just let go and grabbed the opposite one, shifted her weight into the horse's side and threw him to the half frozen ground. The splash was like having a chocolate milkshake poured over your head, except it wasn't a milkshake and it didn't taste like chocolate. I expected the horse's eyeballs to come floating to the surface without the rest of his head. When he did get up, she proceeded to nail on some shoes that weren't exactly fronts and certainly not hinds. The horse never moved a muscle, though he seemed to be wheezing pretty badly. I took him inside the barn and tied him to the wall next to the door. Wasn't exactly sure about what I just witnessed, but figured the information could be useful later. No, I don't know exactly how.

Leroy returned about this time, minus the two hospital cases. "Well guys, the hospital said they'd have to stay over. That Indian kid…Jesus, must have some kind of pain threshold, you should've seen his left…anyway, Carlos is on his way down to look at your work. If it's okay, we're just about done here. Who did the hind feet?"

"*She* did," I said standing inside now. The smell had shifted from rotten meat to something like a muddy urinal.

"Tiffany got him done, huh? Well I'll be." Leroy shifted over toward the door, no doubt seeking some breathable air of his own. Suddenly, a God-awful racket came from the hallway, followed by what sounded like a fish sucking air – a big one.

Tiffany? I was musing about Johnny Cash for some reason.

Outside the entranceway where the horse was tied, Carlos was spread-eagled on the floor, a bent horseshoe stuck in his chest. It appeared to be a hind, based on what he had taught me about the shape. "Is he breathing or just leaking air?" I asked, pretty sure the answer was still under debate.

"Geez guys, I don't know. You better get out of here, we haven't got a license for this sort of thing and well, you know I gotta call the police…look here, you guys and you too Tiffany, ya'll passed! I'll mail ya your diplomas, but right now it'd be a good idea for you to disappear till this is cleared up."

And so school was over. Tiffany suggested we go over to The Lariat and have a few beers to celebrate our newfound professional careers. I caught the nearest bus.

3.

NANCY ARBUCKLE'S HAIR

BACK AT THE ranch, all things had remained about the same. My pitch-fork and wheelbarrow were about where I had left them and when the boss got a look at my horseshoeing skills, he promptly decided that he'd rather pay for bad work than horrible stuff that was free. All things considered, it was probably time to leave the ranch. Besides, Mexico had sort of faded off the horizon, at least in the context of a necessary expedition. I could forget about the husband of the backseat girl. Last anybody had heard, he was doin' 5 to 10 upstate for sticking a gas pump in some guy's mouth that simply tried to check her oil at a gas station. Yeah, that was the abbreviated version. At least *I* was off the hook. As for *Hombre*, the Boss never could correct his navigational problems. It was like the horse's brain was connected to a GPS system that excluded the southern hemisphere.

It was probably for the best. I got to thinking about the ramifications of *Hombre's* rather bizarre aberrations and how they might float in Mexico. Mexican jails are not too pretty. Plus, there was this issue of some white guy sneaking <u>into</u> Mexico. Might be difficult to explain.

"*Señor*, you were clocked at 45 mph in a very congested area. Quite dangerous, if you ask me. And tell me, what's in your saddlebags? Can't be drugs, you're going the wrong direction."

(This was the Chief of Police in Juarez.)

"I'm very sorry, but *Hombre* lost his mind."

"*Hombre*! I hated that movie! Besides, *señor*, you were going back-wards. And then you backed into our best house of...well, you scared those women terribly. And then there was the matter of twelve cases of Tequila smashed in the incident. We are a small town and, well, to be honest *señor*, they are organizing a lynching party."

"Oh my, God! You have to protect me! It's your job – it wasn't my fault! I...I..."

"Ah, I see. No need to worry *señor*. They're going to hang your horse. We don't hang stupid *gringos*. We just put you on a bus and send you back where you belong. It's what you Americans call 'tit for tat,' even though I really don't understand the 'tit' part. I always thought that..."

"Thank you – really, thank you."

That was my vision of bad riding in Mexico. The boss managed to sell *Hombre* to a woman who thought he had a great hind end. Something about dressage. Sounded kind of sexual, but hell, she was thirty-eight and who knows what goes on there. Last I heard, he got loose one day with his saddle on (another one of his bad habits) and took out fifty feet of cyclone fence, a swing set, one picnic table and a neighbor's Volvo. I think the local police were forced to shoot him since he was bucking his way toward a nuclear power plant. I'm sure it was a prejudicial call – an Appaloosa with no spots and probably pink front feet dragging a beat-up Volvo to the front gate of the Satsop Nuclear Facilities. Probably the first time in history that most of the radical left and the undecided were on the same page:

AIM: "Not one of ours."

PETA: "We'll take a waiver on this one. Shoot it."

SDS: "Don't bogart that joint my friend..."

GREENPEACE: "We're checking to see if he's on staff here."

BLACK PANTHER'S: "Man, the horse is a white dude!"

KKK: (Remember, they are so far to the right, they ended up on the left.) "Man, the horse is a white dude!"

WEATHER UNDERGROUND: "Hey, look. He'll save us the trouble of blowing up the damn place ourselves."

SOCIALIST WORKERS' PARTY: "What's with this elitist capitalistic Volvo crap?"

GAY LIBERATION FRONT: "Wave girls! The press is here!"

CHEECH to CHONG: "Wow man. Isn't that our car?"

With no horse, no real plan and most importantly, no gainful employ-ment, I needed to rethink my options, which consisted of little and nothing. Most of the jobs out there seemed to involve logistical support for either a cheeseburger or a pizza pie. Low pay and a greasy apron. Probably a funny hat. I answered an advertisement for a school bus driver, and quite sur-prisingly, got a call back. After a pretty serious interview with Ruby, whose main concern was my hormone levels, I actually got the job. Piloting a fifty foot long yellow tube seemed like a piece of cake. Except, I also had to haul the senior cheerleading squad, hence Ruby's matronly concern for everybody's virtue. She said to be aloof. Aloof? Tried and failed. There is nothing more exciting for a young man than to be stuck in a traffic jam with fifteen cheerleaders.

Then came the down side. Early one morning, the dispatcher (a short guy with a bad attitude, which brings up an important detail: Why are all dispatchers five feet tall?) calls me into his cubicle. I thought it was about cheerleader #11. Both of us seemed overly defensive, circling the room like a couple of tomcats out to spray the same bush, ready for combat over a minor indiscretion that only occurred somewhere in my imagination.

"It's like this," he began. "You know Nancy Arbuckle?"

"Yeah. Well, sort of, I mean, not really. Her hair looks funny, like it caught on fire or something." I was fishing.

"Good. Very observant. Actually, she did have a small fire in her hair. Seemed the eighth-grade class at Morgan set her head on fire up on 99, you know, where it crosses over to Richmond Beach Road? Christ, the Wash-ington State Patrol, the fire guys – I mean, it was really embarrassing for the district. I got thirty pages of reports to fill out, workmen's comp crap, a bunch of irate parents, kids hiring lawyers – my butt's in the sling. You have to take over her route."

"Oh."

"Dammit, don't say 'oh.' Here's the routing. These are a tough bunch. Remember, no real discipline. State says we can't throw 'em off the bus, duct tape them to their seats – we're stuck. Just watch your back. Now, get outta here, I'm gettin' a migraine."

Well, that certainly explained Nancy Arbuckle's hairdo. Here I thought the curling iron was a little too hot, but it was really a bunch of lighter fluid and a Zippo. Poor woman. Guess it explains why she wouldn't let go of the fire extinguisher.

Monday morning I took over her route. Rumor had it that she was sucking down Valium in a private hospital somewhere near Portland. All the other drivers cast me sideways glances, oddball winks and goofy smiles. Bad omen stuff. Maybe like vultures circling a guy in the Sahara 'cause they know he made a wrong turn an hour earlier. Here I thought the pool chart on the bulletin board was for the Super Bowl. It <u>was</u> January, but most of the money seemed to be bet on a #45. Thought it might be a player. Turned out to be my bus number. Well, how tough could a bunch of eighth-graders be?

Well, more than one might assume. Eighth-graders are biological oddities of sorts, in that they are somewhere between puberty and a car accident, and unlike James Dean in "Rebel Without a Cause," are really *Rebels Without a Clue.* I'm hoping that some software engineer in Silicon Valley is penning a new book: "Eighth-Graders for Dummies." We could really use a set of instructions.

As a group, they seem to hate everything, including bus drivers. The boys are working out the girl thing, the girls discovering just how disgusting the male gender is. Part of it is the maturity curve. Girls become young women at twelve or thirteen, boys become men somewhere in their eighties, or shortly after death, whichever one comes first. So the inside of a bus turns into Yugoslavia on a bad day. Once they discover a mutual enemy (me), they redirect all this hormonal warfare to the nearest adult, which of course is the person stupid enough to be hanging on to the steering wheel for dear life. I found it difficult to drive 50' of mechanized wonder with my eyes focused in the large mirror that is designed to keep track of arsonists, potential assassins, seat rippers, bombardiers, potential neo-Nazis, sociopaths, extortionists and lunch thieves. This was further complicated by sweet young girls whose mothers encouraged them to be snitches. They'd whisper things in my ear that I really didn't want to hear.

"Mr. Andy. Bobby Watson brought a bunch of snakes on the bus."

"Great Suzy, have a nice weekend."

"But, they got loose, and well, two girls threw-up."

"Uh, okay."

"And I think Margie wet her pants. She hates snakes."

"Uh, okay Suzy. I'll take care of it."

"And a policeman wants to talk to you. He's been following us for quite a while."

Seems three Algebra 101 textbooks and an old dictionary ended up on the hood of a Sheriff's patrol car. I got a ticket for littering. Seems the only person I can throw off the bus is myself. That idea holds a great deal of merit.

Then again, these eighth-graders, *at least those who were boys and graduated high school would have the ability to make choices. Poverty would still marginalize them as it always has, but a third option, beyond insanity, or death, or both could take hold. No draft, no Vietnam, no exile to Canada, no wearing the brand of a coward. Kids could finally grow up and be that astronaut, that fireman, maybe even that horseshoer. They wouldn't have to defend an ideology they couldn't possibly comprehend — with their last breath.*

Maybe the senior prom could become a beginning rather than an end. Of course 'getting laid' and 'going off to war' in the same sentence would sort of lose its credibility. Hell, it never worked anyway.

A couple of days later when I stopped for lunch, I happened to pick up a magazine called *The Washington Horse*. While I was sucking down a bottle of antacid, I happened to glance at the classified section. **'Wanted: Farm Manager for Mid-sized Thoroughbred Breeding Farm. Salary and Housing Negotiable.'**

I thought about *Hombre*. Now *there* was a management problem. Thirty-five eighth-graders was something more suitable for the UN. One of those cases where you send in the Marines and just tell them to shoot anything breathing. I made a phone call.

At 7: 00 that night I was knocking on the door of a rather palatial home in the outback of Bellevue, a small town that was about to become Bill Gates' private playground. A rather tall blonde woman answered the door. She was kind of decorated with all sorts of gold stuff, some accented with large diamonds and other type rocks. Dogs were barking, a cat ran between my legs and the phone was ringing off the hook. "Doc," she yelled. "A young gentleman is here." She was staring at me a little too intently. "Do you have a girlfriend?"

"Well, no, not really...why..?"

"Don't worry, we'll fix that. Doc! You've got company! I'm Elaine. Doc's a veterinarian, but you probably already knew that. I guess it explains all the animals."

"Sir, I..." Doc wandered through the hallway, a phone pressed to his ear. Something about the third race at Santa Anita. He looked like Dr. Dolittle's illegitimate brother. Elaine shone like a star, one of those quasar things looking for a reason to implode and screw up Einstein's best stuff. Both were in their fifties, yet it seemed that they arrived on different space ships altogether. While I waited for Doc to get off the phone, a Brittany spaniel was kind enough to hump my leg.

"Oh, he likes you. That's a good sign. He kills chickens, you know. Alfie is even worse. He kills chickens *and* ducks. Well, actually, that was singular – just one duck. But, if you lump it all together...Doc!" Elaine had this peculiar way of distorting any perspective you thought you owned.

Doc wandered through the hall again. "How do you feel about Nubians?"

"Ah, well... some of my best friends are from Nubia. Sir...?"

"Goats. I've got a bunch of goats. Hang on a second."

The interview seemed like it was going quite well. So far, I had tip-toed through the girlfriend and Nubian part without much trouble.

Elaine finished the review. "Doc needs some help. He's got four clinics and all these office buildings – oh, his dad's bowling alley and we leave for Palm Springs in a week. When can you start?"

"Well, how many horses do you have?"

"I don't know. I don't go out there. Probably too many."

"Well, what are my responsibilities exactly?"

"I think you just feed them and do what farm managers do. My friend Barb has a manager. You could ask her. They're just over the hill, you know, the place with the hippopotamus in the field? We brought in a mobile home and you get a salary and, really, I'm not sure. We've got some accounts in town. Just don't spend too much money. Doc hates it when I spend too much. And you have to drive us to the airport Friday."

"So that means I got the job?" A hippopotamus?

"Doc!"

Doc made another pass through the hallway, nodding apologetically, but still engrossed in the third or fifth race or whatever it was. He tucked the phone to his chest and whispered, "We'll be in touch." Elaine just winked, and said, "See you tomorrow. Don't forget. The airport on Friday."

Suddenly, I was outside. The Brittany still had a thing about my left leg. I could hear horses destroying something off in the distance. I assumed I had a new job, but had no real idea of what it entailed. What I was sure about was that the paramedics wouldn't be dousing <u>my</u> head anytime soon.

I looked up at the stars and thought about Nancy Arbuckle. Every time I hear a fire truck, I'm sure I'll think of her scorched head. Nah. Way too scary.

4.

A HORSE NAMED TUBBY

AT FIRST, MY new job looked fairly easy. I had to take care of seven or eight broodmares, six older horses that supposedly spent their summers employed at the racetrack, some yearlings and weanlings, a herd of goats (the Nubians), Silly the barn cat, and three pathetic and from what I had been told, murderous dogs. In exchange for babysitting this menagerie, I was supplied with a fashionably obsolete two-bedroom mobile home, the utilities and a decent salary. Hardly ego-boosting, but better than having my hair on fire. I also had the opportunity of beginning my horseshoeing career. I still believed that getting paid for having a foot fetish was a brilliant idea. The main thing was that I was assured of eating every day and my food wasn't sharing the freezer with a bunch of equine spare parts.

Lewis and Clark would have enjoyed this farm. (It's a 'farm,' not a ranch – anything west of Montana is a farm.) The terrain fluctuated between hilly pastures, picturesque groves of fir and cedar trees and enough unexplored regions to whet the most adventurous of appetites. Silly the cat was the perfect guide. He (or, she – determining the sex of an altered cat is too dangerous to be worthwhile), followed a regular route around the eighty-acre farm, doing what most cats do: bury a little something here, dismember a rodent there, flail wildly in the air at some winged incarnation regurgitated from the cranial depths of *catdom*, followed by a bladder release into the cuff of my pants – the feline version of cross-species male bonding combined with a real-estate career. Oh, this cat was also quite proficient at catching pheasants. I thought this skill might be a great boon to my menu choices until I discovered that fighting with a cat over a dead bird causes you to lose most of the skin on your face.

On my exploratory visits to Doc's forested labyrinth, I became the perfect sightseer – a camera-bedecked Japanese tourist with a maniacal obsession to finally tell all of mankind where lawn mowers go to die. I found at least six dead mowers. Doc didn't do repairs, in fact, he avoided things like spark plugs and oil altogether. He also didn't seem to go for name brands. He was in favor of cheap mowers that were manufactured in Yugoslavia or Kansas, made of recycled milk cartons and powered by something that Henry Ford gave up on. They weren't into cutting anything. They just wanted a negotiated settlement and a retirement plan.

I discovered the burial ground in a small ravine, shaded by spindly-armed vine maples and ancient rhododendrons, the leftovers of some grand landscaping plan fallen prey to the murderous advance of laziness and weeds. The six were rusted and bent, seeking what dignity they could from a sense of mutual grief. Two were from JC Penney, a third from Sears: a Toro whose Briggs & Stratton engine still shined in black enamel, not yet consumed by the acid touch of falling leaves. The rest were dismembered, unidentifiable, the unknown soldiers of long forgotten campaigns waged to suppress the social and political ambitions of the dandelion. I gave them my crispest military salute and quietly, like a pair of dismissed pallbearers, the cat and I climbed back up the hill.

These first visits to the farm were not state callings. I was merely engaging in that old American tradition of moving, a process by which you throw away the sum total of your existence because it is much easier than trying to cram it in the trunk of a car. The sum total of my meager existence consisted of three or four boxes of instant soup, *Hombre's* old saddle, four or five cases of Rhinelander beer and a collection of rock-n-roll records that never quite made the Top-40. The lavender couch, a going-away present from Mom, didn't complete the move after twice falling out of the trunk. It now contributes to the comfort of early morning commuters at a north Seattle bus stop. Besides, real horse wranglers don't do lavender.

Doc had owned the farm for about ten years. It had had a number of owners, but was originally the Eddie Bauer estate, developed back in the late forties by the guy who invented wrinkled khaki pants and floppy hats for trout fishermen. Doc had a bunch of busy small animal practices in Seattle and Bellevue and racehorses were his hobby...or business, depending on how things were going at the local IRS office. Doc had been trying to run his practices, keep Elaine entertained and maintain the eighty-acres of farm all by himself – a process similar to what finally declined the Roman Empire. I think he should have taken Nero's example and simply burned the place to the ground, but then this was Seattle. Not exactly the climate for arsonists.

I arrived at my new post in late January, a month that is known in the Pacific Northwest as 'suicide season.' It rains, it blows, it rains some more, it gets grey and snows, and then it rains some more. Most people don't realize this, but the dinosaurs didn't perish because of some errant asteroid. They were at a convention in Seattle, and well, if you're cold-blooded, two-weeks in this crap and you're extinct.

Being warm-blooded only helps a little. Anyone with good sense, a little money or even a fragile grip on reality, quickly leaves the state. That being the case, my first official duty as farm manager was to take Doc and Elaine to the airport. They and the ducks were migrating to Palm Springs. Doc gave me a hearty handshake, asked me who the hell I was again and reiterated the notion about not spending too much money. And with that somewhat awkward farewell, the pair promptly boarded a 727 for the California desert. Fragile grip on reality or not, I was stuck in the rain and cold with a farm that looked like it had either experienced a major earthquake or badly needed one – only wetter.

When I first toured the farm, I was overly impressed with the size and number of buildings, in much the same way one is blinded by a well-dressed woman: nice earrings, beautiful dress, lots of make-up. Show up unexpectedly at her house at 7:00 a.m. though, and it's Lyle Lovett's bar stool lament: "She's ugly from the front." Amazing how optimism evaporates somewhere between that first beer and last call. Seems I should have toured the place on an empty stomach, or at least without the image of Nancy Arbuckle's slightly scorched head motivating my flight to the hinterland.

Once my misguided infatuation subsided, I began to inventory 'my farm.' (From here on out, it becomes 'my farm' – farm managers are possessive that way.) I quickly discovered just how much make-up it was wearing. I'm talking about a really bad shade of mascara. As near as I could tell, all the roofs leaked, none of the gates opened, the fences had either fallen down or were giving it serious consideration. Most things were held together with baling twine (yeah, that red stuff), water seemed to be flowing everywhere, except through the pipes and a babbling brook was babbling through the barn. That explained the boat tied next to the hay. A good two-acres surrounding the main barn looked like San Francisco Bay at low tide. Kind of smelled like it too.

Further inspection revealed that the main barn was actually a lot taller than I'd assumed, the result of Doc's overzealous attempts to control mud with additives. Most of the time, the horses wallowed around on their kneecaps, high-centered in this swampy morass, unless the ground happened to freeze, elevating them above the barn like prehistoric leviathans, home for the weekend to reclaim their planet from a meddlesome mankind. It was like "Jurassic Park" played by a bunch of hairy B-movie extras that were tossed out of a John Ford western.

Maintenance had also been lacking for the horses — a prison run by the inmates. Most acted as if they had just come off a six-month stint with one of Kit Carson's Wild West shows. The broodmares appeared amiable enough, but everything under five years of age stood back in shock, a case of post-traumatic stress disorder induced by the sight of a human being. They looked at me like I had broccoli growing out of my head. Maybe I did. The amount of carnage before me was so extensive that I couldn't see the end to it, and as I stood in front of the barn with mud oozing over the top of my tennis shoes, I couldn't see the beginning either. It was the apocalypse, with dirty four-legged carrion eaters picking through the rubble of what had been a grand civilization. It wasn't a farm, it was an urban renewal project. If I could have found some toxic waste, it probably would have qualified the place for the EPA's Superfund. Unfortunately, cat hairballs don't quite qualify. Neither do dead lawnmowers.

My only hope was a nuclear strike, but Nixon and Brezhnev screwed up that prospect by inventing the acronym of the cynics: MAD – Mutual Assured Destruction, which for those of you who never did a nuclear war drill basically means that when you flush one toilet, all toilets flush.

Plumbing or nuclear catastrophes aside, I was still stuck with an agriculturally-impaired farm inhabited by ADHD afflicted vegetarians intent on upholding an uneasy status quo. Feeding the horses Ritalin was one possible solution except that it wouldn't help in this case. Hadn't been invented yet. However, swallowing Drano showed promise. No, not the horses, me.

Later that evening, I had a long conversation with Silly the cat – you know, the usual sort of one-sided talk where you tell the cat all your problems while it's slowly shredding most of the upholstery in the house. First, I told the cat I was going to quit this job, hang it up right then before I got in any deeper – literally. Then, I stroked his back for a few minutes, felt a little better and changed my story. I'd quit the next Tuesday instead. Then it was February, or maybe March. Pretty soon the cat had me talked into making a go of it. I made lists and formulated plans, trying to visualize a little Kentucky in the middle of a landfill. By two in the morning I was convinced this was no ordinary cat. This was a super cat.

The following morning, I burned my resignation speech and marched to the barn, ready to do battle with the elements. I was armed to the teeth. I had new rubber boots, a Sears Never-Break shovel, and that look in my eye – the mercenary look, I called it — teeth gnashed together, eyes kind of pointy, fists coiling and uncoiling in some sort of western Washington *Ninja* gesture, my heart and soul united in a singular quest: to put the fear of God into nature.

Nature was impressed. I wasn't so sure about God. Somehow, I had to convince a great deal of water that it could indeed, run uphill. Since the barn was almost underground and the babbling brook was at ground level, the plan was to either raise the barn or lower the brook. Since the barn weighed at least 150 tons, it was a short debate. Besides, if Moses could part the Red Sea, I could certainly dispatch one babbling brook. Or, so I thought.

Four hours later, my ditch was a monumental three-feet long, which left only forty-seven feet to go. As it turned out, Doc had been filling the area around the barn with what people in the dirt business call 'pit run.' To get an idea of pit run, just picture a mountain broken into four or five pieces and dumped in your yard. A Sears Never-Break shovel is no match. Neither is a pick, or a crowbar or even trying to beat the stuff to death with a claw hammer. Swearing at it only makes it mad. The only true adversary for pit run is a Case 180 backhoe with an ill-tempered driver. An hour later I had both, though I suspected that my budget was already in deep trouble.

The backhoe operator, as I was to ultimately learn, belonged to a disappearing race of American entrepreneurs: the neighborhood mechanic. His name was Chet and he stood about five-feet, three-inches tall and almost as wide. He wore black Frisco jeans, a striped work shirt with 'Bob' neatly embroidered above a grease spot on the chest pocket and a black welder's cap turned backwards, which disguised a head that resembled a bowling ball with a flat spot. I don't know about the 'Bob' thing. Maybe shirts with 'Bob' were cheaper than ones with Chet. One less letter. His lips always sported an unfiltered Camel cigarette and for the most part, he seemed disgusted with humanity in general.

His garage, which bordered on the backside of the farm, was a white-washed wooden structure converted from an old cow barn. It sported a hand-painted sign over the door proclaiming his domain: **CHET'S REPAIRS – TUNE-UPS & WELDING**. Below it was another sign that stated: **TOOT HORN FOR SERVICE**, which was a bad idea if he happened to be lying under a car.

Chet's marketing strategy was simple. He just hung around his shop drinking coffee until someone showed up with a problem suited to his skills. If you wanted quick service, he just doubled the price. If you wanted service at all, then it was necessary to listen to a twenty-minute dialogue of his previous career of driving oil tanker trucks over the Cascade Mountains. And, if you showed any impatience at the progress of the story, or failed to laugh at the right times, then he would simply wander into the house on the pretext of getting another cup of coffee and never come back. Considering my desperate need, I not only listened to three complete *novellas* on the gear ratios of Diamond Reo trucks, but laughed on cue to everything he uttered – including a good-bye to his wife who seemed to be missing at least twelve teeth and in the final throes of a nervous breakdown. Even so, he came straight over.

The Case 180 made quick work of the pit run. By six o'clock, the babbling brook was flooding the neighbor's carport and I was pulling the boat out of the barn with a winch. My first success! I had actually wounded the enemy and it had only cost me one Sears shovel and $215 dollars in backhoe time. Tomorrow, I decided, would be the second offensive. I congratulated the cat and went to bed.

Up at dawn, I swallowed a cold cup of coffee and headed once again for the barn. This time I took a buggy whip, because <u>today</u> the horses were to receive their eviction notice. No thirty-day grace period, no second chance and no pleading insanity, even though most of them would easily qualify. From this point on, they were going to live in the pastures like real horses. I felt like I'd just left a Billy Graham Crusade and was going to convert the entire world to a new form of animal husbandry. The farm figured that living with the current dysfunction was just fine.

Doc's idea of equine management was based on a fast food restaurant. Instead of formal seating (the stalls), Doc felt the horses would be better off just mingling with the other customers. So rather than dining in just one particular place, the horses lived in *all* the particular places: in the stalls, in the aisle ways, the driveway, above the garage (this really pissed the cat off), next to the boat, pretty much wherever they felt comfortable. The place was like a Motel 6 run by the local chapter of the Hell's Angels. In Doc's mind, it was the perfect system. After work, he would simply drive down to the barn, throw some hay over the fence and like a pack of hyenas, the horses would divide up the carcass. Which meant that horse 'A' got the leafy parts and horses 'B' through 'F' got the stems. And, of course, if I tried to negotiate some sort of equitable seating arrangement, the horses would cry bias and rip me to shreds. I could suffer their indignation more readily than their table manners.

It was also quite apparent that the younger horses needed to become acquainted with humanity, especially a certain grey yearling who hid in the woods during the day trying to pass himself off as a moose.

His name was Tubby. God knows why. He appeared to be height/weight proportional as far as horses go, though I was rapidly learning that names and horses rarely share a common purpose. Elaine had given me a brief cocktail party type of introduction prior to flying south and I tried my best to apply the name association rule, but it wasn't working.

"Andy, this is Toad; Toad, Andy. That's Chrysler, she's one of our broodmares. Over there is Woodpecker, Crazy Eddie and I think that's Next Week…no it might be Spit. Spit is short for something. Foghorn is one of my favorites, but I don't see her."

"Well, great. Say, what time did you say the flight was?"

Tubby had lost his halter at some point before my arrival at the farm. For most horses, a halter is simply a handle that humans use to exert some influence on a horse's direction in life, but for Tubby, a halter seemed to imply a slow and miserable death at the hands of Mr. Broccoli. I could only get within about twenty feet of him before he'd spin around and bolt off, giving me one of those smart-ass looks that sends any normal thinking male in search of a shotgun. I tried trapping him, roping him, coaxing him and chasing him. Each time he found some way out of the trap and would run back to the comfort of the trees, laughing the whole way.

That kind of attitude, I decided, was unacceptable. I was the human, the farm manager, chairman of the board. No horse was going to treat my male ego like a stale bagel. I became obsessed with catching him. No matter what task my mind was working on, my heart was up on the roof of the barn with a giant net. I absolutely hate being outsmarted by an animal with a brain the size of a persimmon.

Finally one afternoon while I was feeding the other horses, Tubby wandered down from his forest retreat to steal a bite of dinner. I had left a five-gallon bucket of grain in front of one of the small sheds while I hiked out to feed the broodmares. Tubby spotted this free meal right away and seeing that I was out of sight, quickly stuck his mouth in the bucket. In the process, he managed to hook the bucket handle over the top of his head. Naturally, this proved to be a very exciting way to get dinner, and he took off full speed across the barnyard with the bucket still stuck on his head. It was only a matter of time until one of the buildings got in his way and, sure enough, he hit the machinery shed head-first at about 28 miles per hour, knocking himself unconscious in the process. From my viewpoint, I was convinced that he had managed to kill himself. As I ran to the shed, I suddenly felt marginally guilty: on one hand, I was applauding *my* good fortune, on the other was the whoops/guilt/explanation part. "Damn horse!" I kept yelling. "How could you do this to me?!" It is always easy for the living half to complain this way – never mind what the dead half thinks. What was I going to tell Doc? "Gee, one of your yearlings got hit by a building."

As I leaned down to get the bucket off Tubby's head, I quietly asked God to take care of this stupid horse. God didn't answer, but Tubby did. To my delight/dismay he was breathing. Yahoo! I ran behind the shed, grabbed some lumber and a hammer and boarded up the area where Tubby was sprawled in a heap. Then I slipped a halter on him and sat on his neck until he woke up. He was so shocked that a human being could do so much damage to him from so far away that he never ran from me again. Of course, he never ate out of a bucket again either.

God, I felt cocky. Tubby, on the other hand, probably needed some aspirin. It's not how you win, but if you win. I slept pretty good that night.

5.

THE LOOK OF EAGLES

BY FEBRUARY, THE cat and I had established a shaky truce with the farm. As far as I knew, Doc and Elaine were still in Palm Springs working on their skin cancer, so with cold days and long nights I prowled Doc's library searching for the *Holy Grail* – the theoretical meaning of why perfectly normal looking people would fiddle around with racehorses. I could easily understand why someone would like horses, since they are large, warm and not particularly hard to look at, but I really needed to understand the big picture – the mortgage on the farm, the $10,000 stud fees (a dating thing), the trainers who get $100 a day to supervise the also-rans and, of course, the really important question: Why do I have this job? So I studied long into the cold February nights, concluding that it was something we mortals rarely get to touch: greatness. That elusive, mind-boggling, ego boosting, look-great-in-a-tux thing that normally gets super-glued to some actor dumb enough to show up at the Academy Awards, even though he or she is going to be nothing more than two hands clapping. This 'greatness' thing apparently also applies to guitar players, Panamanian army generals, certain members of Congress, the Joint Chiefs, Madonna, the entire Marine Corps Marching Band and most women who end up on the cover of *Cosmopolitan*. And, from what I can surmise, racehorses, the primary difference being the source of all the applause. Apparently, Andy Warhol was right. Fifteen-minutes of fame is all you get and it just shows up when you least expect it. However, none of the books mentioned fifteen-year old juniors named Paulette, which leads me to believe that there is more than one kind of greatness.

I was particularly struck by what one book referred to as 'the look of eagles.' Beside this epithet was a beautiful portrait of a chestnut stallion named Man O' War. His eyes were fixed forward, ears alert, every muscle flexed in anticipation of a rendezvous with immortality; well, maybe just an unattractive mare. Who knows? But, I had seen that look before – on my mother's face when she opened the box with the hairy spider inside. Sex and terror seem to dilate the eyes in about the same manner. I'm not sure what Man O' War was thinking when the shutter snapped – how naive – I know perfectly well what he was thinking about. The breeding shed was only fifty-feet down the road. My mother simply had a thing about lower life forms – large hairy ones a little more than she could absorb.

Doc's horses didn't seem to resemble that portrait. Maybe once, when I gave them too much grain and the weather turned cold, causing the whole bunch to turn into agitated rats on a meat hunt. If I didn't know the source of all the sudden manic glee, I would swear the bunch showed talent. Of course once the carbohydrate level evened out, they reverted back to a herd of muddy, somewhat regular looking horses. Took about fifteen minutes. What a coincidence!

Genuine greatness seemed to be doled out in the same manner as the Silver Star: posthumously. Every famous breeder mentioned in the books I read somehow managed to die just prior to owning something great. It was like the Mummy's Curse: the only way to stay alive was to own something mediocre. As far as I could ascertain, the fastest thing around this farm was whatever the cat was trying to add to his menu. Or her menu. I still hadn't figured out the cat-sex thing.

I slowly came to realize that Doc had spent the better part of a decade and countless thousands of dollars at the task of trying to produce something great, like Secretariat. Since Doc was still alive, I assumed he had failed miserably at his goal and would probably be punished by a longer life. I wasn't sure where that left me as far as curses went, but I certainly had no intention to alter current affairs. The last thing I needed was a pissed-off mummy tearing my trailer apart. The cat already had that job.

Another theme that seemed to be repeated in the books I read was this overwhelming desire to win the Kentucky Derby. That's the big race in Louisville, Kentucky where everybody drinks too many mint juleps and stammers their way through "My Old Kentucky Home." In this particular case, most of the winning owners were still alive, but according to their comments after the big race, they must have known about the curse, as they all insisted they were the luckiest people on earth. They thanked God, their wives, ex-wives, their trainers, the weather, the Marine Corp Marching Band, Howard Cosell, a kidney transplant or two, the dog down the street. They knew. They threw greatness around like it was a rabid bat. They either immediately checked into a maximum-security prison, joined a monastery in Tibet or entered a witness protection program. You ever wonder why the Triple Crown is so hard to win? Check the steward's box at Pimlico. The funny looking guy on the left with the Velcro face wrap? Guess who?

In all fairness though, horse breeders, like Doc, face enormous obstacles. And it doesn't seem to matter what form of genetic material is involved, be it horses, dogs, artichokes or cats that lack a sexual preference – the problem is roughly the same: how to put the attributes of the parents into the body of the offspring. Now listen parents, or potential parents. You meet, you fall in love, each assumes that some God has ordained your union as the biological future of the world. Forget it. Mrs. Manson ran with that assumption and got blessed with Charlie. The difficulty is that recombinant DNA is like a parking lot with 3 million spaces. What are the odds of a blue Toyota finding a black Bentley on the same night that the salmon start spawning?

All this convulsive musing has *to do with 'The Theory of Eve.' Anthropologists love this stuff because it's contentious. And you can keep writing books on it forever because nobody can absolutely prove you wrong without writing a book of their own. This is how you insure tenure. Write slowly and you make it to retirement and grab the pension. Sell 100,000 copies for the old alma mater and you get a Chair with your name on it. Kind of like a tombstone, only utilitarian.*

According to the theory one can only trace the female *genome in reverse. Guys were too promiscuous or something, but it apparently has to do with the fact that women give birth and men just contribute some stuff. In anthropological terms, 'stuff' doesn't amount to a hill of beans. So the entire history of mankind, as we assume we know it, had to do with a pile of female bones dug up in Africa by the Leakey's some time ago when they were young, bored or optimistic — or simply trying to avoid paying back their student loans. Carbon dating on this bag of bones threw the evolutionary history of mankind into a decades-long spasm. All it did for me was to give me a headache and a C+. But if you consider a few hundred-thousand years of famine, war, pestilence, more war, the Crusades, various nasty plagues, A-bombs, country-western music and light beer, it is amazing that any of us are even here. Think about it. If my great-great – to the tenth power if you like – if she or he had got in the way of the Scythians (not nice people) in 500 BC, I wouldn't exist. Think about that the next time you're feeling impatient about a sloppy waiter. Because a soldier died on the field at Gettysburg – your neighbor, and perhaps your best friend – doesn't exist. And your chicken-fried steak is going to be later than you ever imagined. It's as simple as that.*

So now you know why there is no 'Theory of Adam,' though there is evidently a theory of 'It.' I only point this out to clarify that marriage, monogamy and I suppose decency, are little more than social constructs – other predators willing to eat their own young in a bad economy or a competitive relationship. It would seem then that we're an organism under constant restraint, the ropes and chains that bind us to this moral plateau in conflict with the instincts that got us to this point in our evolutionary history. Neither idea seems right and both can't be wrong. What then?

But back to horses. Combining the attributes of the parents into the offspring is no more difficult than getting a ham and cheese omelet back into the eggshell or the pig's…well you get it. It goes a long way toward explaining all those three-legged frogs in Louisiana. Don't understand? Okay, everybody thinks the problem is pollution. Fat chance. It's really a bunch of DNA-infatuated scientists who want to open fish farms in South America where a few well-placed pesos negate any worries about four-eyed salmon or 72lb prawns. You really don't want to know what they have planned for oysters. The more complicated the organism, the more opportunity for producing a cabbage that speaks three languages and can fly an airplane. Useful maybe, but nothing for the family album.

Other than the overall complicated nature of the organism (the horse, not the bi-lingual cabbage), one other major problem exists for horse breeders, (well, two if you believe in the curse): breeding horses requires a person to plan the future in rather long-term increments, at least by human terms. Horses have a gestation period (time in the oven) of eleven-months. A baby horse doesn't get to the track until two or three years after that, which means that horse breeders must weigh their decisions years prior to their actual goal, as muddy as that might be. In the fast moving world of equine fashion, a foal could be doomed to mediocrity before it even gets to try on the clothes. It gets even worse with children. Two brilliant software engineers have an only child. They're thinking MIT. In the next eighteen years the world manages to have two nuclear wars and global climate collapse, resulting in most of the world's oceans congregating on the outskirts of Kansas City. The kid is brilliant at calculus, but the only viable skill needed is an ability to digest dirt and salt water.

Racehorses are however, great proof of why we should pursue genetic engineering at all costs. A sire with great racing ability bred to a mare with great racing ability has a fifty/fifty chance of producing: 1) absolutely nothing, 2) all legs and no brains, or 3) something related to a blender. Of course, there is always the remotest of possibilities the mating will produce a star. In the peculiar mathematics of horse breeding, that dim light of potential shines like an economic beacon over the skies of Kentucky. Just a horse? Never. Horse breeding elevates man to the level of a cheap Greek god, twisting and manipulating the clouds of fortune into bolts of crisp lightning – the final unification of ego-born self-delusion and contagious arrogance in a brown fuzzy coat. A kingly sport for common kings. And we've got idiots cloning sheep. Geez.

After hours of careful study, I couldn't help but wonder what would happen if we really did combine our meddlesome nature with a little lab work. I pictured a horse with all sorts of Velcro attachments, allowing for the quick replacement of anything that either wears out, like the legs, or bombs out, like the face. I also imagined the altered horse with reptilian skin to facilitate cleaning – kind of like that double-jawed lizard that tried to eat Sigourney Weaver in the movie "Alien," only rideable. I also wanted it to have the tongue of a frog (to deal with the fly problem), the speed of a small Italian car and a brain devoid of all those cells responsible for mischievous behavior. Those would be sent back to the cat family where they belong. All this engineering would necessitate a new and demanding language. Dismal terms like 'lame,' 'rearing,' or "Gosh, he's an ugly horse," would be replaced with programming language and microchips. Training would be supplanted by downloading and horseracing would become little more than a competition to see who could get to Bill Gates' secret laboratory first. Most horsemen would have to trade in their Stetsons for laptops, which really could have saved the technology industry from its current, and, well, chronic slump. Of course, that still leaves the little problem of: **You have performed an illegal operation and this program will be terminated.** Trainers just go, "Which one?" Just goes to show what happens to your brain when you spend long, cold nights in an empty library.

Maybe Doc did have a plan. I figured he was, like many horse breeders, trying desperately to improve on Nature's tedious approach to product improvement. I mean, really, thirty-five thousand years to design a sports model of the cow, when the real idea was to be filthy rich in six months or less? I liked the idea of filthy rich. Ten-percent of filthy rich equals one Mercedes 500SL or something. Beats the hell out of a Toyota.

Even so, there still appeared to be something amiss. As I checked the pedigrees and racing records of Doc's ten-year battle with the forces of nature, one theme bubbled to the surface with enthusiastic regularity: the results. Doc's horses were mostly $3200 claimers – just fast enough to make you want to train them another week, but not fast enough to warrant an Egyptian curse.

A claimer is what the racing industry refers to as a cheap tart. It basically means that if you fall in love with a particular horse you can put your checkbook where your heart happens to dwell. It's a little bit like prostitution, but with a more subjective value system. A $3200 claimer is unlikely to win a $5000 race. Same thing with a $6200 claimer that moves up to the 'allowance' ranks. Allowance? I've always wondered about that term. An allowance race is somewhere between the cheap date thing and a stakes race. It 'allows' an owner to find out just how bad his horse really is without having somebody even more optimistic claim him. Don't look for common sense here.

A 'stakes' race is one of those black-type get-togethers where the equine elite fatten their resumes by getting to the finish line first. *Black type?* God, this book is far more complicated than I ever imagined. 'Black type' is different from black tie. Well, maybe not. Black type can mean anything from winning the Kentucky Derby to the $1500 Taco Bell Stakes in Bermuda. If a horse wins a 'stakes' it's basically the same thing as a two-for-one stock split at Microsoft, only in this case it is 'preferred stock.' That's why the Daytona 500 carries a bit more weight than Bubba's Friday Night Beer Bust and Backyard Demolition Derby. It makes the distinction between quality and just a curious form of mayhem. And, if the horse's genitals happen to be intact, an end-of-the-year bonus is a sure thing. However, if you run dead last in something like the Derby, 'stake' becomes 'steak,' at least as far as the French are concerned. Just look at black type as a MA from somewhere like Harvard. Maybe Yale. Parents should explore this issue – the costs are just about the same. Buy a racehorse? Educate your child? Tough call.

The following morning I tried doing a little genetic exploration of my own, based on my newly acquired knowledge. Still, the theories seemed a little opaque. One popular thesis centered on *measuring bone* – which bone, I don't know. I also wasn't sure if you measured the bone on the horse, or sometime later when the horse didn't need it anymore. I assumed it was an on-the-horse type of undertaking, but most of the bones I measured had a leg attached that didn't want to humor an idiot with a tape measure. One leg would measure six inches around and the other would come in at just under thirty-five feet, the latter determined by the degree of fright generated by a flapping metal tape measure.

I immediately moved on to the theory of *tail tension*, which, from what I could gather had something to do with Einstein's space/time continuum. The 'time' part had to do with how quickly you'd be killed exploring this theory, 'space' was the burial plan. Seems you yank a mare's tail up and see how much pressure she exerts clamping it to her ass. Now, this is bound to piss her off. And if she's pretty good at the 'clamping' part, then the next move is to see how quickly you can extricate your hand from a mare's backside at about thirty miles-per-hour. Not quickly enough, really. But the theory does have merit, for any mare that can drag a 160lb man for a couple of blocks by her tail, definitely warrants a second look. I'd like to know how long the author of this asinine theory spent in traction. By the way, the neighbors really enjoyed this experiment.

I also explored a few of the *classic* theories, which appeared to be based remotely on Italian cooking, obscure sections of the "Old Testament," British nobility and some horse named *Mumtaz Mahal*, which the "Encyclopedia Britannica" identified as the sole resident of a concrete vault in the *Taj Mahal*, somewhere in the outback of India. Classic theories also require the practitioner to be 'currently rich' as opposed to 'hoping to be rich,' an arrogant assumption whether you happened to know what the hell was going on or not. So said the experts: Varola, Tesio, Wall, a couple of British Lords with large trust funds. I mean really, we won the 'big war.' How come we're stuck with $3200 claimers? I had a sore foot, a creeping headache, one finger was two inches longer than the rest, and the cat decided my bowl of popcorn made a great litter box.

Later that evening I settled on the theory of *breeding the best to the best*, allowing a very liberal interpretation of what I considered to be the best. Even so, it turned out that the best had a $250,000 price tag, which was just slightly over the farm's budget for the next 127 years. That only left dumb luck as a business plan. Well, at least that was something that appeared manageable.

Before I turned in for the night, I came to a couple of pertinent, though idiotic conclusions. One was that no matter what we tried, sadly, we would be stuck with $3200 claimers, thereby saving some mummy countless sleepless nights haunting our barn. And secondly, if I ever grew weary of our humble contribution to the future of Thoroughbred racing, I would do the honorable thing. No, I wasn't going to commit my spirit to the afterlife with a Japanese sword, even though the cat had a rather unhealthy interest in mammalian intestines. Instead, I'd simply run down to the local video store and buy Doc and me a pair of 3D glasses...that way any old thing we happened to breed would look like an eagle.

6.

MUD

AFTER A FEW nights of exploring theoretical nonsense by people who could afford to publish their *own* books, I decided it was time to re-engage the enemy – that meant I had to go outside. Chet's backhoe work helped a great deal, but I was still stuck with approximately 482,586,000 tons of mud. Most of the world's supply. Felt like Saudi Arabia on a cocky day. Trouble was, nobody was buying. Nothing worse than owning the world's entire supply of mud and it's a buyer's market. Even the cat was depressed. You ever try to bury a bowel movement in a pile of goo? Keeps floating to the surface. Drove the cat nuts. I was going to see about putting him on medication, but he discovered my laundry basket. I guess good mental health comes in many forms.

I'm not sure anyone really understands western Washington. Sure, Seattle gets its fair share of 'rain' jokes, normally perpetrated by California weatherpersons who don't have anything to talk about anyway. They sit for hours staring at the Doppler radar looking for one cloud with some sort of potential. Most of the year, a chipmunk with an alcohol problem could do the weather. "Geez, itttsss goin' to be sunny and...where the hell did my tail go?" Whereas, Washington weather people are on the front line of bad news. Hail, rain, snow, ice storms, flooding – average life expectancy on the job is eleven days. They bury them faster than they hire them. The interviews give a slight clue:

"So, Marlene, you've been doing the morning weather in Kansas City, for let's see, three years?"

"Yes, but I wanted to find out..."

"So, Washington is a little different. You've probably heard it rains a little out here."

"What I heard was that the last person had a sort of..."

"Well, good. I've heard enough to make a decision. We liked your tape, the producers thought you had great screen appeal. Start tomorrow?"

"I haven't even moved. I'm in a hotel! I've got a rental car!"

"No problem, HR will handle the details."

"What about my husband?"

"Not a problem. We're used to dealing with next of ...I mean, spouses."

Washington creates these kinds of problems. It's an old family recipe. Take one part low pressure system, two parts Japanese current and add in one mountain range. Then mix well with 500,000,000 tons of dirt that the last ice age left lying around and stir well with any month of your choosing. Turn a few horses out into it and what you have is a collector's version of *espirit de mud*. I'm not kidding here. Our stuff is world class. Forget a few dead weather people. We're talkin' collectibles. People in places like Las Vegas or Phoenix love this stuff. They can't produce it on their own. It either gets blown away, or it's too hot to touch, or the gangs steal it. It's an envy thing.

Still, I seem to have more than I either need or could possibly market. People in San Francisco drive up to Napa or Calistoga and plunk down huge amounts of expendable income to look like most of my horses. They shove slices of cucumber under their eyelids and then get lowered into a vat of pureed, well, dirt. Maybe it's designer dirt and mine is just generic, but selling that concept to urban Seattlites, most of whom believe that fall fashion includes being shrink-wrapped, would probably leave my spa with a lot of empty rooms. Still, part of the tonnage is what I call 'mud in motion.' Ronald Reagan had a similar idea when he suggested that nuclear missiles be put on trains and shuttled around the country in a rather macabre shell game with the Soviets. Greyhound buses would have been better. Amtrak never could keep a schedule, which just might have been the whole idea anyway. Or then again:

"This is General Rawlins, Colonel – we have the 'go' code. President says launch."

"Uh sir. We have a slight problem with that," says Colonel Pickens, head of SAC's Amtrak division.

"What's the holdup Colonel?"

"The Central Limited, sir. It's stuck outside Milwaukee."

"Well Colonel, make a stationary launch dammit. The Russians may launch any minute!"

"Uh, sir. The train's stuck in a tunnel."

"Shit! How long?"

"Milwaukee says two hours. Freight train derailed outside Chicago. The whole system's backed up."

On the other line: "Mr. President. You have to stall. Missiles can't be launched for two hours. Say, ever tried negotiating?"

Here's how it works: (Horses, not missiles.) First off, horses don't mind the weather as much as one would think. They have six inches of hair, reinforced with two-inches of well-caked mud covered with wood shavings from the sheds. They look like Almond Roca bars with legs. As their body heat warms and cracks the mud, steam vents pop out all over their bodies. Early in the morning they look like small volcanoes on maneuvers. Twice the neighbors called the fire department, convinced that Satanists were running around my pastures torching the horses. The horses were just in the second phase of relocating some of the mud. Once enough heat was generated, the dried mud would crack and fall off. Preferably somewhere else. It was like watching snakes shed their skins, only messier. After the dried mud fell off, then the search was on for new mud, which naturally wasn't too hard to find. I figured they managed to relocate about 1500lbs a day in this process. I'm not sure it improved their complexions. But then that's the advantage of having all kinds of body hair. Nobody sees the wrinkles or the cellulite.

Oh. Reagan changed his mind. He decided to hide them in submarines and then hide the submarines. They're still out there, but we have no idea where.

Chet's work on the babbling brook was marvelous. Money well spent. I stayed away from the western property line though, since that particular neighbor seemed to be on a really serious hunt for the source of the Nile. I could see a few ducks on the hood of his Lexus and some guy wearing a tie and writing on a clipboard. Not a good time to introduce myself.

With the babbling brook out of the way (actually it didn't babble, it was more like a wet stutter), the next job was to stop the salmon from spawning in the tack room and scrape the frogs off the walls. With the tide out, I needed to figure out how many stalls I actually had to work with and where the hay had beached itself. Foaling season was just around the corner and a need existed to get the maternity ward into usable condition. Thoroughbreds do not foal outside, particularly in western Washington. Between womb and world is something called air. Nothing worse than drowning the first night in a new town.

It quickly became apparent that the barn roof leaked terribly, which was pretty hard to notice when the barn was underwater. Eighty-five roles of Saran Wrap would solve that problem. Then, there was the situation with the lake, which was really our new training track. Only about a third of it had found its way into the neighbor's carport. Not quite fast enough for my purposes, so I started checking around for another neighbor. Somebody must need some really dirty water.

Now I had to convince a bunch of recalcitrant horses that the barn was really a barn. Not an easy task when you have a group of surly outliers that figure that all forms of civilized dining are literally punted out of the trunk of a Cadillac. All except Tubby, who seemed to be permanently glued to my shirt tail. He was starting to annoy me. I couldn't even sit down to read *The New York Times* without him sticking his head through the bathroom window. I once read something about obsessive behavior, but I wasn't sure I could get a restraining order on a horse. The judge would end up like my sister – trying to cut down the oxygen flow to his brain with a paper bag. I'd have to buy the guy a new diaphragm or a lung or something. And probably from jail.

With the others, I'd just have to deal with their suspicions. I guess after years of watching ducks and trout fishermen cruise through the place, this sudden architectural rise from the bowels of the earth must have appeared to them like a giant horse trap. Okay, it was. But it was clean and dry and it didn't make those strange sucking noises anymore when you walked through it. All of which would convince a smart horse to spend the night elsewhere – maybe a Holiday Inn with a mud hole nearby.

I managed to convince two of the dumbest broodmares to come into the barn. However, they got so panicked that I had to put them both in the same stall for mutual support. They kept looking at me like the barn had wheels and the next stop was...*Dachau.*

...My family, on my mother's side was German, with a few Russians thrown in to confuse matters. My father's side was Norwegian, though in truth, the Germans killed off what few second or third cousins I might have had on that side. Twice-removed has a totally different meaning for me. My father was a corpsman in the US Army, stationed in Western Europe. He gathered up the limbs and tried to match them with the other parts so that they could all be sent home in one bag. My mother was an only child, a survivor, eventually a war bride. My father survived the war but like a lot of veterans, never really completed the journey home. Somewhere over the Atlantic 'what was, became what is.' And no bottle was large enough to wash the images away.

My grandfather was born in Bialystok, which in 1904 was considered East Prussia. My great, great something, Andreas Hofer, defeated Napoleon at Innsbruck. So the story goes. East (Polish) Prussia was contested ground, what we would refer to today as a 'frozen conflict zone,' only a little more fluid than most. Pre-World War I Europe was little more than bad marriages and crooked auctions. My grandfather was fluent in both Russian and German because the town was swapped back and forth for a decade between the Hapsburgs and the Czar. When the Russians finally cemented their position in eastern Poland, all the Germans got to spend their school years east of the Urals, guests of the Romanovs. After the Czar and his family made that final trip to the basement, things still didn't improve for a couple of years. Finally, the Bolsheviks emptied the camps and sent all foreign nationals home. Of course some, like my grandfather, no longer had a home. It was now part of what would become the USSR.

They settled in central Germany. My grandfather married, became a highly skilled machinist and life began to make sense, but only if you ignored 2000% inflation and the Treaty of Versailles. Then Hitler got out of jail. My grandfather ended up in the Luftwaffe, serving on the Russian front. The irony in his assignment wrapped up in a bi-lingual education compliments of the Russians, the same folks he was now trying to kill. Back home, his town was being fire-bombed by the Allied forces, an atrocity rained down due to the proximity of the Messerschmitt works which manu-factured aircraft nearby. Yes, atrocity – all around. Industry required work-ers, cities supplied the workers, B-17's and Lancaster bombers controlled the rate of unemployment. Still, he managed to survive another war and live long enough to see a man walk on the moon and the Berlin Wall come crashing down. For a guy who started out with little more than uncertainty and a few chickens for pets, he experienced more of twentieth-century his-tory than most people would care to absorb.

But, there was a nagging problem. The trains. The God-awful trains. Germans of that generation don't care to discuss it openly. Maybe we can't hold them as accountable as we would like, for time erodes the pain and silences the witnesses. Some of my relatives were of questionable descent, that determination contained in Himmler's little book on racial purity. Seems a "biomedical vision" existed, whereby mass murder needed to occur in order to heal the "racially diseased body of the German nation." That policy was often dictated by who you were, not what you happened to think. Russians, Jews – even Catholics. Those labeled deviant, recalci-trant, diseased, disabled. Of color. The road to Auschwitz wasn't as dis-criminating as one would think, the rails subject to the whims of political body snatchers or the expediency born of a full-scale conflagration.

My grandfather in his broken English denied knowledge of The Holo-caust. Who could blame him really? War creates this unnatural tendency to uncouple the personal reality from the greater truth – overwhelms it really, creating a schism between personal accountability and the mass guilt generated by the greater association. "I didn't, but I did." Perhaps survival demands a bifurcation of the spirit, for in order to live, one truth must dominate the other.

My grandmother was of Russian-Jewish descent. She somehow sur-vived the war, only to have her mind shut off the world around her. When my grandfather died, I traveled to Germany to settle his estate and my uneasy curiosity about where I came from. Dachau was 35 kilometers from his house on a main road. Dachau was the first camp, a lovely little model for what was to come. Fear and tyranny get married every week. They are a successful, professional couple. And you know, they always live just down the street a bit.

Later, the mares settled down. Reminded me of most female gatherings. I used to hang out in a bar in West Seattle, which was kind of an industrial-going-Bohemian section of the city. Men wander into the restrooms as rivals and leave with that same attitude. Women go into *their* restrooms and come out as best friends.

Women will eventually straighten out this dysfunctional planet. Men need to trust them a little more often with the job. Or not.

7.

THE LATE SHOW

STOMACH STARING. HOW do you fit that into your resume? The barn was somewhat usable and sometime after everybody got over the New Year's epidemic of allergic reactions to gin, vodka, Tequila, cheap beer, Champagne, Scotch, whiskey – what have I missed? – oh, Bourbon, the one necessary ingredient for a mint julep — the mares were moved indoors according to their due dates. These 'due dates' aren't the same as the ones Visa sends out. This is total abstraction roughly based on the last 'cover' date, which is a polite way of intimating an intimate encounter only with horses it's about as subtle as a train collision. So there might have been two or three of these covers over a period of ten days, or maybe it was the previous cycle and the mare was just killing time at a farm that was much nicer than ours. What you then do is subtract all these unknown variables from 12, then add a month to make eleven (the gestation period) and you have the inexact date within three or four weeks of actual birth. That is of course, an approximate time frame and if you happen to be dyslexic like myself, then the actual date comes up in either early Egyptian or Cyrillic, which for me is much prettier than English. Most mares just multilaterally decide to give birth at a point in time where a hangover crosses that thin line of merely being a nuisance to something requiring four or five paramedics and some speedy transportation. Trust me, there is a weird connection between blood alcohol levels and water breaking.

I had been studying up on this impending birth thing. My career as midwife to the stars depended upon it. I actually felt a maternalish radar developing in a portion of my skull normally reserved for female anatomy and fast cars. If I looked closely in the bathroom mirror (yes, Tubby's head was still stuck in the window), I saw a paternal figure with graying hair and bifocals, wise as the ages, committed to the role of ushering new life into a cold, harsh world. If I opened my eyes though, I saw the truth – two cratered eye sockets containing the world's entire blood supply. Mares don't give birth until they have driven the nearest human insane. I didn't need a doctor, I needed a coroner to find out if I was still alive or merely twitching because of a biological resistance to embalming fluid. Stoicism and insomnia are the midwife's curse. Later comes the insanity part, but only if you're awake.

I was however, the perfect martyr. Swept up in self-sacrifice and humility, the cold winter nights bore witness to my humble wanderings. From the coffee pot to the stall, back to the coffee pot, outside for a cigarette, then to the wall with the clock: 2:00 AM – back to the stall – whoops, side trip to the bathroom. Damn coffee. Then, to the television, back to the stall and then it was 3:00 AM, the silence of the night broken only by the tired scrapes of worn boots on cold asphalt and the toilet flushing. Look, even James Herriot went to bed occasionally. The really ironic part is that males don't normally do 'responsibility.' Fishing or showing up for the birth of your first child? No contest. With a two-week salmon season your wife better just cross her legs and hope the guy limits-out in one day. The fact that I cared one wit about these mares really made me wonder if my chromosomes were out of synch. I wasn't into cross-dressing, had no real interest in men unless they owned a backhoe, and I really didn't picture myself as a male nurse in an intensive-care unit. Oh, now I remember. No foals, no paycheck. At least it wasn't a sexuality crisis.

I quickly became a late-night television critic. Johnny Carson was always the best, David Letterman only seemed funny once my brain turned to mush, which occurred on a pretty regular basis, and Jay Leno seemed to have a future if you could get past his lower jaw. It was so big that it seemed like it should have its own brain to operate it. Reminded me of one of those nutcrackers my mother used to collect. She didn't crack nuts though. Put an eight-year-old's thumb in one and it became truth serum. Conan O'Brien might have been entertaining as well, but he was still doing stand-up routines for his parents in front of the Christmas tree.

Commercials on the other hand, prey on the nocturnal victims of sleep deprivation: "Sure, I need a Ginsu Knife and a Vegematic II." All those youthful memories of dodging parental authority, staying up late, dashed on the rocks by the political correctness of a new age and cable TV – no Indian Chiefs on the late night test patterns, no stirring inspirational messages from the electronic heaven, no fighter jets or battleships carrying the banner of nationalism to distant non-combatants. Just a computerized print-out that looked like a box of Wheaties that caught fire. Designed, no doubt, to keep the night shift alert and motivated. Oh, cable TV? Forget it. My TV had one of those sophisticated signal interceptors made out of a coat hanger. Coat hangers do two channels at best. Well, sometimes if you made a real creative pretzel out of the thing and hung a beer can on the left side you might pick up Wolfman Jack who was illegally transmitting from somewhere over the Mexican border, but most of his show consisted of the forms of profanity found next to the urinal in a bad bar. You know it's a bad bar because the 'F' word never has a 'c' in it. I once had a dog with a better vocabulary except he took to chasing airplanes and well, shucks, Boeing *is* a Seattle company.

Not much of this idiotic stomach staring made sense. In the death throes of insomnia, it had about the same effect as the test pattern in that you actually do fall asleep with your eyes open though you're pretty sure that's not the real problem. Doctors call this advanced catatonia, though in our case it's more like combining chain smoking with snoring. You cure sleep apnea with lung cancer and part way through chemotherapy the mare finally foals allowing you to either die in peace or change the channel.

Humans have an endless list of chores that must be executed in the last month of pregnancy. Shopping for baseball gloves. Could be soccer shorts. Disposable diapers. Hemorrhoid pads. Anybody with a quart or two of morphine – Bill Cosby's wife once described labor pain as pulling your lower lip over your head. Yeah, more morphine. Maybe a couple of *Lamaze* classes taught by naïve organic-types that actually gave birth once or twice, but can't actually remember because it was the fifties, and doctors just didn't do screaming in the fifties. One guttural utterance and by God, you got a *Caesarian*. The Ides of March *were* going to thunder across your abdomen.

Maybe a *Lamaze* class would be perfect. I could bring all 1200lbs of Princess whoever, that would knock over most of the furniture and leave hair all over the floor. Rhythmic breathing would be replaced by spontaneous deposits of ...horses don't *go* to the bathroom, they just sort of go to the bathroom. Even if I got into one of those classes, I'd probably have to pay a damage deposit and deal with all those strange looks that humans love to throw around whenever you date a female just slightly out of your general species.

"So, you two met where?"

Instead, I just watch, a voyeuristic spy in a goose-down vest, sleeping in the barn, consuming multiple pots of coffee until my bladder explodes, never out of sight unless I need to call the Crisis Clinic, manned in the late winter months by specialists in caffeine poisoning, alert to the repetitive, somewhat disconnected sentence structure of a person on the brink:

"Hello, Crisis Clinic…Hello?" Normally manned by a stern, older woman. And she actually volunteered for this assignment.

"Pepperoni and olives. Uh, did I pick up my dry cleaning?"

"Hello?"

"Heeeerrre's Johnny!"

"Hello, this is the Crisis Clinic. How much French roast have you had?"

"Oops, can't talk now, my shoe's untied."

"Do you want us to send an ambulance?"

"Sure, can they bring along the pizza?"

"Have you considered de-caf?"

"Wasn't he the president of Israel?"

"We're trying to help."

"Help? I admire that in a pizza parlor. I need five stalls cleaned and somebody who can figure out how to determine the sex of a cat."

"Hello? Hello?"

It is the scourge of modern animal husbandry. Laws that forbid the birth of domestic animals without the proper degree of meddling. Which of course sends Darwinian social scientists crawling up the wall. I don't recall any waiting rooms full of anxious hairy men in the Neanderthal epoch. I don't think drugs had been invented and a spinal tap was something you did with a spear when dinner was a day or two late. Women would just wander off somewhere and show up a few hours later with a small friend who was kind of noisy and well, familiar in a really weird sort of way. Nowadays, nothing can end gestation without $15,000,000 worth of assorted medical hardware, four or five malpractice lawyers and a husband who would rather have his testicles eaten by a mentally ill kangaroo than actually watch you give birth. I'm not kidding. Few men can deal with this. Suddenly this rival shows up and like the VCR, (DVD's get invented in chapter 22) the instructions are lost. And gorgeous has become 'mom' – hell, just wander off for a decade or two until the damn thing gets a life of its own.

Psychologists tend to think that long hours spent in cold barns lead to a number of mental health problems. Mare watchers become overly fixated with mathematical equations: the number of knotholes in the ceiling; calculating how many craters are on this side of the moon or solving the mystery of a seven dollar overdraft that has been haunting the checkbook for a decade. Chronic boredom also encourages one to check in with old friends, often at odd hours – like 3:00 AM. "Oh, were you sleeping? Listen, what do you know about cats?" Or really dedicated scientific inquiry, like studying the migratory habits of dead spiders. The advanced cases deteriorate into cleaning obsolete bits of broken tack or compulsive stall mucking, which so upsets the natural body rhythms of the rat population that most seek asylum at another farm. It's the Timothy Leary thing without the need for an illegal substance. It probably explains why the neighbors surrounded their place with razor wire. I had developed the Frankenstein walk, occasionally bumping into random trees and parked cars. Twice, the UPS guy found me asleep with one hand in the mailbox. It was as if Ted Bundy suddenly lost all his murderous ambition. "Not now Gail. Let me pencil you in for August. Okay, late July."

The lack of sleep also activates the more sinister side of the brain. The part that likes to put flies in the microwave oven just to see what happens. Okay, if you just do defrost, they fly upside down. Hit the 'high' button and they explode like little firecrackers. Fun, but really hard to clean off the glass. I should probably feel guilty about nuking flies but I don't see them suddenly appearing on the Endangered Species List.

Nuking humans though, that seems to have a lot more potential nowadays. More than one can imagine. At one point the Soviet Union boasted 27,000 nuclear devices. The US about 32,000. The population of the world was approximately 6.3 billion in 1990. That meant that there was one nuclear device for each 913,000 men, women and children. Cost-effectiveness didn't seem to be the goal in this process, though considerable mayhem apparently was. And here the teachers said I was hopeless at math. I also learned that a fifth of whiskey was one-fifth of a gallon and had a similar effect on women and children – though probably fewer of them than an atomic bomb.

Before long, nefarious plots are hatched, driven forth in a desperate desire to force the impending birth. The barn is filled with the cajoling threats and lies of a man whose eyelids are pitched in battle with a brain too wounded by coffee and Ginsu knives to fight back. Believe me, I had more knives than Wolfgang Puck. My UPS driver figured I was a frustrated pirate intent on overthrowing five or six Caribbean islands. I get sea sick in a bathtub. Plus I didn't have a one-eyed parrot with a wooden leg. The cat eats mascots. It's just that tele-marketers love to talk and deranged farm managers love to listen. That's how you end up with fourteen Chia Pets. Good thing Enzyte was still in the R & D phase.

While I didn't have a real plan to expedite the process, I was determined to get visiting hours with my bed. At first, I would try to have a sensible conversation with the mares. Something along the lines of a cheap, insincere grovel, "Pleeeeaase get on with it. I'm due at the blood bank in fifteen minutes. You know little Margie with the multiple metastasizing ear tumors? Come on." Then, I'd move directly to threats: "I'll plow the whole damn farm! You'll never see grass again!" Or, "If I don't see a foal in ten minutes, you're getting a bath!" I'd also put my hands on my hips and look stern and determined, a posture I observed my mother to use whenever spinach (or liver) found its way on my plate. Her favorite expression was, "Eat or die." She could be pretty convincing. I think it was a leftover German thing.

If coercion failed, I tried scaring the daylights out of them. I know from watching late night movies that pregnant women always give birth as soon as they get stuck in an elevator between floors, or on an airliner with two engines on fire over the North Atlantic. Since both of these scenarios are difficult to duplicate on a farm, I was forced to develop a system based on available resources. The first technique involved sneaking up to the stall in a rubber Richard Nixon mask. If the mare feigned interest, then I played three hours of back to back favorites by Alvin and the Chipmunks, followed by a rendition of the world's favorite accordion polkas. That caused the neighbors to pull down the razor wire and move to Australia. I don't think upper class refugees really care where they go, as long as they get away from either an opposing army or a slightly psychotic farm manager.

Some nights, if I was particularly cranky, I forced the mares to watch Barbara Walters interviewing Tammy Fay Baker on television. The blubbering gave *me* labor pains. I mean, I've never seen a woman waste so much makeup. No matter what she was talking about her face looked like a seagull after a visit to the Exxon Valdez.

The trouble with all this late-night insanity is that it rarely produced a foal. Instead, I am plagued with the false-alarm. The mare circles the stall 47 times, starts sweating like a linebacker, breaks water without spilling a drop, finally throws herself down in a heap and boom! A bell goes off in her head and everything crashes to a stop. Meanwhile, I have on my rubber pants, the long plastic sleeves and my bottle of iodine, looking like a cross between the guy who sells fish sticks on television and the Surgeon-General's definition of safe sex. The only sound competing with my pounding heart is a gentle snore drifting up from the floor of the stall where a whale lies beached in the amber tide of straw, immune to the danger lurking a few feet away: a man, a monster, a mad lemur driven to unreasonable acts by a lazy uterus.

Farm managers share a common look during foaling season. The Romans referred to it as *in articulo mortis*, that brief moment or two before Brutus leads a chorus in "Hail to the New Chief." Or Keith Richards on the last Stone's tour. Either way, everybody in town knows your occupation by the ashen color of your whole body, lending to speculation that Hollywood is either filming a zombie redux nearby or you've stumbled into the middle of a hepatitis convention. The cat tries to bury you, but like everything else, you float to the surface. Unlike normal people who get home from work around six in the evening, farm managers start the second shift around that time. Dinner is a bologna and peanut butter sandwich, with or without bread – the bed is a recliner. An alarm clock, set at two-hour increments, is placed on a hay bale next to the chair. Every two hours it bursts alive, sending one's heart into wild palpitations, finally forcing me to construct a self-defibrillator made out of two TV dinner trays wired to the electric fence charger.

The brain is in the saddest shape, but I guess I already proved that point. Dreams become withered remnants of a hopeful seed, robbed of the time needed to bear fruit on their own, pushed along by an impatient cop or a broodmare who has figured out that the easiest way to commit homicide is to do absolutely nothing.

Think of all the bullets we'd save if armies could figure out that simple principle. If no one shoots first, then nobody would shoot back. Of course, there would still be the problem of 100,000 or so well-armed guys with nothing constructive to do. Humanity and boredom always seem to be a bad mix. In some ways that might explain that quiet decade after the truce in Korea. Television was invented. We didn't seem to have another war for...gee, fifteen years?

Doc and Elaine flew back around the end of February looking rested and somewhat carcinogenic. Doc began to notice my slurred speech, the disheveled clothes, my inability to tie my own shoes and the fact that the neighbors had mysteriously disappeared. Elaine caught sight of the backhoe bill. Doc offered a solution to my chronic insomnia, vested in the outstretched arms of modern technology: closed-circuit television. Instead of being jerked awake every two hours in a cold damp barn, I could be jerked awake from the comfort of my own bed. Logic wasn't an issue in this debate, but money was about to play a role. Doc had been quoted a price of $2200 for an entire system, wired from a camera above the foaling stalls to my kitchen and *his* bedroom — yes the priority was noted. Each of us would have a color monitor and remote control. In the budget hearings that followed, Elaine convinced us that we didn't need two monitors, a remote control, color or a professional technician to install the system. So Doc and I sped down to Radio Shack with our $500 appropriation and spent the weekend bringing the farm up to technological speed. The result was a video image of a stall, a large brown thing in the middle and a snowstorm that would have looked much better in Fargo, North Dakota.

Doc was trying optimism. "Yeah, see if you get the vertical right...there, you can see the mare now. Over in the corner."

"That's the cat."

"Oh. You sure? Here, see if that's better."

"Still a cat."

So instead of actually seeing what was going on in the barn, I could only guess what was going on in the barn. I would end up putting on my muckers, my coat and hat and trudging to the barn anyway. Then back to my old chair (now sitting in the living room contaminating the air), a fitful two-hour nap followed by another heart attack. It was an equitable arrangement. The mares had finally managed to trade *their* misery for mine.

Everything did work out in the end. All the mares foaled, none of the babies sprouted antlers or extra legs and most medical authorities agreed, that with time, my heartbeat would return to normal. No guarantees on the brain though.

8.

BREEDING THEORIES EXPLAINED– OR FURTHER COMPLICATED, DEPENDING OF COURSE, ON YOUR POINT OF VIEW. BUT FIRST:

I DO NOT stay up all night with bloated female horses because my social life is lacking. I stay up all night with bloated female horses because my social life is nonexistent. Agriculture has a long and lonely history that runs contrary to the romantic wailings of a few Midwestern singers, or one of those cowboy-poet-get-togethers in Nevada where people get roaring drunk and try to convince other drunks that eating beans and hanging around with 30,000 poorly trained bovines is as good as it gets. *Americana* aside, I'll take along some Gas-X and a steak knife.

Sure, bright green corn fields and grazing cattle do offer a wistful respite for a victim of urban decay, but cows and corn do not drop from the heavens to soothe the cancerous breast of a New Jersey stockbroker. He may think of it as God's work – an exhalation of evil thought and mounting temper, offered and received by a humanity gone slightly mad with progressive enrichment. Any clue what I'm talking about? Me neither. I'm pretty sure it has something to do with taxes, sleep deprivation and entrenched guilt about the neighbors. Still, if we're going to cauterize the senses and cleanse the souls that crawl around big cities like well-dressed cockroaches, we should charge admission. Those kind of props don't come cheap.

My farm had a predilection for attracting urban refugees and people addicted to take-out food. We had one of those long mysterious driveways with bright red 'No Trespassing' signs, which are really an invitation to ascertain the obvious contradiction wrapped up in the word 'no.'

Overdressed people clutching Egg McMuffins and coffee would wander down to the creek to watch the sun rise, stopping off to steal my newspaper or ask for a refill. Others would bring the kids and have a picnic in the woods. When confronted over their wild assumption that they had discovered a previously unknown state park they invariably grew defensive and surly.

"The gate was open man. Why don't you put up a damn sign?" First customer of the day.

"I've got six of them. You know the red ones that say 'no.' Is that the *New York Times* you're reading?"

"Yeah, I found it. You got a problem with that?"

"No, no. Like a warm up on that coffee?"

Seems that trespassing and the *Bill of Rights* are in conflict when it comes to farms. People tend to assume that the gates, fences and signs only apply to *Latter Day Saints* and aluminum siding peddlers. Not 'regular' people who just stop by to steal apples, newspapers, corn, trout, hallucinogenic mushrooms, or in the fall to ground-shoot exhausted ducks.

The movies have done little to discourage the loopholes that exist in the laws concerning private property. Opposing armies are the greatest violator of the trespassing statutes. In the average war movie, tanks, artillery, personnel carriers, personnel without carriers, airplanes, flame throwers and jeeps just show up somewhere in France and have a war in some guys bean patch. He's inside having a cup of tea and when he glances out the kitchen window all hell's breaking loose out by his barn. He's pretty sure he remembered to lock the pasture gate and it *is* Tuesday so it's not the garbage man. Plus, he doesn't seem to recognize anybody in the crowd. Puzzled, he turns to his wife. "Bernice, were you expecting company?"

"Well, no. Not really."

"Better call the police."

Aha. War is against the *law unless you hold it at your* own *farm. If not, then it* is *trespassing and the best thing to do is call the police and have the army arrested. That's how a civilized society is supposed to behave.*

Without the rule of law, society would fall into anarchy, chaos and, well, war. That <u>was</u> after all, the whole purpose of civilization. Wasn't it?

Of course the worst offenders are the westerns. Here the whole idea centers *on* violating the trespassing laws. In a good western, the main characters always steal land, water, cattle, horses or gold – then trade them up for women or whiskey. Forget stealing land from Indians. They never quite grasped the concept anyway. Some westerns also took the antithetical approach whereby the bad guys were those putting up the fences in order to stop cows from trespassing on land that they were already trespassing on themselves shortly after stealing it from some oddly dressed fellows who failed to read the fine print. In this case 'good guys' were fully interchangeable with the bad ones. Kind of a morality play with some disinterested cows as the audience.

Disaster movies take the whole concept full circle. Whether it's a tornado, tidal wave, hurricane, earthquake, volcanic eruption or an alien defecating killer spores, everybody's farm gets wrecked. Disasters pay even less attention to my little red 'no' signs than the guy who stole my newspaper. Hollywood needs to reflect reality a little more. Instead of armies, cowboys and defecating aliens, they need to produce more lawyer movies. Men and women battling to the outskirts of delirium with writs, depositions and expert testimonials – a jury of average looking non-partisan, racially diverse middle class semi-retired real estate agents handing down the only verdict possible: Pay the man!

Some of us know how expensive this soothing backdrop is to produce. The portrait isn't just a one dimensional brush stroke painted by the inarticulate hand of hard labor — calloused, swollen, probably underpaid. Instead, a masterpiece, the tiny steps of a magnificent work in progress, destined to become the eighth or maybe ninth wonder of the world.

The viewer, diseased by an imagination starved of color and light, sits and stares at my creation, thanking God in some roundabout way for an intermission from a terribly long and boring movie. One with a shallow plot, unattractive characters and a bad soundtrack. Before I can get his five bucks though, he disappears down the driveway, pointing his mid-size, non-smoking rental car back toward Jersey. I spend the rest of the afternoon re-arranging the scenery again.

__A lot has to with__ the decades of urban/rural warfare in this country. I was raised in suburbia, a kind of bastardized, dysfunctional, hybridized cultural compromise lodged between the zealots of the opposing camps. Lawn mowers were invented there. Micro-farming of sorts. A Twelve-Step program for people struggling with the horrible need to grow their own beets. Of course, like all addictions, this one is most damaging to the children.

"Andy! I thought you were going to mow the lawn this weekend!"

"It's not my stupid lawn."

"You said you'd do it. It's getting really long. The neighbors are starting to talk."

"Let them mow it."

"Here's five bucks. Mow the damn thing."

"Ten."

"Fine. Do it __now__. Or else." The 'else' part was where it always got interesting. This was normally sub-contracted out to a male individual who showed up one day with his own set of keys and a strong desire to restore order. Somewhere between the end of the honeymoon and the definition of 'else,' we went out the window only to find ourselves deposited at the front door once again. In our case, we weren't interested in the __movie__, just the intermission. That's when you get up to use the restroom and the cops find you two weeks later in Nevada.

Future farmers. Little more than childhood victims of the dynamics of agricultural withdrawal, lawn maintenance merely a substitute for fond memories of the Dust Bowl. We'd water it so it would grow, fertilize it to make it greener and then have to mow it because we were too successful with the first part of the process. We couldn't eat it, smoke it or sell it. It just sat there. About the only thing it really did was make the septic tank hard to find when it backed up, or somehow facilitate a transition from angry resentment to marginal envy for no apparent reason – other than cigarette money.

Growing up in suburbia had other drawbacks. I assumed a Massey-Ferguson was a pair of democrats making a run for the White House. Also, like most kids, I had no idea where fried chicken came from or why watermelons were so expensive in February. Everything just showed up on my plate missing the feathers, hide, bone, roots, skin, beaks and scales. In school books, all the farm animals were smiling like happy idiots. They evidently didn't know what we had planned for them.

NOW FOR THE CONFUSING PART:

There is of course, an earthly purpose to all the midnight madness suffered for the sake of welcoming a new Thoroughbred into the neighborhood. Far from the realm of ethereal self-sacrifice lies Churchill Downs, splendidly dressed for the first Saturday in May. A spot where every breeder of every Thoroughbred would one day like to stand. Smiling broadly in the winner's circle, red rose clamped gingerly in their teeth, casually and confidently recounting to Jim McKay and sixty-million television viewers the genius behind their dumb luck. It's generally a short speech. ABC needs a break to sell a few Pontiacs, the horse doesn't speak English and a musty smelling guy is off in the corner booking a flight to Baltimore. Better to just grab the check and sneak out the back gate. Wouldn't want to end up under a rock pile in Egypt.

It's important to remember that it is a race for three-year olds. Three! When I was three I was being spoon fed my dinner while I was sitting on my lunch. It took me another twenty years to elevate most of my bad habits into something more sophisticated – bad behavior. It's a matter of semantics. People tend to be a little more sympathetic when it's about behavior. They also figure it's treatable with the right medication. Habits appear to be a matter of choice, most of the choices involving the downside of other kinds of medication. Doctors and bartenders have a lot in common.

The race itself is contested over a mile and a quarter. I'm not sure why that distance was settled upon. Couldn't be the British, they measure in kilometers and race in the opposite direction. Given our distaste for most things British, we probably just invented the mile because it was easy to spell. Another quarter was added to make sure that any horse that won really earned the money. Any longer and the network would break for a commercial half way through. That's what happens with NASCAR – all the good accidents take place during a Pennzoil commercial. And forget instant replay. If the driver gets ejected out of the car and lands in the grandstands the network censors get in the act and block out all the good stuff.

Personally, I'm opposed to excess exercise. Folks in the city join clubs, spas, diet programs – they climb indoor mountains – indoor mountains? They also jazzercize, aerobicize, tai chisize, power walk, jog and ride bicycles in an outfit that closely resembles a car with too many bumper stickers. All so they can look younger and live longer. Farmers get plenty of exercise. It's known in agricultural circles as *work*. So that being the case, living longer fails to be a desirable goal.

I did try the bicycle thing once, but my butt and spandex didn't mesh. I looked like one of those black plastic trash bags filled with lawn clippings. Women assume they hold all the patents on undesirable body parts. Guess again. Men have the bulge thing which spandex greatly accentuates, or well...the way some men are built it almost appears as if your crotch fought to the death with a vacuum cleaner. I tried adding a ball of Mozzarella cheese to increase my crotch image, but I ended up smelling like a two-day old pizza and being constantly chased by a drooling pack of dogs. I mean, women have it great. They don't have to do the public urinal thing where men do the sideways glance to reinforce that their equipment is on par with everybody else's even though nobody really knows what that means anyway. Cup size? Theirs or ours? A 34-A guarantees you won't need a chiropractor for at least twenty years. Besides, we don't have time to read the label because we're fiddling with the fastener. Once you get beyond the blouse, then it is probably okay to proceed to the mechanical engineering part. You know you have permission because you've been fumbling with it for twenty minutes and she didn't bother to tell you that it snapped in the front. I don't get it. I once called an escort service because, well, I was...well, I was just curious. The woman on the phone described a potential partner as a 38-D. I did a few uh huhs, agreed with something I don't remember and promised to call back. The 'D' threw me. Normally a D is one step from an F. I had to either go to the library and look it up or find a *Victoria's Secret* catalog to figure out what that meant exactly. Turned out her breasts were a D going on F — part of a class-action lawsuit involving some kind of window caulking. Didn't want to schedule a date during a factory recall. But overall the conversation was interesting – no, more like renting a car from Hertz. "You want a mid-size or a luxury?

What about the discount on bondage?" I finally chickened out. Ah, well. Some guys do breasts, farm managers spend so much time staring at mammary glands that the whole thing kind of seems irrelevant.

FINALLY...

...back to breeding theories at last. Is it really that simple to end up on *The Wide World of Sports*? Breeding a great racehorse is a task burdened by traditions, superstitions and rules, not to mention the occasional curse. Added to this pile of veiled obstacles are the actual odds: about 50,000-to-1. (That's the average foal crop born in the United States each year, adjusted for inflation and the few immigrants that wander over from Europe for a fast buck.) It would appear a simpler prospect to fall off a ski jump and land on your head, immortality gained in 'the agony of defeat' rather than the same 'agony of defeat' while you're still conscious and trying to modify the definition of a 'sure thing' in under ten seconds. That's about how long national television is willing to invest in a loser. Ever watch boxing?

"What was it Manny, a left hook?"

"Whasa log yuck whoos it me."

"Over to the winner. So Jesus, you said your hobbies were naked spear fishing and visiting day-care centers? What was it, a left hook?"

The only legitimate tools in the horse breeding shed are knowledge and as much money as you can find. Doc seemed to have the latter. Whether or not he had ready access to it was another matter altogether. Elaine always drove a new Cadillac, was often weighted down with an Aztec treasure in gold trinkets and often wheeled through town like Nancy Reagan on her way to a press conference. If people judged Doc's business acumen according to Elaine's ability to shop, they could only conclude his remarkable genius. Actually it was more like a combination of ransom and a never ending layaway plan. Elaine's idea of "Better Homes and Gardens" was a penthouse above Neiman-Marcus with her own private elevator. Living on a farm required the requisite amenities: the swimming pool, the Cadillac and the winner's circle. Fortunately the former was more critical than the latter. She still dressed for the photographer though every time Doc entered a horse in a race. Oddly, she never seemed to be disappointed when the horse didn't win. I guess a wink from the doorman at the Turf Club said it all.

Money did seem to be the easy part of the equation. Useful knowledge, another matter completely. Even though few subjects in the modern world have been dissected as much as Thoroughbred breeding, the end result is clouded in mystery. A deep, dark, foggy world of contradiction, where no one will admit the results of an experiment until he has coveted the cure, or one of those Nobel things.

A little like the Defense Department when they put 'dignity' and 'withdrawal' in the same sentence. It was a war, not a sexual encounter.

A SUDDENLY FAMOUS BREEDER ON THE SEVENTEENTH GREEN:
(Check out the caddy with the wardrobe problem.)

"Well, I knew that Northern Dancer nicked well with *La Troienne* in the third generation by tail-female descent, concentrating the blood of Teddy in the second dam of my new Bupers mare. By out-crossing to Secretariat the following year, the foal won the Triple Crown."

A YEAR LATER TALKING WITH FATHER MURPHY:

"Gosh, I have to tell you Father, those stocks I bought with the Triple Crown money turned out to be real dogs. The wife wants a new car, my son's gone and picked Harvard so the out-of-state tuition is gonna kill me, the firm's in litigation, gosh Father, I think I'm gonna have to skip Northern Dancer. I had to sell five of my best mares and I swapped a man my golf clubs for a stud fee. You know, the ones I got in Scotland. I got three Buper's mares left and their foals can't outrun me, and well, you know I'm a little heavy. Maybe next year things will pick up a bit."

So the wife got her new car, the kid flunked out of Harvard and started a worm farm in Connecticut and the Buper's mare got hit by lightning. Everybody, except Father Murphy heard the first speech, which sent every breeder on the continent on a mushroom hunt for the same can of DNA in hopes of duplicating a process that was no more difficult than rear-ending a bus.

It is a deflating realization. I had always imagined Thoroughbred breeding as a divine calling for people with so much judgment that they couldn't get rid of it all during the week. Now, I must painfully accept the caustic notion that the bank account is the important part. The good judgment is delegated to the task of keeping the bank account in its bottomless condition. Breeding Thoroughbreds is merely a well-oiled scheme by the Federal Treasury to keep everybody's money from going stale. A few thousand Thoroughbred breeders with no common sense keeps inflation under control and the economy booming. It's the 'trickle-down theory' run amuck. Kind of like what the cat does in his/her litter box, but with more impact.

I was also forced to consider another equally disturbing notion: that money didn't <u>necessarily</u> produce the best racehorse, only that it <u>could</u> produce the best racehorse. This may not make sense, but a horse can look great and still not outrun my Toyota. That begs the point of those after dinner speeches that are normally end-of-the-season Oscar-type get-togethers where you quickly thank everybody and race the mummy to the fire exit. Most of these speeches were based on wildly inflated hindsight, which if it actually worked would mean that most people would applaud the beginning of a movie instead of the end.

Many breeders, including Doc, combined their personal resources and knowledge with classic breeding theories. Ancient dissertations that fell under three broad classifications: Lord So-and- So's theory, Count So-and-So's theory, or more recently, the collected wisdom of Leon Rasmussen, garnered from three hundred back issues of *The Daily Racing Form*. Credibility granted by either royal decree or journalistic confusion. None of these well-intentioned postulations appeared to offer any consistent clue in solving the genetic puzzle, but they did reinforce my own theory: royalty and publishing are excellent avenues toward affording a racehorse.

Theory books have a lot in common with seventh-grade French classes. They offer a new and exciting language, steeped in tradition and culture, and sufficiently perverted to dumbfound logic. And like French, subject to the nuance of misunderstanding:

"Vous désirez votre café dans votre chaussure?"

"I see sir. You wish to have your coffee in your shoe?"

"Excusez-moi, votre ami desire boire votre café dans votre chaussure."

"Oh, pardon. Your friend wishes to have *your* coffee in *your* shoe."

"Oui."

I decided not to argue with a foreign language, opting in favor of my own interpretations, based to a great extent on my inability to understand French, Russian, German, Italian or whatever the hell they speak in Brooklyn. The following are key breeding theory terms developed by Franco Varola, Count Lehndorf, Lord somebody in Wales, Leon Rasmussen, the late Italian genius Tesio (the mummy got him) and two Polish guys named Waddizzxcelov and Zylaboutszi. The terms belong to them, the italicized definitions are mine, adjusted to the realities of the twentieth century:

DOSAGE:

{Pronounced Dow-saaaaage, in a nasally snobbish manner.} The exact amount of money required to buy a horse you can't possibly afford.

TAIL-MALE:

The back part of a boy horse.

TAIL-FEMALE:

The back part of a girl horse. Granted, this may seem painfully obvious, but English aristocracy has a long history of gender confusion.

PROMINENT FAMILIES:

Elaine's relatives.

INBREEDING:

The opposite of out-breeding and not subject to further discussion if you have either a weak stomach or one mare.

OUT-CROSSING:

A buzz word to explain mistaken success and planned failure. Fully interchangeable with any of the above terminology.

VARIABLES:

An overall description of Thoroughbred breeding in general.

Some breeders seek help from industry professionals known as *blood-stock agents*. Quite gifted, these individuals seem to know everything there is to know about a horse. For a small fee (normally ten-percent of all your future earnings), they will accompany you to a sale, buy a suitable mare, find an appropriate stallion and somehow convince fiscally fussy women like Elaine that the whole deal will work out better than a *Fortune 500* stock portfolio. (Blood Stock = BS. Oh, I get it). So did Elaine. Doc wasn't allowed to go to a sale with a live checkbook.

Bloodstock agents have an uncanny ability to sit next to you at a sale, whisper sixteen things in your ear from the catalog page, order a whiskey-sour and engage five other agents in a vicious bidding duel, all with a cell phone pressed to one ear. When the hammer falls, they pump your hand, say something like, "We stole that one!" and rush off to find another victim. The buyer, still in shock, has to sign for the purchase, receive the somewhat sanguine congratulations of the other agents, accept a smile from the auc-tioneer, who has already calculated his commission and then try to digest the exact meaning of the word 'stole.' The two security guards over in the corner giggling don't help with this part of the process. Evidently in the Thoroughbred world, 'stealing' is anything within $100,000 of what you wanted to pay. All expectations and no common sense. It explains why all Thoroughbred auctions have a well-stocked bar.

With the acquisition of a new mare, the next order of business is a suit-able mate. Unlike cousin Sibyl, few female horses become pregnant through divine intervention. Most mares need to date a little, talk about the future and then have a passionate interlude in the backseat of somebody's car. Preferably with a guy that has the right sort of qualifications.

When seeking out a stallion, there are two principle characteristics to debate: speed versus stamina. Since racehorses have an obvious need to get places in a hurry, speed is a good choice. As long as they save their sta-mina for the breeding shed, everything should work out fine. Well, steril-ity is also an issue, especially with all the controversy over athletes and steroids. Steroids make for great muscles, but they also turn most testicles into one half of the Raisin Bran combo. Those little sperm guys do the lem-ming dance and run downhill till they run out of Alaska. Yes, steroids are

common in racehorses. The veterinarians do more training than the trainers in some cases. I suppose that if it was all legal and ethical, the vets
would show up in the winner's circle for the photo. But they don't.

Seeking out the perfect stallion is not as easy as it may sound. Granted,
most stick out like a sore thumb in a crowded elevator, but that is only the
surface of the animal. Lurking just below is the real challenge in modern
husbandry: deciphering the resume. Which is why most major corpora-
tions hire a human resource specialist. Someone who can keep a straight
face when forced to read <u>my</u> resume. (Okay, so I didn't write "War and
Peace." I didn't think anybody would check.)

Bloodstock agents are, as a whole, a very honest group. Somehow
though, when the stallion they represent (they're like Hollywood agents),
gets in front of an audience and the "oohs" and the "aahs" reach a towering
crescendo, they take a slightly dishonest left turn. This affliction is known
as *pedigree padding*. It leads to all forms of wild claims, unsubstantiated
innuendo, false testimony, perjured documentation, prejudicial puffery and
an assortment of scandalous tales last heard at one of those get-togethers
involving Congress and a Special Prosecutor. Including:

*OLYMPIC CHAMPION, THREE YEARS RUNNING

*BRED EXCLUSIVELY TO YASSER ARAFAT'S PRIVATE MARES

*KIDNAPPED IN IRELAND, RECENTLY

*A FULL BROTHER TO THE BLACK STALLION

*QUEEN ELIZABETH'S FAVORITE HORSE

***ACQUIRED SECRETLY IN ONE OF DONALD TRUMP'S
DIVORCE SETTLEMENTS**

*WINNER OF THE INDIANAPOLIS 500

*THE ONLY HORSE RONALD REAGAN EVER RODE, TWICE

Doc tended to support a good many of these wild claims. He had to.
Since he was always on the verge of having his horse budget reapportioned

by the nearest diamond salesman, a viable interest surfaced to inflate the credentials of any horse he showed an interest in. Often, inadvertently selling himself on a wild claim in the process. One such case emerged from the resume of a recently imported stallion from Australia, claiming to have won the Melbourne to Auckland Cup in record time. Turned out that a mere 800 miles of ocean separated the two cities and somebody confused the horse with a sailboat. We still sent a mare to this horse to be bred, but it meant that Doc didn't dare renew Elaine's subscription to *National Geographic* until sometime after the foal was born.

What really hurt Doc's breeding program was the Federal Tax Code. The time to choose a sire roughly coincided with the time of year when Elaine was putting the final spin on the year's books. That hair-pulling, "Oh, my God!" sort of masochistic mental gymnastics act that people endure because it is easier than making new shower buddies at the state pen. Doc would start out in November, budgetarily confident he could get a booking to Nijinsky as easily as dialing the phone. (Remember, this is a conversation between two enablers addicted to supporting the bad habit of the other addict to the same substance sold under a different name but with the same ingredients and the same tragic results. And when caught, both go, "What?") Recovery is rare. "God grant me the serenity" doesn't work with racehorse breeders. We're into adrenaline. We only do humility if the mummy is around

Before heading off to Palm Springs, Doc would have collected the evidence for his case: parchment style pedigrees, computer print-outs of the race records, Leon Rasmussen's latest fashion statement from the *Daily Racing Form* and eight-by-ten glossies of Nijinsky, shining like black gold on the kitchen table. By the day of departure, Nijinsky's attributes had dropped dramatically, no doubt the result of Elaine's uncanny ability to use an adding machine. A $50,000 stud fee to produce a $3200 claimer? I guess she really did earn that Cadillac.

Doc was a proud man, but then again, he was a realist. We never called these economic second-string stallions, 'cheap.' We referred to them in the vernacular of the sport – *long shots*; gifted sorts that never got the breaks of the great ones. It was a lesson in the intricacies of marital and agricultural diplomacy. Doc would remain the husband, I the employee. For down in the right-hand corner of my monthly check was the true meaning of life on this farm: Elaine's signature.

9.

BAPTISMS & INQUISITIONS: THE RITES OF SPRING – OR, MAYBE JUST A MOVING VIOLATION

THERE ARE QUITE a few rituals that announce the arrival of spring. Some invoke Nature's more subtle face: barn swallows on their annual migration to the light fixtures outside the barn, mice building maternity nests in the air filter of my truck, allergies that produce enough nasal fluid to drown a bull elephant. I mean, where does that stuff come from? Does part of your brain melt? Does your nose engage in a hostile takeover with your bladder? How can a human manufacture enough snot in one day to fill a bathtub? Sometimes I'd sneeze so hard that it felt like my kneecaps blew off and I started leaving a slime trail behind me. People put salt on my back because they thought I was a slug about to ravage their lettuce patch. Allergy tests came back positive for pollen, hay, mold, horses, mud, the presence of women and cat dandruff. Nothing about dead pheasants or dismembered rodents and defunct lawnmowers, but my tissue bill was starting to outrun my salary. I was thinking about having a vacuum cleaner hose permanently installed in my nose, but I figured everybody would think I was a *Star Trek* groupie. I didn't just have nasal drip, I had a full-blown case of nasal volcanic activity – a lava flow trying to construct a new island in my handkerchief. It seemed that I was allergic to everything in my job description, including the cat who insisted on sleeping on my mouth at night. I was too gutless to throw him (or her) out the window. Geez, I have to settle this cat-sex issue. Maybe I could be more assertive if I knew it was a guy-cat. We could have a couple of beers, fight to the death in some obscure parking lot and I could get my bed back. Considering how the competition went over dead pheasants, I've got a pretty good idea who would end up on top. It was easier to wake up with a mouth full of cat hair.

Another spring ritual can best be described as 'frog thawing.' Thousands and thousands of these little green amphibians all wake up at once, orating their displeasure over a cold, bugless world. I know that frogs hibernate, but I have no clue where. In trees, underground, at a Motel 6? How do they synchronize the wake-up call? How do they go from narcolepsy to mass insomnia in one night? And further, what's all this frog conversation about? Sure, it's a sex thing, but they all sound alike. The girl frogs are probably doing most of the talking, the guy frogs thinking about a quick get-together. Think of the all frog scoring going on in the pastures. Talk about an amphibious orgy. Then again, some frogs are known to be hermaphrodites. Cash strapped bars should consider that anomaly before they schedule the next 'Ladies Night.' Why be so selective in a bad economy?

Maybe I sympathize a bit too much with frogs. As a small child, I engaged in that pre-pubescent pursuit known as tadpole collecting, a process by which you dip an old mayonnaise jar into a pool of swampy water in hopes of catching a wild animal. Trust me, you don't want to try this in Florida. Alligators don't do mayonnaise jars. They eat mayonnaise jars and the idiot hanging on to it.

Tadpole collecting was a transition from bee collecting, only much safer, especially if you forgot to put the lid on the jar. I have never figured out why a kid would want a jar full of pissed-off bees. Why not collect hand-grenades? My friend Bobby Evans tried to shove an entire nest into his jar. The service was nice, but it was definitely a closed-casket affair.

Most of us at that tender age of exploration had already figured out metamorphosis, whereby a tadpole suddenly sprouts legs. Our science teachers went to great lengths on this subject, vainly hoping to remove the "Yech!" from the word 'biology.' Few of us fell for this obvious trap, but the idea of a fish growing legs and walking off, sounded too fascinating to be completely ignored. So the jar of swamp water found its way to a bedroom shelf, gently placed between a box of marbles and my rock collection. Here, the tadpoles would swim vigorously near the surface of the jar, while I waited impatiently for the frog transformation thing. By the third day, the tadpoles suffered what I considered to be a major setback. They died. I was forced to facilitate the usual goldfish-toilet-bowl funeral ceremony.

That experience caused me to develop a severe distrust in the principles of biology. No longer would I casually accept a teacher's painstaking explanation of cellular division or photosynthesis. Science was flawed — tadpoles died for no apparent reason without converting themselves into a frog, and a 'D' in science wasn't the end of the world, even if it did affect my television privileges for extended periods of time. Sure, I felt bad about their sudden demise, but given my allowance at the time, an autopsy was out of the question.

The great frog conspiracy returned in the eighth-grade. By then, biology had advanced from "Yech!" all the way to the throwing-up phase. Captured frogs were imprisoned in large terrariums, held hostage by the diabolical Mr. Cudgel, a coke-bottle bespectacled science teacher determined to pound into our young minds the difference between an amphibian lung and a Bunsen burner.

Each of us was supplied with a scalpel, a long needle and a terrified frog. With the cunning of a man obviously immune to God's displeasure over frog murder, Mr. Cudgel demonstrated proper 'frog anesthesia,' known in the frog mayhem business as 'pithing.' Pithing requires you to insert the long needle in the back of the frog's head, upward toward the brain. In human terms, it's like a total lobotomy. As Cudgel explained it, this piece of work would alleviate the frog of any suffering and make him more cooperative for what was to follow: frog open-heart surgery.

My frog was having none of it. Evidently, he had heard Cudgel's speech before. The fires of rebellion quickly spread through the classroom, the 'pithers' on the wrong end of the French Revolution. When order was finally restored, three people had thrown-up (one in my backpack), two were in tears and science had taken a long leap backward. My frog found its way into my shirt pocket. It would live free, far from the mad plots and schemes of men like Cudgel. Men who assumed that science and frog murder were somehow connected. Yeah, I got another 'D.'

For farm managers, the true rituals of spring are definitely adversarial. Man against nature, nature against man and sometimes man against man. Progressive thinking is not always a universally shared concept when two males try to possess the same fem…well, farm. Think if you had two captains piloting the same cruise ship. Hawaii! No dammit, Alaska!

"Honey, do you think I look fat in this bikini?"

"Ah, gosh no, Madeline. You really goin' to wear it on the glacier tour?"

"*Glacier?* Was thinking about it. Are you sure it doesn't make me look fat?"

These are all organic tasks like field mowing, tree maintenance, mud management – a sort of social reform that must be conducted in secrecy. I was re-arranging Doc's farm without Congress's permission. I now understand the whole Oliver North thing. If you already know that the answer is 'no,' then you simply rephrase the question so that 'no' becomes 'yes' and further clarification is followed by 'what?' The CIA learned most of its tactics from third-graders. What I had to do was find some scrap of credibility for my new government. It wasn't like I could fire the Prime Minister. He was a cat. Oh, Doc clarified that issue. The cat was a 'he,' minus certain accessories. Even so, I had to work out a sales pitch whereas cause and effect were somewhere on the same page or at least the same acre.

For some people, excuses come naturally. I never pictured myself as a particularly gifted criminal. I found lying difficult, thievery revolting and, as you know, I can't even con the cat into sleeping on the floor. Yet, I felt compelled to offer anything but the truth in defense of my spring assault on the farm.

"Yes Doc, the babbling brook is missing. No, I'm not sure where it went. The boat? What boat? Oh, *that* boat. Your son-in-law took it." God, I hoped he actually had a son-in-law. We glossed over the thing with the neighbors.

We also discussed the backhoe bill, the missing mud, certain aspects of *Rastafarian* culture and the need for a Republican president. Throughout most of this, Doc's eyes remained fixed on the barn, his lips gingerly rehearsing a disapproval speech. It wasn't that he liked chaos, it was just that chaos seemed so much more manageable. He was about to speak when Silly the cat mistook his leg for a scratching post. Once he stopped jumping around in circles, I used the opportunity to take the conversation in another direction.

"Well, you know Doc, I saved about three tons of hay by getting the water out of the barn and you know, you can actually walk in there without hip-waders." I felt my voice rising into a subordinate whine, the excuses sounding very much like…excuses. I was trying to figure out a way to turn off his mental digestion. "And besides, it was such a damn…"

Suddenly, from our distant vantage point, we both heard a familiar, "Doc!" coming from the direction of the main house. That was immediately followed by an ominous question: "Who's Nijinsky?!"

"Oh, God," Doc muttered under his breath. "I forgot to cancel that breeding contract." He quickly spun around, marching toward the house, no doubt ready to face the wrath of a bookkeeper-wife defiled by an overdrawn checking account. I pounced on what I saw as a political opportunity.

"Tell her I forgot to cancel it," I deadpanned. "That's my job, right?"

Doc's pace slowed to a crawl, then abruptly stopped. Turning, he took a broad visual sweep of the new barn area. "This actually looks pretty good," he stated, his objections suddenly swamped by the notion of self-preservation. "I better get to the house," he continued, raising his voice as he departed. When he got to the front door, he turned back towards me. "Dammit, I wish you had remembered to cancel that contract! What do I pay you for anyway?!" Then, with a grin, he disappeared into the house.

For the next two-weeks, I skillfully avoided Elaine. All I had to do was hide in the barn. That was the one place she'd never go. I limited my confrontations to the plant family: grass, trees, shrubs – species that harbored no great influence over my future employment.

In Washington, grass grows very well. In fact, most everything does. With an abundance of rain, a few warm days and not enough fat broodmares to eat the stuff, pastures rapidly turn into equatorial Africa. By trading *my* imagination for the cat's, I was able to churn out a vast zoological portrait of skulking wildlife: lions and Kodiak bears, zebras and gazelles – large, ugly, ravenous snakes – hunting and hunted just beyond the sacred boundary of the pasture gate. Not to mention a few unlucky pheasants. It was really more than a farm manager could stand. With a tractor and a field mower, Africa could be tamed, brought to its domestic knees by the implements of advancing civilization, or if necessary, churned into compost. Sounds like one of Queen Victoria's speeches. The cat liked the compost idea. Mouse *mousse*.

I failed to realize though that Washington gives up winter a lot more reluctantly than equatorial Africa. Under that innocent covering of grass and weeds was an earthly substance capable of stopping Patton's Third Army: wet clay. A 50/50 mix of dirt and Elmer's Glue. Probably a few frogs as well.

I started out my mission feeling a bit cocky. No, arrogant. No, cavalier; brazen with a little bumptious swagger thrown in. I mean, hell, I finally had my hands on some real farm machinery. I made one swipe around the fifteen-acre broodmare field like a hot knife through butter. Okay, that's a cliché, but all authors are allowed one per book. Just ask Leo, my agent. He's the guy at the end of the bar, sleeping in a plate of spaghetti. I stood up on the tractor as I drove. I had seen real farmers do this in the movie adaptation of Steinbeck's, "Grapes of Wrath." (Only later did I realize that was because tractors didn't have seats in those days.) I surveyed the battlefield. The enemy was on the run. Everywhere weeds were running up little white flags or bounding the fence into the neighbor's pasture – hoping to surrender to a more benevolent foe. Too bad, they moved.

"What power!" I yelled to no one in particular. Within a week I'd invade Idaho. I quickly decided to grind up the grass in fourth gear instead of third and save myself an hour or so in the battle. "Piece of cake," I mused, as I slipped out the clutch and roared down the fence line for a second slice of agricultural immortality.

History is rarely kind when it comes to situations where overconfidence collides head-on with the forces of nature. Few people remember the great victories of General Cornwallis in the Carolinas during the Revolutionary War. However, everybody recalls his humiliation at Yorktown. My Yorktown, equally desperate, terminated the spring campaign about a hundred yards from where it began. The tractor veered into a tire rut of the previous mowing swipe and unceremoniously sank in a bog hole. Being a little new to this farming stuff, I figured that 3000 rpm's were better than 2000, so I hit the accelerator. That accomplished two rather unfortunate things. First, it managed to sink the tractor up to its axles, and second, it flung about fourteen-pounds of wet clay and dismembered frogs on to the back of my shirt. Neither of which moved the tractor an inch.

Spirit bent, but not broken, I headed for the barn and appropriated ten feet of chain and Doc's Jeep Wagoneer, a vehicle whose only purpose was to haul around a bag of golf clubs and his three murderous dogs.

Once I had the Jeep hooked to the tractor, I assumed my problems to be over. I began backing the Jeep slowly away from the submerged tractor, watching carefully through the open tailgate window as the chain gradually gained tension. Once it was taut, I gently pressed the accelerator, not wanting to repeat that rpm thing. I expected to see the tractor slowly lift from its muddy tomb, a bit like reversing what happened to the Titanic. Instead, I felt the Jeep wrench and groan, the suspension creeping downward toward the center of the earth. I decided right then that I better have a look at the situation before I ended up with more clay on my shirt. What I saw appalled me. The tractor <u>and</u> the Jeep were now sharing a puddle that was swiftly becoming a pond. Even the chain was under water. The tires on the Jeep were coated with a thick layer of yellowish-brown clay, worn absolutely smooth by three seconds of spinning. There also appeared to be a few dismembered frogs stuck in the treads. Trust me, dead frogs don't increase your traction. If you get caught in a snowstorm without chains, try dead hamsters. Frogs are no help whatsoever.

My first thought was to use *my* truck to pull out the Jeep so I could once again try to use <u>it</u> to pull out the tractor. My second thought had to do with the law of diminishing returns, whereby my prospects would diminish considerably with three drowned vehicles versus two. Besides, the puddle/pond was slowly becoming a lake. And the frogs, well, they were beginning to circle the mess and looking a little predatory. With the bug shortage, there was no telling what they might do.

I trudged the half-mile to Chet's Garage, skipping the 'Honk for Service' admonition since I didn't have anything to honk anyway. He was off in one corner of the garage swearing at a piston, grease smeared all over his forehead as if a midnight parachute into hostile territory was planned. I greeted him politely, listened once again to the 'gas tanker over the Cascade Mountains' story and meekly explained my predicament. I gave him the usual lame excuses: sudden monsoon, radioactive clay, Florida sink-hole, communist frogs – the whole nine-yards. He wasn't buying any of it. Under his breath, I vaguely heard the words 'moron' and 'idiot' used in the same sentence. Even so, he came right over.

The sad part was that his evaluation of my agricultural skills roughly paralleled the truth. He preferred moron to incompetent as it involved fewer syllables. I was forced to admit that I was the apprentice, he the master, each of us incapable of surrendering our pre-ordained roles in life. No matter what, he would always be older and wiser, a frustrated Aristotle trying to pound some common sense into the most pathetic of students. I tried to view the whole thing as fatherly concern, cloaked in a few four-letter words, but the adoption papers never came through. He was far too well-trained in the subtle connection between capitalism and stupidity. His whole career had been based on certain men's inability to figure out a screwdriver or how many vehicles are allowed to occupy a mass grave.

Since most crime has its punishment, mine was an afternoon spent trying to unglue a whole bunch of clay from the inside of Doc's Jeep. I had left the back window down in order to be able to view the tow chain. The spinning tires managed to telegraph most of this crap into the cab. Even the ashtrays were full. Chet did manage to pull all this machinery out of my new lake, but I was still stuck with a Jeep that looked like it had tried to spawn in the Mississippi River.

All that rain that falls on Washington is often accompanied by a good deal of wind. Our (my) farm was one of several old estates in the area, most dating from the 1930's and 40's. As such, most of the landscaping was old, vastly overgrown and according to one local botanist, on the wrong continent entirely. The farm was originally a much larger estate, but a downturn in the wrinkled khaki pants industry caused it to be chopped up into smaller chunks. According to the legend, Bauer imported about a hundred illegal Philippine landscapers along with about 5,000 trees and shrubs shortly after World War II. Really, it was a wonder to behold. Rhododendron trees, magnificent star magnolias, azaleas, lilacs and virtually every kind of maple known to man.

Intertwined with this botanical menagerie were the tentacles of the Northwest blackberry, the closest living relative to barbed-wire in the plant kingdom. These things can grow a foot a day, making it a really bad idea to fall asleep next to one. Blackberry management had definitely been lacking around the farm. I was faced with a giant, cancerous, thorny growth from the depths of hell, or maybe Canada, intent on overthrowing all forms of civil society. Nothing, short of Agent Orange was capable of killing the stuff. Napalm only stunted its growth for a day or two. I could injure it slightly with the field mower, but most activity involving that implement was under a feasibility review.

Spring weather actually prevented me from any further embarrassment in the fields. A typical spring storm cancels planned incompetency in favor of the unplanned version. On old estates, it is a three-part disaster: first the rain loosens up the roots on those old trees. This is followed by a wind storm which causes the tree to lose interest in living. The tree then falls on either A) a brand new fence, B) across the driveway, or C) into the middle of a blackberry patch, where the thorny arms of the green octopi curl around the trunk in a fatal embrace. It then becomes a farm manager's duty to convert these former monuments to landscaping purity into something that will fit in the fireplace, without dying a prickly death in the process. And regardless of what you're thinking, the field mower is no match for twelve-thousand board feet of old growth whatever.

My favorite tool for the job is a chainsaw. Most models consist of a smoky engine attached to a sharp bicycle chain that maniacally spins around, throwing wood chips into my eyes, my shoes and in some cases, my underwear. That is, and here is the big hitch: *if* it wants to start that day. I think everybody knows this drill: a couple of warm days and every land-scaper wants to invade a foreign country with a pull cord. You've heard about those rotator-cuff injuries that professional pitchers get? It's not pitching. It's trying to get some damn machine started on a short weekend when you're up on the rotation list. The first thing professional pitchers ask a real estate agent has to do with the front lawn: "It's plastic, right?" Of course with a salary of $3 million a year it doesn't seem likely they'll be yanking any pull-cords. Not with their agent in the spare bedroom.

I really think that an unemployed orthopedic surgeon invented that piece of rope. I'd spend more time cranking than actually doing any work. My left arm was at least six inches longer than my right. I'd set the choke, I'd crank, I'd unset the choke (reverse psychology), finally, I'd scream at the damn thing. More psychology. Machines don't seem to get involved in verbal negotiations. Instead they just sputter like a fish trying to inhale air for the first time. It's a lose/lose proposition. I mean, humans should have the right to intimidate machines. It's gotta be somewhere in the *Bill of Rights*. Right to bear arms? Right to defame all sorts of machinery? What's the bloody difference? I don't think the founding fathers anticipated the arrival of two-stroke engines, though the similarity to an ill-tempered mule might have influenced the ultimate design.

The truth is that most chainsaws won't start in an emergency. If a close relative is trapped in a burning Ford by a renegade birch tree, it won't start. Same goes if you get a sudden urge to carve a totem pole. Want to take a trip into the wilderness to cut a Christmas tree for the grandkids? Forget it. Better off taking a 357 magnum and just blowing the trunk off. Odd, but guns always seem to work. The only time chainsaws show any consistency is when you mistakenly set one on the hood of a brand new truck. It will not only start all by itself, but it won't shut off until it's chewed its way through the engine block.

Disposing of prostrate trees always sounds much simpler than the actual job. Even if the chainsaw does happen to start, there are a number of rules that professional loggers never share with local idiots. The foremost is what is commonly called the 'pinch.' According to the specialists (guys with red suspenders – no, I don't know why they wear them), this phenomenon is roughly equivalent to a pair of elephants in an amorous embrace. The weight of the log causes the cut to turn into a giant metal-eating clam that won't give up the saw blade without a long and vicious altercation. This rather disrespectful act occurs on the first slice, leaving about eleven tons of tree trunk stuck on the end of your saw. You can't yell for help, because every logger within five miles will show up to question your intelligence. Not that intelligence has anything to do with it anyway. It's an ego thing. Columbus wandering around the Atlantic? A bunch of guys with dysentery, no women, no beer and God knows what for dinner in sudden agreement with the flight plan? No, ego is a big part. No tree that didn't have the guts to stand up to a little bad weather is going stop the...my God, I'm starting to sound like the Post Office.

The other problem with these inanimate, incompetent things is 'chain tension.' Too much or too little? Too much and quite literally, the chainsaw imitates a frozen pizza. Too little and it has this nasty habit of flying off the bar and doing a bolo-knot around your belt buckle, usually removing a little denim in the process. If the chain is exceptionally loose when it parts company with the saw...well, don't plan on having a lot of fun with the grandchildren.

The last problem has to do with prostrate trees versus trees that need to assume the position. It is easier to get a felon on the ground than a tree. Real loggers ponder the height, their blood-alcohol level, the limb load, which way it is leaning (normally toward a house, a car that is about to suddenly increase in value or a couple of 200,000 volt power lines), and finally, whether to ponder the whole escapade at the nearest bar. I always vote for the latter, especially when Elaine took issue with a fifty-foot cedar that had the audacity to cast a shadow on her swimming pool. I guess that's where the suspenders come in: loop one end around a rafter in the garage and the other end around your neck. Since they stretch, you can always change your mind part way through the exercise. Sure, it's gutless, but it beats the hell out of explaining it to the pool guy.

Elaine did manage to finally corner me one afternoon about the stud fee indiscretion. She was getting pretty good at the old Indian trick of following wind-borne expletives. She suggested a new activity for my duty roster: washing her car. She also thought it might be a good idea for Doc to help out. So every Sunday for the next month, Doc and I scrubbed her Cadillac. We nicknamed it Nijinsky.

__Later that evening my sister__ Dana called to tell me that she was breaking up with the produce manager at Safeway and planning to marry a Hispanic coke dealer from Canada. Sister had gone from tomboy, to neighborhood mercenary and then to man collecting. A psychiatrist could probably explain this activity better than I can.

"Don't you think that's a little dangerous?" Congratulations seemed, well...too happy?

"Oh, gosh no. It's not like Canada's a foreign country or anything!"

Three months later hubby was found in a Vancouver motel room shot, stabbed and decapitated. They didn't need the dental records since they couldn't find his head. All sister could say was, "This isn't supposed to happen in Canada — not Canada!" I skipped the funeral.

10.

IT'S ALL IN THE NAME

MAY 30TH IS the official close of foaling season. By this point all the mares have safely given birth and been shipped off to meet their new boyfriends. Since the gestation period for a girl horse is approximately eleven months, few mares get to stay home until their figures improve, which goes a long way to explain why the national conception rate for Thoroughbred mares is a miserly 52%. They're just not ready for romance. They all want to be a size 2, when in reality they are somewhere near an eighteen. It's a female thing.

Since few foals are born after May, a little arithmetic will show that few mares date after June 1st. In the wild (when horses were known as 'food'), most foals were born in spring or early summer, nature giving the best possible advantage to the baby by providing warm days and an abundance of fodder. However, this system was extremely inconvenient to a number of people in New York who wanted to race their horses at the same time of the year that the barbecue was being unpacked. This led, in the 1800's to the formation of *The Jockey Club*, an organization similar to a Turkish court but with fewer executions and a lot more paperwork.

In order to insure that an afternoon of racing could be followed by beer and ribs, these early organizers implemented a universal birth date of January 1st for all Thoroughbreds born in North America. Actually *The English Jockey Club* came up with this plan in the 1700's and it's one of the few archaic English customs that survived the Tea Party. Since the *Brits* aren't big on barbecuing, it probably had something to do with either the Cod season or the Irish. By January, half of Ireland had already starved to death, so it was quite natural to move on to something more gratifying. It was a case of jurisdictional arrogance on a grand scale, but it made it a lot easier to plan all those birthday parties.

The tradition has held weight to this day, reinforcing the unpopularity of a foal born in June, or the idea of a mare getting overly amorous in January. Since Mother Nature wasn't consulted by *The Jockey Club*, 'Mom' has responded by enforcing the old-fashioned tradition of identifying real maturity according to actual minutes spent sucking air. Think if they did this to people. All the restaurants would fill up on January 1st, Hallmark stores would go nuts and everybody would spend the day singing *Happy Birthday*. It would be like a cross between a mass escape from the local zoo and a polka festival with a no-host bar. The entire country would come to a standstill because everybody would be too hung over the next day to even sort the mail. Trust me, the old Soviet Union would take advantage of this guttural orgy and overrun Europe. Before everybody digested enough aspirin and tomato juice, the Red Army would be dining in Paris. Once Russians tasted real food, they'd never go home.

Washington State used to have this unusual custom where everybody had to re-license their vehicles by January 1st. I mean everybody. Procrastinating is built into our culture. Just ask all those Post Office guys on April 15th. The local license bureau looked like a food stamp convention five days before Thanksgiving. Lots of foot tapping, nervous glances, line cheating, lame excuses – staring at watches. A lot of folks were worried about their jobs, not realizing that the boss and the whole HR department were in line somewhere behind them. Oh yeah, I was number 345 on the left. They finally abandoned the practice because most of the agents went out on permanent psychiatric leave the following day. Some needed an exorcist with a background in profanity extraction. I hadn't seen that much wrong-way enthusiasm since the '73 oil embargo, which proved to the world that Americans had a lot less patience than anybody ever imagined. Those two issues constituted the political and social origins of 'road rage.' Without the tags on your car or gas in the tank, you couldn't go out and illegally tailgate, drive drunk, or do the "guess where I'm going next" routine. Seems everybody wanted the ten feet of asphalt just in front of *your* car and once they accomplished that goal, they'd discover another ten feet in front of another car and another and…sounded a little like horseracing without a specific goal in mind. Awfully competitive considering the lack of prize money involved. The winner gets what? A $485.00 summons to traffic court? Seems a little counterintuitive in a culture that embraces embezzlement as a viable business plan.

What this all comes down to is that Thoroughbreds race at a fairly young age and they don't get to feel special on their birthdays. Imagine doing that to a child. Little Billy sharing his special day with three or four million other little Billy's. Plus, how would you handle the invitations? Little Billy #1 couldn't attend Little Billy #2's party since he had to host one at his house. Little Suzy couldn't come either because she needed to welcome the no-shows at her own gala event. The only presents would come from relatives, which meant that everyone got socks, school supplies and pants that didn't fit. A whole generation would grow up unable to grasp the subtle nuances of self-gratification, external validation, conceit, avarice, jealousy and selfishness. Sulking would still be an issue, but then you do get to eat a whole chocolate cake by yourself. How bad can that be?

The issue of physical maturity in racehorses is a lot more contentious than simply deciding who gets to blow out the candles at the non-event. Horse owners haven't adopted the 'dog system' (1 year = 7) as yet, primarily because of the universal birth date. That causes the math to be a little fuzzy and as horses and people get a little older, we get a little testy about the topic. In addition, horses race year 'round and a clear distinction in class and eligibility exists – particularly between three and four-year-olds. That's when *fillies* become *mares,* and *colts* become obnoxious or endowed with racing's generic enigma: *horse.* I'm not sure which party is getting the sexual snub here. The vernacular indicates that once a mare is four years old, she stays a mare. No upgrade possible. On the other hand when a colt hits the magic number, he becomes an *older horse.* He only gets to be a *stallion* when he shows up on a farm. So sex means a promotion for the guy, while the mare just stays a mare. Geldings don't seem to gain any new distinction at all. One little surgical procedure and you've hit the glass ceiling. If they continue to race, they get lumped in with the older horses and are deemed *handicappers.* And everybody knows just what kind of handicap we're talking about.

So no matter which system you adopt (one birthday or 40,000 simultaneous birthdays), foals born after June 1st might as well seek out a career as a pony, for it is really tough to win a race when your legs are five inches shorter than everybody else's. Plus the teasing by the other horses is almost unbearable. And think about the jockeys trying desperately to win a race while their boots are dragging along the ground. Jockeys have an enormous ego to support. Next to weight, a little excessive self-assuredness is not a bad attribute when you're piloting 1100 pounds of over-enthusiasm at 40mph. Especially when you've got ten other jockeys determined to get to traffic court ahead of you. Not a good time to bother with civility or turn signals.

Most people should also refrain from picking a fight with a jockey, even after they've hung up their spurs. They are pound for pound the toughest athletes on the planet. *Sport's Illustrated* proved this point when they tested athletes just prior to publication of the Swim Suit Edition. (That was both an incentive and a rather sly marketing scheme.) Willie Shoemaker beat out Walter Payton by approximately two to one. *SI* claimed that the judging criteria was confidential, so we never found out if Willie's horse was included in the equation.

At some point in the grim, cold, bitter months of winter, I had made a solemn vow to the cat that during the spring months some attempt would be made to organize my herd of hairy anarchists. Procrastination notwithstanding, my vow was in danger of colliding head-on with the chores connected to summer. If you could call it summer. In Washington the sun is a shy woman with a broken mirror, clouded in a veiled mystique that might be lifted sometime in the waning days of August, if at all. Added to this was a personal problem: I'm not particularly adept at tasks where organization is a critical requirement. Most of my socks don't match, I change the oil in my truck when the engine freezes up and I pay most of my bills once something has been shut off, or an out-of-state collection agency leaves me ten messages in three languages on the same day. Normally, it's not about money. More often than not, it is because I tend to clean my mobile home with a weed blower. Anything not anchored down ends up somewhere in the Ionosphere. On top of *my* defective business acumen, the cat loves to shred anything made of paper. He was always in training for pheasant season. Try giving that excuse to a collection agency. They'd repossess used toilet paper if a market existed for it.

What I had in mind was to produce an information bank on all these renegade horses. Stuff like inoculations, foaling dates, breeding history, voting records and bad habits. Data a person wouldn't give to the IRS without a subpoena. Even after a few months, the horses and I were still in the 'dating' phase, trying to figure out who was a star and who might be replaceable with a parakeet. This is a really mundane task that involves spending $50 on pre-printed forms designed to record all the pertinent information outlined above. I had a ball with the 'bad habits' section. What an opportunity to drive some stallion owner insane. "She won't breed until she's kicked the hell out of a least one testicle." That always resulted in a long-distance call from a frantic horse breeder.

"Should we hobble her?" he'd ask.

"Sure," I'd say. "Handcuff her to the bed. She'll love it."

Each of these pre-printed dossiers had a spot on the top for the most critical of all notations: the horse's name. I had never given names much thought until I began scribbling notes on these forms. Suddenly, names began to stand out like beacons of self-serving *sophism*. For my needs the intention wasn't to provoke excited conversation at a cocktail party or to make one kid more important than another. Names were simply a way to separate one brown horse from another. Evidently, that isn't always the case. Names also resemble bumper stickers slapped on the back of a Volvo station wagon. They gladly answer the question of, "Who am I and what do I believe in?" That leads to all kinds of political statements wrapped up in a four-legged billboard. Racehorses were named *Pro-Choice*, *Peace Now*, or *Bomb Serbia*. Unless the name was particularly profane, *The Jockey Club* would pretty much go for anything. Creativity played a major role, a little like personalized license plates. Unless *The Jockey Club* had a couple of English majors around, the occasional slip or mutated consonants tended to glide by. The whole process turned into a jigsaw puzzle with certain conspiratorial overtones. One well-known Italian entrepreneur, known for 'that San Francisco treat' turned most of his racehorses into four-legged advertising campaigns. Even Doc named one weanling after a female acquaintance's breasts. Something about Charlie's *Boom Boom*. Private jokes are kind of confusing, so I guess the conservative bastion in New York misses a few. However, the locals get it. This woman was thrilled to have a racehorse named after her chest. I'm not sure Elaine was amused, particularly since nobody seemed to know who the mysterious Charlie happened to be. It wasn't her husband. Imagine though, a racehorse named for a famous bra size. I loved it. Wait until *The Jockey Club* reads this book. Boy, are they going to take a serious look at policies and procedures. We're going to end up back at the "Bob" and "Joe" thing. Creativity is going to be set back decades. Conservatism is not necessarily a good thing for racing. Racetracks need bad English and X-rated innuendo far more than a dress code. Think of the hunch bettors who would latch onto something with an overly obtrusive name. I bet the handle would increase by 80%, without the need for a pay-off of any kind. I once bet on a horse named *Blubberbreath*. It was just so damn irresistible. I wasn't betting on the horse, I was betting on the creativity of the owner. So what if the horse was a twenty-to-one shot? Hell, two bucks wasn't going to cripple my over-drawn bank account. I looked at it like buying an Andy Warhol print. The guy is dead, he paints soup cans and dead sex symbols and they do nothing except escalate in value. Nobody seems to be overly concerned about Warhol's art school credentials – formal justification or royal breeding would just ruin the appeal. Blubberbreath is really a traveling art show for Americans with bad taste and I'm part owner! Where else can you get acculturated for $2.00 except at a racetrack?

I tried to make an analytical connection to dog names, that process peo-ple engage in to make a political statement with a part Beagle. There are Irish Setters named Chardonnay for the upwardly mobile, black Labs named Bubba for the beer-drinking, Ford pick-up, NRA, I–hate-everybody crowd, and of course, the Orange-County-always-vote-Republican poodle, named something like *Newt.* Currently the trend is a Pit bull named Vulcan Electrified Deathhead Gangsta Mojoo. You can figure out the rest. Ani-mals are a rather cheap extension of our political leanings or some people's inability to read and write. Most dogs don't bother to vote and the major-ity will agree with any stupid notion if raw meat is involved.

Horses are a bit different. Oh sure, someone will engage in ego-exten-sion with a monumental masterpiece like King Fritz of Norway, but the majority of the time, the names are a subtle pattern of intellectual sword-play, not unlike a *New York Times* crossword puzzle.

Since racing is known as the Sport of Kings, royal titles lead the long list of abused wordage. 'Sir' this, 'Regal' that, 'Princess' something else, or even a combination of the sire and dam's names: 'Sir Regal Princess.' The trouble is that nobody knows whether to call the horse a he, or a she, or a maybe. A lot like San Francisco on a Saturday night.

Mischievous breeders always go for the tongue-twister. They hope to live long enough to hear a track announcer cope with a stretch duel between 'Tananabanana' and 'Pickinpurplepeppers.' Oral gymnastics that will require a tongue surgeon and a crowbar to untangle. "And down the stretch they come!" Followed by a lot of choking noises and a call to 911.

The most popular names incorporate a hidden meaning. Sometimes, well hidden. In *The Jockey Club Foal Book*, a 500-odd page printed mon-ument to abstract thinking, every foal born in the last thirty years or so is listed. The purpose being that no race is going to have ten horses named Secretariat. That would definitely screw up the betting. Every name ever forced upon a racehorse is listed in alphabetical order, published no doubt to help rid the world of four-legged redundancies. The book has had limited success. Breeders will stay up all night to create the perfect name, or more accurately, a name that nobody in their right mind would take credit for unless it first went through an announcer. How about 'Cheyenne Showdown,' 'Monkey Madness,' or 'Donut Head?' Remember, intelligent, educated adults actually filled in the boxes on the registration form.

On page 112 is a horse named 'Coincidence.' Sired by 'Questionnaire,' the mother is none other than 'Small World.' Also worth mentioning are 'Compassion' (out of a mare named 'Humane'), 'Compliance' (out of 'Requested') and 'Double Ugly,' whose grand-sire is 'Stefan the Great,' though he is probably too embarrassed to take any credit. 'Double Ugly?' It's that Wildebeest thing, but more complicated.

A good many breeders fail to take name choosing seriously enough. In the 1940's the book highlighted the 'Little' dynasty. Among the group was 'Little Action,' 'Little Beauty' (which probably explained the former), 'Little Flush,' 'Little Hussy' (probably not related to 'Little Action'), 'Little Snail' and finally, 'Little Lost,' a condition most of us in the Thoroughbred business are acquainted with on a daily basis. The line seemed to end in 1956 with a horse named 'Little Little,' no doubt a victim of the great noun drought.

For those of us indentured with the task of simply managing these magnificent animals, pomp and ceremony take a back seat to practicality. Standing at the barn gate at five in the afternoon yelling for 'King Fritz of Norway' to come for dinner would undoubtedly prompt the neighbors to call the police. I'm talking about the neighbors that do the lawn chair thing every time I step out the door. The other neighbors are long gone. They're probably basking in good mental health on the outskirts of Melbourne. The *other* neighbors watch me because they can't afford cable. For them, I'm the agricultural version of *Saturday Night Live*. They even bring popcorn. I end up like a drive-in movie with five customers.

So the spring months gave me an opportunity to attach a new name to each of Doc's broodmares. Sure, I used their registered names whenever Elaine was around, which wasn't too often, or when *The Jockey Club* called for some form of clarification, that normally being twice a day. Clarification was important. Between me, Doc, and *The Jockey Club,* none of us were capable of matching the paperwork with a likely candidate. The high court of paperwork in New York noted this fault in their system and finally initiated blood typing for all Thoroughbreds. That led to some brilliant conversations around the farm:

"Say Doc. Says here that that horse isn't Spit. It's some horse named...I can't read this. What does that say?" I'm trying to read the fine print.

"It says 'sterile.' That's the label thing." Doc had glasses, I only had eyes.

"Well if it's not Spit, then who is it?" I was thinking we'd just call one horse 'Sterile' and mail the shit back.

"Ah, you know I think it might be the neighbor's horse. When we took the blood samples I only had fourteen kits and there were fifteen horses in the barn if I remember right. Or it could be one of the dogs. I had a lot of samples in the refrigerator."

"So..." I wondered how this filing system worked when he was neutering a cat. "What do you think we oughta do?" And here *The Jockey Club* thought they had finally closed the last great loophole.

"Why don't you give 'em a call. Oh, here's another one. I don't think I own this horse anymore."

"Really?"

Either way, I needed a system of organization and discipline that involved fewer syllables. It's one of the reasons that "Whoa!" works a lot better than, "Could you please stop here." Horses are one-word animals. Convoluted syntax is not on their list of relevant concerns. Crappy hay, yes. Verb/noun junk, no.

Nicknames proved very useful. Freudian slips notwithstanding, the system definitely had some advantages. I mean, really, horses don't know their own names. They don't have driver's licenses, or a Social Security number, or a MasterCard. "Hey you!" would probably work, but let's face it, that's a pretty boring system. Farm managers have this sick need to think creatively, mostly because we're bored to death with cleaning stalls and destroying tractors. And as I explained earlier, during the spring months we're pretty deranged anyway and paperwork is the one chance we get to prove we went to high school. And it's better than trying to quantify sanity after someone has found you talking to a fence post for two hours. Are you mildly insane, mediumly insane or a flaming lunatic? According to the convenience store down the street, I'm definitely in the flaming category. Apparently because of the company I keep. Most farm managers have a couple of mean cattle dogs or something. I only have a cat.

I nicknamed our mares 'Hippie, Boo Boo, Char, Fat Broad, Mouse' and 'Sieve-Head,' based on their temperament, destiny or unexplained eating disorders. Since few of the mares spoke English, none seemed particularly offended. There were a few others, like Chrysler and Spit, but they already had ridiculous nicknames.   Couldn't really improve on the existing effort...or affront? You see, personal dignity is a human vice. Horses will trade any sort of insult for a bale of hay, lending credence to my long held theory that wars are primarily the result of over-educated combatants:

"You're a multitudinous receptacle of crapulous coprolites!"

"Say what?"

'Hippie' came by her name by being born during the last fitful gasps of the great counter-culture revolution of the 1960's. Since her birth date (the same as Ken Kesey's), was almost as prominent as her exaggerated pelvic contours, the name stuck. I nicknamed her first foal 'Dopey,' due to its propensity for aggressively attacking other mares when it was only three-days old. In the horse business, this usually results in what we call 'terminal behavior correction,' whereas a pissed-off mare kicks this thing in the head until it is either dead or endowed with some table manners. Dopey embarked on life as a disturbed rodent of some kind, evidently born with a list of entitlements she didn't care to share with the rest of us. I decided to name future foals 'Sneezy, Wheezy,' and of course, 'Snow White.' Okay, so I was being overly optimistic. It turned out that most of Hippie's foals were gifted with an assortment of aberrations, the majority not particularly pleasant. You could have bred this mare to the entire membership of *Moral Majority* and they still would have ended up pillaging a small country. I began to think that the mare's ovaries belonged on the *X-Files*.

'Boo Boo' was a mistake. Just possibly the ugliest yearling ever to qualify for a summer sale, she was purchased because Doc was staring at the wrong catalog page. Since Thoroughbred breeders are required to be good sports, she came home anyway, though probably with a paper bag over her head. After winning a few minor races, she entered the farm's broodmare ranks and abruptly founded a new line of odd-faced foals. I named one 'Insect Eyes,' a second 'Llama Lips' and I was going for

Beetlejuice, but it was already taken. I guess I wasn't the only one stuck with an equine anomaly factory.

'Fat Broad' was your basic dietary disaster zone. Following a Darwinian path of dysfunctional evolution, Fat Broad skipped the salad fork entirely and became a caloric predator. A living example of metastasized fat cells, she stayed grotesquely obese on a diet of dirt and Presto logs. Often grunting like a wounded warthog, she was the farm's social outcast. Doc wanted to sell her, but I didn't think I could find anybody gullible enough to buy a cross between Hampshire sow and a termite. Even her foals seemed to be embarrassed to hang out with her. If she didn't get enough hay in one day, then she'd order take-out. That probably explains all the pizza boxes behind the barn and why my MasterCard was always over the limit. If she got especially desperate, she'd eat poisonous weeds, plywood, whole trees and small foreign cars. Fussy was not on her résumé. She could throw a little ketchup on your shirt and suck it down like a Komodo dragon.

'Char' was a different story altogether. A multiple stakes producer (a *stakes producer* is a cash machine that breathes) is a mare that has produced one or more foals that have won major races. That means the mummy is not far behind. I always called her "Mrs.," and if she wanted to live at the Hilton, Doc would have booked her a room. In the vernacular of the business, we picked her up 'dirt cheap' from a farm in Kentucky. While she was on the van headed west, her first foal started tearing up the tracks back east. She was a Bupers' mare, which was one those variables in breeding racehorses that cause geneticists to self-medicate. Her sire was a bit of a dud as stallions go, but <u>his</u> daughters were gold plated. In our case her value was connected to the odometer on the van as she headed up the interstate. She was a three-in-one deal: a foal by Groton at her side, one in the oven by *The Axe II. No, there wasn't an *The Axe I. His dad was Mahmoud. And the asterisk? That means he was imported. From England. So now you know almost everything I do about this sordid affair, which was probably no more than dumb luck anyway. Just imagine if you had to explain this to an immigration agent and this paragraph had something to do with your children.

When she arrived at the farm, I wanted to put her in a rubber room, mostly because I had no experience with quality. I was used to broodmares whose only real value was if they died and we collected the insurance. To be quite honest, this mare scared me. Every time her water broke, it was a $250,000 event. I was so paranoid that I'd have fifteen vets on call, a couple of major universities and the Mayo Clinic on standby. We weren't having a baby, we were birthing a stock portfolio.

'Mouse' was an example of first impressions gone painfully amuck. When I first met her, she coyly feigned timidity and social restraint. As time went on, she began to exhibit a number of aberrant characteristics last seen at one of Charles Manson's parole hearings. A tougher mare would be hard to find: she hated people, other horses, dogs, most waterfowl and on occasion, her own food. No horse in its right mind would go near her, and every stallion that ever tried to whisper in her ear ended up petitioning for geldinghood. Her only redeeming attribute was her infatuation with foals, anybody's foal. She loved them whether they happened to belong to her or not. Somehow, these babies were granted immunity in a war that nobody really understood. She was a walking day-care center suffering an allergic reaction to anything that resembled an adult. All she had to do was grind her teeth and every horse for five-square miles was scrambling to get into the nearest bomb shelter.

The Queen of the Hill

Matrons and mothers, and sisters and brothers,
An uneasy still, demanded by will,
They watch and they worry, the Queen of the hill.

The others all know, for if she should show,
That infamous scorn, be it always well worn,
A look that could kill, from the Queen of the hill.

When the oats and the corn, arrive in the morn,
Trues that prevail, with none to curtail,
Others must mill, not the Queen of the hill.

The foals gather 'bout her, without any bother,
For they know not a scare, from this pompous old mare,
They mingle at will, with the Queen of the hill.

Lastly, was poor 'Sieve-Head.' Raised as an orphan, she insists that she doesn't belong out in a field with a bunch of other horses. She'd rather be in the house watching television. Orphans always have a tough life: raised by people, they suffer marginality — not quite a horse and certainly not a human. They stumble through life like a Rodney Dangerfield monologue, misunderstood, drowning in disrespect, serving as a repository for most of the world's tasteless jokes. Sieve-Head's only saving grace was a divine grasp on motherhood, oddly intact in spite of being raised by a 62-year-old retired electrician. Confusion is apparently a human malady. Needless to say, I'm the new surrogate dad. Every time I get near her, she gets all dreamy-eyed and slobbers on my jacket. Between her and my friend Tubby, bringing a girl home would require more of an explanation than a second date would warrant. "Meet the folks, honey. Don't mind mom, she always drools."

Most breeding farms also own a stallion. In fact, no self-respecting breeder would be caught dead without one. Since our farm fails to put respect on a high plane of affordability, we thankfully send out our mares to somebody else's stallion. I say that because most of these 'Guy Horses' fall into a narrow genealogical classification under the heading: hormones, screaming. Most of these testosterone machines end up with interchangeable names according to the season or whom they might have maimed lately. In the calm of early winter, most stallions answer to the "Hey you" thing. Breeding season converts the "Hey you" into something like "Back, animal back!" or an equally derisive collection of adjectives and verbs. These confrontational episodes are really not the stallion's fault, for as anyone can tell you, sex is a lot more fun than running around a racetrack. The real problem seems to be us humans, who somehow get taken along for a ride and then resort to all kinds of name-calling. It's a good thing most horses can't afford a lawyer.

After many years of relationship counseling, man and stallion come to some sort of compromise on semantics. Since the bond is barely in the realm of tolerance, a name like 'Cabbage Head' seems perfectly appropriate. I don't think it is a bad name. Not vulgar, or obscene, it really speaks of the insensitivity of male procreation: 400,000,000 little sperms willing to die for one female egg and loving every minute of it. Not a regret in the bunch. Besides, the neighbors will appreciate such a name when it's four o'clock in the afternoon and I'm screaming "Cabbage Head!" at the top of my lungs. It's two syllables shorter than 'King Fritz of Norway.'

After four days of intense struggle, I had a short pile of completed forms. Every horse had a name, a birth date and a somewhat fictionalized history based on Doc's recent memory and whatever forensic evidence I could dig up. I would have been extremely proud of my organizational skills except for one minor detail. As far as I knew, the farm owned 37 horses, yet on the desk in front of me were 39 files, the extra two belonging to one horse named 'Busy Bee' and another called 'Foghorn.' According to Doc, 'Busy Bee' and 'Foghorn' were on the farm – somewhere.

"Where?" I queried in disbelief.

"Uh...over there," Doc stammered, as he waved a finger toward the missing neighbor's house.

"What are they doing over there?" I asked, marginally amazed by the whole conversation, but still caught between curious and just where exactly the train was headed.

"Listen," Doc said in a whisper. "I sold those two horses three years ago. That's how I could afford the tractor. Elaine doesn't know a thing about it. So if it comes up, just tell her that 'Busy Bee' had a colt and 'Foghorn' had a filly. She always liked Foghorn."

So, 'Busy Bee' and 'Foghorn' joined the pile of paperwork. I gave them inoculation dates, a foaling history and a quiet spot in the back of the filing cabinet. I also made up new files for their non-existent foals. I named 'Busy Bee's' colt 'Boring Bob,' and I thought I would call 'Foghorn's' filly, 'Foggy Bottom.' It seemed like the logical thing to do.

11.

INTELLIGENCE TEST FOR THE NEWBORN

WHEN I WAS born, few people wandered into the maternity ward of the hospital to offer me an IQ test. Uncles and aunts probably pressed their faces up against the glass partition and made grotesque expressions, but I seriously doubt they held up a flash card seeking the answer to: $x - y = ?$ Most of us newborns were trying to figure why it was so damn white outside and why our pants kept filling up with water and other disgusting stuff. We had not yet grasped the fundamentals of language, opting for a number of gurgling noises that sounded like a broken garbage disposal. Relatives really got into this abstract vocabulary. They'd respond with mindless statements like, "Oh, coochie, coochie, coo, whas a cutey pie." I mean really, when you're two hours old they might as well be explaining the Heisenberg Principle to you. Besides, most of us didn't want conversation, we wanted a full breast. Once they cut the cord, food becomes a major issue. Backstroking around the uterus was definitely fun, but life on the outside required a friendly fast-food restaurant. All we wanted to do was eat, sleep and somehow avoid a semi-frozen rectal thermometer.

Our nurses offered little in the way of enlightenment. Most of the time they were overly concerned about what was going on in our pants, which were very bulky, causing most of us to grow up bow-legged. I tried to look at it like a pre-qualification for a life as a cowboy. If you're going to ride a horse on a regular basis, then being bow-legged is a definite advantage. Otherwise you're looking at ligament adjustments on a major scale. When you ride a horse, your legs have to go out and then in, thereby giving you some degree of control on the accelerator and the brakes. If you happen to be duck-footed, then it is quite likely that you'll end up somewhere north of the International Date Line. Just ask *Hombre*.

When our nurses did speak, they rudely ignored us, as if we had absolutely no idea about world politics or the rain forest.

"Oh, would ya look at that Dr. Widlow. Ain't he somethin' else."

"Forget him. Did you see that new orderly on the seventh-floor. I mean a hunk or..."

"Orderly, smorderly! A doctor, girl! Ya gotta pick a doctor!"

"Geez, if I look at one more dirty diaper, I'm gonna puke."

"Oh, come on Cheryl, you ever seen a clean one around here? They have a life expectancy of thirty seconds."

Most of my relatives had narrowed my career choices to two: President of the United States or a United States Senator soon to be elected President of the United States. Either way, I would be living on Pennsylvania Avenue in a three-story white house with a dog, a press secretary, the First Lady and a bunch of guys with guns who would check the toilet every fifteen minutes to see if the lid was up. When I wasn't busy with Congress, I'd be exchanging sly innuendos with the President of Russia, whose aunts and uncles probably made grotesque faces at him as well. Two-hundred million Americans would look to me to guide the country, maintain peace and order, guarantee prosperity for every man, woman and child, abolish homework, fix healthcare, subsidize cheap beer and to not launch thirty-thousand nuclear warheads without a very good reason. Awesome stuff for a guy who started out life with flooded pants. Think of the fun: days spent arguing with Congress, nights on the hot-line driving Boris nuts, dispatching aircraft carriers and submarines to places I can't even spell, being pampered on Air Force One, making the Vice-president feel like a schmuck – the possibilities are endless. And the pay isn't too shabby either. Think of all those state dinners where you are fed like a steer on the way to a slaughterhouse. Oh. I think I just stumbled onto the downside. Maybe I'll hang onto the shovel and skip the Oval Office. Damn! I always wanted to play with that red phone. "Hey, Boris, checked your radar lately?"

Fortunately, few aunts and uncles ever get their wish. Children grow up to be firefighters, janitors and cowboys, electricians, fry-cooks, truck drivers and brain surgeons. Some even become farm managers. One or two make it to the White House, though after four years or so, they wish to hell they had learned how to push a broom. The paths all start out the same, but end at different conclusions. The higher you go, the further potential for a serious fall. If I did become President, I'm pretty sure I'd end up bailing out of Air Force One with the nuclear codes and no para-

chute rather than making that final choice for mankind. Before I hit the ground, the Vice-president would be redecorating the executive bedroom. Of course, I would receive a great state funeral where a bunch of horses haul a casket full of presidential road-pizza to Arlington National Cemetery. I wouldn't lie in 'state,' I'd lie in a shoe-box with whatever they could find. Probably two or three fingers and a nice tie.

I often wonder if any president could once again execute the nuclear option. Psychiatrists (and maybe movie producers) probably enjoy rolling this notion around in their minds. Hiroshima and Nagasaki were really experiments in a whole new sector of our assumptions about what constitutes reality. After we took a look at what we did, no playing field of our imagination could ever contain the boundaries of what we could do. Our protection, our defense really, seems to be predicated on the notion of 'willingness.' Not right or wrong. Just the level of our pride, the depths of our fear, or worse yet, our savage insolence.

Like most offspring, I did *seem to have a mother around the place, though it appeared she experienced some difficulty with the paternity question. A few rumors were bandied about, (facts were troublesome in those days) so it appeared that my real father served in World War II, died in Korea, somehow got resuscitated whenever one story or another unraveled, and then managed to fall asleep in the Sacramento River thirty-five years later. Kind of like Spock with the dead/undead thing. In exchange for this man, I got many others. Or they got me. That's why my sister and I referred to them as 'It.' We'd say to each other, "It's coming." I don't think we knew why at the time, but it seemed like if we let them be human – called them by name, then they might escape our imagination and become something real.*

If you are born a Thoroughbred, all such familial prognostication is tossed out the window. No distant relative is going to be brash enough to question an alternative career, and quite frankly, few owners are going to spend fifty or sixty-thousand dollars to help a foal explore its real niche in the world. After losing five races in a row, an owner may subtly suggest a task normally associated with 40 acres and a plow. But in the wildly optimistic world of racing, full of people not thoroughly schooled in defeat, alternatives simply do not exist – at least in the beginning. There is always a plausible explanation: Jupiter was rising, the horse stumbled coming out of the gate, the track was muddy, the jockey didn't follow instructions (like right, a 1200lb hyperactive horse listens to a 98lb guy in a funny shirt), the distance was too long or too short, he threw a shoe, he swallowed his tongue, he got cut-off in the stretch (never mind that he was running twelfth), he bled, she was in heat, the girth slipped, the jockey lost his whip, she sucked air, etc., etc., etc.. Racing is simply an excuse factory running on overdrive. I promise I'll provide a detailed glossary in this book, so that every potential owner can understand how 'losing' works. I'm pretty sure I'll end up like Salman Rushdie, slammed with a universal death threat by a secret society of trainers that suffer from an inability to commerce with the truth. At $100 a day for training a total flop, these folks have a lot at stake. They live in a world where the glass is always overflowing. If a horse runs dead last in the *third* race by 35 lengths, then technically, he just won the *fourth* race.

When a foal is born, it resembles a disjointed pile of bones with some skin strung over the ragged parts. Kind of like a frog that fought to death with a dust bunny under a couch. They also make the same gurgling noises as their infantile human counterparts. They cannot seem to find their mothers, the udder, the difference between a right leg or a left, or whether x-y=? is a question or a statement. Yet, owners like Doc will press their face against the glass partition, make the same grotesque faces and pronounce the newborn the next President of the United States – whether the Electoral College has anything to say about it or not.

"Boy, would you look at those stifles," Doc would say, his finger rotating counter-clockwise in the general direction of a knee. "Secretariat had stifles like that."

"Secretariat was by Bold Ruler," I would shoot back, trying to take a little flotation out of his cloud.

"Coochi, coochie, coo, whas a cutey pie!"

Geez, where did I hear that before? "Gosh, hope his knees straighten out. He looks like a duck walking backwards."

By the middle of June, most of the mares were back at the farm, each with a uterus carrying the next President of the United States. Naturally, they also had the next president running alongside them as well. And out in the pastures, there were a few more presidential aspirants in the wings. We were president-poor and losing ground. I considered making a strong argument against such breeding optimism, but all I could focus on was my Grandmother's crinkled up face steaming the glass above my crib with her loyal breath. How could I possibly disappoint such a woman, such a saint?

She was the only one who stuck around. Played the sidelines. Delusional it seemed, at least to me. Not willing to give up on her youngest son – or the greater truth of his son and his daughter, dematerialized by a lie. Wars do that though – they corrode the foundations of hope in those poor souls unwilling to live inside the façade. They don't see killing as the necessity of war, just the killing. Semantics. The difference between a casualty and a victim? None. They're both dead. Those left animate inhabit the shadows of what was, or perhaps never was, in a constant, almost frantic re-enactment of a single moment. And those who love them stand outside the circle – seen and heard, but never really acknowledged. And the mothers and grandmothers of those shipwrecked children memorialize the evasion under the selfish guise of saving the wounded, when they should have really been saving themselves.

Farm managers aren't normally plagued with the emotional burden of trashed dreams. Most of us are janitors and purveyors, content to operate the doors of commerce with somebody else's money. Secretariat stifles do not impress us nearly as much as common sense and brains – *the intelligence test for the newborn.* For it is our burden to keep the day-care center out of the bloody throes of baby anarchists, foals who haphazardly assume their powerful destiny. I have to chuckle occasionally, since I know perfectly well that their overblown stature involves running around in circles. It's a corporate thing whereby you extract your revenge sometime down the road. They think they have inherited an idyllic life – I know they can't outrun a dirty sock. When they are forced into retirement, I get to turn their self-esteem into a salted slug. Once these little presidential aspirants falter, I get to reverse the playing field. Like a bad afternoon at Wimbledon, I get to say, "Advantage, Andy." I had the power of an impending impeachment trial and I had little doubt that I couldn't prosecute. Lose ten races in a row and no lawyer could defend your overwhelming inadequacy. You weren't a racehorse, you were a four-cylinder Yugo trying to merge onto a major freeway. Outmaneuvered at last! First comes the patience, then the revenge.

The first test comes immediately after birth. Since it is always 3:00 in the morning, I put an extreme amount of weight on this one examination. I call it the *bag test*. The first duty of all newborn creatures is to appease their sleepy host (me), by consuming the first meal. It's right there on my clipboard next to the coffee stain. Personally, I really don't care if they eat or not. I'm just following proper animal husbandry protocol whereas every box on my pre-printed forms gets a check mark. First milk contains the colostrum. That's most of the immune system and an industrial strength laxative meant to unplug the plumbing. When you're in the womb for eleven months, a lot of baggage has piled up at the station and…well, you get it.

The mare also has a vested interest in this early exercise. She also has a few suitcases on the station platform, primarily in the form of a full *bag*. Or bags. Like most mammals she has two, though it really looks like one large angry one when the water gets backed up behind the dam. The situation is also pretty painful from what I can ascertain. I've personally never had a full breast so I'm assuming it is somewhat like a full bladder with a different kind of expediency to it. The mare is basically ready to feed most of India and the foal is playing hard to get – get 'it' really.

Next on the pre-catatonic farm manager's list is a little thing about checking the placenta. That only occurs when she is finally willing to give it up, which shouldn't be construed as a positive event. It normally weighs about thirty-five pounds and resembles an alien egg sack. If you hung it up on a stop sign it would probably force the evacuation of an entire city. My immediate task, once I have possession of this biological oddity is to ascertain if it has all its parts. Naturally it is torn to shreds since that's how the foal escaped in the first place. It's a little bit like folding sheets all by yourself, but a lot messier. Not a good time for the UPS guy to show up.

With the foal now ensconced in the material world, the next step is a three-part exercise, composed of *standing, locating the mother ship, and grasping the matronly faucet* firmly in its mouth. I discount actual drinking, since if the foal drowns itself on the first gulp, it is an automatic 'F' anyway.

Fillies are much better at this task than colts, a point not lost by the feminist movement. Colts tend to suck the wall, the feed bucket, mother's hock, even their own knee. All taste equally *unmilklike*, but fail to discourage this misguided nomad from its quest to drive the nearest human insane. It reminds me of those rocket tests in the 1960's where the only thing the missile could manage to hit was the oxymoron known as Mission Control.

A lot of this has to do with the *Farm Manager's Code*, a quasi-religious-cult whose manifest dictates that nobody gets to go to bed until a mammary-impaired foal connects eating with some sort of future. Owners like colts, farm managers appreciate fillies. That is because colts tend to compete in richer races more often than fillies and few owners suffer from sleep deprivation because they have idiots like me around that stay up all night on a nipple hunt just to get paid. You ever wonder what the FICA deduction on your pay stub stands for? 'Finally Incapable of Communicating at All.' Our deductions don't go to Social Security, they go to our future home at an asylum in New Jersey. We trade in our pitchforks for a cute little number that buckles in the back.

Desperate people like myself, desiring something resembling unconsciousness, engage in a dance of contorted body movements, agonizing with each foal's near miss and fitful, useless grasps. Closer, closer, then no...wrong way! The whole thing turns into a frustrating obsession, as aggravating as watching a near-sighted tailor attempting to thread a needle. We strive to circumvent the crisis by rushing into the stall and pointing at the udder, shouting, "It's right there, stupid!" The colt responds by falling down, digressing the new lesson back to the previous one on left leg versus right and why these damn things don't seem to work. Of course, by now it is 4:00 AM and I am considering a career as a benevolent drunk. At least you can sleep in a ditch or under a park bench – by yourself.

This scenario rarely occurs with fillies. Girls are born with an extra piece of chromosome, the so-called tail of the male 'Y' giving them a 'XX' rating – a lot like Five Stars if you happen to be a hotel. This extra particle of DNA is responsible for memory, good taste, common sense, color coordination, balancing a checkbook, raising males, finding the udder and keeping world wars and freeway altercations from escalating into something far more unpleasant. It also allows farm managers to get to bed before dawn. Evidence of this superior biological gift is both widely disputed (by males), and broadly accepted by the available testimony:

FEMALE: The shoes match the belt, the belt offsets the scarf, which blends nicely with the blouse. The earrings engage the outfit completely.

MALE: "I wore this tie because it is powerful."

FEMALE: (Following a near accident with another automobile). "Oh, he must have needed to get in that lane so he could get to the dry-cleaners."

MALE: (Similar scenario). "You dirty #&!!#@!$?&!! I'll kill ya! I'll wipe up the street with your face! I'll run over your dog, your next of kin! I'll put a cigarette out in your eye!"

FEMALE: (Preventing a world war). "Yes, I would really like to hear your side of this dispute in the hope that we can negotiate a settlement."

MALE: (Same war). "Fly this up your ass, buddy!"

Males rarely admit their own limitations. Mostly because they cannot remember what they thought they were limited to, or why someone would ask such an asinine question anyway. Hey, we're busy invading Iraq, defending the West from hordes of...well, a bunch of guys who seem to own most of the world's oil. No oil, no Lexus. Seems like a perfectly good reason to send 100,000 troops and some heavy hardware 10,000 miles to insure bad mileage and cheap air conditioning for another decade or so.

Male behavior bespeaks the Holy truth: male dogs claim real estate by peeing on it. Male men do the same by leaving dirty socks on the bedroom floor. Bulls will crash through a fence to fight another bull who is mad because he didn't think of it first. A stallion will fight to the death to acquire one more mare, even though he can't handle the twenty-three he already has under contract. Compare that to most female spiders. She lures in a male, has some incredible sex, then kills him and eats him. And she gets a good night's sleep in the process. Guilt seems to be reserved for males and really serious Catholics.

Or as General Douglas MacArthur might have said concerning that little conflict in Korea: "If you're going to spend the gas to get there, you might as well shoot somebody." Probably explains why Truman fired him. MacArthur wanted to take on China, which is like attacking an ant-farm with a box of toothpicks. Other than suppressing the spread of an opposing ideology, what was the payback? Cheap take-out? MacArthur did have a point, but then again, MacArthur was an old warrior who couldn't quite comprehend that future wars would never be won – or lost really. That war – MacArthur's kind of war – was obsolete. 'All or nothing' was mutually inclusive.

Still, governments rely on this 'warrior class.' They spend immense sums of money and countless decades in molding this perfect killing machine. The warrior will execute the policy of the tribe, protect the borders of the empire, and in some cases attempt to redefine the very policy he champions. He looks forward, not back. Strategy, not diplomacy. When the will of government falters and the goal drifts from sight, what becomes of the warrior? And who will be willing to take his place when the stench of some monstrous evil once again permeates the rarefied atmosphere of our glorious and always unobtainable dream? Our ever elusive Elysium — with a knife at its throat.

War only became an arbitrary pastime after man acceded to its horror and regulated the process. The plan mimicked professional sports. Rules. The Geneva Convention. "Crimes Against Humanity?" The same humanity that creates governments, whose members formulate policy, whose policy-makers instigate conflicts, which escalate into wars and please remind me again about crimes levied against innocents. Who might they be? Is the problem the puzzle or the puzzle makers? Generals were given new speeches: "Remember boys, no shooting until after 11:00 on Sundays. And no land mines. That's considered sneaky. So go out there, have a good war and win one for the…"

War is about attrition. The 'other' guys' attrition. Nice is not an option. In war, the victor must be nastier and more willing than the enemy in order to prevail. Oh. The Geneva Convention? Only useful if you happen to win.

And before you fire that first shot, please try to remember that there are (were) children in the audience. They always appreciate a good (or bad) example.

The third major test for a newborn is the *motor-coordination-memory-capacity exam.* This test begins on the second day of life, when I find it necessary to move mare and foal from Point A to Point B, normally from the stall to a small paddock. The mare, being female, has little trouble with this exercise. However, <u>this</u> test seems to cross the gender gap in the foal. Both male and female babies experience roughly the same sort of puzzlement over the proper way to fulfill this requirement.

One method is to allow the foal to simply follow its mother to the new destination. For some, this is fundamentally impossible to comprehend. First, they lose their mother, who is not really lost herself, but just standing three feet away next to a wall. The foal immediately develops hysterical blindness, causing it to scream horrifically while it runs full speed back and forth in front of its mother, who now either smells or looks like a creature from the deep recesses of another solar system. Finally, I am forced to return to the familiar surroundings of the stall where the foal suddenly regains its lost eyesight.

Failure to follow in an appropriate time frame is overcome by the *buttrope*, a four-foot circular rubber band that functions like a sling-shot. One end is placed over the foal's butt, while the other end is looped through a farm manager's elbow. This leaves the other hand free to lead the mare, open gates, or answer the phone. A foal's reaction to this device is immediate and severe, for after spending eleven-months confined in a uterus, restraint is an unpopular concept. Colts either flip over backwards in a heap, or sit down like unhappy mules. Fillies vote with their feet, trying their upmost best to fracture my skeleton. If that doesn't work, then they try to gum a person to death. No matter which way I pull, they push the opposite way. Brute force finally succeeds where gentle persuasion fails and I collapse on the ground thankful for such a labor-saving invention.

The *memory* portion of the test is conducted in the middle of June when mares and foals return to the farm after visiting the stallion. Since my elbow still aches from the rubber band lessons of spring, I assume that a lasting impression has been made on their small equine butts as well. Not so. Three out of four do not even remember my name and one has arrived home missing its halter, a sure sign of medium to severe wrath from one of the lesser gods – the one who handles last minute reservations. They have also grown, ballooning from a birth weight of around a hundred pounds to somewhere near four-hundred pounds – agile and quick, like giant squirrels. This is the point in farm management where anybody with a functioning brain re-establishes contact with the word 'no.' There must be someone out there who specializes in basic etiquette for fairly large, frenetic and hydrophobic lactose-dependent rats.

Then again, no guts, no glory and no perceived manhood as identified by overly confident movie producers that have discovered the connection between gore and profits. Geez, I'm starting to sound like a Sylvester Stallone movie: "Rambo 4 1/2 – The Nightmare Continues." The plot's simple: Rambo parachutes into Redmond, Washington intent on rescuing five equine POW's held prisoner by the diabolical Mr. Manager. After shooting up the barn and Doc's swimming pool, he kills the farm manager with a corkscrew through the forehead. He jumps into the pen with the foal/prisoners while a helicopter circles overhead. No, it's not the CIA, it's a local TV station desperate for news – any news. Redmond is a small town. Rambo machine-guns a couple of communist rats, tosses a hand-grenade into the tack room, rips off his shirt and shoots off the gate latch. Hell, it was unlocked anyway. Meanwhile, the foals are having a conference call, convinced that they are going to end up strapped to the wings of a B-52. A quorum is reached and the foals decide to eat Rambo, along with his machine-gun. All that's left is one bicep and an ammo clip. A sequel seems out of the question.

Internalizing. *This is how you kill time before it becomes time to get killed.*

Before these adolescent delinquents get returned to the pastures for the summer, they will have to be *processed*, a purposely vague term which is roughly equivalent to developing civilization in 1200BC. For this purpose, I had constructed over the winter a *bull-pen*, aptly named for its structural integrity. It is a thirty-foot circular corral with seven-foot sides, set on eight-by-eight-inch thick railroad-tie posts. Strong enough to contain an unhappy hippopotamus or four *unprocessed* foals.

The first order of business is to adapt certain military stratagems credited to Napoleon Bonaparte or the Republican National Committee – divide and conquer. One mare and foal are placed in the pen, the others in an adjacent paddock.

Rope in hand, I bravely enter the ring. The music roars in my ears, cymbals and drums crashing like a flooded waterfall around me, applause thundering from a thousand hands in the grandstand seats. Sweat dripping down my chest, eyes locked on the opponent in a struggle of granite wills. My ears ring as the crowd demands blood: "Toro, Toro, Toro!" The cat smiles from a nearby fencepost.

"Yes, Toro!" I shout back, waving my cape to an enthusiastic crowd, reduced now to a single face, grizzled and wise, smiling from between the wooden rails of my arena.

"Yeah, what's wrong with the Toro – I need to mow the grass out by the pool," Doc was asking, his voice producing text-book English for a guy fresh out of a Barcelona bull-ring.

"I was just going to pick it up from Chet's, as soon as I get a hold of this one foal. It came back without a halter. It's a wild little sucker. I'm not quite sure how I'm goin' to do this without getting killed," I confessed, hoping Doc would be more interested in retrieving the lawn mower. Some tasks are better done without witnesses. It's like the first time you try sex. It's a good thing Siskel and Ebert aren't in the same room. Can you imagine the revues?

"Boy, look at those stifles. Secretariat had stifles like that!"

Look at those teeth, I thought.

"I'll give you a hand," Doc said. "We can corner him in here."

"Uh, Doc, this one's the filly. Remember? The one that bites so bad? The one they called about." I had gotten three calls from the other farm (where the stallion lives), about wounded grooms, maimed veterinarians – victims of this foal-turned piranha.

'Oh' was all he said. I was hoping for a longer sentence, maybe even a paragraph or two.

"So, how are we goin' to handle this?" Hope was vanishing on the lawnmower option.

Doc reached into his pocket, producing a fifty-cent piece. "We'll flip. Heads or tails, whatever you call, you get – literally." He threw the coin in the air.

I called 'heads' figuring it was my duty to accept the most dangerous end, what being younger and likely to heal faster. The heavy coin plopped to the ground. "Tails," Doc sighed.

Or, maybe it was a silent Norwegian angst prayer. I thought about having him inhale into a paper bag, but he seemed determined. A little frightened, but determined.

"Damn!!" Doc yelled, throwing the coin into the woods.

"You want me to..." I started to offer, quite comfortable doing the slave-master guilt thing. Okay, so I lied. If the boss got killed, the notion that I would get paid was pretty slim.

"A deal's a deal. We'll gang-tackle him."

"It's a her." This was beginning to look like a re-run from horseshoeing school, only in this case I wasn't a curious bystander.

Like a big rope, we slowly closed in around her, using our outstretched arms as a moving fence. When we were within about five feet of her, Doc yelled, "Now!" and we both sprung like lions on to her back. Doc had one hand through her mane and the other curled around her head, his fist squeezed tight over one ear. I had her tail and one hind leg, too afraid to let go and too scared to come up with a plan B or C. The filly was leaping in the air and bellowing like a moose, her newly acquired baggage, a collection of torn shirts and flailing limbs, whirling madly through a vortex of dust and piss. Yes, she peed on my head and anything else she could hit.

After a number of staggered circles, our combined weight finally overcame the laws of gravity and the filly crashed to the ground, Doc under her neck and me laying half over her back, one hand tangled in her matted tail.

"I got 'er, I got 'er!" Doc yelled, but from my viewpoint, the filly had him, her teeth locked on to a tender portion of his upper thigh. "Gimme the halter, quick!" he screamed. "Aaaaaaah!!"

As I pulled loose from her tail the halter fell from its perch on my shoulder, landing about two feet away in the dirt. As I stretched to reach it, the filly, feeling a sudden shift of weight on her back, gave a giant heave, lashing out with one back hoof in my general direction. I heard a sharp crack, like a gunshot, coming from the direction of my shin. The pain got there about two-seconds later, momentarily causing my brain to instruct my hands to grab the maimed part. When I rolled over, the filly was standing again, with Doc draped over her back like a sack of potatoes, one hand still in control of an ear, steering the pair oafishly through an inebriated version of *Swan Lake*.

Getting to my feet, I charged the pair like a deranged linebacker, throwing my entire weight into the filly's rib cage. The impact threw her to the ground, Doc and I landing on top of her chest, the force of the impact causing her eyes to bug out and her lungs to aspirate most of the oxygen left in her body. None of us moved for a few minutes, Doc finally breaking the silence.

"I think my leg's bleeding," he gasped between mouthfuls of air.

"I think mine's broken," I offered in return.

Doc wiped the dirt out of his eyes, staring at the filly's nose, which was whistling like a tea kettle. "I think he's dead."

"Her. I'm going to halter her anyway." I crawled to my knees, slipping the leather noose over her head and buckling the strap. I gave Doc a hand getting to his feet and the two of us lamely stumbled out of the pen.

"I think I'll go lay down for a while," Doc said, as he gimped his way back to the house. "If he lives, I'm going to sell him!"

"Her."

When I returned from investigating the large crease in my shin, the filly was standing and nursing, as if nothing really happened. I walked into the bullpen and effortlessly attached a rope to her halter. If I asked her to walk forward, she followed. She would also back up, circle to the right or left, or stand quietly while I brushed her. Her appetite for human thigh meat had also mysteriously disappeared, prompting me to consider the value of chest crushing as a viable training tool. Doc, however, was not so forgiving. Two-weeks later, he still had a slight limp and by the end of summer the filly was sold. In a way, it was a shame. She might have made a great little president – getting me off the hook for another four years or so.

Everything you ever need to know about the art of persuasion can be learned from a 240lb horseshoer named Tiffany. Wish she could have been here. No, not really.

12.

ROMEO & JULIET? (HOPEFULLY WITH A DIFFERENT ENDING)

[AHEM...AHEM. BEFORE we embark on this particular chapter, certain clarifications need to be addressed concerning the physics of lust and/or that other stuff that involves human courtship. It goes much deeper than that planetary nonsense about Mars and Venus. Earlier in this century, two very wise men (Thomas Edison and Albert Einstein) spent a week together on Long Island, in New York. Both were troubled over how their research had been transformed into a couple of ominous and rather disturbing inventions: the A-bomb and the electric chair. Their collective research was beginning to have a detrimental impact on their marriages. You know, too much time in the lab, that sort of thing. So like Newton in his quest to quantify God, the two scientists sat down to expose scientifically, at the nuclear level, why men and women can't agree on the same restaurant: apparently, women are Gluons and men are W & Z bosons. Men get the Electroweak Theory, while women own the Theory of Everything. Knowing that should help all of us get through this difficult and troubling chapter.]

As the spring months gave way to summer, a celebration seemed in order. Break out the sun-screen, slaughter a few virgin sheep, invade somewhere easy, like Nebraska; maybe scrape the mold off the patio furniture. Trouble is, Seattle honors no tradition born of true chronology. It may be the summer solstice, but out in the Gulf of Alaska where the gods of Gortex reside, Neptune is busy drowning everybody's barbecue. You don't roast chicken in Washington, you kind of par-boil it until it develops the consistency of a bag of rubber bands. Then you jump in the truck and head for McDonald's. That is, if the windshield wipers aren't burned out.

June has a reputation for being wet, humid and yet somehow nurturing the immature blossom of romance. Breeding season has come and gone,

Elementary Particles

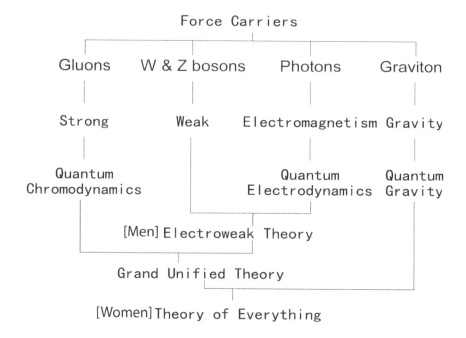

Force Carriers

Gluons   W & Z bosons   Photons   Graviton

Strong   Weak   Electromagnetism Gravity

Quantum Chromodynamics   Quantum Electrodynamics Quantum Gravity

[Men] Electroweak Theory

Grand Unified Theory

[Women] Theory of Everything

Forces

Physics Never Lies. It Just Verifies Most Inconvenient Truths

geese mated for life, have either migrated north or to the nearest public park where they enforce the 'no barefoot' rule. Really, I don't get it. Geese mate for life even though one goose pretty much looks like every other goose. Americans stay mated only about 50% of the time, opting for someone younger, richer, or less boring. And the courts support this concept by adjudicating "no-fault" divorces. No fault? Hell, it's got to be somebody's fault. If I smash my thumb with a hammer, is it the hammer's fault?

The June newspapers are filled with wedding announcements – brides in white chiffon and newly capped teeth grinning in blissful rapture, unaware of what their baited line caught: a man. Somebody that will eventually snore, pick their nose in public, never shave on the weekends and by age forty will have hair sprouting out of their ears in some genetic reversion to the Paleolithic era. Or buy shirts that look like a case of Salvador Dali having second thoughts. But hell, if they can change the oil in the car in less than four hours, maybe they're worth it. Someday, they may even figure out how to clean a bathroom or turn on a vacuum cleaner. Nah, not likely. Men don't live long enough. We die young just to avoid any form of housecleaning.

I too feel the urge in the sweet, damp air – a rush of warmth, a sudden urge to pollinate a brightly colored flower. The cat doesn't experience these urges since he is fixed and far too busy with his hobbies, most of which center around murdering things. I'm surprised that the avian world hasn't put out a contract on him. He gets the prime parts of the bird, while I'm stuck trying to figure out what to do with beaks, feet and feathers. The left-over parts have the same protein value as a rock and quite frankly, barbecuing pheasant heads is about as appealing as attending a cannibal's convention in a Speedo. Think of the recipes though: human Newburg, sautéed ear lobes in white wine sauce, brain omelets with wild mushrooms, barbecued adult-back ribs with beans, Cajun lobe of liver, shish-kabobs with onions, tomatoes and toes, eye-ball soup, numerous butt roasts, Irish ankle stew with cabbage, nose-hair fettuccini, finger food (no pun intended), broiled lip in cream sauce and finally, lung marinated in lime juice and cilantro. Maybe I should quit <u>this</u> book and work on recipes. I wonder what the market is like for a cannibal recipe book? I better give Indonesia a call. Maybe Borneo Information has a listing for: "Cannibals – take-out."

Under my plastic rain suit (you know the type: yellow and leaky), the humidity tip-toes over my flesh like a probing mosquito. God, my underwear itches. In fact everything itches. When the temperature hits around 60 degrees, wearing rain gear is like being shrink-wrapped and tossed in a sauna. You don't sweat, you slowly slime. All your pores are trying desperately to evict that sweat stuff, but yellow plastic's efficiency rating is ranked right up there with oysters. Nothing gets in and nothing gets out. Instead of leaking on the outside, you leak on the inside. I enjoy steaming vegetables, not T-shirts and jeans. By four in the afternoon, a weird smell surrounds me. A combination of melted rubber, dirty socks and something that can best be described as deodorant failure. At first I thought it was fermenting pheasant guts until I went to the local store for a coke. After we did the smelling salts thing, the clerk wanted to know if I worked at a morgue. I think that was a hint and probably about as subtle as store managers get on a weekday. I just mumbled, "Yeah," and crept out the door. Later that night, I burned my rain gear and all the leftover pheasant parts. The cat kept trying to jump in the barrel after them. Burning cat hair didn't add much to the evening's ambiance.

All this animal husbandry stuff had finally managed to overwhelm that strange kind of safety one finds while building a ½ mile long fence. The desire I held to engage the opposite sex was held in check by an equally strong inclination to avoid those parts of the adventure that included conversation. Conversation would have to entail honesty – that meant giving up information beyond my name. This was a lot different from dating hookers where most of the conversation centered on what time it was and that they don't accept post-dated checks. Insincerity was fine under those kind of house rules, but it seemed like it was time to develop something less cynical, though I wasn't really sure why that was important. Actually I did know. It was Elaine. One of her new hobbies was centered around socializing one of her employees; her only employee. I thought that just maybe she was trying to whittle down the lumber bill by forcing me to recreate, but she was too complicated a person to stick to a single motive. That was great. I had one woman conspiring with another woman who as yet hadn't been identified as the woman at the center of the conspiracy! Or did I? Or did they? Gets a little confusing when the conspirators haven't met yet.

Unbeknownst to the learned members of my private Warren Commission, I *had* developed a viable case of lust toward a certain young woman who helped manage an adjoining breeding farm. The one with the hippopotamus. So far I had only managed to share this terrifying notion with Tubby and the cat. Both are great listeners, though I tend to think the horse is faking it. Horses can sleep standing up and with their eyes open. Here I always thought he was reading the back page of the *Times* through the bathroom window and he was really sound asleep.

Now, I always look at these situations in their true light. Love is a wonderful, stunning, ecstatic, somewhat crazy emotion, but more often than not, it manifests itself in those parts of the body below the chest. The heart only gets involved after the rest of the hormones are exhausted. Then it falls into this oxygen-deprived bliss that is similar to climbing Mt. Everest, only easier on the legs. But invariably, love starts with lust. I mean, come on, physical attraction triggers the whole courting ritual. Eyes, a certain walk, a curve to the hip, an irresistible smile, a BMW – whoops.

Actually it was a Datsun pick-up. I had my projections mixed up. I was confusing upward mobility with what was going on in my shorts. Forget the car. I was long gone before I even knew I was missing. Just ask Safeway – within a week my face was plastered on shopping bags with a notation to call home. When the bug hits you, don't operate moving machinery. I mean, a guy suddenly in lust, given a chainsaw, could easily mow down Canada before he comes to his senses. Maybe that's why the minimum age for a president is thirty-five. A sudden case of lust at middle age and there goes the State of the Union Address. Deal with the deficit? Too busy buying red roses.

Her name was Jessica. Jesse for short. Jess if she was in a good mood, back to Jessica if she was testy and headed for something worse. Formality is supposed to defuse anger but mostly it sounds patronizing and self-serving. Well it is actually. You can't be in love and dead at the same time, so self-preservation plays a key role in the operation of your mouth. That is probably why men start out with exceptionally good manners and then misplace them somewhere around the third date.

She had glorious brown hair, hazel eyes and one of those lithe little figures that looked smashing in any sort of outfit. Plus, she liked horses and hated eighth-graders. It was a perfect combination. There was absolutely no prospect of her ever asking me to drive a school bus. The big problem was that while she managed to barge her way through my heart like a clumsy burglar, I wasn't confident that my obvious charm (that's singular – I could only think of one) had made a lasting impression – or any impression, really.

We met casually at the March *Two-Year-Old in Training Sale*, a blustery event held at Longacres Race Track in Renton. This sale was designed to give potential owners a head start on the racing season by selling them a young horse familiar with the term…*saddle*. Most of these young horses had received a perfunctory lesson or two on these leather accouterments, but not with the guy who insisted upon sitting atop of said accouterment. These guys and gals are known as *exercise riders*, which basically means that they are too fat to be jockeys, but thin enough to get bucked-off on a regular basis. In Thoroughbred racing, weight is a big deal. Jockeys spend long hours in sweat boxes until they look like freeze-dried raisins with legs. They eat big meals and then excuse themselves and go outside to throw-up on a bush. Some have a questionable pharmacist, others just don't eat on a regular basis. The lucky few are just naturally emaciated, or like Willie Shoemaker, born in a Leprechaun suit. Everybody gets into the weight thing. Racehorses wear aluminum shoes – skinny little things first made by *Tiffany's* in New York. Saddles are nothing more than a hot pad with stirrups, and quite frankly if the trainers could convince the jockeys to ride naked, then hell, they could shave off another sixteen ounces. Of course that would place a whole new perspective on the odds, not to mention a letter or two from the *Moral Majority*. But anyway, mornings were spent brushing, bathing and saddling our young prep-students and afternoons out at the track digging up the remains of small *Hispanic* guys who fell off in the morning. Kind of like a combination of avalanche rescue and clam digging.

By sale day, I had only managed to blurt out the occasional, "Hi there," normally as I was being dragged through the barn area by a horse that objected to bathing in front of a crowd. Both Jessica and I were in our best goose-down coats and ski hats, insulation against the forty-degree cold. Goose-down is a wonderful defense against a blizzard, but it defies those anatomical explorations men engage to build strength and courage for the campaign ahead. However, as luck would have it (actually I searched for a good hour) we ended up sitting together in the pavilion as our respective horses sold. Hers brought $13,000 and mine about $8800. I guess that shows the difference between working for a large construction magnate with a hippopotamus in his front yard versus working for a veterinarian with a chronic limp. I ate a hot dog that tasted terrible and she finally took off her ski hat. It was intensely romantic for me, but then again, men can find almost any ridiculous situation charming, especially if it involves a brunette.

That was March. Now it was mid-June and I had already exhausted every rotten manipulative male motive I had gleaned from my older peers in high school. "Jesse, I've been drafted. I have to go off to war. I may not come back. This could be our last night together." I guess I forgot that she knew how to read a newspaper. I couldn't think of any country that Congress was particularly pissed-off at. I finally invented one: Pakislovakia. Somewhere in central Asia. I made out like it was highly sensitive and given my connections with the CIA, I couldn't divulge anything more. I tried to pawn off this story to the cat – a bit of a rehearsal. The cat left a deposit on my pillow. How do cats know when you're lying through your teeth?

Abandoning the old "off to war" offense, I tried throwing around charm, intelligence, virility, sensitivity, vulnerability, *machismo* – beating up a purse snatcher while saving a baby bird – even a certain degree of aloofness, even though the idea of ignoring her made my molars ache. She just backhanded my volleys over the nearest fence. My confidence was reduced to a pool of tepid oil, marking a lonely spot on a vast ocean of despair, a grave where a grand ship had silently dropped from sight. Here I was exploring manhood with a broken propeller and no lifejacket. You know the Mariana Trench? So do I.

Really, it wasn't for a lack of effort. I had visited the farm where she worked at least 27 times on a variety of pretexts. "Just came by to borrow a sparkplug," or, "Say, I'd really like to see that new manure spreader of yours!" Earl, the general manger of the farm, was getting a little suspicious. During my many visits I had learned all about his three kids, his wife having her tubes tied, grandfather Ned's by-pass surgery and Earl's ordeal with a herniated disc in 1961. I was invited to dinner occasionally, shoveling food into my mouth while I stared out the window for a glimpse of...her.

This situation could have been quite tolerable except for one minor detail: Earl and I didn't really like each other. Earl was obsessed with murdering ducks, Monday Night Football, beer drinking and a kind of really old world male-eating ritual, the latter displayed by a priory claim to any food on the table not consumed in the first round. To the Hun went the spoils. While Earl shoved mashed potatoes through his tightly clenched teeth, his emaciated family stared at my plate, drab and silent, too proud or too submissive to simply steal my food.

Dinner always ended quickly. The scraping of dishes was a signal for the men to retire to the living room, where after-meal conversation rotated between gun talk and guttural discharges, each followed by a one-sentence critique on the dinner menu. Hell, I was still staring out the window. For all I knew, I may have eaten an Aardvark.

"Now Andy, what kind of gun you shoot?"

"Well, kinda...it's a Hutton 3000."

"BAAACH! Tastes as good the second time. A Hutton, huh? Never heard of that one."

"It's brand new." (Actually, it was the name of the can-opener in the kitchen.)

"Over and under? BAAACH! Good barbecue sauce, honey!"

"Ah, no, not exactly."

"BAAACH! Pardon the pig! Ah, side by side. Bring it over some time, we'll murder a few ducks!"

"BAAACH! BAAACH! BAAACH!"

After about twenty-minutes, Earl would drift off to sleep, snoring like a cow with a hole in its lung. I would wander into the kitchen and thank his rubber-gloved wife, who would nod and smile, no doubt plotting in some way to sneak into the living room and plant a butcher's knife into Earl's chest. It was <u>that</u> kind of smile. Earl might have been a doting father and husband, but he was also a living commercial for Gas-X. Plus, he had this tendency to take his boots off prior to passing out. The whole place smelled like a *Feta* cheese factory that never invested in refrigeration. I shared this critique with the cat. He wanted the address.

One of those evenings, following my usual habit of pretending I couldn't remember where I left my truck, Jesse pulled into the driveway and strode up to the house. She was returning an old and dusty book to Earl, some *treatise* that looked older than he did. Unable to form a logical sequence of words (known as a sentence), I clumsily complimented the book, even though I had no idea about the title. Could have been "War and Peace," or "Five-Hundred Ways to Destroy a Pizza." I'm not sure it really mattered. I did notice her eyes light up when I mentioned old books. I had blundered onto a viable subject. She liked old horse stuff! Paintings, sculptures, even books. And I just happened to have a pretty substantial collection of old horse books stacked in boxes in the mobile home – discards from Doc's massive library on dysfunctional Thoroughbred breeding. Some of them were quite old, mostly because Doc was kind of old himself.

I did my best Van Gogh imitation, painting a vivid portrait of my mobile home as the western annex of the Smithsonian, but without the missing ear part. Her eyebrows curled a little, her palms looked sweaty; twice she looked back at her Datsun pick-up as if it was going to leave without her. Finally, she took the bait. I had her talked into stopping by the next evening after work to look at my collection. Yes!

The following morning, I was up at first light. I was determined to make a good impression. I vacuumed, dusted and swept. I don't think the place had been really cleaned since it was manufactured during the Great War. Probably explained the mosquitoes hatching in the toilet bowl. Everything was spotless, including the cat, who got a thorough vacuum job himself, which set him off full speed for the woods. Of course the horses didn't get fed, the mail collected, or much else, but I had the cleanest kitchen counters in town.

Doc was suspicious. The horses were getting pissed-off. I could hear a lot of hoof tapping and throat clearing out in the loafing sheds.

The postman didn't cometh, the hay evidently lost in the mail. I figured they were too fat anyway and probably in need of a day of fasting. I told them the farm was going Buddhist, so get used to it. They responded by grinding their teeth in my general direction. Horses can send telepathic death threats that way. They can travel six, maybe seven miles on a clear night.

Doc's curiosity finally got the best of him and he stopped by the mobile home. The stench of Pine-Sol just about knocked him out the door.

"I thought the appliances were brown," he said as he pointed toward the gleaming white stove.

"They used to be."

"Company coming, huh?" He was on to me.

"Uh, no. Just some spring cleaning."

"It's summer."

"So, I'm late! What's the big deal!" I was defensive, he was doing one of those fatherly grin things old guys do so that you can confess to something they can't quite remember. I'm sure it's pre-Alzheimer's.

"What's her name?"

"I gotta go feed the horses." Death by hoof stomping <u>was</u> an option here.

"I'm going to tell Elaine. She was getting worried about you."

Around seven o'clock that evening, Jessie showed up. She was cautious, polite and rather quiet, clutching her purse as if a wild animal was about to leap from it. Mostly we talked about the books, a musty collection from the 1930's. I was trying to find the courage to ask her out. She was playing impossible to ask. She was almost out the door when I blurted out my real desire. "Dinner, ah...I mean would you like to have dinner sometime?" I said stupidly, deciding it was a bad idea to rehearse a speech. "I mean, just go out sometime?"

Silence. Total silence. Minutes passed, hours passed. We stood staring at each other in the doorway. Perspiration was beginning to bead-up on my forehead. My legs were weak and rubbery, palpitations vibrating through my rib cage. When would she answer? How long would she force me to stand here?!

"Maybe," she said calmly. "Call me."

With that, she was gone, the taillights of her truck vanishing down the driveway. I collapsed in my recliner, positive my heart valves had just reversed direction. "Yes! Yes! Yes!" I could hear something though that sounded vaguely like a cat suffocating.

Then the phone rang. It was Elaine.

"She's cute."

"She just came over to borrow a book."

"Whatever you say." Click.

A first date shouldn't be one of those instances where your life feels like it is being sucked out the front of your shoes. Sure it's a little tense at first, what with your whole life seemingly at stake, but it's just a date. Two people, scared shitless, eating something messy like spaghetti in a public place — with other people watching. Other people that instinctively know it's your first date because you're both eating too much garlic bread. And the waiter – he smiles a lot for somebody on minimum wage. Don't forget the valet. He parked two vehicles. One with a dog and another one that smelled funny and had a cat inside. And you're sitting face to face. Distance. No chance of accidental body contact. *It's just a date!* Besides, I read somewhere that you can't get dumped on a first date. Abandoned in a parking lot, but not dumped.

Being the man, I felt some sort of eighteenth-century need to produce a suitable itinerary for the evening. Which meant I had to guess what *she* might want to do. Movie? Dinner? Music? Theater? My God, I didn't even know what I wanted to do. Then I had to decide on what to wear. Casual? Fashionable? Wait a minute, I didn't own anything fashionable. I owned mostly agricultural goose-down sort of stuff that wouldn't work at most restaurants. I needed the Ralph Lauren look – polo shirt, sport coat, hair *moussed* back in thoughtful masculine sensitivity. I needed a new mirror.

I finally settled on my only clean shirt, jeans, tennis shoes and a sweater. I would reject being fashionable as an elitist propaganda tool of the financial institutions that issued my credit cards. I would be an individual — unique, unburdened and somewhat sophisticated as farmers go. I still checked myself in the mirror at least fifteen times.

Our date started like most first dates: long periods of uncomfortable silence followed by pointless observations on the weather. Common ground sacrificed for safety. We went to a small bar that sported dark tables and a loud band, too loud to dissect Pacific cold fronts or much of anything else. I suggested we leave. An hour later we found a seafood bar that made great Irish Coffees and steamed clams. We stayed until it closed. Irish Coffee and steamed clams? Only a human would put together such an improbable combination.

Over the next month we dated a couple more times. It wasn't my idea. Jesse firmly supported the new 55mph speed limit, which meant that even if the road was long and straight, there was no need to speed. An idea worthy of respect if my heart hadn't been carrying a load of perishable goods. What is it about the start of a relationship that makes it impossible to drive a tractor? I hit gates, fences, buildings, trees, seagulls – nothing was safe. Field mowing produced crop circles or giant 'J's' that turned into 'U's' then big 'O's.' You can't do reverse with a field mower. Not only is it mechanically impossible, but even attempting the process is normally fatal and pretty messy.

Doc was starting to worry about the deductible on his insurance; Elaine knew perfectly well what was going on and having far too much fun at my expense. She wanted to do the 'dinner thing,' where the couple meets the opposing parents. Okay, so Doc and Elaine weren't the folks, but they definitely found a comfort zone when it came to gross manipulation of any kind. What irritated me the most was that they were having more fun than I was and I was picking up the check. Life was imitating television.

By the third date, I began to notice a certain pattern developing – small things really. Jesse pointing out that my shoelaces didn't match, that I forgot my mother's birthday (little did she know that I was disenfranchised by an electrician from Texas – and that was a <u>good</u> thing) that the reason my phone didn't work was because I never paid the bill, and something about unidentifiable life forms in my refrigerator, some of which moved when the light came on. Good thing she never found the toilet seat up. Co-mingling toilets only happens after seven, maybe eight dates. For now, it was off-limits. I was in toilet etiquette training anyway. Little Post-Its that read, "Flush – Lid!" plastered on the mirror along with horse snot from you know who. Funny, but she could probably accept a horse in the bathroom, but not the lid thing. Or was I projecting? You know, I'll do this because she'll be anticipating the opposite in hopes of me noticing her anticipation and thereby adjusting my behavior because I noticed her discomfort in what I was thinking about doing, but didn't. There. Makes perfect sense.

In her own subtle way, Jesse was demanding that I clean up my act. Granted, my act was a little tarnished, but as near as I knew, a third date should be no more than exploratory surgery – digging around in the body of the beast, checking out the spleen, maybe squeezing a kidney or two – non-threatening encounters easily closed with a couple of well-placed sutures. Instead, she was going after my pre-fabricated ego, something I concocted like most men do in order to avoid long drawn out confessions with the pathological liar that shows up every morning in the mirror.

Most of the time I ignored her off-hand assaults:

"Listen, don't you think you need a haircut?"

"Pass the salt."

"Sideburns have been out of style for two years."

"How 'bout some pepper."

"Are you ever going to throw out that red sweater?"

"How 'bout some Tabasco sauce."

"On broccoli?!"

I really felt I was being prepared for something in slow motion. Marinated might be the right word. On one hand I was being told we needed to let time and space dictate the speed of the relationship. On the other, I couldn't help but notice that I was being remodeled, shaped, influenced and molded into a specimen worthy for display – to her parents. Stuffy old Bellevue conservatives intent on having their daughter marry a stockbroker or somebody in the Reagan administration. Being in lust was tough, but if I ever wanted a fourth date, I was going to have to play her game, even if it meant losing my sideburns. Geez, the red sweater?

Though really, a fourth date might be a record. Continuity wasn't on the virtue side of my attributes list. Unless you consider my uncanny ability to end a relationship before it might be requested, or maybe before it was identified as such. It's so much easier when you accept the blame prior to the crime. Less testimony that way.

Still, something held me at the outskirts of this new town. How much would I have to give up? How close is too close? Lonely or alone? Only one person can really keep a secret and most of mine were classified. I didn't sleep with the window open because I enjoyed fresh air. When the truth showed up unexpectedly, the window was quicker than the door. That's what happens when you spend too much time in the company of strangers.

Jesse was a little tight-lipped about her family. She had a somewhat mysterious brother and my only clue on their political leanings was that her mother drove a big Chrysler. Not too many liberals drive Chryslers. She had a father, since that is considered a biological necessity in these things, but most questions there left a cold trail. So cold he didn't appear to have a name. However, she did graduate from high school and it appeared she wasn't accident-prone around trains.

Sometimes her resistance seemed like a good thing. I couldn't quite figure out if the attraction – that pull I felt – was all hormones or some other kind of risky behavior. The kind where you drop the defenses just long enough for a sniper to find the distance. Somehow though, that morbid fear never went full circle. Every time one of us peeked over the neatly stacked sandbags, the other ducked. If Cupid was going to launch some foreplay here, he'd probably need a machine gun.

Part of my trepidation had to do with intimacy. I never really understood that part – where the physical meets the other stuff – where emotion and intellect start altering the rules of an encounter. I always thought that intimacy had something to do with lingerie, or a lack thereof as the situation took a favorable turn. Then again, maybe I had intimacy and anonymity confused. Or honesty maybe? Thought that was why sex seemed to be conducted with your eyes closed. Either you were handing the experience over to your imagination, or neither side really cared to watch. Or worse yet, one person kept their eyes open because they knew yours were closed. God that was a scary thought.

What was she so afraid of? Couldn't be me. *I* was terrified of *her!* Hell, I was terrified of *me*. Me? Someone define that for me. Five million words or less please.

Maybe I do need
a new mirror...?
No, the cat looks fine.

Dennis Haskett

13.

ADVENTURES IN FARMING

I FEEL IT on my forehead first, subtle and warm, sneaking out of my pores like a careless burglar. A twinge, a single drop of sweat skiing down the bridge of my nose, hanging there precipitously for a second, then falling thousands of feet to the valley floor, the cracked and mud-caked basin lying just in front of my LL Bean muckers. Soon my skin begins to crawl under my wool shirt, an itch that wanders around my nervous system playing hide and seek – a cat's dry tongue searching my back for a lost bowl of milk. The skin, long denied the radioactive joy of the sun, revolts, spreading a rose-colored cloud over the pale, tepid landscape of the human form. No, not another bout of lust about you-know-who. The first real sign of summer? A rash.

Some people would argue whether summer ever does arrive in Washington, especially weathered and wind-blown types who made the mistake of reading a travel article written by the desperate staff hunkered down at the local tourism office – folks who madly search the adjective vault for upbeat alternatives to horizontal rain and gale-force winds: "June in Seattle is brisk and exhilarating, the senses renewed by cool Pacific breezes, seagulls gliding on the gentle winds, sailboats plying the inland waters." Ha! June in Seattle is vulgar and decrepit, the sinuses washed out to sea by a bitter Pacific typhoon, the seagulls crash-landing at the nearest high school, sailboats upside down on the rocks, tourists wandering the streets in hypothermic dementia, vainly searching for space heaters and hot chocolate. The truth is that June is fickle, mean and oddly, forgiving – capable of spawning seeds from the ground, umbrellas from the closet, Calamine lotion from the medicine chest – all in the same day.

Farm managers love summer. Unlike normal human beings who are content to water a potted plant on the balcony of a condominium, farm managers view the extended day as a holy campaign against a bunch of organic infidels intent upon overthrowing the forces of democratic agriculture. Those of us running point-guard against left-wing weeds, subversive blackberries and manic pastures must hold the line against a counter-offensive designed and implemented to break our collective will. We can do it! Why? Because we have tireless will and a whole collection of power tools. Not to mention a few chemicals.

Yes, I was in bed with the chemical industry! Had a whole collection of stuff that was destined to be banned, discarded or sold to the developing world within a decade. Topping the list was creosote. It had two appreciable attributes: the first was that nothing on the planet would eat the stuff. The second had to do with its uncanny ability to sterilize seawater. One was marginally useful while the other was hotly debated. In the case of the latter, most of the witnesses didn't contribute much to the dialogue since they were floating belly up on the morning tide. Kind of like behavior correction by the mob, but without the cement.

Creosote was a by-product of the petrol-chemical industry. It is made from crude coke oven tar and is full of polycyclic aromatic hydrocarbons. Also a few phenols and cresots. The stuff is a known carcinogenic. This is determined by shaving a rat's ass and then repeatedly painting it with creosote. The chemical company hires a frat party to conduct the research.

Creosote is primarily a preservative used to treat telephone poles and railroad ties. Mostly it sheds moisture, thus reducing rot, but it also kills wood-eating insects and in my case, discouraged wood-eating horses. Subsequently, everything on the farm was coated with the stuff. I used a 50/50 mix of creosote and tar. Without the tar, the horses assumed the creosote was just an appetizer. The stuff burned your lungs, blistered your skin and you had to use another carcinogenic substance to wash it off. Maybe the combination canceled out the effects, or like asbestos it just lies dormant for a decade or two and then kills you. The alternative was something called penta, but instead of cancer, you got miscarriages. Tough call. "Say Eddie. Got some good news and some bad news I'm afraid: You're not pregnant, but you've got a 'mess o' thelioma.'"

Another product we used was dimethyl-sulfoxide (DMSO – a polar aprotic solvent) which originated as a by-product in the pulp and paper processing business. It was normally discarded in an environmentally unfriendly way. It was either pumped into the rivers or got lost somewhere in transit. Lot of this stuff got lost and since the EPA was in the conceptual stage of its development, nobody was really looking for it anyway. The great part is when a by-product finds a profitable use. Instead of just dumping it in one place, you can sell it to farmers and they'll dump it every-where. We used it as a liniment. DMSO had the capability of carrying other substances rapidly through the skin. You could mix it with cyanide and squirt it on your neighbor's dog and it would stop waking you up at night. Highly toxic to a developing brain so if a child gets ahold of it, for-get the third grade. Also suspect as a possible carcinogen, but only in female mice. No, I don't understand the distinction other than maybe most of the guy mice got bumped off in the creosote test. The rest weren't talk-ing. National security or something.

We had an excellent collection of herbicides, desiccants and defoliants. None of them managed to kill blackberries, but they pretty much killed everything else. Most were glyphosate-based since we couldn't get the good stuff. They only sold that to places with a slow legal system, like Guatemala. However, we did have monobar-chlorate which not only killed all forms of vegetation, but tended to migrate every time it rained. It was just as efficient as a plague of locusts and equally hard to control.

We also used naphthalene. This nasty substance was mixed with tur-pentine and used as a local anesthetic on horse's hooves. Very effective if you ignored the possibility of hemolytic anemia. Oh, just in case you didn't know, most people store this stuff next to their Armani suits and silk blouses. Mothballs.

My personal favorites were the anthelmintics. These were used to eliminate internal parasites. Animals that eat off the ground get worms. That's why people use bowls and plates. We had quite an arsenal to use against these freeloaders. On our team we had benzimidazoles, pyrim-idines, piperazine, fenbendazole, oxibendazoles, praziquantel, dichlorvos and my favorite: ivermectin. They were meant to discourage the visiting team: blood worms, tape worms, round worms, pin worms, thread worms and bots. Bots are like little armored personnel carriers that dream of becoming real worms. Any way you look at it though, that's a lot of worms. The idea was to make the inside of the horse's body so toxic that the worms would choose to leave. Of course, when they did leave, they took the chem-icals with them. That was a little hard on garden worms and trout fisher-men. Kind of the same principle as creosote. Kill the termites by destroying the entire planet. Ivermectin worked a little differently in that it traveled through the liver, thus making the blood toxic instead of just the digestive tract.

I'm pretty sure I also had some old DDT around. Farmers are like that. We hate to throw anything away. Especially if it's about to be banned.

I've attached a chemical breakdown of ivermectin in case there are additional questions that I have no intention of answering:

Certainly glad we got this cleared up.
If you're a worm, watch out for this guy

Our fixation (mechanical, not chemical) is brought to fruition by pounding nails, shoveling manure and mowing down weeds – an army set loose against a corrupt and ungovernable society, bringing civility, godliness and a new coat of paint to a heathen land. The world was not tamed by war and technology, but by maintenance – by self-effacing guys in overalls and tool belts changing light bulbs, mowing lawns, cleaning gutters – leading the huddled masses down the righteous trail of extended warranties and 3000-mile oil changes, never seeking more than a handshake and a smile from these grateful millions. And they dare to call this work!

***Well, I'm glad that speech** is over. Maybe I should have been a Baptist preacher moonlighting at Home Depot. The cat applauded politely.*

To have a farm, it is necessary to farm *something* – hence, the horses. Some of Doc's friends tried cows, others pigs, a few even tried chickens. The true visionaries combined all these animals into one and created the multi-purpose farm, which I guess cut down on agricultural boredom while fulfilling a desire to be the *complete* farmer. It is far more impressive an undertaking than a few petunias on the back porch.

Naturally, the best kind of farm is a horse farm. There is a certain stature (actually, it is unbridled snobbery and arrogance – cheap and disgusting) associated with raising Thoroughbreds that simply cannot be acquired with chickens. And farm managers appreciate a parallel rise in social stratification. Sure, we still shovel manure, but it's *pedigreed* manure.

GOLFER #1: "Well, you know Jack, that filly of mine won the Tidy Bowl Stakes by three lengths yesterday. Got a nice trophy from the Governor!"

GOLFER #2: "Yeah, that reminds me Bob, one of my hens laid a triple yoker on Monday. Damndest thing."

CADDY: (Under his breath.) "Geez, if I wanted a three-egg omelet, I'd go to Denny's. At least I wouldn't have to smell a bunch of stinkin' chickens. I bet this guy tips with a dozen eggs and a couple of drumsticks."

GOLFER #2: "Damn! Hooked it again."

Nope. No comparison. Thoroughbreds are noble animals and the presence of such royalty in the neighborhood not only raises property values, it also plays pretty well on the ninth hole. Besides, social stratification demands a certain degree of neighborly tolerance, giving one of Doc's little princesses a free shot at stampeding over a neighbor's rhododendron bush. An ounce of grace rarely offered to a bunch of no-name chickens. In the vernacular of the business, this is known as nose-sniffing patronage last practiced shortly before Louis the something parted company with his head. I'd practice it myself, except I have this image of a bunch of shabbily dressed chickens constructing a *guillotine*. Might explain the missing lumber.

Such self-gratification has a price however. While chickens may be a little ego-deflating, horses tend to be large, fairly clumsy and easily bored, not dissimilar to a bulldozer going through the *terrible twos*. Most of the destruction wrought upon a farm revolves around the big three: chewing, rubbing, or kicking...or, kicking, rubbing and chewing, depending upon the preference of the individual horse. Collectively, they can do more damage in a single afternoon than an unhappy rhino. And since most of this damage is buried in mud or fungi most of the year, summer presents one of the few opportunities to assess the damage – a process similar to cleaning up Europe in 1945 after everybody got done trashing the place.

You think war is sloppy, *try a few horses that can't afford cable TV…and that was a big part of Vietnam's undoing…television. Every night, somewhere between the macaroni and cheese and the Ice Milk (it was cheaper than ice cream) we got to review the carnage from Hue or Khe Sahn or the Ia Drang Valley. The first televised war in real time. The broadcasts had commercials and of course, the local weather. My father's war (WW II – not Korea, my mother confused quite a few things in those days) had movies. John Wayne, Richard Widmark, Humphrey Bogart. All winners. Movies had hopeless heroics, endless victories, great racial overtones – we never lost focus in the movies – we never lost. When somebody yelled, "Medic!" the prop guys threw some catsup around and the actors grimaced in Oscar-worthy agony. I guess when my father got summoned it was a matter of figuring out whose intestines he was holding in his hands. Unlike World War II however, Vietnam wore out its audience.*

♪ *"Come gather 'round people*

Wherever you roam
And admit that the waters
Around you have grown
And accept it that soon
You'll be drenched to the bone.

If your time to you
Is worth savin'
Then you better start swimmin'
Or you'll sink like a stone,
For the times they are a changin'"

©Bob Dylan, 1963

But did they, Bob?

On Doc's farm, the abuse generally centered on the fences. In fact, that old song, "Don't Fence Me In" was probably put to music by one of our horses, its melodic ideologue handed down from one generation to the next so that fence-wrecking was easier to determine genetically than racing ability. And when it came to demolishing fences, the same theories launched in the breeding shed, *speed versus stamina*, found new credence in their destructive, moronic behavior: some of them did it fast, while the rest could do it all day. Doc's emergency response team, which consisted of him and whatever was in the trunk of the Cadillac, preferred baling twine or wire whenever an escape was in progress. Some of the fences had highly technical repairs which I was to learn were mattress sutures. One section had an uncanny resemblance to a hernia patch. Seems veterinary medicine and home repairs had a lot in common. Good thing he wasn't a dentist, otherwise the whole place would have been wrapped in dental floss.

I discovered, at least in the beginning, that a great deal of energy has been exhausted over the years to support the various fencing lobbies – loose confederations of grizzly looking wire peddlers who have researched the pros and cons of all kinds of exotic and organic materials, from old-growth cedar, to recycled Michelin radials and weird plastic posts made from melted- down dashboards, some with the speedometers still working. Each professed to know *my true needs*, the opening salvo of their sales pitch, playing on either my naiveté or my ego. "Well, see here, you got some mighty expensive animals here, and well, I don't profess to tell ya yer business, being a manager and all, but I wouldn't consider anything but the best. Now look here at this Bolivian teak..." Little did he know that what I really wanted to do was dig a mote and hope that two out of three drowned trying to escape.

We also covered electric fencing, something called, "The Bull Tamer," that plugged into your dryer outlet. It didn't shock you, it blew off a limb.

"Don't you think that's a little severe," I asked.

"Why, hell no. Them horses of yours will only touch it once. Once they get a handle on 240 volts, they'll develop a whole new attitude. Now, about that Bolivian teak?"

"What about the rain forest?"

"The what? Ah hell, you mean down there in South America? Did I say Bolivia? I meant Alabama. I keep gettin' those places confused. Damn, I never was any good at geography."

A field trip to some neighboring farms revealed a number of options, from four-board plank to an assortment of woven wires – some square, others claiming to be especially designed for Thoroughbreds: triangular. I didn't think most horses did geometry. I figured it was a fashion thing. I stopped by to ask Earl, but he only shouted, "She ain't workin' today!" One neighbor was sold on electric fencing, but when I inspected his system, the sight of a half-dozen squirrels, frozen like rigored trapeze artists suspended from the wires, made me a little uncomfortable. Smelled pretty bad too. I did get a vote for this system – from the cat. I never knew cats could drool. I locked him in the truck.

I even considered barbed-wire, that nasty stuff that turned the Great Plains into a giant bovine parking lot. Granted, revenge did enter my mind in considering such an option, but I figured the cheap horses would con an expensive one into putting its leg through it, sort of like an initiation ceremony into a motorcycle gang. I finally decided on woven wire – non-climb – not the pricey triangular stuff designed for Thoroughbreds, but a cheap brand guaranteed not to rust, splinter, break, attract lightning or kill squirrels. At least until you got it home. I bought ten rolls, each weighing about two hundred pounds. I never did understand the 'non-climb' thing. Our horses were too lazy to climb anything. If they wanted out, they just put the transmission in reverse and rammed the fence with their butts. Their excuse was an unreachable itch. I should have bought them all back-scratchers instead.

I had planned on being environmentally sensitive by using the old fence posts, split-cedar relics from another age (when wood was wood and men were...), but the termites had eaten the bottoms and the horses the tops. (No, I don't know why horses eat wood, other than to irritate the hell out of me.) A guy down the road had a semi-load of old railroad ties, soaked in creosote and made from 'Erk' trees and was willing to part with them for three bucks apiece, a bargain by local standards. I asked him what kind of wood 'Erk' was, but he just snarled and counted the money. Why does a guy with a fourth-grade education who uses diesel fuel for cologne always feel inclined to insult a guy who is trying to give him money? He probably stole them from Burlington-Northern and the Chicago-bound West Coast Limited was going to end up in a ditch outside Missoula, Montana.

Now I had the wire and the posts. The only thing missing were the holes, which deductive reasoning told me might involve a little digging. A search of the farm failed to produce anything suitable for the task. I did find two boxes of duck decoys, the motor for the barn boat and somebody's clam sucker, a long tubular device designed for catching Pacific razor clams. It showed a lot of promise until it hit a rock. I headed for the feed store.

"Hey, how ya doin? How's that *Moomud* mare you guys bought doin?" This was Maynard speaking, the owner of the feed store. Actually, the mare was a distant relative of Mahmoud. Something got lost in the translation.

"She's fine, but I gotta dig some post holes. You got somethin' for that?"

"Sure, try this." He handed me a two-handled shovel that looked more suitable for pulling an infected molar on a gray whale.

"Say, you guys ever heard of a wood called 'Erk?' I got these railroad ties, the guy said they were..."

"That pile on Novelty Hill? Geez, those things weigh about 400lbs a piece. That's Bobby Williams that has them. He's from Georgia. They're oak, not 'Erk.' He just kinda talks funny."

"Well, I actually didn't buy them, I was just thinkin..."

"That's good, it'd take a stick of dynamite to get a nail in one of 'em."

Great. I just paid a fortune for petrified wood. And just think, there are only 300 of the damn things.

Back at the farm, the cause and effect of stabbing the earth with a weird shovel and the need for good mental health were at odds. I had figured that good, honest labor would negate my need to curl up on a psychiatrist's couch and discuss my infatuation with Julia Roberts, Susan Sarandon, Madonna, Cindy Crawford and Lyle Lovett. Okay, so I hum along with Lyle and have sexual fantasies about the others. Really, it's inexpensive entertainment when you're faced with punching holes in an unforgiving planet.

The first two holes went rather well, but by the seventh or eighth, the notion of an hour on the couch confessing old insecurities began to develop a certain appeal. My shoulders felt like Joe Namath's knees and I was even developing blisters on my forehead. Considering I had 292 earth penetrations to go, it was time to go high-tech.

Another trip to town produced a true wonder of modern, technocratic farming: the auger, which is little more than a truck rear-end with a milk-shake mixer attached. The thing fastens on the back of a tractor, gets hooked to the power take-off and while I sit and drink frozen daiquiris, it burrows its way to Shanghai. Perfect, except for one minor problem: it could dig the hole, but it couldn't decide where the hole should be, a conclusion clouded by tall grass and natural indecision. A male thing. Men are not natural planners, we're executors. Ever watched a B western real close? Women load the guns, men pull the trigger.

There are certain exceptions though, most involving stuff like betrayal, toilet lids, bedding other women – that sort of thing. Since the man was kind enough to teach the woman how to load the gun, the next step goes pretty quickly. The big difference is that women keep shooting until the gun is empty. Oh, and they try to shoot the man on the porch, not inside the house. Less mess that way. That's the planning part.

After an hour of circling the field, I took the coward's way out – I asked Jesse. Women always know where fences belong and they always show up on cue when something needs clarification. You turn around and there they are! Women love to confuse men with clarification.

She took to the task right away, explaining the importance of strict boundaries, honest lines of communication and something about parallel thinking. I tried to explain that parallel thinking was on a collision course with a forty-five foot alder tree. She dismissed my argument abruptly. "I think you need to re-evaluate your priorities. Maybe I should re-evaluate a few for…"

"Hmmm." I killed the engine on the tractor and swung around to face her. "We *are* talking about a large tree?"

"Really," she plowed forward. "You haven't considered what it means to set distinct boundaries. If you did, you would know *exactly* where this fence belongs." By now, she was waving her hand in the general direction of one of the outer planets in the solar system.

I kept looking at her, then outer space, then back to her. "Oh bloody hell," I mumbled.

"What?"

"Nothing. The bloody well. You can't put a fence there. The well is in the way!"

"Then put it over there!" she yelled, gesturing toward the neighbor's driveway. "In fact, why don't you stuff it in...never mind, I'm leaving."

Suddenly the clouds split and God's long right arm slapped me alongside the head. "I completely forgot about last night...I'm really sorry."

"You only remember what you want to remember. You'd forget Mother's Day, the phone bill; you'd forget Christmas if it weren't for all the decorations! It was my birthday!"

Mother's Day I could understand. The last thing I wanted to do was encourage my mother. I'd already tried twice to get the local paper to print my obituary. "Wait a minute," I interrupted. "I haven't known you that long. How am I supposed to remember everything in your life? I have enough trouble with my life!" Bad choice of words.

"Every? I sat in that restaurant for two hours – in a dress! The waiter started buying me drinks because he felt sorry for me! Like I said, put the stupid fence wherever you want. You'll forget where it is in ten-minutes anyway! I knew I shouldn't have...whatever!"

A dress? I missed that! I figured she'd only wear a dress for the Queen or something. "But, but..." Never could finish a sentence in this circumstance. However, I did have clarification.

With that she was gone, leaving me to my own devices, parallel thinking and all. Actually it was an historic moment: our first confrontation, man and woman sorting out the intricacies of our lives in front of God and a few of the neighbors. Somehow, it felt a little premature. According to my count, we had gone out approximately five times, not including one romantic rendezvous having the oil changed in her truck. I had gone from being invisible to patently irresponsible without ever having left any shaving stubble in her sink. "It's not fair!" I yelled. From a distant porch, a neighbor yelled back, "I agree with you!"

After an hour of finger-drumming on the hood of the tractor, I made a bold decision. In reality, drumming your fingers is what professionals refer to as 'anger management.' Kind of like counting to ten, but spread out over sixty-minutes or so. That way you can assertively answer all those angry statements in the privacy of your own brain. As far as fences went, I would simply follow the creek on one side and the old fence line on the other. Plus, I'd whack down that damned alder tree. Somebody or something needed to pay a price. In this case it was a tree, which on further examination, turned out to be dead anyway. Probably a suicide. A much better way out than watching me try to start a chainsaw.

I ran a string between the two distant points, insuring a straight line. At eight-foot intervals, I stuck a stake in the ground to pinpoint ground zero. That's where the auger would quickly chew up grass, loam, rocks and probably a few unlucky worms, producing a perfectly engineered project. Right? Wrong. Somehow, every hole ended up at least six inches off where it was supposed to be, reinforcing my long held belief that you can't draw a straight line on a round planet.

A hole is a hard thing to move. A 747? At least it has wheels. Holes just lay there sucking the life out of you. My choices were limited: either buy a two-foot wide auger or digress to a little corrective work with the manual model. But then, I figured that by the time the horses got done doing the 'big three,' the fence would probably be a little crooked anyway. So why bother? Besides, Jesse was going to take one look at it and wrinkle up her nose anyway. I had gone out with her just long enough to recognize when I had been dismissed by a facial twitch.

Now that I had all the crooked posts in the ground, it was time to string the wire. Contrary to what they told me at the feed store, there is nothing simple about a two-hundred pound roll of woven wire. The first step is to unroll the wire. The second step goes a lot quicker, as the wire decides to re-roll itself with me inside. Step three, which was probably step one in reality, is to anchor one end, then unroll it. Once I had it unrolled again, I discovered it was three-feet short of the end post, which might as well have been a mile, since all I had was a two-inch staple.

I tried hooking it to the tractor and stretching it the extra three feet, but that pulled it off its anchor, causing it to re-roll itself quite smugly underneath the tractor. A good jack and an hour of cursing finally brought the wire to its senses. It was now time to stretch it tight, giving it that *professional* look. Oh, I decided to ignore the problem about the missing three feet. It was a lot easier to shrink the farm than risk another session with the jack and a bunch of obscenities. Any more noise and the guys with the red suspenders would show up to sell me a brain.

The guys at the feed store told me that the best way to stretch wire was with a tool known as a *come-along*, a device that makes a wimpy farm manager into the Charles Atlas of fence stretchers. His instructions seemed simple: attach one end to a stout tree or the tractor and the other end to the wire. Vigorous cranking should make the fence as taught as piano wire. Evidently in the farming bizz you couldn't have a fence that looked like fifteen mesh bras on a clothesline. Not really acceptable.

There *is* a problem with the cranking though. A *come-along* is really a power trip – singing wire and all that – so guys want to do just one more crank. It's irresistible. Do it, surrender to your ego and boom, either the posts all pop out of the ground, the tractor tips over, or, in my case, the wire breaks, once again re-rolling the whole mess under the tractor, causing the neighbor to throw up his hands and disappear into his house. I wish the guy would get into down-loading pornography or something.

About nine o' clock that evening, I scraped up the courage to knock on Jesse's door. Mostly the dog barked, but after about ten minutes, two or three towels and a body showed up at the door. She had been in the shower.

"I'm sorry about this afternoon," I offered. Actually I was.

"No, *I'm* sorry," she returned.

"I'm sorrier," I shot back. I was still thinking about the dress.

"Dammit!"

"I brought you a present." I stuck out a bouquet of flowers and a can of corn. The kind that has little bits of red pepper tossed in.

"Corn? *You brought me a can of corn?"*

"Yeah, Mexicorn. And flowers! Focus on the flowers."

"Mexicorn?"

"Well, I read that when a relationship gets down to gift-giving, each period of time dictates a gift made of a particular material. You know, five years equals wood, twenty-five equals silver, that sort of thing. I thought I should follow the tradition, so I looked it up. Four dates and an oil change equals corn. I wanted it to be special, so I got Mexicorn."

"This is really stupid – well, actually, it's kinda sweet, I guess. Come in and I'll...yeah, I'll put it on the stove or something. You could have wrapped it. And this isn't a relationship, it's something...something else...to do. Okay?"

14.

GUIDO: THE GODFATHER OF GOATS

GOATS ARE SCHEMERS. When I first took this job, Doc mentioned something about Nubians. I figured it was either an enquiry into my feelings about the Arab/Israeli war – series actually, since they were on at least the fifth one, or that *he* was really a Syrian disguised as a Norwegian. I couldn't initially get a handle on the goat collection. Some racehorses, plagued with a neurosis or two have goats for company. The goat facilitates mysterious therapy sessions where no one speaks – they just chew. Seemed slightly plausible except for the fact that Doc had about thirty therapists on staff. That's a lot of issues for one farm.

Turns out the Nubians were research goats. No, not sub-atomic particles. Cancer and communicable diseases. And to clarify matters, Doc and I wore the white lab coats, not the goats. Now I'm pretty certain that at least one person from PETA or the National Defense Fund for Maligned Goats, or whatever, will get their puritanical hands on this chapter and...I don't know, smuggle arms to the world's goats? Better read the chapter first. You might want to reconsider supplying arms to these guys.

In many cases animal research is the only option short of human research. Creates kind of an ethical dilemma unless you happened to be Dr. Joseph Mengele or perhaps Karl Otto Koch and your office was just inside the front gate at Auschwitz or Buchenwald. Koch's hobbies were nearly as odd as his day job. He made lampshades out of the skin of dead, tattooed former patients. Doc Mengele? He conducted most of his autopsies on the living. Without anesthesia.

Now that we all understand the ethical dilemma, we'll move on to what the goats did for a living. About every three months they were injected with a substance that caused a reaction in their blood. Once a month, they gave a little blood back. This was sent to a lab in Canada, processed for the medical community and used as an antigen medium in cancer and communicable disease research. The end result was a diagnostic tool that just might save your wife, husband, child, mother…whomever — at a stage where they might actually be savable. We weren't shoving Oil of Olay up a rat's ass to see if it cured hemorrhoids, even if the idea did hold a certain economic, though slightly disgusting appeal. The marketing could be problematic. Besides, each goat was worth about $35,000 and received better care than half the world's children, which by most accounts seems like a better repository for our indignation and self-serving contempt. That's just a suggestion though.

And *that* about covers *that*.

However, what I had was a goat *mafia*. These were all 'guy' goats – wethers, I think they call them in the goat business. They were missing the same accessories as the cat, which basically meant that they weren't dating on a regular basis. So instead of worrying about the opposite sex, they were engaged in an ongoing plot to break out of prison, or to eat anything even remotely connected to the human race. As far as I knew, they ate four or five leg wraps, two gallon jugs of vinegar, one small building, an unfortunate mare's tail, one gate, 400 feet of electric fence wire and thirty-five pounds of horse wormer. I also made the mistake of leaving the tractor in their field one day while I went to get some lunch. They ate the distributor, all the plug wires, one front tire and they were going after the battery when I got back. Oh, I forgot. One duck, though I'm not sure what that was all about. Seemed it belonged to one of the neighbors and you already know the difficulties I was having in that department. The leader of this gangsta' pack was a one-horned Angora named Guido, or in the secretive world of animal research, No. 56. Not sure why since we only had 32 goats. For all I knew, the extras were also at the neighbor's place along with Foggy Bottom, Busy Bee and the rest of the off-shore accounts. Guido had a pretty substantial history for a goat. He had a rap sheet with the SPCA, frequent death threats from our few remaining neighbors (the duck thing) and at least one moving violation for driving without a license. Seems Doc was driving him to the farm from his previous place of employment (a petting zoo at a mental health facility) when he got his horns stuck in the steering wheel. The jeep careened into a ditch with Guido at the wheel and Doc buried in a pile of golf clubs. That apparently was how he lost one of his horns. The police also cited the two for violating the seatbelt law though they did manage to pass the field sobriety test.

Guido seemed to be always plotting something. He had that look in his eye. He would normally be standing alone staring in the direction of the feed room next to the barn. This was a pretty good distance away. Down one hill, across the bridge, a good hike down to the creek, up another hill, then a 200-yard sprint to the grain room. Plus, he had to deal with two fences, a hundred feet of electric wire and me: the warden. I didn't have any machine guns, but I did own a few power tools and extra batteries for the electric fence. Still, he stared in that general direction often enough to make me believe that a *coupe d'état* was simply a matter of time. There's nothing worse than a goat with revolutionary tendencies. Ché Guevara? A goat in disguise. Fidel Castro? A closet goat guy. The CIA needs to take a serious look at these little beady-eyed goateed bastardized ovine mutants that feign being dumb animals. They are <u>not</u> dumb. They may even have nuclear devices. The federal government worries constantly about Iran, North Korea, and the Democratic Party – goats. They need to focus on goats. We're talking about weapons of massive dental destruction. They could eat a B-2 bomber in under twenty minutes. That includes the pilot, co-pilot, the engines, most of the munitions and the more succulent portions of the landing gear. If they ever got loose at a commercial airport, most flights would be announced as "eaten en-route."

Okay, call me paranoid. But, I've seen these guys in action. Hell, I buried the duck. It was not pretty. No head, no feet. Very few feathers. The body was intact, but I guess that is a goat thing. They only eat spare parts. Some kind of brotherhood initiation-family-ritual-eating-disorder sort of problem. Still, I knew Guido was up to something sinister. It was just a matter of time before he'd strike. And strike he did.

June 11th dawned as most days do in Seattle. Overcast with a hint of rain and two million people sacrificing virgin sheep and sucking down *lattes* in hopes that the Sun god was listening. If he was, it was via a cell call from Jamaica. The farm had a certain nervous character to it. The horses were ignoring their breakfast, geese were flying west toward Hawaii, the cat feigned interest in whatever was scheduled to die that day and turned down flat a fresh can of some sort of kitty gourmet delicacy made from ground-up Tuna heads. Doc was at the track evaluating his collection of B-movie re-treads and hopeless cripples. Elaine was planting spring flowers behind the house (we do that in summer since spring normally gets canceled) a spot directly in line of Guido's *blitzkrieg*. I was busy calling Chet to see if he could come over and weld the field mower back together again for the 27th time. Yeah, we did the tanker over the Cascade mountain thing again. This time he swerved just in time to save a busload of Mormons from sure death. Last week it was the University of Kentucky basketball team. What's next week? The population of Lithuania?

Around 11:30, I heard a blood-curdling goat-like scream, then two more. Through my binoculars I saw three young Nubians hanging by one leg each in the forks of two trees. Goats do this occasionally, mostly because they are either trying to eat the tree or are simply desperate for attention. Once they have decimated the ground, then they go after trees, shrubs and poultry. I thought about calling 911, but it would be hard to put the whole thing in proper perspective.

"911 Operator. Please state your problem."

"I've got three Nubians hanging in a tree!"

"Nubians, you mean Arabs?"

"No, Nubians! They're like from Nubia or somewhere!"

"Sir, you need to be a little more clear on this. This sounds like a hate crime. I'm dispatching the Swat Team immediately."

"Really, a veterinarian would work better."

"Are you a Skin-head?"

"No, but I've got a pretty good rash at the moment."

"Sir, I'd suggest you just lie prostrate on the ground with your hands behind your head when they arrive."

"But, what about the goats?"

"Goats?"

"Yeah, the Nubians are goats and they are hanging upside down in a couple of trees! What the hell did you think I was talking about?"

"1052 cancel the 10-19. Transfer the call to Fire and plan on a 5150 with restraint. Sir, you need to calm down. Help is on the way. By the way, are you on any sort of medication we need to know about?"

"Just a triple *latte* with mocha."

"Ah, hell. You again?"

After rehearsing my speech for the local authorities, which was bound to result in another interview in my trailer, I made a mad dash for the far side of the farm to gallantly rescue the young Nubians from the clutches of an angry red maple. I never thought that trees could hold a grudge, but I suppose if they are surrounded by goats intent on amputating their limbs from the bottom up, I could get a little testy myself. Ever piss-off a tree? The first thing it will do is fall on your house or your BMW – whichever is in range.

As I sprinted down the hill toward the bridge, I stopped to turn off the electric fence charger, figuring that it might save me the hundred bucks or so it would cost to have my hair re-straightened. Then I simply vaulted over the gate in perfect sub-Olympic form, hooking my boot through the top wire. The audience gasped as I completed my three-point landing – one foot, one hand and my nose. The boot landed about five feet in front of my forehead, which was gently cradled in a pile of goat excrement. Good thing, it broke my fall. I think this acrobatic maneuver disrupted Guido's overall strategy or the judging committee simply couldn't decide on a score. While I started extricating goat limbs from tree branches, Guido and his lieutenants were doing a conference call about fifty-feet away. Lots of rapid chewing noises with a few guttural discharges thrown in to prevent eavesdropping.

With the gate still closed, they had no choice except to work out an alternative plan. They took my lead and settled on mass gymnastic goa-tracide. Every time I got one Nubian out of a branch, three more would leap into a tree and start screaming. It was like the lemmings jumping off those precipices in Alaska and then changing their minds halfway down. There is nothing worse than botching a suicide. Get a better gun, find a faster train, try jumping off the Empire State Building instead of a one-story Motel 6! The whole mess looked like a convoluted Christmas tree with screaming goats for decoration. A few blinking lights and the whole crew could be on *The Twilight Zone*. I can almost hear Rod Serling's opening monologue. No, actually I can't.

Meanwhile, Guido and his mob had reached a consensus. With me busy hauling down the decorations, they charged the gate. Guido assigned the goats with horns to tear out the electric wire, not knowing that the damned thing was turned off anyway. Regrouping, they formed a flying wedge and rammed the gate. It held. Back in formation, they hit it again. It still held its ground. I would have been extremely proud of my carpentry skills, but then, I was a little busy. The third assault tore off the hinges and the gates crashed to the ground. I turned around in time to see them sprinting toward the bridge. Within a minute, they were clattering across the deck and heading up the hill toward Elaine and her petunia garden. I could only watch in abject horror.

Elaine spun around, shovel at the ready. The mob was on her. She was totally outnumbered. Petunias were being ripped from the ground, torn and dismembered. All I could hear was the sickening sound of molars gnashing the life out of innocent petunias. In little more than five minutes, the flower garden was reduced to a few scraggly stems. I'm pretty sure they even ate her shovel. The only other sound was one I hated to hear: "Doc!!!" Of course, he was still at the track picking up the weekly excuse roster.

Elaine sort of dropped and sat on the ground, her hands over her face. I thought she might be crying, but I knew better. Elaine never cried. She did retribution, not tears. Somebody was going to pay for this and I had a funny feeling that it wasn't going to be Guido. I avoided her glare as I too sprinted across the bridge. The goats, having digested the landscaping were moving toward their main target: the feed room, scarcely two-hundred yards from their initial assault. Guido led the pack. I just topped the hill when they burst through the barn door. The cat was already at the top of the power pole next to the barn. Too late, I thought.

Everything was eerily quiet for a few seconds, then a sudden flash of light. The doors flew back open belching out a cloud of acrid smoke and ash. Guido came out first, missing his lone horn and kind of smoldering around his head, a little like Nancy Arbuckle, the bus driver. The rest of the pack followed, trudging rather forlornly in the direction of the bridge, Napoleon's great army evicted from the gates of Moscow. The barn continued to exhale a great deal of smoke. Out of the haze came a guy wearing a welding hat and holding an arc welder tip with a goat horn attached. It was Chet. He had been welding the field mower together.

He was yelling in my general direction, "What the hell was that? I turned around and all I saw was a bunch of beady eyes and the next thing I know the whole place smelled like a burnt mattress! It was like a flashback or somethin' – Mormons runnin' everywhere, basketballs bouncin' around! This is goin' to cost you."

Well, actually it *was* going to cost me. About two hours later, I meekly knocked at Doc's door. Naturally, Elaine answered the call. She had a look on her face that can best be described as hysterical blindness shortly after one has regained their sight and is seeking out the source of the hysteria. It wasn't particularly pretty. I had four flats of new petunias and a shiny shovel. Her eyes softened a little, but not enough to avoid the gallows. Women are good at that. She just said, "You keep 'em."

We all know what that means. Next morning at around seven, shovel in hand, I was in the back yard re-establishing petunia heaven. Doc thought it was pretty funny. Later that day, I rebuilt the gates in the goat field and re-strung the wire. It didn't really matter. The *cartel* had been broken. Guido was a shattered shell of his former greatness. He stayed off by himself, hornless and despondent. The others, without a leader, seemed content to resume eating small buildings, errant ducks, stray saddles and various tractor parts. Law, order and civilization had been returned to a chaotic planet.

Oh, Chet added $25 to his bill for what he called 'de-horning his welder.' Sounded like something machinery does when it gets amorous. I just paid the bill.

15.

ADVENTURES IN FARMING, PART II: THE *DIRT* ON DIRT

I ONCE READ about the joy that has always been associated with working the land. I don't really remember if it was Stephen Gaskin or perhaps Mao Tse-tung that coined the phrase. I do know that regardless of politics, ideology, exorbitant ideals or simply a desire for agrarian simplicity, at the end of the day, everybody wants to sit down to dinner. Maybe that's why pot roast, politics and history seem to be a lot like farming. Food has always been an antecedent for migration, a trophy of war, a maker of revolutions and sadly, the ransom of kings. Farmers seem to be the custodians of more than the land, perhaps in older days, the very harbingers of peace and stability in an uncertain world. Just maybe that's the appeal for me, though I sometimes wish I could trade in the racehorses for turnips. Regardless, I can claim one triumph: the land remains the land. The pastures and trees cleanse the air, the animals fertilize the ground and no commerce will asphalt my optimism. Not here.

In a circuitous fashion I could understand Mao's philosophy – he was busy putting the final touches on that little red book while fighting to the death with the US-backed Nationalists. Most of his political philosophy was based on turning society upside down, which he viewed as a way to empower the peasantry and break the very long tradition of internal serfdom and the shorter historical reality of external interference. It was a bold plan, born from centuries of an imperial system of emperors and warlords. In spite of the fortunes of a world war raging around him at the time, he knew that a victory by either of the great antagonists would result in a divided and lesser China. The Long March was exactly that – and it covered the whole of China. Few people know that Mao never allowed his troops to confiscate materiel from the locals, even though the Red Army was starving about 80% of the time. Most people also do not know that the seizure of Tibet was a personal matter, not political.

You see, the various 'tribes' of China did offer what comfort they could to the vastly outnumbered and ill-equipped Red Army. Except the Tibetans. They viciously tore his army to shreds as Mao traversed the high country. He did not forget the affront.

Fewer still fully comprehend the tribal nature of the People's Republic, nor bother to consider the social burdens of the most populous nation on earth. Or puzzle over Mao's decision to have all the birds in China killed because they ate the grain. All personal research began and ended with the word 'communist.' Yet at its most basic level, communism is a lot like farming – production by the many for the benefit of the whole. But two things differ substantially in that equation. Communism evolved from a social construct to a Godless political will, while farming slowly embraced the corporate/capitalist model. Only in the case of America's sophisticated approach to farming, the ransom happens to be food. We could fill the world's bellies, but always at some indeterminate price. A vote here, a gesture there. Such a cavalier outlook fails miserably when you have 2 billion guests for dinner and the next night's reservations are already piling up.

The Nationalists under Chiang Kai-shek never seemed to have a problem with pillaging the locals. They treated their own people like a shopping spree at Safeway without the need for a cashier — this while being bankrolled by a very edgy West. China's fall (or rise) to communism would mean that two-thirds of the world's population would toil under the godless tyranny of socialism. A fate viewed by many as far more horrific than the slow rape resulting from God-fearing imperialism. Did the ignorant savages not get it? Or did they?

The end of the first round of the Nuremberg trials marked the opening salvo of the Cold War, and for the next 40 years America supported a host of despots, dictators and barn burners for the sole purpose of stacking the UN against the Soviet Union and China. All this human energy consumed over an ideological debate mutually reinforced by over 50,000 nuclear devices. Agreeing to disagree had never been explored with this much at stake. A living, breathing hell restrained only by words – the interpretation of a single sentence in a difficult conversation. Diplomacy with a loaded gun. Percussion and repercussion crammed into a single chamber.

And so began the "Great Game." The pimps of Washington, Moscow and later, Beijing began the arduous task of buying the prettiest girls in the countryside. Some were from Africa, others from Central and South Amer-

ica – the best were to be found in the Middle East and southern Asia. Even comely girls were welcome if the address was right. Location, location, location. All they had to do was like us…for now anyway.

We gave them gifts. Bridges without roads, airports without planes, great reservoirs without pumps, pipes or water. We even picked new enemies for them, started their wars, sold them the guns. If they lost, we walked away. If they won, we sent them a bill. The payback was simple. Plough your sorghum, raise beef – we'll buy it at under market value, sell it to a third party. Maybe sell it back to you. What? Can't afford it? Well, go back to eating sorghum. Oh. Plowed under, huh? Well, how about a nice bridge?

Turned out the old girl wasn't as pretty as everybody thought and most bridges, pipelines and air strips weren't edible. China had no hope of feeding China in a free-market system and no hope for true world autonomy without the mantel of socialism.

Gaskin, on the other hand, was probably digesting hallucinogenic mushrooms somewhere in the southern hills of Tennessee. He was way ahead of Timothy Leary in that for him, enlightenment was merely the clarification of simplicity, minus the clutter of modernity. The world really was sensual, unsophisticated and rather forgiving – i.e., governable under physical law. No gates, no locks, no garrison manning the parapet. One need not protect what can never be controlled. Stephen Gaskin? Led a great caravan of buses to Tennessee in 1971. Formed the largest commune in the United States. It lasted until the late 1980's. It was named for Don Quixote's horse Rocinante, though everyone knew it as The Farm.

Ah, the skinny war horse Rocinante and his pettifogger knight off on a prodigal quest to slay the sour-breathed dragon of the Hypocrites – that race of dogged assassins that left the dreams of Camelot in ashes and despair. And vanquished the believers to the wilderness of Tennessee. The foolishly impractical pursuit of ideals — marked by rash, lofty, romantic ideas and extravagant chivalrous action.

Yeah, that sounds pretty accurate. Beat the hell out of a bad haircut and a M-16. 1971 also ushered in the 26th Amendment to the United States Constitution, that "living document" that took a deep breath and threatened Congress with the unemployment office. Pretty hard to press an 'unpopular' war to a 'dignified' conclusion when the business-end of policy throws down the gun. Romantic ideals made a lot of noise, but the real power showed up in the ballot box.

If the Cabinet and Joint Chiefs had ever "tuned in, turned on" and per-haps "drop[ed] out" even momentarily, they might have realized it takes a lot more guts to plant an acre of lettuce in the desert than to run over an elementary school with a tank. Ask a farmer. They lose one war or another every six months – sometimes sooner. And yet oddly they return to the task, re-work the ground, rarely holding an ideology accountable for a bad freeze or a lack of water. In some ways communism and America's counter-cul-ture followed the path of the farmer. The work of the many for the benefit of the whole – the caveat found in the price of lettuce. And both aspired to conquer the twin evils of humanity: the malignancy of personal ambition and the psychosis of absolute power. Neither proved to be what we'd call sustainable farming. Both crops withered in the field.

Still, I liked the idea of creating life and being the only witness. I felt no danger here, just awe. The only prisoner in this wondrous green jail.

I think my first introduction *to dirt sniffing was a sixth-grade essay I was forced to author on Thomas Jefferson, penned in a feeble attempt to turn another potential 'D' into something respectable – a grade a mother could look at and say, "Well, at least he tried."*

According to Jefferson, the joy was best viewed from the rear balcony of Monticello, which offered an expansive view of his vast holdings, includ-ing about 125 slaves, one of who wandered into his bedroom occasionally, certainly by mistake. Naturally, 1958's interpretation of history was subject to the political correctness of the time, not to mention the intellectual capacity of sixth-graders, but the concept, as sheltered as it may have been, was not totally lost on me. Managing joy is a lot less labor-intensive than executing such joy, allowing the joyer the pursuit of higher office, while joy-ees deal with the plowing. The players have changed, but the game, per-haps even the relationship, goes on.

There is a feeling of kinship with the elements of nature that are rarely granted entrance to the lofty isolation of the balcony – the smell of freshly cut hay, the Arctic elegance of frost on early morning air, the faraway cry of southbound geese seeking shelter in a neighbor's field – images and sounds that filter out the harsher side of life's commitment to asphalt, avarice and expediency. On the other hand, there is the reality of working such land: the romance of broken-down manure spreaders, the exhilaration of getting down to nature with 400 railroad ties, and of course, the acrid smell of creosote and rotting straw – all of which manage to etch a joyous path into the senses of urban man and leave us farmers bewildered at the notion of perceived charm. I guess that's because we commune with nature the old-fashioned way – with tall rubber boots and a shovel.

To our city-raised counterparts, farming seems as capricious as the weather: an endless mélange of disconnected affairs, thrown together by the singular need to nurse something, anything, from the ground. It is a passion that cannot be explained or defended as a completely rational pursuit, not to those people that put success and an ulcer in the same sentence.

Odd and slightly unorthodox as it may seem, at least in the agrarian view, Doc's horses were undeniably a crop – given the result of what *his* land could bear. About the only other stuff we could grow was skunk cabbage, seaweed or alligators, though the latter would probably need thermal underwear and an electric blanket. Well, frogs too, but ours were too skinny-legged to warrant planning a meal around one. I am into legs myself, normally those further up the food chain, but after four hours spent trying to get enough protein out of a bunch of emaciated amphibians, I'd switch to cannibalism. I could cruise the bus stops squeezing forearms to check the fat content. Same with crayfish. A huge pile of miniature crustaceans and two hours later you're starving to death because you expended 2000 calories just trying to figure out which part you eat and which part you throw away. That's why frozen dinners are so popular. You don't need a forensic biologist, just a fork.

Compared to lettuce or cabbages that merely lie around all day getting a suntan, horses require a far more intensive investment in energy, even though a Nebraska wheat farmer or some other high priest of agricultural purity may laugh it off as little more than fluff farming. Actually they're probably right. Most horses won't contribute much to the developing world as a dinner item, but according to well-established tradition, farmers are identified by *where* they shop, not *what* they grow. Places like the John

Deere dealership, the feed store, Monsanto, the lobby at Dow Chemical. I've got the Bib overalls, the green baseball cap, calluses and the most important badge of inclusion: dirty fingernails. Ones with real dirt, not just stuff you pick up around the house.

American farmers could benefit however from the French example. France's farmers are not only unionized, but pretty temperamental as well. They don't get their price and most of the *Brie* ends up in the Atlantic shipping lanes. How much wheat could the Mississippi River handle on a good day before the cesspool backed up all the way to Toronto? And eating racehorses might not be that undesirable in the long run. Since they don't get paid $4 million a year for playing a kid's game like baseball, the also-rans might get the hint. Just filling a spot on the Tote Board would no longer constitute a career choice. Throw in a nationwide turnip strike and everybody would know that we're pretty serious guys. Of course I'm not sure if the horses would really appreciate the distinction since they don't get paid anyway. They're more like eccentric rock stars with trust funds. The trustees make all the important decisions for them. Stuff like what color of Cadillac to buy.

Even so, I don't see horses delighting guests at a Texas barbecue, barring either a worldwide shortage of cows or a large and unlikely expansion of French cuisine. Having snails as an appetizer normally limits any further menu exploration by an American diner addicted to mashed potatoes and gravy. And we do have this romantic infatuation with the old West, where feral horses denude the landscape and trample on 30 or 40 legitimately endangered species that actually do belong in North America. Still, cowboys eating horses? They might boil up a stirrup or two, but not Ol' Baldy. Just try to picture John Wayne and Julia Childs swapping recipes:

"Too much oregano, John."

"Ma'am, you know how old my horse was?"

Perhaps part of the disconnect lies in crop presentation. Instead of horses tromping on top of the ground, foals would pop out of the earth each spring like ripe melons ready for market. Each could be washed, waxed, dusted with God-knows-what and shipped in cellophane to the Keeneland sales ring and offered to anxious buyers like a Christmas fruit basket. Farmers respect that sort of thing. It's known as marketing. That's how a pear that looks like an apple became an 'Asian Pear.' Mostly it's a defective pear. Marketing transformed this humble mutant into a mystic symbol of oriental mysticism at $2.59 a pound. Same with 'Irish' butter, 'English' gin, 'Chinese' parsley – translation: butter, rot gut and Mexican cooking. Of course if you happen to believe that everybody got to North America via the land bridge from Siberia, then Hispanics, Navahos and Sioux are Asian anyway. The food is about the same, the only real differences are the out-fits and the language. Still, better than calling something 'wheat' I guess.

"What are ya growing this year Orville?"

"Wheat."

"What kind?"

"Just wheat. You know, wheat dammit!"

"Simmer down Orville. Just askin.' Know what I planted?"

"Don't care."

"Nijinsky Thoroughbreds. Eighty acres of 'em."

"Now what the hell is a Nijinsky Thoroughbred?"

"Don't know really, but sounds special, huh?"

But alas, the concept is *probably flawed. Since I would have to dispense with the usual 50 tons of herbicides, pesticides and fertilizer (thus saving at least one major river), all forms of mechanized harvesting, ozone-eating refrigerated shipping and the entire population of a small town in Mexico, agricultural conformity would probably be compromised. Then, of course, trying to harvest the little beggars on a hot September afternoon might be as frustrating as trying to weed-eat a path through Brazil, even though that hasn't stopped a bunch of environmentally impaired slash-burners who think their children are going to develop a taste for carbon-dioxide.*

I think I'll just let mothers be mothers, foals be foals, and simply accept the notion that I'll never be sanctioned by the guys who hang out by the coffee machine at the local John Deere dealership. I mean, it really hurts my feelings. Every time I wander in, it causes a lot of throat-clearing and mumbling about getting in the turnip harvest. Nobody grows turnips in Washington! I feel like I opened a leper colony next to a Nordstrom's. Why? I don't have a John Deere tractor. I have something a little different.

My first introduction to high-tech farming (not to mention the purpose of this chapter which seems to have gotten lost from the first paragraph), revolved around a 1953 Ford 8N tractor, brilliantly negotiated for when Doc sold Busy Bee and Foghorn to the neighbors, the ones that mysteriously disappeared. The people that is – the horses, well they disappeared after they were already gone. (The horses that is – prior to the other disappearance.) So. The 8N possessed every option that 1953 had to offer: a contoured steel seat, indicted for doing odd things to your backside according to the season (a subject best left to the privacy of a doctor's office), a six-volt electrical system (which meant that the tractor would not start if the temperature was below thirty or above eighty-degrees), and a patented scoop-loader on the front that dropped most of its load on the engine. It had three gauges on the console, but the letters had worn off, so it was difficult to guess which one was the oil and which was the water, made completely redundant by the fact that two gauges were broken anyway. The engine consumed about three quarts of oil a week, and if I didn't throw in a pint of STP every Sunday, the pistons would refuse to come out of the oil pan.

It also had power steering (the same kind Arnold Schwarzenegger has), no brakes, and bald tires, which meant that I avoided any tight turns that happened to be near a building. My inspections also revealed: no radiator cap, assuming too, no anti-freeze, a hydraulic system as powerful as the Russian economy and a mufflerless tail pipe that vented itself under the seat, lending further evidence to the mysteries afflicting my jeans. The tractor was also home to a small family of mice, who occupied a small apartment between the gas tank and battery, engaged in trying to sabotage world order by chewing up all electrical systems first. No, I didn't evict them. Jesse thought they were *cute*.

I should have felt fortunate to have any tractor at all. Doc's desire to promote economic privation was rooted in Rockefellian socio-economic illogic: the male who writes the fewest checks will sleep in the house. Elaine understood $300 azalea bushes, remodeled kitchens and the need to keep the local Cadillac dealer employed, but her vision stopped short at mechanized farming. Thus, every time a wheel fell off or the engine began to cough uncontrollably, Doc would secretly hand me a pile of well-laundered cash and tell me to get it fixed...no receipts, no estimates and certainly, no questions. Like going to the Cayman Islands for a *vacation.*

Some farms had it a lot worse. They had to get by with little more than a riding mower and a lot of imagination. Still, the 8N was not the gift from heaven Doc first implied. Some days, I felt that in order to simply get a day's work done, I would need two or three mechanics, a priest and a stiff drink. Or, just a little refresher course at that asylum in New Jersey where they re-align your thinking with a battery charger. With farm equipment well to the south of adequate, the day always begins with a list and ends with a new one. First, the tractor won't start. Forgot. It's 82 degrees out. Try the chainsaw. No deal. Weed-eater? Somebody fixed a fence with the string. Jeep? At the golf course. Shovel? Damn! Right where I left it.

However, if it happens to be 79 degrees then field mowing is back on the list. Normally it is a job riddled with a productive sort of boredom, unless one tries it in early spring, which has been pretty much explained, or the mower happens to shave off the top two inches of a hornet's nest. In Washington, we have ground hornets. They're economically disadvantaged I guess, or they don't know how to construct those complicated paper condominiums that look like angry footballs. These folks are as tenacious as an insurance salesman in tornado alley. They dig a hole in the ground, excavate out a baby hornet factory and invite over about ten thousand guests. Run over a nest during one of their pot-lucks...well, don't stop to apologize. Head for the nearest lake and drown yourself. These guys don't take prisoners. They'll spend two hours trying to sting the tractor to death even though it's a little tough to kill 1100lbs of scrap metal. Me? I'm under the bed with a can of Raid.

Other possibilities can and do exist with geriatric tractors. I normally mow about fifteen acres at a shot. Since the tractor is quite noisy, I pop a Walkman in my ears and play a little Bruce Springsteen. Since I tend to sing along, the neighbors are tortured by "Boooooorrrnn in the USA!" accompanied by a broken muffler. The combination is just loud enough that I rarely hear those pieces of machinery in the final throes of metal fatigue. Normally what happens next is that a number of rusted bolts all decide to cancel their warranty at the same moment – in fact, it always occurs during the second verse of "Tunnel of Love." Unfortunately, these bolts are normally in the *major structural category* of importance: holding the rear fender to the axle, the three-point to the frame and the power take-off to the main body of the tractor. So while I'm hitting a high note on the chorus, the mower, now operating on a new agenda, spins around and begins digesting the tractor by climbing up the rear wheels toward my seat, not unlike the misunderstood shark in the movie "Jaws." Disaster is averted by thoughtful neighbors (the only ones left), who, much like their movie counterparts, wave frantically from the beach to warn me of my impending death. They watch because they are bored, they use binoculars because they're either old or don't want to miss the details. I wave back until I notice a cold breeze whistling through my underwear.

Sometimes the inside of the tractor breaks — Korean War vintage gears and sprockets that have served countless masters. All this machinery suddenly loses interest in doing the same, mundane task. *Gearbox schizophrenia* is such a disease, manifested by the transmission's desire to process information in the same manner as the IRS. First gear becomes third gear, second turns into fourth, reverse becomes fifth, and neutral, well it just acts disinterested. All this mechanical confusion is just fine until the mowing is finished and I need to exit the field, preferably through an open gate. To open a gate, one must dismount the tractor. Lacking neutral, dismounting a moving tractor normally results in being crushed, ground into mush and catapulted into the cat's dish. Most health insurance companies frown on this sort of behavior, so I end up circling the field for an hour or so until somebody shows up to open a gate...an experience shared by airline pilots trying to land in New York on Christmas Eve. Eventually, I invested in an early model of the cell-phone. "Hello, 911? I need the gate opened. It's the gearbox again!"

"Drop dead!" Well that was another option.

Actually, that was what I was trying to avoid. The most aggravating problem was the brakes, at least when it came to building those important personal relationships that require some form of communication and trust. If the farm had been composed of purely flat land, the need for brakes would not be critical, but we did have a few hills and it was often necessary to scale these heights in my pursuit of maintenance. I got in the habit of carrying a large rock in the bucket of the tractor and would attempt to get it under the back tire before it could get a head start on the laws concerning gravity. Of course, if I was a little off in my timing that day, then the tractor would roll back down the hill and hit either a loafing shed or a yearling, two things that weren't bright enough to get out of the way.

I thought Jesse might like to help with the rock.

"You just put it under the tire when I say, 'Now!'"

"I don't think so."

"Really, it's easy. I do it all the time."

"What about my head?" She was bent over and gesturing at the rock. "See, my head is right next to the wheel. I'll get mushed!"

"No, you won't, just..." At that second, the engine died. "Now!!" Jesse just dropped the rock and it and tractor rolled down the hill, grinding to a stop on top of a watering trough. The horses scattered in the nick of time, followed by you know who.

Next, I tried Elaine, thinking it would be a good idea to show her that I actually worked during the day. Doc was busy tying the tubes on most of the neighborhood dogs, the choice of rock-tossers being a little limited. The first two rock throws went rather well, considering Elaine's unfamiliarity with rock technique, but on the third attempt, the tractor lurched to one side, displacing the rock and rolling over her foot. Cats scream like that just before they die.

Once she stopped squirming around on the ground, I attempted to explain the faulty brakes. She was more concerned about why they repealed the death sentence. When I further clarified Doc's reluctance to fork over the three hundred dollars to pay for the brakes, her expression turned dark and a little menacing. I never knew women could put together that many obscenities in one sentence. A couple of them appeared to be in Romanian.

Three days later, the old 8N was gone, in its place, a shiny new John Deere. The brakes worked, the gauges followed the rules of honest reporting and I had serious doubts that any revolutionary mice would be living next to the battery. The carcinogenic smell of diesel fuel tends to discourage most tenants. Or, the mice get so high from the fumes that they practice birth control by accident. Doc never said too much about the whole affair and after about a month, Elaine's foot started to improve. In a way, I should have been thrilled about the outcome – kind of like when the Smithsonian gets a new bag of old bones, but it just wasn't the same. I'd plug in Bruce Springsteen, turn up the volume, "Boooorrrrnnnn in the..." and the rhythm, cadence, the grating, mashing groan of failing machinery just wasn't there. It seemed like a damn shame. But then, I could get free coffee for life at the John Deere dealership and maybe even one of those official green caps. I'd be one of the 'guys' at last.

In China, all foodstuffs consumed by a city are grown in the surrounding countryside. The roads in and out of the cities run 24/7 with dog and horse carts, overloaded bicycles and small tractors pulling ten times their own weight. In America, a New York apple is shipped by train and truck to Washington State. Washington State ships its own apple by truck and train to New York. Same apple.

16.

THE HORSE SHOW

She was about thirty-five. Her hair was dirty-blond, jeans faded, whatever figure that might exist, hidden under a wool Pendleton shirt. Sometimes she chewed tobacco and it was a rare event to see her without a Diet-Coke in one hand. She had chicken-tracks around her eyes, a vocabulary last heard at a thumb-smashing contest, a nasty Australian shepherd-pit bull sort of creature named Meatball and a Ford pick-up with one headlight missing – not broken, just missing, as if some long-planned repair had suddenly been postponed. She was Jesse's *horse show friend*. A person who cleans tack, saddles horses and mends wounded egos. And this week, she was sick. Her name was Sue – Diet-Coke Sue.

Summer had taken the edge off my romantic combat with Jesse. She was following the show circuit (weekly get-togethers of the equine-impaired), and I was busy dismantling the farm. Every so often I would miss her, bemoaning to Doc the melancholic pit my existence had become. Sage-like, he would try to impart his long years of wisdom to the manic-depressive student. Socrates driving the short bus.

Doc: "Don't be too eager."

Jesse: "Where the hell have you been?"

Doc: "You have to be assertive with women."

Jesse: "How can you be so insensitive?!"

Doc: "Let her stew on it awhile."

Andy: "Why the hell doesn't she call?!"

Doc: "Women are a pain in the a..."

Jesse: "Men are a pain in the a..."

Doc: "Just don't give in."

Elaine: "Doooc! Who's Nijinsky?!!"

What is it about assuming that you're suddenly in love? I mean, the heart is supposed to ache, but the only thing I feel is a knot in my spleen. God, maybe it's cancer. Ah, geez. Here I think I'm infatuated with a woman who 'fixes things' and it could really mean that I need six months of chemotherapy, radiation and a new barber. Really, I like her – no, I more than like her. Why???? "Hello, Crisis Clinic? What do you know about spleens that involve women? I think I'm dying!"

"We're sorry, but no one is currently available. Please leave a number and a brief message and we'll get back to you as soon as possible." Beep. They blocked my phone number.

My thoughts were interrupted by the phone ringing. (Mine, not the Crisis Clinic's.) Naturally, I was up on the roof of the barn, for phones never ring while you are staring at them. Jesse spoke rapidly while I tried to catch my breath, suddenly realizing why women get phone calls with nothing but heavy breathing on the other end. It is not some weird male pastime, but the strain of trying to get from the roof to the phone in under five rings, that way avoiding listening to your own message explaining why you're not there at the moment when you really are, but are busy listening to your own explanation of why you're not. Plus, the pack-a-day Marlboro habit that the woman receiving the misguided message and lung exhaust hasn't been informed of quite yet because a few other questionable habits are still locked in hopeless arbitration.

"Andy, Sue's sick and I've got a show tomorrow. She said she'd leave the keys for her truck and trailer and I need somebody to drive over to Bainbridge, 'cause the show is kinda important, what with year-end results and all, and I just don't think I can..."

"You mean Meatball-Diet-Coke Sue?"

"Yeah, she's sick with the flu or something."

"Probably swallowed her wad."

"What?"

"Nothing. Sure, I'll drive ya. Doc won't mind. Isn't this a two-day show? I mean, we have to stay over?" Oh, oh. This just turned interesting. "What time do you need to leave?"

"About five and we're sort of camping."

"Five? In the morning?"

"Yeah. Oh, one more thing. Brownie needs his shoes reset. Would you mind...pretty please?"

"Geez." This was sounding like hard labor combined with infinite possibilities. Camping? Nah, I was confusing optimism with...optimism?

"Oh, thanks."

"I didn't say yes... and what about..."

Too late. The line was dead. Show horses are, well, foo foo. And what's with the 'pretty please?' I'm going to try that the next time I need a human emergency brake.

Men can't say 'no' because the line is always dead, as if all forms of electronic hardware are monitored by shrewish potential mothers-in-law in the basement of AT&T, their sole purpose to disconnect any line where a male starts to say 'no.' "No, no, no, no!" I screamed into the receiver. "No!"

By five-fifteen the following morning, we were on the road. It was still dark and Meatball-Diet-Coke Sue's single headlight peered down the road like a weak flashlight. Jesse was obsessing over what we had forgotten – a notion that seemed completely absurd in light of what we hadn't forgotten – no, not the kitchen sink, a refrigerator.

I had no first-hand experience at horse shows, which Jesse assured me would continue if we failed to make the 6:30 ferry. She was digging around in the cab of the truck searching frantically for some buried item. Finally, a brown head popped out from under the seat. I let out a scream.

"You brought Meatball!!"

All I could see was a set of wolf-like incisors. I pictured the dog crushing my skull as I raced for the 6:30 ferry. My left hand gripped the door handle. I'd jump at the next curve.

"It's not Meatball – it's Emily."

My grip relaxed. Emily was Jesse's Jack Russell terrier, a depraved little beast that was born with a tennis ball stuck in its mouth.

"Yeah, I knew it was her. I was just teasing." I stared down the faded roadway, pressing my chest against the steering wheel. My heart pounded. I patted Emily on the head. She growled. I figured that a four-way by-pass was just around the corner. How much fear can your arteries handle when they've shipped most of the blood supply to your intestines? Or was it the coffee? We made the ferry by a mere five minutes. Jesse was marginally impressed. Her compliment went something like: "You could have driven a little faster." Given the Meatball thing, she should have felt lucky. If it was United Airlines, a lot of folks would be hard pressed to find their luggage – especially if it was spread all over Kansas. Why are men so doomed to such absolute mediocrity – damn it, we can fly airplanes, bomb small irritating countries, change light bulbs, figure out the toilet seat thing – some of us even know how to turn on a vacuum cleaner. Still, we're declared incompetent. We're not men, we're a biological redundancy that only gains some degree of existence if a woman happens to need one of those sperm things or a 6:30 AM rendezvous with a ferry. Otherwise, we are merely an annoyance.

The ferry ride turned out to be a lot longer than I imagined. No, it wasn't the tension level. Seems I failed to examine the geography involved in our expedition. After an hour or so I was thinking Europe. After two hours, it was time to have a serious conversation with Columbus. Even the porpoises that had been following us turned around. I started rummaging around the truck looking for oranges – figured we might need to fend off dysentery or beriberi or something. At 2hrs. & 37 minutes we struck land. The locals seemed curious, but not overly friendly. I considered sticking a flag in the ground and claiming the place for God and America, but a Denny's restaurant had beat me to it. The ferry crew was busy hosing Brownie's urine and other stuff off the deck. They gave us a cheery one-fingered send off. Local custom I guessed. After a quick greasy hamburger we hit the road again. Smaller road, fewer inhabitants.

"Uh, just where exactly is this show?" I swore I saw a sign that said, 'Last Gas for a Hundred Miles!' I was hoping it was just a marketing stunt.

"Other side of the island."

"Okay. Just how big is this island?"

"Relax, it's a couple of hours. We'll get there about three, maybe four."

So it *was* Europe. About then the dysentery hit. Or maybe the hamburger.

Three gas stations later we arrived at the show grounds. Yeah, the sign was a shameless marketing ploy. I figured that the next time I toured Europe I'd bring my own hamburger. Between emergency roadside stops Jesse and I talked about the subjects of her choice. I asked a question and received an answer disguised as another question. She must have studied counter-intelligence or male interrogation techniques since after two hours in the truck I wasn't even sure if Jesse was her real name.

"Why'd you get into horses?" Seemed like a safe question.

"Wasn't supposed to."

"Me, it was school buses and…some other stuff."

"Other stuff?"

"Yeah, stuff."

"Home, huh?"

"I didn't say that."

"Yes you did."

"Look, are those Canadian geese?" Wondered what they were doing in Europe. Next time we stopped I planned on going through her purse. Probably find fifteen fake passports, the miniature camera – maybe a Walther PPK. Oh, the official fingernail pulling manual.

"Have you ever been arrested?"

"Where'd that question come from?" My eyes were doing the darting thing. "Wow, see that! One shoe by the road. I always see those and they're always a right shoe. Makes you wonder what was going on…like roadside amputations by deranged foot collectors or…least they could do is leave a pair or something."

"Well?"

"What?"

"I thought so."

Well, there was that small *misunderstanding about the 54lbs of marijuana. Really belonged to the one-armed guy they handcuffed to the banister on the patio. Naturally he escaped, dragging twelve feet of iron railing behind him. You would have thought that he'd be pretty easy to spot. Might have clarified things with the judge, though it really didn't matter since the evidence had mysteriously disappeared anyway. No, not corrupt cops. The stuff had some quality control issues. It had this really peculiar odor to it. A little like sitting next to a live skunk that had eaten moldy sauerkraut for lunch. You see, 1970-era marijuana was still in the pre-product improvement stage. What that meant was that the whole plant got ground up — seeds, stems, maggots, roots – might even find somebody's finger in the mix. Then it was distributed to consumers in a sandwich bag, affectionately known as a 'lid.' A lid was a pretty subjective form of measurement. Kind of like a 'furlong' in racing. Nobody seemed to know where the term came from or what in the hell it meant. (Furlong, not lid.) The end result was that when you smoked a joint of this awful stuff, two things were bound to happen: either a seed would explode and take out your left eye, or the heat generated in the joint would magically turn all the maggots into happy little flies. And about the only way you got high was to smoke the marijuana* <u>*with*</u> *the plastic bag.*

Then there was that other matter of the Beatles' private jet. But they decided not to press charges. Or the coast-to-coast dine & dash expedition or maybe the Richard Nixon near-miss tomato, or just possibly when I burned my fourth or fifth draft card. Sure, it was a federal offense, but so is ripping off those tags on pillows. The government just sends out a new one. No, not the pillow tag, the other one. You know, there could be more than one reason to take a Tuesday off and ride to Mexico.

[Okay, a lid is roughly 1 to 3 fingers short of a full sandwich bag of weed* and each finger was considered to be about an ounce unless you were either near death from smoking plastic and dead maggots or you had fat fingers. The term 'lid' was derived from the fact that an ounce of marijuana would fill an average sized Mason jar lid. As for 'furlong,' we can all thank the British again. The word is derived from the Old English words furh (furrow) and lang (long) and originated in the 9th century. That's probably why it is 'Old English' rather than something we can actually understand, like Hungarian recipes. Originally it referred to the length of a furrow in a one acre field. Never mind what shape the acre was in because it appears a couple of oxen were doing most of the math. So it comes out to 1/8 of an international mile, 220 yards or 660 feet – though none of that matters since the term isn't recognized as having any real meaning anyway, particularly if you're building a house or outrunning a cop. Just hang onto this example: five furlongs is approximately (British ho-hum math again) 1 kilometer. (Really 1.0058 km.) A meter is one-quarter of one ten-millionth of the circumference of the Earth, measured where it passes through a well-known boulangerie in Paris, France. I'm not sure why Paris claimed this distinction, but if you ran a race that began and ended in front of Gustave Eifel's odd little monument, it would be a 200,000 furlong race. No, I don't think I'd wait around for the winner, much less a potential windfall on the daily-double.]

*Or, if you were a novice shopper, three fingers of oregano, basil & alfalfa. Never happened to me though.

My first reaction to the horse show was one of incredible awe. Before me was a regal procession of well-groomed horses ably piloted by some of the most capable riders ever assembled in one place. Everybody seemed to get at least one ribbon, and if a person was exceptionally talented at *equitating* or something, then a famous person (usually Elizabeth Taylor), would present a giant, useless bowl to put over the mantelpiece. At the end of the day, the riders simply handed their well-tuned horse to someone with a grooming fetish and headed for the nearest watering hole to congratulate themselves for being so awesome. Right?

Well, not quite. Once I was allowed into the horse show inner circle (I was introduced as Jesse's *friend* – aka, a non-committal appendage of the opposite sex, just a little above casual labor), I quickly learned the actual reasoning behind the exodus to the watering hole. It had much more to do with awful than awesome. Horse shows were not about winning, but about competing with one's self – or in Jesse's strange analogy, "just getting that *distance* right, just once." I stared at the brightly decorated show ring.

"*Distance?* Looks like about eighteen feet from here."

Jessie walked Brownie away, no doubt searching for a second opinion.

The next day started early – about 4:15 in the morning, which according to my figures, still constituted night. I figured we had a national emergency. Who gets up at four o'clock something unless an armored car has rolled over in front of your house? Jesse was coherent and focused. I was babbling about a dream I had that seemed to have the potential to end badly. Since I was awake, I'd have to get the bad news later when it might actually be an improvement over the current situation. Details were sketchy, but I vaguely remembered something about decaffeinated coffee and a Portuguese rabbit. Who knows? The only thing I was sure about was that it was entirely too early to face life in its current form. Maybe it would have been different if we had had incredible sex the night before, but she slept in the cab and I slept with two bales of hay and a sweaty horse blanket. Talk about romantic. I smelled like the inside of a shoe.

My first job was to reset Brownie's shoes. I skipped the hinds since they were fairly tight and if I bent over too far, I'd just fall asleep. The second job was to unload the truck. This was a two-day show, which meant unloading and loading basically took place in the same twenty-four-hour period. Added together, this amounted to relocating about six hundred pounds of 'stuff.' Among the collection was a tack trunk the size of a coffin, tack room curtains made of lead macramé, saddle racks (plural), potted plants, rugs, brooms, brushes, hay, grain, buckets, bridles, tent stakes and a refrigerator.

"This must be for the beer?" I quipped.

"It's for Brownie's medication. He has arthritis."

"You're going to make this poor arthritic horse jump over fences? Boy, we both better get some beer."

"It's illegal."

"Beer is illegal?"

"Not for you, for Brownie. They test for drugs. All this medicine is organic. This is aloe vera, this is biotin, and this stuff is yucca. Brownie has a little arthritis in one hock and it really helps."

I read the price tag on the Yucca. $32.95 for three ounces. Heroin was cheaper.

Backing up for a minute, I'd like to describe our arrival, which was definitely more dramatic than our departure: once we arrived at the show grounds, the *stuff* is scattered on the ground next to some other lucky slob's *mess*. The *mess* must now be organized into something that will make everybody else's *mess* feel envious. This is accomplished by three or four hours of hard labor and bad language. By the time it is completed, most of the local real estate agents have dropped by hoping to list your creation with their company. I told Jesse that it would have been much simpler to merely tow the barn to the show. She smiled like women do when they don't want to bother giving exact directions to hell.

I had just sat down on one of the monogrammed folding chairs when Jesse walked up with Brownie. He was saddled, bridled and had wraps on all four legs. "I gotta go *school*. Why don't you come watch? Besides, you're not supposed to sit in those chairs. I've got some others in the truck."

"What's wrong with these chairs?"

"They're just for show. They match the curtains. If you sit in them, they get worn out. I'd rather save them."

I stood up, suddenly feeling guilty for being so insensitive about chairs. How could I be so stupid? Then again, how could I be so patronizing? It's a damn chair! I was beginning to picture a bonfire of major proportions. I'd cruise around the show and steal every chair I could find and torch them. It'd be like a Third World revolution, the consequences last seen in *Les Miserables* on Broadway. Chairs would die. Every pathetic male on the show grounds would don a beret and with a little lighter fluid would convince women everywhere that chairs are the property of the state. I mean, it is so obvious: one doesn't sit in a chair, one sits on the ground, thereby preserving the chair for <u>not</u> sitting, and the curtains for <u>not</u> shading, the hay for <u>not</u> eating – virtual non-reality run amuck!

__Revolution. Always happens when the__ door opens just a crack. One little possible, conceivable, even laughable expectation and this over-whelming force, this collective and unpredictable animal rises off its cal-lused knees and slays the monsters of an oppressive conformity. But never when life is at its lowest. And perhaps that was America's problem in 1969. We still had a middle-class and the middle-class never riot. They just com-plain. Their children though, they prided themselves for marching in the streets, by joining the SDS, by flying the American flag upside-down...they resisted. A few even took up arms only to discover that the cause was too vague, too splintered and mostly ill-defined. Peace was the mantra of these masses, but what kind and how do you institutionalize a desire? A wish really, for an entire planet, when in truth, far too many children were sim-ply trying to survive another Friday night with the folks.

Yeah, peace sounded good. Though it did seem that you couldn't prac-tice it in a crowded place.

"You're mumbling," Jesse said.

"Thinking."

"Well, you mumble when you think. It's annoying. Why don't you try whistling."

"Sounds too happy. Rather mumble."

"Were you able to reset Brownie's shoes? They looked kinda loose."

Anybody who gets up a four in the morning to go to a stupid horse show has every right to mumble. "Mumble, mumble, mumble." I'm not a boyfriend, I'm a double herniated slave stuck building a monument to a god named Brownie. I mean we're talking about 1200lbs of hairy mammal parts. This is an animal that passes more gas than Chevron, sheds enough hair to produce ten-thousand bad toupees, craps on my shoes, pees in the trailer, pees on the ferry, pees on the freeway — pees on the State Patrol when they get curious about the headlight thing. He's a felon searching for a crime! Yes, I'm mumbling. Horse shows do that. We're non-combatants!

What happened to the Geneva Convention? Who ran off with my white flag? Which way's Switzerland?

"Yeah, I reset his shoes. You're good to go school." The previous speech is reserved for the cat. A can of Tuna and he'll listen to any damn tirade. Jesse was starting to look a little odd though – *rigor mortis* with no apparent cause of death. You could have played something by Bach on her spine. I was afraid that if I touched her, NASA would have to fish her out of the ocean somewhere south of Hawaii.

Schooling is the exact same thing that Jesse spent $5000 a year to do at home, only in this case, she gets to do it somewhere else in the rain. It's practice really, and the horse knows it, for most horses can see backwards and if Jesse's not wearing a hunt coat and breeches, everything is copasetic. Bring out the good clothes and Brownie goes lame, Brownie goes mad, Brownie disappoints the judge. Brownie's no fool.

At about the same time, the trainer shows up to facilitate the *schooling* process. Most trainers are kind and generous people under normal circumstances, but at a horse show they tend to become strict and red-faced, likely to rip out their student's intestines at the slightest infraction. Jessica's trainer was a woman named Louise. (We're switching to 'Jessica' here because I feel we've crossed some invisible line where questionable mental health is becoming an issue.) The trainers always wear khaki breeches, a turtleneck and one of those thorn-proof British field jackets. I made the mistake of comparing her to Field Marshall Montgomery – the salute didn't help. I spent the next two hours hiding in a Sani-Kan.

By four o'clock, there was not an ounce of human self-esteem left on the grounds. We headed back to the *mess* to wrap Brownie's legs and give him a bath, two things rarely done without a great deal of peer pressure. The bath I understood, as most people don't like to go to bed with their leather all sweaty, but the only plausible explanation for wrapping the legs seemed to be that we wouldn't have to start the morning by staring at all the lumps on them.

Bath time was designated as *official horse show communication time*, which meant that the level of mental depravity circulating around the grounds had finally dropped to a decibel level that allowed rational conversation.

"How'd the *schooling* go?" I asked, knowing full well that Jess had got dumped twice in the schooling ring.

"He was a little spooky out there. Didn't you see him? He spooked at that yellow oxer and dumped me!"

"No, I missed that. I'm sorry. You okay?" Of course I didn't miss it. That's why I ended up behind a barn on all fours trying to regurgitate the Marlboro I sucked down one lung.

"I'm all right."

"Tell me something," I said, wanting to change the subject before I surrendered to the giggles. "Why do you do this? I mean, this doesn't seem like it goes too well, and like I thought this was supposed to be fun? You get horribly nervous, the trainer chews you out, the horse dumps you and you hardly ever get a ribbon or money or anything. How come?"

Jessica paused, tossing the sponge into the bucket of shampoo. "I don't know. I guess it's a challenge. To take something like Brownie, with no training, no manners or anything, and convert him into something usable." She tossed her hair out of her eyes so she could stare straight at me. "I like *fixing* things."

"Oh," I deadpanned. I had really hoped she wanted to ride in the Olympics or something. 'Fixing things' tended to make me more than a little nervous. The last thing that got 'fixed' was the cat. I guess though that it supported my overall opinion that Jesse and Chet had something and nothing in common. Chet fixing those broken pistons was one thing, but why would a woman sort of pick a man and then try to turn him into some other kind of man? Why not keep shopping? "So winning doesn't matter?"

"No. Has to do with a poem I read once. Something about 'the value of the journey' as opposed to the destination — something like that. Besides, I can't afford a horse that wins and it probably wouldn't be that much fun anyway. I bought my first horse when I was thirteen. Couple of hundred bucks. My father said no…" She suddenly straightened up, gently tipped the bucket over with her left foot, handed me the horse and walked off.

"So, Brownie, now what in the hell did I say?" I thought about just sitting there and waiting, but there was still that issue about the chairs. So instead Brownie and I took a tour of the show grounds. I did most of the talking.

Jesse showed up about an hour later and didn't bother to finish the sentence she left hanging. I didn't get a new sentence either. So once we had Brownie put up in his stall, the day closed on the usual note, only this time it was to a motel for a shower, dinner and a good cry. At least we weren't sleeping in the truck. Sorry, no sex. I still sleep on the couch. It's much safer. Sex = commitment which = marriage. I'd rather be an astronaut during a budget crisis at NASA. Don't get me wrong – sex is definitely fun, but it ups the ante considerably. I needed to preserve my 'waffling' status until I could sit down and sort out my feelings. That was bullshit by the way. The truth is that I wasn't invited. Men don't 'sort feelings,' or laundry, for that matter. We ask another guy who gets our version of a different story orchestrated from the beginning to support our view that the woman is being recalcitrant about some subject that will appear on the docket later. That way the next surprise is a lot less stressful and the current altercation gets lost in the confusion. The only trouble with this system is that you have to keep notes.

We did talk a little though. Something was rattling around in Jesse's head and couldn't seem to fall out of her mouth.

"I've gotta see my brother next week. He's in the hospital in Cle Elum."

Ah, the mystery man. "He okay?"

"Yeah, but I should see him."

"Need some company?" Details were not forthcoming. Neither was an invitation.

"No! Sorry, no. Listen, I'm tired. I need to make some phone calls and lie down. Would you mind feeding Emily? Make sure she gets some…"

"Cottage cheese, I know." I fed Emily and pushed a couch over next to the window. Old habits die hard. Emily took up a surveillance point on my chest. She was probably hoping the motel was rat infested. As I drifted off to sleep, the oddity of the situation struck me. No, not the carnal stuff, the fact that I fed Emily and *she* was sleeping with me. An hour later I was still awake. I was waiting for Jesse to realize her horrible mistake and get the dog. She never showed up.

The following morning was D-Day. Jesse had on her best attire (the one hunt coat that Brownie hadn't slobbered on), and we hit the show grounds at top speed. Conversation was limited to things like whether or not to use the windshield wipers. The tension level in the cab caused the radio to go dead. Emily cowered under the seat – the tennis ball rolling around the floor of the truck. Terriers might be depraved, but they are also rather telepathic. I'm pretty sure she was on my fourteen-pound cell-phone with a behavioral psychologist discussing the problem with humans – the part about who's dispensing the cottage cheese and why. That colloquial notion that pets are some sort of subservient species that *we* choose to hang around with is totally flawed. They pick us. Most of these folks used to be wolves. A few probably ate a couple of our distant ancestors. After a few centuries of competing over rabbits and stuff, they perfected the art of manipulation. All they had to do was wag their tail and the rabbit showed up on its own. Beat the hell out of chasing something that could outrun a BMW. Women and small dogs perfected the art of 'cute.' Why work when you can just wag something?

As we approached a stoplight on our quest to reach the show grounds, the tennis ball lodged itself under the brake pedal. Jessica only stared straight ahead, her lips quivering as if she was about to speak, but didn't. Two red lights later, we arrived. It must have been 'donut hour' for the local police since I didn't end up with a lecture or a pile of expensive paperwork. Or maybe God's will. God always fools with the brakes when someone is racing toward a bout of humility. Hence, the Biblical overtones of the 'tractor and the rock' fable. The tractor was a metaphor. No, I don't know for what, though probably something to do with Moses and the Red Sea since parting water or breaking water has a lot of relevance around a farm.

Once again, we bathed Brownie (he likes to be dirty), and I checked his hind shoes. One was loose, a large piece of hoof ready to fall off. I decided to ignore the whole thing. Jessica put on Brownie's shin boots, bell boots and a set of polo wraps. She tells me she needs to *lunge* him.

Lunging is a process by which the horse runs wildly around in a circle while attached to something immovable, like your arm. After an hour of this nonsense, the horse is either A) permanently bent in a circle, B) grazing quietly in another county, or C) somewhat rideable. Jessica decides on C and informs me of her need to go *school* again. I feign stomach cramps and head for the Sani-Kan, unwilling to risk my Zen on Louise, the dragon slayer. I really think that most horse trainers had a previous life in the *Gestapo*. Get the *distance* right or it's off to the showers.

Distance is this weird mathematical equation based on a horse's stride. I think it is something like twelve-feet to a stride, so the fences are set up in increments of that denomination. Five here, six there. Some are called *verticals* and the fat ones are called *oxers*. No, I don't know why. I'm assuming that an *oxer* is like jumping over an obese cow. If I get time, I'll call the British Embassy – England apparently invented this pastime.

Finally comes the moment of truth. Battered, bruised and with Brownie's shoe ready to fall off, Jessica enters the ring. The first three fences go rather well, considering that Jesse ran out of oxygen about 60 seconds into the class. The next fence ends up a little long (I knew this because even the judge gave out a gasp), and the next three are *chips*, because by this point Brownie has decided to find his own way home. A *chip* is the same thing as a bluff in poker, in that you add an extra stride assuming the judge or the other players won't notice your facial distortions. The last fence somehow works out just right and is thankfully only about six strides from the out-gate. Louise and I offer our solitary applause, both quite thrilled that Jessica is still alive.

After waiting around to see if the judges gave a ribbon for twenty-third place, we took Brownie back to his stall, bathed him and wrapped his legs in forty-five pounds of cotton and Velcro. Jessica swallowed a couple of aspirin while I organized what was left of the *mess*. I slid into the cab of the truck and put the key in the ignition and turned it. Zip. The horse show had taken the last ounce of our dignity. After spending the early morning hours braiding Brownie's mane in the one good headlight of the truck, the only thing we earned for our efforts was a dead battery.

The ferry ride home was cloaked in a noisy silence.

"So, Jessica, where does this leave things, like with the year-end standings and all?"

I thought she might have said something but it was just the prop churning the water. Maybe teeth grinding.

"Okay then."

17.

A PRETTY FAIR FARRIER

THE WARM (AS opposed to hot, naturally) days of summer proved to be a boon to my fledgling career as a professional farrier. Each week brought greater confidence, more money and a cocky realization that I could succeed at a difficult and demanding task. Like a baby bird tossed out of the nest, I was ready to eat some bugs on my own. Oh, I still had a few reservations, but I hid them pretty well. I just lied like hell. I always told people that I had been shoeing for at least five years. Nobody in their right mind would confess to just starting out. Doctors do the same thing – just check for white-out on their diplomas. "This is your lucky day. I've always wanted to take out an appendix! Now, where is that little bugger?"

I also kept all my old shoes piled in the back of the truck, even if I had to borrow a few from another horseshoer. I told them I needed some ballast for my sailboat. They knew what I was up to. I was buying into the accepted *gestalt*, which in horseshoeing means the messier the truck, the better you must be, because you don't have the time to do all that anal sweeping and vacuuming stuff. I would also postpone a potential client for at least two days, even if I was starving and down to my last package of Top Ramen. Women do this all the time – aloof and disinterested, even if they really want to personally audit your taxes. Believe me, this takes hours of practice for a guy. You say, "No, no, no!" while the brain screams, "Yes!" And while you're having this internal crisis, the woman vanishes anyway.

Doc didn't seem to mind my time away, as there was a direct connection between the balance due at the lumberyard and my absence. He also didn't mind that he got all his horses trimmed for free. I think this weird precedent got started because I hated trying to hold one of his yearlings while it dragged another horseshoer around the barn. It seemed easier if I just got dragged around the barn. Lot less embarrassment that way. Part of the trouble of being a horseshoer though, is that the last thing you want to do when you get home is trim your own horses – especially for free. So they become a bunch of renegades operating on the untamed fringes of society. Try to pick up a foot and it either grows roots and attaches itself to some metamorphic rock at the core of the earth, or the horse does the snap-and-pop routine where the foot comes off the ground at the speed of sound, either slapping me in the forehead or shoving my fingers into my elbow joint. The screaming is hideous, especially if they catch you on the end of your fingers. The forehead doesn't matter, that's just cheap anesthesia anyway. Young horses also think that you are trying to steal their leg. Hell, that's the last thing I want. They respond by sitting down, falling over (preferably on me), or hopping up and down on the other three legs like a renegade pogo stick – with me attached. Think if dentists had to work that way. The tooth fairy would end up in bankruptcy court.

My mother wasn't a real fan of this secondary career. She figured I would probably not get killed, but injured critically, forcing her to keep me on life support till the electrician ran out of money. Some days, I figured she wasn't too far off the mark. I think she hoped for something different: a scholarship to UCLA, a couple of those Pulitzer things, maybe even a dental practice in Beverly Hills, sucking out the saliva of the rich and famous. Mom did have a point, which she was always happy to point out, but it normally lacked any real sincerity or what I really needed: clarity. That was provided by a bank manager when I tried to apply for a Visa card.

LOAN OFFICER: "Let's see, you're self-employed as a...farrier?"

ME: "Yes, a professional farrier."

LOAN OFFICER: Strumming through a pamphlet entitled: *Adjusted Salary Expectations in Isolated Trades.* "Farmer, framer, ferry boat captain, furrier...you're not a furrier? Hmm. Furniture, fraud investigator...well, no farrier. Just what is a farrier?"

ME: "A horseshoer."

LOAN OFFICER: "A horseshoer? So you toss horseshoes? Is that something people do professionally?"

ME: "No, actually I nail them on horse's feet. I'm a highly skilled professional." I felt a few beads of sweat rising on my forehead.

LOAN OFFICER: "People still do that, I mean the village smithy, sinewy arms, that spreading chestnut tree, all that? I just didn't think people did that sort of thing, I mean, not as a business?"

ME: "You wouldn't do it for fun. Trust me."

LOAN OFFICER: "Are there that many horses?"

ME: "About three-million or so."

LOAN OFFICER: "Really? You must stay pretty busy."

ME: "Well, actually, I don't shoe all of..."

LOAN OFFICER: "I'm going to have to get back to you on this application. I just don't know enough about the current business environment for farriery. How long have you shoed horses?"

ME: "Shod, the word is *shod*. About two years."

LOAN OFFICER: "Listen, I just don't think we can do this right now. Perhaps when you can show a track record, a couple of years of good solid tax returns, maybe some part-time employment with a *real* company, that sort of thing. Have you tried American Express?"

ME: "They suggested Visa."

As I left his office, I pocketed the booklet on *Adjusted Salary Expectations in Isolated Trades*. It was published by the American Banking Information Clearinghouse in Elgin, Illinois. The loan officer was right, farriers weren't listed. But if I had applied as a magician, a road-reflector technician, an ice-cream man, or a greeting card author, I would have been issued a card. There was even a card with a $500 limit for 'people currently incarcerated by the United States government.' But no farriers.

Horseshoeing is never going to compare with a sibling's degree in psychology...a point my mother would probably support under opposing circumstances. No matter how poignantly I described my chosen profession, Mom probably gauged it somewhere between real-estate sales in the Australian outback and fighting oil-well fires in Saudi Arabia. "Oh, it's such a dangerous job," she might moan. "Why can't you find a good job like your sister Dana? She works at the University of Washington in a nice office. You should really talk to her." Actually, she didn't work there. She had taken a leave of absence from reality and talking with her was normally entertaining, but rarely informative. Fifth floor, Room 512.

Mothers tend to exaggerate. Most of the danger in horseshoeing occurs when one of the side-effects of the job ruptures social norms – the smell in particular, a combination of hoof and fire that reeked like a flock of chickens caught in an electrical storm. It was hard to hide (even after bathing in Irish Spring, Pine-Sol and mothballs), but even harder to explain, particularly when standing in line at the bank, tossing a load of clothes in the wash at the Laundromat, or meeting a certain woman's mother for an accidental lunch – or rather, inspection. Turned out my bank was next door to a pricey Italian place known for harboring Bellevue Republicans.

"Oh my god, what is that smell?"

"What smell?"

"Have you had a death in your shirt?"

"Whew, you're right. I think they put too much Parmesan in the Caesar's."

Fortunately, Jesse was *horsey*, a condition that allows the most ungracious of *faux pas* if it involves a horse, especially *her* horse. Somehow, in the broken logic of Jesse's mind, her mother could be offended as long as the offense first traveled through Jesse's horse. I could not offend either one directly, without the horse, and further, I could not offend the horse unless it had first offended Jesse, but not her mother. Fathers were out of the loop completely and I was never able to clarify third-party horses or offenses aimed at groups in general. However, I could be offended equally by all, including Jesse's horse, and retaliation was considered the worst sort of response, bringing me full circle as far as offenses went. It was a little like doing the seating arrangements at the UN. "Hey Kofi, let's put Syria next to Israel – see if they trade recipes or something." The rules were so complicated I had to write them on my arm before I dared pick up a fork.

Physical danger was ever-present – by now, that should be obvious. Even after some additional experience, I still managed to end up one index-finger short occasionally, do the anvil toe-drop thing and once, I cleverly nailed my apron under the shoe of a nervous two-year old. That required me to undress in a rather public and speedy manner while still holding up one leg. The woman who owned this young horse admired my agility, but not much else. Odd accidents came with the business. One day I actually drove three blocks with a pony still tied to the door handle of my truck. According to the cop that stopped me, I had violated either the seat belt regulation or two or three sections of the leash law. And if not the police, I got the fire department. I kept a coal forge in the back of the truck – always somewhere between smoldering and a full conflagration. Public concern over my well-being was appreciated, but I did have a schedule to keep – preferably without an official escort.

One debate always permeated my overall business approach: owner present, owner absent? A lot of owners treated their horses like oversized Beagles. They'd pat them on the head, feed them carrots, teach them how to bite people and pretty much excuse all forms of deviant behavior under the heading, "He's frisky." Yeah, right. I got goober soaked carrot chunks dripping down my back, a butt that looked like it went to a hickey convention and large bald spots on the top of my head. If the owner runs out of vegetable matter, then they decide it's a good time to get out the old curry brush and excavate the horse's back. Everything a horse collects on its back is normally heavier than air, and since I'm working on the basement end of the horse, I end up being bombarded in a cloud of emphysemic fog composed of dried mud, dead hair, horse dandruff and lice. The lice were the best part. I loved to capture a few and present them to the overdressed owner of a $20,000 show horse.

"Ma'am, see these little buggars. They're lice. They suck blood you know." One of those rare moments when getting fired is more fun than getting paid.

But that's the whole problem nowadays. Most horse owners evolved from dog owners. As I explained in an earlier, more desperate chapter, horses do not suck up to people. Doesn't happen. Most horses try to ignore you, which is pretty easy when your eyes are on the side of your head. Best you're going to get is the side-ways glance – yeah, you're dismissed. It's a much better idea to watch the ears. More information is telegraphed by these sensory attachments. In fact, if you happen to be talking to a mule, pay special attention. They telegraph stuff pretty fast. Here's how it works:

EARS FORWARD: Signals the approach of food, sex or a predator. (Humans fall under the last heading.)

ONE FORWARD, ONE BACK: Sometimes it is a case of watching both you and the road. If they turn both ears around then you have gone from a curiosity to an annoyance. Relocation is imminent.

EARS SIDEWAYS: Actually it's a genetic anomaly or the ears are broken. Otherwise, it doesn't mean a damn thing.

EARS FLAT BACK: Unabashedly pissed off. Good time to walk away quietly.

Another problem with having owners around is that they tend to share things with you that they wouldn't necessarily confide to a priest. It has to do with body posture. Same thing occurs with barbers and bartenders. Confessing is so easy when the audience is staring at the back of your head, bent over backwards working on a hoof or shortly after you've fallen off a bar stool. Women seem to be the worst offenders.

"Judy, I think we need to do Sparky at four weeks instead of six. His feet grow pretty fast. Probably be better for him."

"You know, I haven't had an orgasm in fifteen years."

"Well, so that's…maybe we'll stick with six…whoops, there goes my beeper. Better run."

Owner-absent has its own set of problems. These horses are always labeled as perfect to shoe, gifted with no appreciable bad habits and will stand quietly in the cross-ties while I re-balance the tires. Horse + perfect = suspicion. Cross-ties are a human invention designed to negate the need for a human. It's like self-service parking. A rope is attached to the horse's halter, one on each side, those in turn, attached to the wall. Their biggest advantage is a reduction in questionable conversations.

Owners though tend to construct cross-ties out of whatever happens to be available, or is somehow related to their real job. They either use logging chain attached to the wall with a thumbtack, bungee cords anchored to the engine block of a 1957 Buick or an extension cord that's still plugged into a toaster. What they fail to realize is that horses stay in one place by choice, so if the honor system breaks down, whatever the horse was attached to is going to fly past your head like a runaway garage sale. NASA couldn't launch the stuff any faster.

The last problem with absent owners falls under the liability umbrella. It seems that horses (and perhaps children) fall under some vague law of humanity (and what, equusanimity?) that exists under the old jailer's term of, "care, custody and control." The assumption here is that the nearest adult holds some responsibility for either a child or some other species. I'm not sure about children, but horses can get a little tricky. Things <u>do</u> happen. Leaving a note before engaging a good attorney rarely satisfies the situation:

> Dear Mrs. Fielding;
>
> I've enclosed my usual bill for Bucky.
> As you will notice it is only for the two front feet.
> Bucky fell over dead about 1:15 this afternoon.
> Sorry I couldn't finish. Have a nice day.
>
> Andy

Hmm. Too formal?

A bloody finger or a mashed toe did have certain advantages. They created sympathy. On those days when a child's pony maimed some portion of my anatomy, I didn't go directly home to the farm. Instead, I would bandage up the offended part in some filthy bit of rag and stop by Jesse's to say, "Hi." Jesse would spot my gored thumb, launch into a lecture about developing lock-jaw and spending the rest of my life sucking food through a straw, then head for the medicine cabinet. She would take my damaged part and stick it in the sink. Then, she'd clean out the wound – like my grandfather used to gut fish – rip it open and pull out what you don't want to eat and then drown it in iodine – the strong stuff. It was worth it. The two of us, just inches apart over the kitchen sink. It was so damn romantic. Well, excruciating too.

Horseshoeing offered other insights about the equine mind unavailable in my duties as Doc's janitor. Simple things really: like how a horse can break three of my ribs while merely shaking off a fly, or how a horse that was securely tied to a hitching post ended up two blocks down the road in the lobby of a Safeway store. Or how to remain dignified and adult-like while a ten-year- old critically analyzes your just completed job and fires you – skills only useful if you plan on being the only paramedic at a schizophrenia convention.

Horseshoeing was not supposed to be complicated. If I had desired confusion, excessive head noise and personality disorders I could have just as easily become an orgasm counselor or a mercenary in Central America. My view of horseshoeing encompassed a horse, a few tools, fresh air and sunshine, and of course, money. Not what follows:

***Andy's day starts the night** before, with the answering machine. It's Debbie Delay on the tape: "Arlo," she starts out. (Arlo was her last horseshoer.) "I waited all day for you to shoe Velvet. You know I have a show tomorrow and Velvet's moving funny because her toes are so long. I mean, REALLY, if you can't get here, I'll just have to call Andy!" Andy shuts off the machine. He decides that he has a split personality and he's not sure which one to have dinner with. Besides, her appointment was last week and he had to shoe Velvet tied up to the neighbor's barbecue because Debbie was missing. But of course, Debbie is always missing. That's why her picture keeps showing up on milk cartons.*

The next morning over breakfast (bourbon and Alka-Seltzer – no ice), Andy checks his appointment book. Three house calls and a meeting with a veterinarian, one Dr. Grisly, a man who is positive that the word 'farrier' is derived from 'fairly stupid.' Andy cringed. Everybody liked Dr. Grisly because he was...well, because he was a doctor and Andy wasn't. It's called a credibility gap aggravated by what appeared to be the truth. Andy's professors after all, were Leroy, Bub and Carlos the non-Mexican guy with the horseshoe stuck in his chest. Not quite the same résumé.

Already late, Andy roared to his first appointment, positive that he had already been fired. Standing in the driveway was thirteen-year old Buffy Gallagher, daughter of Justin Gallagher, CEO of Gallagher Electronics.

Buffy is so spoiled that if she stands near a loaf of bread too long it grows hair.

"Where have you been?" she demands through Andy's rolled up window.

"Oh, stuff it in..." Andy mumbles into his appointment book. "Sorry," he continues. "My girlfriend's appendix burst; what a mess, all over the kitchen floor..."

Buffy's already moved on to subject number two: A small crack under one of the nails. "Brie has been lame since you shoed her last." (Which was four months ago.)

"Oh," Andy mumbled. (Horses are normally shod every six weeks.) "Did the vet look at her?"

"Oh yeah. He said for you to pull out that nail where it cracked. It's probably putting pressure on something."

Andy's face starts to look like a ripe tomato. "When did Dr. Grisly look at her?"

"Oh, I don't know, a couple of months ago. I've been kinda busy."

Andy pulls the nail, picturing his nail pullers attached to the end of Dr. Grisly's lip, big toe, scrotum – right ear.

Fifteen-minutes later, Andy pulls into stop number two: The Double Lucky Lazy-U Ranch, a Quarter Horse farm that specializes in halter horses. (Halter horses occupy the same niche in horsedom as the Miss America pageant – straight legs and no premium on talent.) Puck Johnson, the resident trainer, brings out Double Lucky Moon Shot, one of his rising stars. Puck never holds a horse for a farrier – NEVER!

Andy starts pulling the front shoes. Puck is quieter than a dead cat. Finally, he clears his throat, one of those phlegm induced noises that begs a follow-up. "You know," he starts, like he's talking to no one in particular. "We didn't win at Tucson last week." Which is a little like saying that the Pope got booted out of the Vatican. "The judge kept staring at Moonie's front legs, like thar was somethin' wrong," Puck continued, easing his way into the point of all this conversation.

Meanwhile, Andy stops working, but continues to stare at his shoes.

"I think we oughta lower those outsides a little more, what da ya think?" Puck blurts out as he snaps Moonie in the cross-ties and takes a couple of steps backward. "Yeah, I think we should do that." Puck was now backing down the aisle-way rather fast, like a guy on the bomb squad that knows he just cut the wrong wire.

Andy starts rasping the outside of the foot. And rasping and rasping and rasping, until the floor is about four-inches deep in hoof shavings. About the time the shavings start to look a little pink, he nails the old shoes back on and leaves, with Moonie still standing in the cross-ties. Well, sort of standing. Grimacing would be more accurate.

Andy arrives at his next stop, a show barn that he started servicing about three months before. A note on the shoeing board tells him to check Buddy, who is lame. It doesn't say front or back, left or right, just lame. The trainer is gone and the only source of information is a groom who is somewhat notorious for being unemployable in most other occupations. First, she tells Andy that she knows nothing. Then, after a few minutes of careful thought, she decides she does know something – the vet looked at the horse the day before, but she doesn't recall what he said or if Andy was supposed to do anything. Now, thirty minutes behind schedule, Andy runs down to get the second horse, but it has disappeared. The same groom when questioned on the whereabouts of horse #2 informs Andy that she never heard of the particular horse, but that she did know a horse in Florida with a similar name. Andy's eyes begin to cross.

Andy streaks out the driveway, heading toward a farm he was going to stop at the next day. Stepping out of his truck, he is alarmed to see that all the horses have been turned out in the pastures. The farm manager is apologetic and begins the arduous task of re-catching all the broodmares. Since it is totally inappropriate for the mares to come back in after they have just been turned out, they punish Andy by sitting on his toolbox, urinating on his shirt and generally acting like...eighth-graders. Meanwhile, four cats (the manager's wife likes cats), break into Andy's truck and mutilate his lunch, shred the lining of his coat and spray the steering wheel. After trimming three mares, Andy decides it is time to get to his meeting with Dr. Grisly.

Hunched over the steering wheel, Andy keeps rehearsing his speech: "Who did he think he was?! Do you think I'm stupid?! I haven't seen that

Velvet horse in four months!! That nail wasn't the problem! Blah, blah, blah!" The windows of the truck were starting to steam up and other drivers were beginning to stare. "What are you looking at?!"

Andy turns into the driveway of an expansive estate, his lip quivering in anger, disgust and nah, nah, nah kind of stuff. As he steps out of the truck, he spots Dr. Grisly talking with a rather well-dressed couple. Andy was so tight that you could have played a tune on the back of his neck.

"Doc," Andy started, ready to make THE speech of his life.

"Oh, Andy," Dr. Grisly says. "I'd like you to meet the Connors. I've been telling them all about you. They wanted the best man available at any price and I told them that you were the man for the job."

Andy's mouth drops. His neck muscles collapse so fast you could hear the vertebrae snapping.

"But, but..." Andy stammers, not knowing which direction to go. "Well, I guess I could fit them in."

"Good, good!" Dr. Grisly beamed. "That's great. Listen though," Dr. Grisly said as he steered Andy over to the side. "Make sure you're careful with those nails, WE don't want another terrible mess like the Gallaghers. They were really upset at ME."

Andy sighed, "Yeah, sure Dr. Grisly, I'll watch those nails."

One evening over a beer, I asked Doc why veterinarians were always picking on farriers.

"Envy," Doc stated without even hesitating.

"Doc, I had a horse pee all over my shirt. What's to envy about that?"

"No, not about that stuff, but about money and pressure and long hours and stuff. I started out doing horses and cattle, but I ended up standing out in some muddy field freezing to death at two in the morning and then never got paid for catching pneumonia."

"So, cats are the way to go."

Doc scratched his head and took a sip of beer. "No, actually real estate is. But I went to school with Grisly. He flunked anatomy three times. He's also scared to death of cats. When he was doin' his residency at the school clinic, a tom cat got hold of him and tried to pull one of his eyeballs out. Grisly swore he'd never work on them again."

"Yeah, but what's that got to do with me?"

"In ten years you'll probably be making more money than he is. That'll drive him nuts. He's pretty insecure, you know. Runs on bullshit most of the time. He'd fit right in at the track 'cept he can't get a license. Felony conviction. Mann Act or somethin.' Underage hooker in Spokane. Motel happened to be over the border in Idaho."

"Well, I wish he'd get off my ass." Hooker? Grisly? Geez.

"So, tell him you know me." Doc's mouth broke into a giant grin. "Tell him you know me *really* well. Then, just smile and say nothing. Don't go into the other thing. She was like 17 ½ and he was like, well senior year anyway. Took a bunch of money to keep him in the university. Just tell him I said 'howdy.'"

I took Doc's advice. A week later I ran into Dr. Grisly at one of my stops. I casually mentioned the mutual acquaintance from vet school, smiled innocently and headed off to the other end of the barn to work on a horse. Grisly never brought up the subject directly, but suddenly I was the hottest farrier in town. Oh, I still dropped the occasional anvil on my foot, except that the act, no matter how painful, never diminished my stature as a true professional. Bolstered by my sudden credibility, I confidently chided Jesse's mother, telling her quite frankly that what offends her nose today is in the checking account tomorrow. She told me she could just as easily do lunch without me.

Really, who needs talent when you've got the dirt on somebody.

18.

THE *OTHER* THOROUGHBRED

A FEW DAYS after Jessie's triumphant day at the self-esteem slaughter-house, the subject of horse shows came up. Doc and I were stacking bro-ken lumber by the barn. It's how depreciation is calculated on a horse farm. It allows us to determine how many National Forests we'll need to clear-cut the following year to accommodate our horse's questionable habits. Actu-ally, I started laughing to myself, no doubt recalling Jesse's aerial ballet in the schooling ring. Doc seemed quite curious about horse shows, surpris-ingly so, since a certain snobbery exists among racing people about the prospects of Thoroughbreds finding job opportunities in other markets. You see, the majority of racehorses are geldings. Simply put, they might be able to retire from the track, but the pension plan got cut – along with a cou-ple of other things. Unlike human sports – baseball or pro football – retired racehorses can't go into coaching or broadcasting. They don't speak human, and cheering on another horse would violate the 'herd ethical code.' Imagine the chaos if 5,000 buffalo were randomly wandering around San Francisco without a leader? Why, you'd need to construct …freeways?

Naturally a lot of mares race as well. Most don't face the surgical dilemma. Their limitations are a little more esoteric in that the value of their ovaries is subject to the whims of fashion or the good fortune of a dis-tant relative. Mares also seem to attract optimism a lot more regularly than their male counterparts. Gee, what a surprise! Then there's the built-in escape clause when a mare turns out be slower than the five minutes just before recess. "Well, you can always breed her." Geldings hate that speech.

Sure, there are dumb-bloods around – I mean Warmbloods, but most have an IQ normally associated with poultry and have feet the size of garbage can lids. Am I prejudiced? Yes. Emphatically. These horses are bred in Europe, basically mongrels that end up with some royal tattoo on their butts in a wild attempt to get them adopted by Americans with more money than sense. Europe is the dog pound of the horse industry. Every farmer has two or three of these brutes just waiting for the adoption papers to be finalized. They are basically a cross between a heavy horse – say a Percheron and a Thoroughbred. The idea was to gain size and soundness from the heavy side and a little heat and ambition from the Thoroughbred influence. The plan actually seemed somewhat reasonable if you ignore the 'Irish Setter Syndrome,' another human experiment in DNA intervention that scientifically established that an organism could fetch and drool whether it had a brain or not. Now that kind of mental acuity may not seem important if you are a tail-wagging potted plant, but the story gets a little more frightening when you are trying to make eye contact with a 1500lb pile of indifference.

How they manage to get them on an airplane is only answered some-where down the yellow brick road. Most five-year olds haven't even grasped the rudiments of leading, much less any mental connection with something as basic as a saddle. If I were the pilot, I'd ditch the plane in the Atlantic and let mankind focus on some other virus. It's a lot like the Bureau of Land Management's 'Adopt a Wild Horse Program.' Why not adopt a rabid wolverine? Bring it home and watch while it eats your pets, your children, most of the neighbors and everything in the refrigerator. The key word is 'wild.' Wild = potential death. "Hi honey. Guess what I brought home?"

Warmbloods are classified according to geographic locale, which is a little silly since Europe changes its borders every forty years or so. Natu-rally, Germany has it down to a precise abstraction.

That isn't surprising since German scientists went so far as to publish body disposal manuals in World War II. Actually calculated burn times for fat versus skinny people, complete with graphs and pie charts. The scien-tists and technicians, when questioned at their trials about the task seemed to have a great deal of difficulty with the answers:

"Well, you see we had this problem with disposing of all these bodies."

"Don't you mean 'people?'"

"Yes, yes. Well no. They weren't people anymore. But we still had this problem...I mean, we didn't kill them ourselves...we were just told to solve this problem."

Thorough folks, those Germans, though I don't think they personally invented the craft of de-humanizing a nuisance. Maybe that's why at certain holidays, with certain relatives, with certain questionable credentials and with an assertive certainty known only to them – my sister and I ate in the kitchen with the dogs.

Every district creates a new breed: Hanoverians, Westphalians, Berliners – *Buchenwalders maybe*. They are all the same horse: big and not known for intelligence. Dutch horses seem to be the worst. "Big, dumb and Dutch" is not a label I simply made up on my own to support an obvious bias. It's universal – their skulls are so thick that the brain simply atrophies into something resembling a raisin. Even an amoebae has a better memory.

I do like French horses, which might seem odd since I don't particularly feel any affection for French people. Part of the problem is that they're people. The rest has to do with those 8th grade French classes. The horses are okay because they are 75% Thoroughbred versus the Dutch things which are probably about 1/16 Thoroughbred, the rest generic DNA scraped from the armpit of a three-toed sloth. I'm trying to be generous here, when I really don't want to be.

Ah. A little equine bigotry seems to be floating around this chapter. Well, I did confess to being a half-German working my way toward American snobbery, so in order to be fair when I also don't want to be, I am forced to cede an uncomfortable, but necessary point: God didn't create the Thoroughbred. The British did. Boy, that acknowledgement was pretty painful.

And it gets worse! The British actually stole horse racing from the Arabs. What's more, they also stole the horses, which was probably a little noted side-bar since the British were stealing entire continents anyway. In order to make horse racing seem like a British idea they had to invent a new horse. Racing Arabian horses outside Buckingham Palace would seem…well, touristy?

So three Arabian stallions were brought to England and assigned the task of having sex with every mare in Great Britain. They were the Godolphin Arabian, the Darley Arabian and in some negotiated deal with Islam, the Byerley Turk. From the loins of these three immigrants sprang the English Thoroughbred, whose ancestry and purity was closely guarded by *The English Jockey Club*, a somewhat stodgy and paternalistic association composed originally of aristocratically anointed males.

That wasn't unusual given the time frame of the *Club's* formation but it did bring up certain questions about the other half of the experiment: the mares. Who were these female horses and what did they do for a living? Seemed at the time that it didn't really matter to the *Club's* brass as long as they could claim the Thoroughbred as their own. Of course, they didn't dare say that a foal looked like its mother, as that would bring up a whole host of awkward questions, none of which were particularly palatable in a mixed audience:

Lord Balfour: "A fine specimen by the great Godolphin!"

Lady Blinkenbush: "And the dam, why she must be spectacular sir."

Lord Balfour: "Ahem, ahem…more tea me lady?"

Lady Blinkenbush: "Lord Balfour, surely she must be…oh, I see!"

Same thing in America. Cowboys invented the Quarter Horse in a marketing strategy designed to dignify the mongrels they rode to chase cows. Once 'cowboying' became a high-profile, high-paying spectator obsession, they needed to have a name for the partner that did most of the work and at least half of the thinking. So the Quarter Horse was invented, the name derived from the shorter and stouter animal's great speed over a quarter of a mile. Kind of like 'Ford' if you happen to be a pick-up truck.

So now that I've given a somewhat biased note to the opposition, I'll add a further *caveat* to my unbridled enthusiasm for the Thoroughbred: refinement. Without that the Warmblood would merely be another unflattering face pulling a cart…and America's Quarter Horse? The breed registry opened their stud book to Thoroughbreds in the 1970's because they were having some 'quality control' issues. Seemed that the public no longer wanted a short, muscle-bound horse that ran a pretty fast quarter-mile. Same public opinion that finally doomed the Edsel.

Funny how confessions can go clear around the block and return as something better. As I was saying, Thoroughbreds are a little hot-headed and prone to throwing fits, a bit like a spoiled child. But you can work through that minor setback and move forward. A Warmblood on the other hand, is a lesson in digression. Run into a problem and you have to regress ten steps and re-teach the animal that you stay alive by inhaling. I think the term is 'developmentally impaired.' However, a horse born in the Bavarian region has a second option. If he fails to make it as a horse, the French are more than willing to sneak him across the border and serve him for lunch. I love it. Talk about the perfect revenge. "Yes, I'll have sautéed Brownie with mushroom sauce."

I tossed another chunk of lumber. "Yeah, most of the horses at the show were Thoroughbreds."

"Off the track, huh?" Doc was chewing on some kind of mental bone.

"Uh huh. Saw one sold at the show for $10,000. Didn't look like much to me." I changed the subject, asking Doc if he planned to enter any yearlings in the August sale. He wasn't buying it.

"Ten-thousand?"

"Yeah, but he won quite a few classes. Now, Brownie's a Thoroughbred too, but he's worth about five bucks...I mean, there's training and showing and they go lame..."

"Ten-thousand, huh?" Doc was circling the solar system, a craft out of control in the cosmic dust. I swung a two by six around smacking him in the shin. It was all I could do to bring him back to *terra firma*. "Ouch!"

"Sorry, I misjudged."

"When's Jesse coming over again," he asked, rubbing his leg.

I was tempted to say that she died in an automobile accident. "Well, maybe this afternoon. She didn't say. I know she's leaving for Oregon next week, so maybe before then." I felt like giving Custer a ring and see if he wanted some help at Little Big Horn.

"Bring her over. I'd like to ask her something."

I honestly believed that Doc liked Jesse for the wonderful person that she truly was, but I was beginning to suspect an ulterior motive. He, like most racehorse owners invariably end up with a few spares hanging around in the *remuda* – six-year old geldings that never won one, broodmares whose ovaries only produce despair and the occasional stake's winner that wants to go to Reno every weekend because he's bored. Doc saw an out, a convenient path to get out from under the thirteen or so equines hanging around the farm digesting most of the profits. In Jesse, he had found something more than my girlfriend. What he saw was a career counselor, a commodities broker, a loan officer with unlimited imagination and absolutely no idea of what constitutes truth, ethics or good eyesight – someone who could convert a liability into an asset – a hay bill into cold, hard cash. SHOW HORSES! And lucky me. I'm just stupid enough to end up as the intermediary. Custer didn't return my call.

Doc wasn't alone in his desire to get rid of the burden of equine in-laws. Most Thoroughbred owners face a similar dilemma, brought to a nasty head around tax time, when accountants start asking impossible questions:

"How is it that two racehorses managed to consume 27 tons of hay last year? And this receipt from the blacksmith – these two horses were trimmed 143 times!? And I don't understand this thing about the tractor. How can you depreciate something that doesn't seem to exist? What's a Foggy Bottom? And who is this Andy guy? He doesn't have a W-2 or even a birth certificate. His Social Security number belongs to an 82-year old woman in Nebraska! Look, I don't work for the mob or dope peddlers. I'm outa here!"

The truth is tough, especially if you have a heart the size of Australia. Confessing to the sad fact that you still own every horse you bred since 1962...well, we all have our secrets. You see, Doc was the 'softy,' Elaine the pragmatist. Anything that cut into her credit limit at Sak's was history. Even I could be traded in on a size-2 silk pant-suit. Do I feel cheap? Not a chance. Have you priced that stuff? I think it would be easier to get a new accountant, maybe somebody with a couple of parole violations on the horizon.

Sadly, animal owners are suckers when it comes to big brown eyes and a cute smile. Doc knew it, Elaine knew it, most of their friends knew it, and I imagine that Doc's kids knew it too, for every time he wrote a check to the feed store, their inheritance shrank. Okay, I'll confess – I'm not much better. I'm a sucker for lost baby birds, stray kittens, dogs that have a problem with the Fourth of July, moronic horses, gassy sheep – you name it. I go to AA every week: "Animals Anonymous." I sit down and bare my soul to a bunch of people who own way too many poodles, lizards, canaries, burros, orphaned gold fish and the occasional black-headed rat.

"My name is Andy and I'm an animal nut."

"Hi Andy." Nothing like a chorus to reinforce your defective behavior.

The problem is that old racehorses never die. Other things go terminal: optimism, hope, checking accounts, microwave ovens, even favorite cats and the miscellaneous pheasant. Racehorses keep breathing no matter what happens to the rest of us. We grudgingly pay the bills hoping that life expectancy will take a turn for the worse...nothing traumatic mind you, just a quiet death in front of the television set. God balancing the books without a lot of teary-eyed eulogies.

Some Thoroughbreds do find employment elsewhere. After years of making one owner miserable, they get a chance to destroy somebody else's life. They become, like Brownie, show horses, which is the exact kind of counseling that Doc thought Jesse could provide: a little pep talk, a pretty outfit – then zoom down the driveway to some other sucker's farm. Personally, I liked the idea. A few less horses to feed, a lot less manure piling up. Why did I have a premonition that the perfect plan had something to do with a jar of honey and an anthill?

Doc's theory though had a fatal flaw. Thoroughbreds are only suitable for certain tasks. They don't like western saddles (much too heavy), they don't chase cows and they never pull anything around, like a wagon – that's what tow-trucks were invented for. Instead they become hunters, jumpers or dressage horses, which on the social stratification scale is about as high as you can go if you happen to be a horse.

It's kind of a fussy business. Racehorse owners tend to be linear thinkers. A horse runs really fast from point A to point B. This is followed by the presentation of a large check. Not too difficult to understand. Show horses follow a more circuitous path, a trail that wanders aimlessly through the forests of love, beauty, talent and desire, all of which are highly subjective. There is a sensitivity issue that rational human beings have no hope of ever understanding or fully appreciating. It's why people go to the dog pound and adopt one-eyed ugly dogs with ringworm. They think they are in love, but what they really have is a bad case of social isolation. Yeah, why date when you can hang out with Buster the Bean Head?

Take *hunters* for example: *Hunters* used to run around with a pack of hounds and a guy who had way too much brandy, looking for a fox. A lot like a fraternity on a Saturday night. Today, most hunters hang around with a pack of trainers and a rider who would rather be tied feet-first to the bow of a sinking freighter. The fox has been replaced by a blue ribbon (the cost of which has been estimated to run anywhere from $1300 to $50,000 a crack), and the whole idea is to impress the hell out of a judge who would rather be in Puerto Vallarta, marlin fishing. It's not sport, but an angst-filled encounter with the alter-ego, little more than a two-month respite from the need for intensive therapy, or that thing where they hook jumper cables to your ears. Either way, it's expensive.

Jumpers are a lot like hunters, except that they jump over brightly colored fences that tend to be a lot higher and wider. These jumps are designed to scare the daylights out of anything with a brain. The curious part: why do humans go along for the ride? Perhaps it is the same sort of endorphin addiction that causes astronauts to happily perch on top of 14 tons of highly unstable rocket fuel and get launched into a hostile oxygen-depleted black hole on the ragged outskirts of public transportation. At least with something like mountain climbing, if you fall you might land somewhere near a cemetery. With jumpers, if you fall, the judge is going to blow a whistle (indicating that you've been declared *persona non grata*), and it is more than likely that you'll spend the next two hours trying to get a bunch of Kentucky blue grass out of your teeth.

Dressage is another matter entirely. I have never understood dressage. I don't think Thoroughbreds understand it either. Most ex-racehorses like action – running away with people, flipping over backwards, that sort of stuff. Dressage is more like waiting for an abscess to rupture: incredible pain followed by two or three seconds of absolute bliss...movie sex really, only in the case of dressage, the foreplay takes seven or eight years. The discipline of dressage (It's not a sport, but a 'discipline.') reminds me of figure skating without the angst of enduring a triple jump that Dick Button would sabotage half way through. He'd always whisper something like, "She fell on her ass last time, let's see if she can put it together for the medal." That always sent the television audience to the nearest bathroom for a mass throw-up session. For many folks it became impossible to watch figure skating. Think about having open-heart surgery and the doctor hands you a mirror so you can watch. The last thing you'd hear on earth would be, "Ah shit."

The other thing wrong with dressage is that nobody except a 'dressagee' knows what in the hell is going on. The horse does a little jig here, a pirouette there, a two-step followed by a phantom kick in the air and then it's over. The rider isn't allowed to show any emotion until the whole dance is finished and even then the audience isn't quite sure if the smile is sincere or homicidal. The rider also has to salute the judge, who has had the good sense to have his jaw wired shut just prior to the show.

Back to the scene of the mugging: Doc's linear thinking and Jesse's equine appraisal business. I should have gone to the lumber pile alone.

"He's too short," Jesse admonished.

Doc would rub his fingers through his hair. "He'll fill out."

"He's ten years old. We're not talking about filling out, but filling up."

"How about Zyrtaki? He's grey."

"His knee is the size of a grapefruit." Well, maybe a tangerine.

"But he's grey!" Doc would insist.

"He can't *move*," Jesse shot back.

INTERMISSION

I wandered off to find a bathroom and a good book. I don't do hostility. Coward? Absolutely. If no one can figure out Bosnia, then the best place to go is a men's room with a lock on the door. I bet Madeline Albright used to do the same thing. Well, not the men's room, but...dammit! What is it about women that forces them to be so bloody honest? Men lie more often than they eat and it's accepted as a DNA problem. Even Clinton redefined the meaning of sex by arguing that it wasn't him but his little friend: "I did not have sex with that woman." Right. "My pants fell down because of a faulty zipper. I was really looking for the nuclear codes, you know, the Joint Chiefs were coming over, we had an errant B-52, Canada took over Niagara Falls, Boris was pissed-off over something, Chelsea got a 'C' in physics, we're missing one or two aircraft carriers, the Yankees lost again, my saxophone is corroded, Elvis was spotted in the East Wing, the Republicans just pinched Ross Perot on the butt, the hot line has a busy signal, my limo's in the shop, Hillary's thinking about getting a job...I can't keep an eye on everything at once! Besides, dammit, I'm the President! Say, Hil, what's with the flannel bras?"

Okay, back to the farm. Doc would look puzzled, trying to figure out what the difference was between *moving* and moving, the old idea of point A and point B suddenly in conflict with some esoteric principle beyond his scope. "Yah, yah, yah...the speed of light causes macaroni noodles to curve to the right. Unless you're on the moon, then ha! They curve to the left!"

Who said Einstein didn't have a sense of humor?

"Look see," Doc said. "He's walking over here right now." Zyrtaki, not Einstein.

Jesse would just throw up her hands in despair. "He needs to float along the ground, to look pleasant – a hunter needs to *move* well so that the rider can *equitate* properly."

It was no use. Not only could Doc not understand all these different kinds of *movement,* but he was fighting fate as well. Doc's horses were destined to be mediocre. It was God's will, for Doc was a veterinarian and veterinarians attract homeless kittens, stray dogs and birds with broken wings. Success would spoil that higher order of things. Just ask James Herriot or the guy with too much gauze on his head.

Later, back at the lumber pile, Doc became philosophical. "I think your girlfriend's nuts." Norwegian philosophy gets right to the point.

"My girlfriend?" I just referred to Jesse that way to avoid those questioning looks one always gets when you're supposed to have one, but don't. It's sort of like trying to pawn off the cat in my truck as a dog. Never works. "Gee thanks. Maybe you can tell her that sometime. I'm still in the *friendly* department, whatever the hell that is."

Doc paused, holding a sixteen-foot board in his outstretched arms. "I think you agree with her."

"Well, maybe. I mean, Zyrtaki does have a big knee. Show horse people are a little funny about big knees and stuff."

"Yeah, well I still think she's nuts." Doc swung the board around, catching me just above the knee. The blow knocked me over the lumber pile and I landed on the edge of a large stump.

"Ouch!"

"Oh, sorry," Doc offered, grinning. "Hope your knee doesn't swell up. It'd be a shame if Jessica got a look at it."

He stretched out his hand to help me to my feet. I accepted the offer, not sure if he would let go halfway through the process. He didn't.

"Well, maybe she's right," he offered, shaking his head. "But one of these days, Elaine is going to start counting heads, and..."

"I got a couch in the trailer."

"Oh, that reminds me. About the tractor." Doc took on a rather serious look, one that doesn't wear well on kindly veterinarians.

"Yeah, I…figured I was going to hear about that sooner or later." Later would be better.

Suddenly his face cracked into a grin. "That was pretty good. Running over her foot. Never could have got away with that! I'm thinkin' about buying a *Ferrari*. See if you can think of some way to pull that off would ya?"

Doc kept grinning while he picked up another board. I got the hell out of the way.

19.

ADVENTURES IN FARMING, PART III
LEFT IS ALWAYS RIGHT

Next to a forty-year-old tractor, a weed-eater is one of my favorite tools. I use it for cleaning feed buckets, pulling manes, cleaning out my mobile home and, if I put a sponge on the end that spins around, it does a pretty good imitation of a car wash. I read in the *Wall Street Journal* that the inventor of this tool (a guy named Donald Thump or Whump, or some such thing), now spends most of his time figuring what to do with the profits, estimated by attorneys at somewhere between fifty-cents and forty-billion dollars. The story went on to say that Donald came up with the idea after he guzzled seven gin martinis and flew his helicopter upside-down through an Illinois corn field on New Year's Eve. Shortly thereafter, he was issued two patents by the US government and a stern warning from the FAA. Donald was, by many accounts a genius, but he had one fatal flaw – he was right-handed.

I, however, am left-handed. Theologians, sociologists, psychiatrists, behaviorists, penmanship teachers, Freudian sex freaks – even talk show hosts and political columnists have booted around the argument about dexterity versus intelligence for centuries. The left-brain/right-brain scientists of this decade insist they know the cause and effect of elbowing a foreign ambassador at a state dinner. Right-brainers are concentric,, left-brainers, linear. At least I think so. It apparently operates on opposing polarity: left hand – right brain. We lefties could actually prove this theory except that most righties in the audience are still trying to figure out why there are two commas in the second to last sentence. Case closed.

All I can say is that I see the forest, not the trees. I'm twenty miles down the road while some right-hander is staring at a pine cone. Food gets spilled because a server assumes it is safe to pour soup over your left shoulder, normally the route your fork follows to get to your mouth. Doesn't make sense? Okay, so I made the whole thing up. The only real truism is that left-handers experience severe prejudice. The saving grace is that we're much better looking than most right-handers. Just ask my mirror when you get over the comma thing.

Evidence suggests that much of the research on this volatile issue was produced in a climate of bias and misunderstanding – perhaps even fraud, to further the interests of an uncaring world. Consider the true facts presented here: known right-handers include Richard Nixon, Ted Bundy, Betty Crocker, Scrooge, Moe and Curly, Rush Limbaugh, Chevy Chase, Flipper, Charo, Mr. Black and Mr. Decker, Dracula, most Proboscis monkeys, the Pillsbury Doughboy and the Tokyo version of Godzilla. I could include 'The Blob,' but with no limbs, it was pretty hard to figure its preference. However, it did have a propensity for right turns, especially if it wanted to digest the leading actress.

Left-handers are Mother Theresa, Lassie, Julia Roberts, Benjamin Franklin, Secretariat, Walter Cronkite, Alistair Cooke, two out of three of the guys that walked on the moon, Barbara Walters, everything on the endangered species list, Kevin Costner, Superman, five or six lesser Kennedy's and Judge Judy. Oh, I forgot Flicka, Lee Iacocca, Barrack Obama and most Popes. This goes to prove that left-handers will save the world and the right-handers will simply control most of the world's power tools, including weed-eaters. And it is just here that the conspiracy deepens. Equipment manufacturers always seem have two names, this in order to deflect their well-deserved criticism: Massey has Ferguson, Briggs has good old Stratton and where would Black be without the charming foil Decker?

Mr. Black: "No sir, I think Mr. Decker was in charge of that thar smoky muffler."

Mr. Decker: "Why Mr. Black, you know full well I designed the faulty electrical switch and not that damn muffler. I told ya that it couldn't be next to the gas tank."

Since I was raised with a strong desire to irritate the hell out of my third-grade penmanship teacher, one Mrs. Evans, I decided at an early age to buck the system and be left-handed. In those prehistoric days, such a resolution was viewed by *academia* as an attempt to overthrow the virtuous heart of education itself. The vice-principal was forced to call my parents, my doctor, the school nurse, even the police – you could burn down the school, steal Mrs. Evan's car, or even skip most of the vowels when reciting the alphabet, but you absolutely, positively could not write the *Gettysburg Address* with your left hand. Unthinkable.

I also had this 'It' that was completely opposed to left-handed eating. He garnered most of his parenting skills in the stockade at Fort Lewis. If I tried to eat with my left hand, he would stab me with his fork, a knife or a bottle opener. I'm probably lucky I didn't die of tetanus. The big bonus out of this was that I ended up ambidextrous, which drives most Chinese restaurants nuts. I can do chop-sticks with the left, a fork or spoon with the right – all at the same time. I can shovel food better than a whale sucking plankton. Then again, some fifty years later I still pick up a fork and stare at it. The left wants it, but the right takes it away. Meanwhile the food gets cold.

The *old school* did succeed in a few isolated cases, mostly with wimpy types in thick glasses, Boy Scouts bound to the Wolf Oath, and girls – the latter plotting to overthrow the establishment a decade later anyway. Gender wasn't the real issue – conformity was. Stick a woman in the hand with a fork and your body is going to end up down a volcanic vent.

Teachers demanded conformity as a necessary adjunct to the process of converting a child into something that might be employable in the future. Sociologists had managed to convince educators that no left-handed kid would make it into management because the clipboard industry couldn't design one to accommodate the disability. So teachers would tape my left hand to the desk, rap me with a ruler every time a No. 2 pencil found its way into the wrong hand and verbally exhort me about the horrible life I would experience if I didn't see the light. I would be shunned by colleges, scorned by women, unable to find a job – I pictured myself as the Hunchback of *Notre Dame*, a left-handed bell ringer forced to steal women. It was demoralizing to say the least.

Fortunately, they were, for the most part, wrong. Women weren't overly impressed with me anyway, colleges...well, grades are grades and I did have a job, but I would be forever haunted by the power tool industry: evil, bigoted empires that always placed the button on the <u>wrong</u>

side. I'd have to crank the thing with my right arm, a limb not accustomed to manual labor, meaning my bicep would writhe in agony and then disconnect from the major bones. I'd be left with the Popeye syndrome, forearms that contained most of my muscle mass. And no, I don't like spinach. I was in the Wimpy camp – a greasy hamburger replacing any need to explore a salad bar or chase a flat-chested woman named after a cooking oil.

When it comes to weed-eating, most right-handers could easily weed a couple of acres without spilling a drop of their iced tea. A left-hander though, ends up losing two or three square inches of skin, fried off by the misplaced exhaust pipe, the same pipe that blows smoke up your sleeve until your armpit melts. Left-handers are also subjected to shock therapy whenever their watch makes contact with the spark plug. If I try to counter such unwanted electrical stimulation by say, tilting the weed-eater on its side, then gasoline drips out of the tank into my shoe, causing a three-alarm fire in my socks.

Weed-eaters have another distinct problem, unrelated to the left-brain/right-brain discussion. It is the little organizer on the spool responsible for keeping the string under control and dispensed at exactly the right length for a smooth, professional cut. Doc's weed-eater ascribed to the laws of random physics, assuming that the string should be either long enough to rope the neighbor's cow, or so short it couldn't knock the ash off a cigarette.

String [dis] organizers are also extremely complicated, the result of allowing left-brainers to run the research department. Invented by the same fiendish individual responsible for the Rubik's Cube, a typical organizer comes with enough string to last about a year, which is exactly how long it takes to lose the instructions. Since I'm not particularly agile in mechanical engineering, I end up sitting on the floor with fourteen feet of spaghetti and a box of Kleenex. No, I never cry, I just sweat profusely out my eyebrows. Then off to the medicine cabinet for some pharmaceutical support.

In situations such as this, I try to focus on people with bigger problems than my own. That leads me directly to the third season of "Gilligan's Island." It's been three years and nobody has hooked up yet. You'd think that either the Professor or Gilligan would have made a move on the Movie Star. Or fixed the boat. We've already figured out that the Skipper is gay since he's always hitting on Gilligan. You know, the 'little buddy' thing. Real touchy/feely. Then there's Mary Ann. She's pretty uptight, but probably leaning toward the Professor, but if they don't get off the island then he loses tenure and the big house on campus. She's not going back to waiting tables. Then again, he is a little quirky. Could be a Ted Bundy behind those glasses. The Millionaire has certainly run out of alcohol by now, so Wife has gone from enabler to intensive care nurse. The Movie Star is getting some action somewhere, but nobody is quite sure, leading to speculation that something is going on during the commercials. Rumor has it that midway through the fourth season Erica Kane washes up on the beach with three members of the Brazilian soccer team. Oliver Stone takes over directing the series, leading to more speculation on who really killed Kennedy. The Skipper?

A couple of hours of re-runs and the possibilities are as endless as the project. The celibates of Fantasy Island begin to beg certain questions about other similar relationships involving people of a familiar nature marooned on another island by an equally unfriendly body of water, watched over by a hippopotamus and a duck killer. Yes, the string is finally organized, but not much else. Every time optimism surfaces, a single sentence seems to drown it.

"I'll come by later with the $4 million and the tickets to New Zealand." Checking to see if she's actually listening.

Jesse pauses. "No, not tonight. I've gotta clean some tack."

String facilitation is designed to take your mind off those questions that tend to maim your self-esteem. That doesn't really work though. Once your brain hands off the task to your fingers, it starts re-running the old tape. Where's this relationship going? What relationship? I'm still not sure if we're 'in like,' or just doing an encounter session without the need for a $90 an hour therapist. Anybody heard of the term, 'emotional autopsy?' It involves an ice-pick and most of your cerebellum. Physically, it's painless. Emotionally, well, you simply agree with anything a woman has to say.

"You're stupid."

"Okay."

"You're socks smell like a dead rabbit."

"Okay."

"Ever trim your toe nails?"

"1968."

"Why do you always smell like gasoline?"

"Okay."

I used to think that operating a weed-eater was so simple that just about anyone with two thumbs could qualify for the job, but now I am not so sure. In fact, I believe that weed eating must be approached with the same caution that early man employed when he got the bright idea to eat an artichoke. I love them with a little sour cream and dill, but why did early man pick a thistle with a bunch of dog hair inside? A Neanderthal with a shopping list should have been chasing something with legs and most of its hair on the outside. Woman was pretty clear on the matter. She invented the <u>list</u> just to avoid situations like this. Maybe it is why you never see an auto parts store next door to a Safeway. "Guess what I got for dinner honey?"

Another food thought came to mind, which normally means I must have missed lunch again. I was in the library a while back and found a book printed in 1910 entitled, "The Edible Mushroom Book." I was actually looking for something like a dictionary on women, but got sidetracked. I really wondered about a book that identified poison by having its author eat samples of different stuff from the table of contents, but I guess it was probably the only way to become an authority on the subject. I concluded that it probably took 75 odd years to publish, since most of the previous authors died somewhere around chapter three. And what about the research staff? "Here George, try this one." If George immediately went into convulsions and his liver exploded on the wall, then it was definitely a "no." And here I thought I was naive. But it's not just mushrooms that highlight mankind's odd definition of the word 'edible.' Think about snails, sea urchin (hose slime with spines), prickly-pear cactus, Rocky Mountain oysters, tripe, seaweed, calf brains, bologna (nobody has ever told me if it is animal, mineral, vegetable or left-overs from the local Humane Society), Spam (same deal), Habanero peppers, mutton, chicken butts, runny eggs, fluoridated water, flat beer and Ripple. Oh, I forgot ox-tails and caviar. Ever take a good look at a cow's butt while you're busy eating a sturgeon's first born male heir? Furthermore, why would someone want to eat fish embryos at $200 an ounce and then spend an hour trying to floss them out of your teeth? Sure, it's a highbrow culinary activity, but I'd rather lease a Lexus. At least I could get to the emergency room on time.

WEED-EATER RULES:

First off, never weed-eat a slug. Even though hacking one to shreds is more gratifying than sprinkling iodized salt on its back, it is impossible to get the slime out of your nose. Ditto for those generous gifts left by the neighbor's Lab. Never, ever hit one of those. Same goes for rare Tibetan roses, the coaxial cable bringing HBO into Elaine's bedroom, Cadillac hub-caps, anything recently painted or made of wood, the cat, or any exposed electrical transformers. It is also a good idea to avoid blackberry bushes, as they are the leading cause of strange disappearances among novice gar-deners. One other thing: dismembering a hornet's nest with one is damn appealing, but falls under the category of stupid/*about to die*. Try a flame thrower.

Around a farm, it is also important to avoid wire fencing. There is a certain rivalry that exists between weed-eaters and metal fences. Those people who believe that angry, emotional confrontations do not occur between inanimate objects have never studied non-molecular biology, or read the fine print on the weed-eater instructions, assuming they're not already lost. Indeed, objects devoid of biological energy can, and do engage in titanic struggles of will – exemplified by the inability of televi-sions and VCRs to cooperate in recording a favorite program. You wanted the *X-Files*, you got a re-run of *The Gong Show*, which in my case is an autobiographical masterpiece that I'm sure I'd enjoy if I were already dead and not sitting in the front row. Failure to give credence to these non-bio-logical tit for tat sessions will once again exile you to the living room floor with all that red spaghetti and your little pink pills. The ones that make any sort of amputation palatable – even fun.

I have also discovered that it is a good idea to pay careful attention to *where* you are weed-eating. Especially if your weed-eater is a turbo-charged model. I failed to honor that rule of weed-eating one morning, when in a wild fit of exhibitionism, a neighbor decided to preview her new bikini next to my weed patch. The bikini was awesome – at least a 9.9 on my scale. But as I was trying to write down my score, the weed-eater took a sudden liking for the cuffs of my pants. Before I could hit the 'off' switch (naturally located in the wrong damn place), the machine had pulled my jeans down around my knees, wrapped the string around my ankles like an Australian bolo and sent me tumbling down an embankment next to the driveway. Meanwhile, the woman next door headed back inside, probably figuring she had done enough damage for one day.

As I lay groaning in the bushes, my shirt smoldering against the hot muffler, I saw my name in bold print in the "Guinness Book of Records" listed as the world's first weed-eater fatality. Fortunately, about an hour later a UPS driver stumbled over my body while trying to make a delivery. I only wish he had had the good grace to untie me *before* I signed for the package, but I guess I saw his point. At least Jesse didn't find me.

20.

EMILY

JUNE, JULY AND August have always been known to anyone under the age of eighteen as summer vacation. A time to walk barefoot on hot asphalt, holiday in the Poconos or Martha's Vineyard, or lie on the beach in an outfit that will give a parent a migraine. Traditions as old as civilization itself.

Outfits? Let's talk about bikinis. What is a bikini? Well, I think they're less than underwear and normally pretty impressive. That's probably obvious considering all the trouble I got into with the weed-eater. Now the big question is whether you're supposed to gawk or not gawk. I mean, I'm not into voyeurism, but even a *Victoria's Secret* catalog is worth a quick look before it hits the recycling bin or my sock drawer. Why? Oh, come on, women are beautiful – well, with certain exceptions. Female Russian shot-putters with a steroid habit may qualify as an exemption. If one of them puts on a bikini, I'd swallow razor blades. Same with our broodmares. I just can't picture Fat Broad in a 58EEEE, floral pattern or not. Meanwhile, I think I'll gawk. What the hell, if a woman feels great in four-square inches of cloth, then I'm not going to insult the effort, I'm going to celebrate the view. We're supposed to anyway. Why else would *Victoria's Secret* send out 78 million catalogs a year to men? They get their mailing lists from Home Depot.

So it was of little surprise to me when Jesse informed me that she was going on vacation to Oregon, the purpose being to attend a couple of shows and hopefully turn her body into whole wheat toast as the guest of Meatball-Diet-Coke Sue's wealthy aunt, who just happened to own an Italian villa on the shores of Lake Oswego. Yes, she bought a new bikini. No, I didn't get to preview the outfit. Instead, I got a long and painful speech that seemed to run around in one of those yes/no concentric circles, no doubt the result of my questionable status. Officially I was still classified as 'friend' instead of the more gratifying 'boyfriend.' I guess I have to get promoted before I get to see the bikini. Finally, the truth surfaced.

"There's one problem," Jesse said.

"Only one?" I could already think of at least two: bikini and out of town.

"Don't tease. This is serious."

Ah, she's pregnant. Going off to an isolated Oregon monastery, give birth, then turn the child over to Romanian royalty, kid grows up to be a slightly eccentric Renaissance painter. I get it. "What's the problem?"

"Sue's aunt is deathly allergic to dogs." Jesse squeezed her eyes shut as if she had just confessed to shoplifting a dress.

"Oh, I see." I sounded smug. I was smug.

"I was wondering if..."

"Sure," I said. "Emily can hang out here. I'll chain her to a tree in the backyard."

"You will not!"

"Kidding, just kidding."

"Listen, you'll have to watch her carefully. There's coyotes around and she doesn't know about cars and you can't overfeed her or let her out of your sight. She's very temperamental."

Like her owner, I thought. "Are you sure you want to do this?"

"No, I'm not."

"You don't trust me?"

"No. Well, yes. It's just that, well...she means a lot to me, that's all."

"I'll watch her very carefully. But Meatball isn't part of the deal. No way will I watch Meatball. He's homicidal."

"Meatball's not going." Jesse picked up Emily, kissing her on the head and admonishing her to be a "good dog," something that Emily couldn't possibly understand. Then as if retaking a scene from *Casablanca*, she handed over the dog and fourteen pages of instructions. I felt like one of those adoption agents that cruises the unwed mothers ward looking for business. "I'll call you from Oregon," Jesse stammered as she quickly got into her truck. "Take care of her." I swore I saw a tear or two.

"I'm going to call you Butt-head," I told Emily. She just wagged her tail. I was just another meal ticket and if Butt-head worked as well as Emily, it was all the same to her. Besides, she'd found a sucker. I couldn't discipline *myself*, much less a dog with overcharged batteries.

Emily belonged to a special race of dogs: the Jack Russell terrier. Little known in the continental United States, the Jack Russell is extremely popular in England. Originally created by the Reverend John Russell, the dogs were bred as varmint hunters – rats, weasels, foxes, even badgers – any furry beast that happened to interfere with the crops and needed a speedy trial and a quicker execution. I'm not sure why the Reverend Russell changed the name from John to Jack, but I suspect that the entire population of Britain wasn't overly impressed with his efforts to create a new dog.

Emily seemed to be part Beagle, part Fox terrier, part Pit bull and part alligator. She also had a genetic aberration that caused her to attack vacuum cleaners, brooms and electric fans – any instrument that could even be remotely connected to domestic efficiency. And never mind accordions. This dog did not do polkas.

Jesse told me that the Jack Russell's were carried in satchels on horseback during foxhunts and used to pull the fox from the ground if he was fortunate enough to make it back to his den. The other dogs are Fox hounds, who are a lot bigger, very noisy, run fast and trip the occasional horse, or an overstuffed Lord who's busy toasting the Queen at a full gallop. The crux of the matter is that Fox hounds can't fit down the hole, hence the Jack Russell, who is more than willing to tunnel to China, especially if the fox happens to be vacuuming out the place at the time.

Emily's hobbies included digging up the lawn, Elaine's rhododendrons, or the manure pile, which probably needed digging up anyway. I'm sure she was searching for a wily fox, Winnie the Pooh, or a rabbit with an orthopedic problem. Mostly she ended up with a mouthful of dirt or some other disgusting material, which either ended up on my couch or in the cab of the truck, along with the 487 tennis balls, chew toys and one overworked cat. Yeah, Emily figured the cat was a life-sized squeak toy. The cat went out shopping for a gun.

Miss Em' was about eleven-inches tall with a long back and short legs. She was sort of bow-legged behind and seemed to have some kind of hitch in her back tires. Every few strides, she'd hop a couple of times like a broken yo-yo. I'm positive I'm going to get the blame for at least two broken legs. I should have videotaped the dog ahead of time.

Mostly, Em' was white, but like all Jack Russell's she had splotches of black on her head and body. Or maybe it was dirt. Her hair wasn't really long and it wasn't really short, but it was unique in its texture, somewhere between the bristles of a toothbrush and the dorsal fin of a shark. When she got excited, the hair would stand straight up, making her look like a porcupine in the throes of immature balding. She wasn't beautiful, as dogs go, but utilitarian – attractive in the same sense as George Patton might view an M1 tank. Capable. Of course, she still slept in the bed.

If Jesse had a true love in her life, it was this dog. But it was not a relationship of equals. A conservative responsibility dominated Jesse's life: bills paid on time, lights turned off, shoes carefully cleaned to avoid things like leather rot. Emily bludgeoned her way through life as if each encounter was to be her last – a tormented poet really, seeing peace as a lousy alternative to war and anarchy. She was an assassin, a whirling dervish, a howling lemur that owned a dog dish with little hearts on it. Curled up on the couch next to Jesse, Emily dreamed of grabbing little hamsters by the head and shaking them to death, burying their broken bodies under the house. If she were human, her ghastly crimes would have ended in the gas chamber, a pellet of cyanide for the bad little dog. But of course Emily wasn't human, at least legally, and Jesse's enduring love, her mortal obsession, the absolute contradiction of Jesse's orderly life was the only thing that kept the dog off death row. And suddenly, I was thrust into the role of warden.

Doc's farm was a perfect half-way house for canine criminals. In dog vernacular, the place was known as a *no discipline zone*. Doc's own dogs, a Brittany spaniel, a Golden Retriever and an Afghan formed the nebulous of what was known as *The Gang of Three*. With over 80 acres to patrol, the dogs were constantly on the prowl – chasing horses, executing poultry, or Tuesdays, lying in ambush for our Filipino garbage man, forcing him to sprint back to the safety of his truck with a forty-pound can of trash on his back. The dogs weren't really interested in the garbage man, but his cargo, a disgusting collection of moldy meatloaf and coffee grounds, deemed suitable for a fine meal or a good roll. Most days, he made it back to the truck.

All three dogs were also boys, which meant that a good deal of territory needed marking. Since they had never mediated the territory issue, all three claimed the same assortment of boundary markers. These markers included new bags of oats, all electrical boxes near the barn, Elaine's hubcaps, the right-rear wheel of the tractor and most portions of my horse-shoeing truck, the latter particularly valuable, as in the course of my rounds their territory could be expanded exponentially to include most of western Washington. Kind of like a land grab on wheels.

Also high on the territorial list were bushes under three-feet in height. Most were expensive landscape items meant to enhance the primitive existence that Elaine was forced to endure. Doc would plant something like a rare Ethiopian Foo Foo plant or an Egyptian Boxwood only to see it reduced to a bleached skeleton in a matter of days. Elaine considered having *The Gang of Three* neutered, but Doc refused. The nurseryman down the road made so much money that he retired early to somewhere near Key West. Everybody seemed comfortable with the process, except the Egyptian Boxwoods which slowly joined the ranks of the Passenger Pigeon – fondly remembered, but none the less extinct.

Of the three dogs, the Afghan seemed to have the most criminal mind. The Brittany and the Retriever were simply too dumb to think up a felony on their own, but were more than willing to follow a bad example. Their crime sprees were the subject of conversation among the neighbors, especially those trying to make a fortune by raising chickens. While direct evidence was often unavailable (the dogs ate all the witnesses), feathers of a certain circumstantial nature often littered the driveway. When a body was found, Doc digressed from clinical veterinary science to rural mysticism, tying the dead chicken around the Afghan's neck, assuming that a putrid poultry necklace would discourage future *poultrycide*. However, the accouterment had the opposite effect, raising the Afghan's status among the other dogs to something approaching God-like. In fact, he wore his chicken like a medal of valor, proudly displaying it to anyone who happened to visit the farm – including the police.

One afternoon, the Afghan came limping home. Doc surmised that he had been kicked by one of the horses, since the dog was probably trying to move up the livestock ladder. Why fool with chickens when you can eat a horse? Elaine was beside herself, since the Afghan was her favorite. No matter how pragmatically Doc evaluated the dog's injury, Elaine would settle for no less than radiological evidence. After two or three deep sighs and a lot of mumbling, Doc and I loaded up the Afghan and took him to the clinic for x-rays. When the film came out of the developer the problem was obvious, and not necessarily confined to this one incident. The dog had so much buckshot in his body that it was impossible to read the x-rays.

Doc pulled another set of radiographs out of a file marked 'Lucky' and put them and the Afghan in the jeep. Elaine was given Lucky's x-rays and Doc's most sincere assurances that the Afghan's leg was not broken, just bruised. The Afghan continued his life of crime, no doubt picking up some additional lead in the process, but Doc just didn't have the heart to tie him up. It was much easier to just pay off the plaintiffs.

This information should have discouraged Jesse from seeking day-care at our particular center. I made the liberal argument that trying to rehabilitate one criminal by throwing her in with a bunch of other criminals was the exact thing that led to the development of the electric chair. She explained my position away by arguing nature versus nurture – either I nurture naturally or I get turned into compost. Seemed reasonable to me.

My trepidations were really a cop-out. What I didn't want was the responsibility for Emily. In Jesse's world, there was a clear-cut priority list that started with Emily at number one and radically progressed downward from there. Number two was probably her mother, from there it went something like: God, certain other relatives, anything that had been run over on the highway, chocolate-chip mint ice-cream, her horse, some point she was arguing at a particular moment in time and maybe me. That is if I had been lucky enough to make the list at all.

By the first evening, I began to have suspicions about Jesse's true motives. Maybe Meatball-Diet-Coke Sue's aunt was deathly allergic to dogs, but Jesse had gone to Oregon before and as much as she loved Emily, I was sure she would simply refuse the luxury of an Italian villa. About six o'clock I got a call.

"How's Emily? Is she okay?"

"Gee, I'm fine too." The priority list seemed intact.

"You know what I mean," Jesse said, her voice slightly apologetic.

"Emily is just fine. In fact, she's having dinner."

"Did you remember the cottage cheese?"

"Yes." Actually, she was eating left-over bean soup. Cottage cheese was probably page 12, sub-section three, somewhere between brushing and flossing in the maintenance manual.

"Listen...I was less than honest about this. Sue's aunt isn't really allergic to dogs. In fact, she has three of her own. The problem...well, I don't know how to explain it, but Emily got into a little trouble last time I went to Oregon."

I was near heaven. The truth would free me. "Yeah, like what kind of trouble?"

"She bit a judge."

"Oh?"

"Well, only one. They informed me that she was no longer welcome at the shows down here."

"So, Emily is like *persona non gratis* in Oregon, huh?" I pictured her duct-taped to the front of a northbound bus.

"Plus, it's too hot for her down here."

Why didn't she buy two bikinis? Hot? What's this hot stuff? She's a felon, not an Eskimo. I tried my best not to laugh. Jesse's little darling on the ten-most wanted list. "It's okay, I understand. Why didn't you tell me that in the beginning?"

"Because you would've taken advantage of the situation, of me." Jesse paused for a moment. "I mean, you would have teased me about it, maybe even refused to keep her."

"Ah, hell, she's part of the family," I said confidently.

"What?"

"You know what I mean; two people, a dog...you know, like 'Leave It To Beaver' or something."

"She's *my* dog! I don't know where you're getting this family stuff. Listen, maybe this won't work. I'll cut this short and come back. I don't want you thinking..."

"Okay! Forget the family thing. The babysitter says everything is fine. Have fun, see you on Sunday. I'll watch her like a hawk. Bye."

The rest of the week passed quickly. I had discovered Emily's weakness; really, her dysfunction. She was so accustomed to Jesse's smothering that she became extremely insecure if no one was yelling her name. I simply went about my business on the farm, for the most part ignoring the terrier. This distressed her to such a degree that she always stayed near me, afraid of losing me more than I was of losing her. It was a viable argument on the value of reverse psychology. Jesse arrived at the farm early Sunday evening, almost two hours ahead of schedule. I got a quick "Hello," Emily got fifteen-minutes of baby talk and a tummy rub. I pointed out that she still had all her legs, she hadn't been picked up by the dog police or fallen out of the truck. Finally I got a thank-you. Just a small one, but it seemed sincere.

Jesse put Emily in the truck, rolled up the window and headed down the driveway. She hadn't progressed more than about fifty feet when I saw the brake lights go on and the window come down.

"Oh, God!" she yelled. "She rolled in something dead! How could you let her do that?!"

I just smiled and waved, pointing to my ears like I couldn't really hear the question. Last I looked they were once again heading down the driveway. Through the back of the cab window I could see Jesse's finger shaking back and forth in front of Emily's nose. "Bad doggie, bad!" I could imagine the speech. And I could also picture Emily listening to the tirade, jaw open in a smile, tail wagging. She had heard it all before.

21.

"IF IT AIN'T BROKE...DON'T FIX IT"

THAT QUOTE HAS often been attributed to Mark Twain. There is also some speculation that it came from George Bush Sr., who absolutely did not want to screw up something as theatrical as the Reagan White House. Sure, rearrange the furniture a bit, bomb Libya again, change the sheets in the executive bedroom, maybe even the oil in Air Force One, but nothing serious enough to tarnish the former luster of a presidency that specialized in obtuse answers, anti-communist rhetoric and the ability to knock down the Berlin Wall with an American Express Gold Card. Little did we know that instead of spending billions on things like Trident submarines, we could have just listed the Iron Curtain with a good real estate agent and bought the damn thing. The real conundrum about the Cold War was that we never bothered to check the Soviet Union's credit score. I mean in this country, five bucks over your limit and you get three calls from a hysterical junior accountant at MasterCard demanding that you surrender your passport or a favorite child. Even the hotline was subject to frequent interruptions: "I'm sorry, your call cannot be completed as dialed." AT&T handled the account and you know how touchy they are.

Given Twain's infatuation for hands-on story telling (lying, actually), one can only surmise that he was probably one of the first 'new journalists,' guys like Hunter Thompson and satirist P.J. O'Rourke showing up a little later on the scene. New journalism was to writers what television meant to George Plimpton. It was an opportunity to write <u>and</u> star in somebody else's messy life. Plus, you got a check and if it was a slow year for war, genocide or political intrigue, then maybe a Pulitzer. Probably a few libel suits as well. The biggest bonus though was giving up on objectivity, which was both unrealistic and kind of shallow anyway. A guy walks into a high school and shoots seven pupils and the teacher in the head. They ask a witness: "Tell me, how did you feel about that?" Well? How <u>do</u> we feel about that? Somewhere between the who, what, where and how we lost the 'why' because it crossed the line between objective and subjective, a division no *rational human being can honor and still claim rationality <u>or</u> humanity. Of course the downside was how it evolved into Reality TV. Terrible when an organism gets loose without a predator to impede its progress.*

Reporters should get to cry like the rest of us. They too bear witness.

I'm pretty sure I give Ronald Reagan too much credit in ridding the world of the Red Menace, or at least certain segments of it. It was actually a combination of over-spending, satellite TV and the Internet. Bulgarians were rock'n to Bruce Springsteen, East Germans were watching CNN or the BBC and all over Moscow the average vodka- saturated public servant was downloading porn direct from some web site in New Jersey. Once spam and our telemarketers got to the average Russian, not even the nuclear codes were safe. Boris couldn't launch anything once Playboy went online. And the general staff? Selling used MiGs on eBay. The whole country collapsed in a fit of greed and carpal tunnel syndrome. The only dynasty in history defeated by a keyboard.

Seems I start out with horses and end up rummaging through somebody's closet. Think about that scenario before you send your child off to college. A BA doesn't create a genius – just a kid with more questions than answers and a $150,000 babysitting bill from the federal government. The best thing to do is agree with everything they say (especially if they attended a liberal arts college), restructure the loans and send the child off to graduate school. Meanwhile, put the house on the market, buy a cheap disguise and join the Peace Corps. Off to somewhere like Uganda, where access to clean water, food, education and conventional civility are generally lacking. The old leader, Idi Amin, an overweight despot with a tendency towards cannibalism will clarify all forms of national policy for you: "Don't confuse what I'm saying with what I'm thinking." Or...

VOTE FOR IDI OR I EATY YOU!

Very effective. Redefined the parameters for a landslide election in a country where most of the votes and some of voters habitually disappear.

So remember, in six months anything a plumber, the state department or a college graduate utters will make perfect sense. And probably seem like the same subject.

Still, there are a few *people who passionately disagree with Twain's idiom. They are plumbers and mechanics, two groups that prosper at the sight of anything leaking. They absolutely, positively believe in the notion that everything on earth can be fixed for $85 an hour, and probably more than once. Which naturally brings us back to racehorses.*

In the Thoroughbred world, the terminology gets turned around. Something that is *broke* is actually ready to do something constructive, while those things that are *unbroke* are sent back to the factory for some warranty work. Yearlings are an obvious example of such nationwide recalls.

Where the term *broke* actually came from is a subject of wide debate. Originally it was thought that *breaking* a horse involved some sort of religious encounter in which the horse's natural wild spirit was traded in on a saddle, or some other object of equal worth. Other authorities tend to think the term was invented by a drunken, dyslexic Australian cowboy known to engage in long-term relationships with kangaroos or toothless women who were forced to relocate on a sudden and regular basis. It was also rumored that he was legally blind, since most people can tell the difference.

The breaking process usually involves three or four hours of heavy negotiating during which the *rider* and *ridee* work out the principles of the deal. Something like, "I won't pitch you into a cactus plant if you promise to give me Tuesday's off." If each side works from a position of honor, most of the conversation is confined to the details – who rides who, etc..

Occasionally a dispute arises and no form of mediation can dissuade the parties from settling the issue the old-fashioned way. Then, the discussion digresses to primordial growling, similar to those one-sided conversations with the phone company over the fifteen calls to Austria. *"Por favor señor. No speak inglese…eh, Austriinglese? I from Chihuahua señor!"*

"Ma'am, our records indicate you made these calls. Plus we have a couple of others made to Nairobi, Kenya. To a Mr. Sabou Motogami. We're AT & T. We don't make mistakes."

"But I from Mexico!"

We're talking predatory egos battling with rope and leather (and automated voice-mail in case you're lost here) to make a phone, any phone ring. These Olympian contests may go on for hours; the winner determined not so much in terms of success at the task, but by survival at the end – either who stops bleeding first or who still has a palpable heartbeat. (Or maybe who can identify Mr. Motogami.) Hardly ever do these encounters end in a unanimous decision, each party having decided at some point to fight to the death – or lunch, whichever comes first. Instead, scores are tallied according to apparent damage: broken toes, spur holes, obvious contusions and crumpled hats. A ripped Pendleton shirt is worth more than teeth marks on one ear; if both parties crash to the ground, the one on top gets two points for a pin. Judging is highly subjective (by the cat and the UPS driver) and open to appeal if the ground is exceptionally hard or the horse overly tall. The use of accessory non-motorized equipment – throwing patio furniture, swinging shovels and rakes, or tossing automotive parts is strictly forbidden. However, power tools, riding lawnmowers, chainsaws, feed buckets or bladder releases are not only legal, but encouraged. At any point in the contest, a participant may surrender by exhibiting submissive behavior – the horse might bow his neck and accept the bridle; the horse breaker may choose to depart by ambulance. Decisions of the cat are final since the UPS guy has locked himself inside his truck.

Fortunately, Thoroughbreds rarely end up in arbitration. Being the valuable and dignified animal we assume them to be, few choose to subject themselves to the intimate company of a cowboy who last bathed during the '73 flood. They let their agent deal with such unpleasantries. That is why they never blow their noses without someone's clean shirt to absorb the discharge, kick children or small yappy dogs or drink beer out of a can. That behavior is reserved for Quarter Horses. And if you believe this paragraph, then I'm going to make you a deal on some recalled dynamite. Thoroughbreds are just as hard to break as any other breed, they only get mad a hell of a lot quicker.

There are three basic principles to *breaking* a Thoroughbred, (or, *unbreaking,* as the case may be):

1. **Mutual Admiration:** Which means you don't insult each other's conformation.

2. **Boundless Respect:** No hitting below the belt or above the eyes.

3. **Honoring Another Point of View:** Which gets kind of tricky if the yearling loses track of number one.

Once these issues are resolved, the task falls under the category of 'technical support.' Such hardware is defined in equine terms: the *bridle* contains the turn signals and the brakes, though in the beginning, they rarely work. Next comes the *saddle* (the thing you hang on to for dear life) – it is placed on the yearling's back; anywhere in the middle is fine. It has a *girth* attached to it which not only keeps it somewhat connected to the horse, but also operates the vertical thrusters according to how tight you make it. Too tight and you're likely to have a head-on collision with an orbiting satellite.

The potential rider (or victim) should also take a good look at his or her flight equipment. This might include a hard hat, a flak jacket, proper riding boots and a copy of one's health insurance premium, which can be clamped between the teeth. It is also recommended that all riders say a few non-denominational prayers, for it is a really bad time to take a chance on who the real God might be. I personally use a mantra that goes: "Yadda, yadda, shish boom bungo." This roughly translates from Swahili into something like, "Who in the hell's idea was this anyway?!" Once all this quasi-religious existential groveling has been completed, just hop on board. Within three minutes, there will be a clear view of either A) the yearling's future potential, B) the roof of the barn, or C) St. Peter checking your passport. Any of which would make Mark Twain smile.

There are a lot of things I am willing to do around a farm – that being a given. Breaking yearlings is definitely not one of them. I made it perfectly clear to Doc in the beginning that the only thing I would sit on was a tractor or a bar stool, neither of which was likely to pitch me into a cactus plant. Bar stools are uniquely problematic, more so than tractors. I mean, three gin and tonics (okay, so I'm a lightweight), and the prospect of making a bad landing multiplies by ten. Bars should really design their seating like traditional Japanese restaurants, whereby you sit on the floor to begin with – or they should issue crash helmets for the alcohol-impaired. If you are going to end up on the floor anyway, it never hurts to cut the free-fall distance. That way the fire department can focus on heart attacks and car wrecks.

Admittedly, I briefly considered breaking our yearlings. I still had a little of that 'ride off to Mexico' tune in my head and way too many B-westerns overdue at the video store. I liked the idea of noisy spurs and I figured I could mumble a little like Randolph Scott and if I practiced real hard, I could paralyze my hips and walk like John Wayne. Ever see a cat laugh? He showed up for the rehearsal. I'd need a sidekick though, preferably somebody that could speak Randolph Scott and was pretty current in first-aid procedures.

Now if I did decide to *unbreak* our yearlings, I would of course be violating my own contract (not to mention my body) to pursue a task that had more to do with gender identity issues than common sense. I'd watched a few rodeos. I could almost feel that strong sexual attraction Miss 1968 Chevrolet Hubcap exuded when she spotted a guy that suffered two compound fractures on purpose. The flushed cheeks, the frumpled hair – running alongside the stretcher, clutching his hand while he tried not to scream in agony – she was squeezing the bad arm – oh, holding his hat and giving the crowd a brave, though slightly insincere smile, all the while stuffing her motel key into his ripped and bloodied shirt pocket. Animal magnetism through animal mayhem. Painful, but apparently a successful pastime.

Naturally, I would have considered asking Jesse to assist with the stretcher part, what with all her experience with battered egos and my natural propensity toward masochism, but I kept having a recurrent nightmare where I saw my body stretched out on the beach like a wrong-way whale, a flock of seagulls pecking at my eyes. One of the seagulls had an uncanny resemblance to Jesse's mother, which prompted midnight screaming and night sweats. First time the cat ever slept outdoors. However, unlike Miss 1968 Hubcap, Jesse didn't do animal magnetism, at least not the kind that dealt with a species that wore plaid shirts and spoke English.

I also thought about Diet-Coke Sue, since she kind of looked like she enjoyed breaking things, but I heard she was at the local cancer center having a gum transplant and a new headlight installed. On the good news front, Meatball bit an animal control officer. If he gets the death penalty I'm pretty sure he'll spend eternity chasing the devil around Hell.

Doc was also a possibility, given his gameness when we had to tackle that weanling, but this time he begged off, citing a need to have his hip replaced. The cat was long gone and Elaine was busy interviewing large tattooed guys for the purpose of eliminating the male staff and waxing her Cadillac. We were still parolees in Elaine's eyes and probably wouldn't be allowed off till the petunias got a little taller, though as luck would have it, the impasse was finally broken by a half-off sale at Nordstrom's. Twenty-four pairs of shoes later, a few renegade goats had become just a pothole on the blissful highway of fashion.

Truthfully, under any circumstances it would have been pretty tedious to break the yearlings at home. Without an *arena* (an equine gymnasium), or a real training track (instead of a trout stream) the entire exercise would have to take place in the pastures, which at this point were evolving into something resembling gritty maple syrup. That might not have been too bad, the soft ground guaranteeing a smooth landing, but given the adhesive nature of clay soil drenched by a summer shower, it was highly unlikely that anyone would find me for months. Months? Would probably pitch the lumber store into bankruptcy court.

Given such rigid circumstances, yearling breaking is subcontracted out to an individual who is fully equipped to handle the job, normally at a maximum security facility on the other side of the county. Most of these horse breakers look alike. They are generally small, wiry, chew tobacco (even the women – horse breaking is equal opportunity mayhem), and have a look in the eye that one would offer just prior to being sucked into a jet engine. They show up at a farm with a beat-up saddle, bent spurs and a whole collection of lurid stories about dislocated shoulders, ruptured spleens and assorted compound fractures. Their favorite expression goes something like, "We'll get 'em broke Doc," making you think that the guy has a clone that does the real work. I could never figure out if these speeches were designed to generate a tip or to impress everybody with how much pain and carnage they were willing to endure. These guys didn't look tough, they looked freeze-dried. It was as if the retirement home for ex-masochists suddenly ran out of bed space and the zombies were hunting for day jobs.

One thing was beginning to puzzle me though, and it seemed to permeate the horse business: chewing tobacco. I suppose I could understand the habit in the pre-cigarette world, but there seemed to be something going on beyond the need for a nicotine fix. No, not style and sophistication, what with brown juice dripping down your chin and a spit can in your truck. Yet it was socially acceptable in certain situations. As long as you were standing near a horse, everybody just ignored the habit, though they kept a pretty good watch on which way the wind was blowing.

Yes, I tried it. No, not when Jesse was around. At first it was just awful – kind of like developing a coffee habit. Coffee smells a lot different than it tastes. But unlike coffee, the tobacco experience seemed to get worse with time. And if I happened to go into a store and have an extended conversation with an attractive female clerk – spitting traded for swallowing – then the next step was either vomiting on a bush or hiccupping so violently that most of the fillings jumped out of my teeth. It was one of those rare occurrences in my life where I just couldn't get a bad habit to stick.

I'm really not sure why people break yearlings for a living, or chew tobacco for that matter. There are quite a lot of jobs that seem easier. Being an anchor on an oil tanker is one; working on the bomb squad when your partner is hung over is another; training a crocodile on a low-fat diet also qualifies. Even driving around eighth-graders is…wait a minute, I've seen that look before.

22.

PARALYTIC LOADING DISEASE
AND OTHER AFFLICTIONS

AS ONE CAN imagine, breaking yearlings necessitates that they go some-where else to complete this process. Initially, it is a transportation issue aggravated by the horses' inborn suspicions about jumping into a metal box that invariably exceeds the speed limit. That's probably why I quit most of my frequent flyer programs. Being crammed into an aluminum cigar along with 100,000 pounds of jet fuel and a pilot whose wife just left him for a drummer in an obsolete rock band seemed like a sloppy way to explore death styles with a lot of folks I probably couldn't stand to be around any-way. Suicidal people are really insensitive. Especially pilots. They always want company! Why can't they be like elephants and just wander down to the elephant junkyard and tip over. Everybody wants to die in front of a reluctant audience, or take a few accountants, stock brokers, janitors, over-dressed Hawaiian tourists or a stray dog with them. It really isn't suicide, it's just a way to organize a group rate on a cheap funeral or maybe send the media on a motivation hunt. That's where the guy's neighbor says some-thing like, "Frank always seemed pretty quiet, you know, kept to himself. Nice fella." Only later do you find out about the fifteen prescriptions for depression, the dead hooker in the closet and Frank's incredible collection of Vodka bottles.

"Good morning ladies and gentlemen. I'm Frank and I used to be your pilot. On your left is Mt. St. Helens and on your right is a cornfield. We should be landing in approximately 13 seconds. Please place your tray in the upright position and have a nice day. Thank you for flying with…well, thanks for the company."

Thirteen seconds? You can't raid the bar in thirteen seconds! Nobody should hit the ground at 600mph without at least two drinks. That's totally unfair! Just ask Frank.

So regardless of legitimate fears, yearlings cannot idly grow old hanging around the same bedroom they were born in. Children yes, yearlings no. Naturally, most young horses are somewhat reluctant to leave the divine comfort of the old homestead. And why would they want to leave? Free food, their own room, no curfew and few, if any enforceable rules. They know Mr. Broccoli Head (aka, the farm manager) is a sucker for any lame excuse and more than willing to hide in the mobile home rather than deal with direct confrontations. Chicken? Yeah, check my feathers. Two things I hate: flying a twin-engine plane where one turbine is flopping around on the runway with my missing baggage and secondly, being eaten alive by a bunch of four-legged sharks disguised as vegetarians.

Therapists have no clear-cut answers for youthful nesting, that process whereby a kid who should be at Harvard is instead barricaded in his room with a basketball and forty-seven pairs of rancid socks. Oh sure, for $125-an-hour most therapists would be more than happy to explore the nuances of the youthful psyche stretched out on their leather couch, but their ultimate prognosis would be delivered from a comfortable lawn chair overlooking the Gulf of Mexico. It's amazing how much money one question can generate: "How do you feel about that?"

"Terrible."

"Good, that'll be $125."

"Time," they would say. "The child needs some time. Perhaps we should explore alternative therapy…say, at the Waikiki Center for Supportive Screaming. It's very radical, but close to most of the major beaches."

For $100,000 you can get a good tan and hope your wayward child gets caught in a rip tide and exported to Japan. Just don't report him or her missing. Otherwise, you have to re-claim the body, breathing or not.

Most good parents simply acquiesce. Bad parents ask relevant questions. Kind of like that *broke* and *unbroke* thing. It is a subjective process determined by the ratio of self-generated guilt weighed against a simple parental desire to once again live alone. Guilt normally defeats common sense, one stupid kid who escaped the womb can be more threatening than a potential stint in purgatory. Think about that before you have children. They're kind of cute in the beginning, but they don't come with instructions. They also don't come with a fully developed brain. My yearlings are not too different.

The real enigma lies in the choice of transportation. Children normally go by car – one parent sacrificing a Honda with 142,000 miles on it — yearlings relying on horse trailers or some variation on that theme. Most are utilitarian in nature, well-designed and pleasing to the artistic eye of humans. Just enough chrome to be fashionable, but not so much that someone would mistake it for a flesh purveyor's new Cadillac. Yearlings perceive chrome as a relative of the Kodiak bear and even though Kodiak bears haven't eaten any yearlings in centuries, most young horses won't bet their life on even those arguably long odds.

I think horse trailers should be built with yearlings in mind. Instead of smooth, shiny metal, they should be designed to look more like a yearling's natural habitat…a pasture perhaps. Grass growing on the loading ramp, a few plastic ducks off in one corner. Or, maybe the loafing shed look, whereas the whole trailer looks like a hay manger going down the freeway. My favorite is what might evolve out of the Freudian camp – the womb on wheels; a fiberglass replica of a mare's uterus that the yearling enters from the rear. They know they will be safe in there, swimming in the calm currents of the amniotic ocean. Whatever the design, the end result must be the equation of one yearling, plus one trailer, equals *bon voyage*.

This year's fall itinerary included three yearlings that never quite made it to the early sales. Apparently some quality control issue over at the sales company. Since most of the tribe had been hanging around the sheds all summer, my first job was to re-establish some form of communication. A week before they were scheduled to depart, I personally captured each yearling and placed it in a stall. After a brief trip to the emergency room, I hobbled back to the farm to re-introduce myself. The yearlings reacted to their confinement in a predictable manner: twelve-hundred board-feet of No. 2 fir was immediately downgraded. Still I've always felt that with horses it is important to size up the competition before attempting anything that involves a meeting of the minds – more accurately, the collision of two large rocks. This tends to cut the bloodshed to a reasonable level while allowing everyone's ego a fashionable route of escape. Sort of like being an usher at the UN.

Once I've captured them, I jot down a few notes about their overall behavior, hoping to classify them into one of the four major psychological groups. Most will be either A) a spook, B) an airhead, C) a sulker, or D), some combination involving the worst characteristics of a motorcycle gang. These classifications are critical in ascertaining the order of loading. Obviously, the sulker can't go first, as there would be entirely too much to sulk about. The airhead can't be number one either as that's how they end up inverted in the bottom of the trailer. And of course, forget the one with the motorcycle gang aberrations, as there is still the remote possibility of it developing some sort of terminal health problem before it has to travel. So, that only leaves the spooky one. Jesse appreciated my psychoanalysis, but not much else.

"Hi Jess. Say, have you got any plans Friday morning?"

"Doc already asked."

"Sorry?"

"No."

"It wasn't a marriage proposal for God's sake. Just throwing a few yearlings into a van. I'll buy dinner. Somewhere nice." God I felt cheap and patronizing. Okay, whatever works. I can't lead a yearling and swat its ass at the same time. My arms aren't long enough.

"Like my birthday?"

"Why don't women ever get amnesia?"

"Because men have a patent on it!"

"So…you wouldn't help me out on this? I'm kind of alone on this project."

"I got an idea, why don't you ask me to dinner some time without some kind of near-death experience on the menu? Like tonight. We could go to the Japanese place."

"Okay, tonight." We're talking raw fish spraddled on a lump of rice with really hot green stuff inside. I'm not sure about the brown things that appear to move around the plate on their own, or the microscopic orange ball bearings.

"Alright. Pick me up in an hour."

"What about Friday?"

"I'm busy."

Dinner went fine. She wore a short skirt and some kind of tank top sort of thing meant to resuscitate Rip Van Winkle. I begged off the drooling as a result of that hot, green stuff. The waiter just smiled. He didn't want to jeopardize his tip, even though a plaid shirt is normally a bad sign in the tip business. We had deep-fried green tea ice cream for dessert. Took longer to say it than eat it. I wanted to sneak into the kitchen and see how they made the stuff, but when I pulled the curtain back to peak I was met by three serious looking women with Ginsu knives. The Japanese know how to keep a secret.

Friday came, and that left me with…we'll skip the first and go on to the second: me and a cranky van driver. The guys that drive horse vans all have graphs and charts indicating their overall job description. It's like furniture hauling or a cheap cab. "I only haul the junk. How it gets in the truck is your problem."

Ah, but there is bribery.

I'll get to that phase in a minute. A key issue in shoving a yearling into a van is presentation. The van or trailer should be placed in a strategic location, one that offers convenience and safety for the *loader* while promoting an environment of calm and solace for the *loadee*. Say, the lobby of a feed store. Then, the yearling is led up to the conveyance while the *loader* wistfully hums an old Frank Sinatra tune, which is designed to lull the yearling into thinking, "Hey, this is no big deal." Well, maybe. Invariably, at this point in the parade, the yearling will stop, bug its eyes out and develop the worst case of *paralytic loading disease* ever imagined. All four feet sprout clamp-like tap roots firmly anchored to the Earth's mantle, the yearling's nose directing the rest of its body to stay well to the rear of the metallic monster, aka the Kodiak bear.

So now I have a van, a driver and a paralyzed, somewhat catatonic yearling anchored to the center of the earth. The next step is what the early Egyptians referred to as *tribute*. As the driver taps his foot and checks his watch, I get a wheelbarrow and take a side trip to the house. The phone rings. It's Jesse.

"How's it goin?"

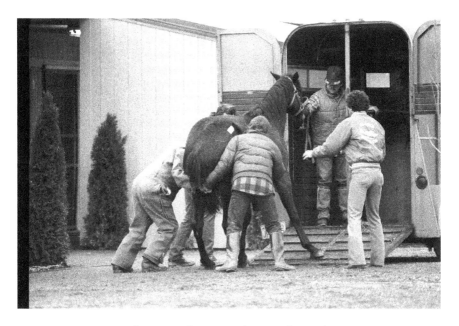

Classic Case of Paralytic Loading Disease

"Fine, fine. Do you remember where I put those cases of beer we got at Costco?"

"No, er maybe the laundry room."

"Great, thanks. Gotta go." I don't have a damn laundry room! She does.

"You sure…" Click.

Two cases of Bud, a carton of Marlboros and two radial tires and I had a reluctant volunteer. He wasn't real impressed with my battle plan, but after a couple of beers he didn't seem to care one way or the other.

Since a yearling's head is responsible for determining the direction of travel for the rest of its parts, the whole process normally breaks down at this point. No, backing the van over the top of the yearling is an unacceptable, though somewhat appealing solution. I also considered borrowing

Chet's tow truck, but that would entail another 'gas tanker over the Cascades' story, not to mention the usual degrading, under-the-breath innuendos about my damaged IQ. No thanks. Humility is good for the soul – I received my lifetime subscription in college. One course I took in the psyche division focused on self-esteem, or a lack thereof. You know those art classes where they hire somebody to pose nude all day? It shouldn't take a genius to figure out how I got an 'A' in Psych 101. Never wrote a paper, never read a book. I just stood in front of the class like a human dartboard. I was a living example of everything chronically wrong with the human race and probably certain dogs. The downside was that I had to date in other divisions, primarily the English department, since most English majors were embracing insanity anyway. It was the only way to get ahead. The guy who wrote "Dick and Jane?" Straight to the poorhouse. Hunter Thompson? Fame, misfortune and an open account at some obscure bar in Colorado. Of course, I can't read him anymore because I think *his* insanity finally went full circle. Or, I've become an insanity snob, intolerant of anybody's insanity more sophisticated than my own. Now, that's an interesting thought – IQ – insanity quotient? I should run down to the local bug house and find out how many residents were forced to read Shakespeare, but then I've got a paralyzed yearling on my hands, and a driver working on his fourth beer.

Back to loading afflictions. There are certain forms of illegal torture designed to break the impasse. One of my favorites is the 'good guy, bad guy' approach so often used by the police to get someone to confess to something – like forgetting a dinner date. Handler A briskly beats the yearling on the backside with a Nerfbat, while Handler B pats the yearling on the head, explaining what a jerk the guy with the Nerfbat really is. In this case, the guy who's now on his fifth beer and strike six in the ass-whacking department. If the yearling is particularly naïve, it will jump into the van and wait, certain that you are going to go back and deal with the guy wielding the bat. Given that the 'dumb animal' rule is in force, few horses are going to know how to spell 'naïve' much less comprehend the theory, making this ploy viable in only about 5% of the cases. And quite frankly, if the horse is that dumb, you wouldn't want him running around a racetrack without a chaperone.

Another technique often used is the 'lazy brother-in-law system.' This revolves around the powerful notion that life in a trailer is not nearly as miserable as life can be at home. In order to make a yearling want to leave home, it may be necessary to become an evil and nasty person. First, I discontinue their phone privileges. Next I put goldfish in their water buckets,

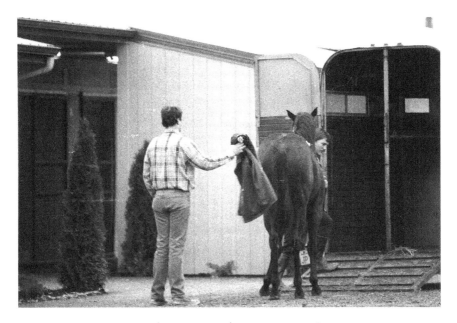

Good Guy – Bad Guy Approach.
You Can Substitute Bat with your Best Coat

anchovies in their grain and only feed them moldy hay. I also trim their feet every day, pull their manes with a dull butter knife and comb their backs with a barbecue scraper – the really rusty kind. If I'm in a really bad mood, I disconnect their cable TV and turn up the boom box extra loud – normally one of Yoko Ono's early attempts at shattering human skulls with her vocal cords. This system works in 8% of the cases.

If that fails to move them, then I progress directly to the 'Clint Eastwood system.' This entails the use of a buggy whip, three or four large rocks, a broom, or a 44 magnum. Whichever utensil is used, it is important to remember that the proper technique will outweigh the instrument by approximately thirty to one.

"Do you feel lucky?"

"Well, come to think of it, not really."

"Did I fire five shots or six?"

"I wasn't counting, but I think you should have that vein on your forehead looked at. Ever thought about opening a restaurant in Carmel? Maybe run for office?"

Using this technique (no, Clint's not willing to audition for the job), I like to begin with an assortment of vague hand signals, waving my arms frantically like a landing officer on an aircraft carrier.

"Left!"

"No, right!"

"Wheels! You need wheels! This isn't a Karaoke bar!"

Ah, hell, he missed the ship entirely. Another $4.2 million deducted from my salary. At this rate, I'm going to be doing this crap until 3030. I wonder if the Navy does instant replay in real-time? I'd rather watch bad landings and paralyzed yearlings from my living room.

Of course, when this nonsense fails, it is appropriate to pick up a broom and pretend that it is the bottom of the ninth, two out and your contract is at stake. It also helps to throw a few rocks around so everyone knows you're serious. If still thwarted, exasperation will lead directly to the buggy whip, a medieval instrument employed for the purpose of spanking a horse – or some recalcitrant slaves, depending upon what century you happened to be stuck in. In the right hands, a buggy whip can be extremely effective, but for the inexperienced there is one important rule to remember: a buggy whip is four feet long; a yearling can kick at least six feet. Retaliation will eliminate the need for dental floss.

Finally, one last-ditch attempt exists when all else fails. It is a true example of the mental powers of modern man. One simply finds six guys (no, not your girlfriend), with incredible strength, great courage and no noticeable health problems. And like a sack of Idaho potatoes, you just pick up the yearling and throw it in the van. That takes care of the other 60%.

Most of this was accomplished by myself, the cat and an inebriated van driver, now somewhere beyond the first six-pack. He must have been a football player in college, for charging full-tilt at a yearling's backside is definitely something that only a drunken linebacker would attempt. I kept waiting for the fight song.

A Guy About to Figure out the Six-Foot Rule

Good Health Insurance is a Requirement for this Particular Method
(Oh, the Horse should be Facing the <u>Other</u> Way – Just a Suggestion)

As I said, I did ask Jesse for a little assistance in this adventure. At the time, she informed me that I had a better chance of being chairman of a dysentery convention in central Africa. I'm not totally sure I got her point. The phone didn't help.

"Well, did you get them loaded?"

"Went fine."

"Fine?"

"Fine."

"Define 'fine.'"

"Nobody got killed, but I'm not sure about the van driver. It's a twelve-step problem combined with abdominal surgery."

"What kind of 'fine' is that?"

"Probably about $500 and thirty or so sutures. Could be jail time involved."

"For you?"

"I'll call you from prison. Bye."

All I know is that the yearlings got loaded, nobody actually lost any real blood and the idea that I could succeed at anything was probably driving Jesse nuts. That appeared to be three positives without an obvious downside. Why does that bother me?

23.

<u>WINNING IS EVERYTHING</u>

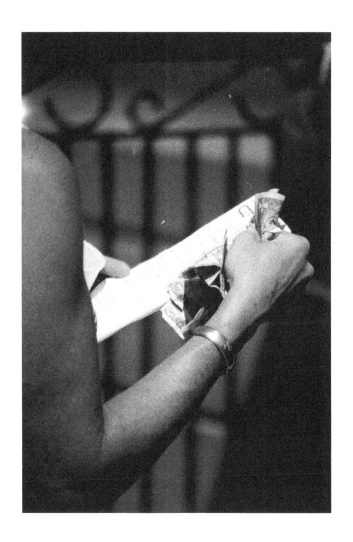

FOR THE FOURTH week in a row, I didn't win the lottery. I thought I picked my numbers rather scientifically: I added the number of times the tractor broke down, multiplied that by the number of moldy bales of hay I was forced to throw away, deducted my salary from the total and added in the inches of annual rainfall for western Washington. I also factored in the dead pheasant count, promised to start going to church, and when I figured God was busy elsewhere, threw in a little Haitian black magic. I was so sure that I was going to win that I called a Mercedes dealer to see if they made a pick-up truck. They didn't and it was just as well. An eighty-two year old woman with Alzheimer's took home the cash. Well, at least her kids were smiling. Boy, were they smiling. The old gal was racing back and forth for the TV crews in her wheelchair yelling for Pat Sajak to give her the keys to the car. The lottery officials looked a little green. Only a commercial break restored order.

With the yearlings off to experience the joys of monastic discipline, I had a little spare time to recreate. I decided that since I was now a member of the racing elite, I should spend a little time finding out what the hell goes on at a racetrack. Doc told me they had a horse in the sixth race on Thursday.

"Yeah, Top Toad's running."

"Good, how about if I meet you guys there?" Top Toad did a lot of running it seemed, though nobody was quite sure in what direction. In the terminology of the game, he was a three-year old *maiden*, though really a gelding, which is a boy horse missing certain parts. The cat will explain that procedure. *Maiden* is evidently a non-gender specific term for a loser. The race was our specialty: a $3200 claiming race for non-winners of one. There were nine other desperate losers in the race. I'm sure the mummy would sit this one out in the bar.

"If you want to come, meet us at the Turf Club around 1:30. We'll have lunch and watch the race. It's a mile and an eighth – Toad should run away with it. Put a few bucks on him and bring Jesse. Elaine wants to ask her something."

"Ah, okay. What does she want to ask…"

"No idea. Remember, 1:30. I'll tell the doorman."

The doorman? Boy, that sounded special. Risking Elaine's pending inter-rogation on the overall status of our courtship, (Elaine had only heard my exag-gerated version as translated by Doc's interpretation of how much I was actually lying about the whole thing, which was probably a lot), I gave Jesse a call.

"Hi Jess, it's me."

"Oh, hi."

"How's Miss Em?"

"Don't ask."

"Good, I won't. Say, what do you think…"

"She attacked the TV set last night. I was watching a *National Geographic* special on wolves. She went crazy and knocked it over. It's at the repair shop. They're re-running *National Velvet* tonight. Can I watch it on yours?"

How tempting. We had progressed a little in our relationship. Holding hands in non-public settings, occasional, passionate necking followed by hours of rabid frustration, and twice, falling asleep on her couch. I'm pretty sure Elaine's inquisition had to do with those missing nights. The driveway has a security alarm and she can definitely read a clock. "Sure, I'll make some din-ner."

"I might be a little late. Earl and I are going to move his yearlings this after-noon. In fact, I'm already late."

"I'll stop by, I need to ask you something."

"Don't. You know Earl doesn't like you. He figured out the can opener thing. He thinks you're gay or something since you don't hunt. Listen, I'll come by about seven or so. I gotta go."

Seven forty-five was more accurate. Elizabeth Taylor and her horse were on at eight and dinner was the house specialty: frozen vegetarian lasagna and a semi-organic salad out of the deli section. Organic was mostly a conceptual thing. People were still trying to figure out what it meant. You know, tak-ing the leap from organs to organic. Tough sell. Besides, lettuce didn't live at my house. I never put anything in those bottom drawers in the fridge. On hot days the cat slept in them with his collection of bird guts. Kept them from spoiling.

The first two commercials were spent shoveling lasagna. Seems it was a breach of etiquette to shove food in your mouth while the young Miss Taylor was talking to a horse. By the third commercial the plates were finally empty. "Want to go to the races with me Thursday? Doc invited us."

"They go to the Turf Club. One dress a year is enough. Besides, I like the backside."

"The barns?"

"Yeah, the backstretch. I used to gallop horses in the mornings. I was the second woman ever licensed at the track. It was pretty funny, they had to build some more bathrooms. Hold on, the movie's on again."

Another fifteen minutes of glassy-eyed interlude. The Kleenex was just around the corner. I kept waiting for Elizabeth Taylor to shoot the horse because it had rabies, but I must have been thinking of a different movie. This one didn't have the right kind of dog in it.

"Why don't you come down with me in the morning. We'll get some breakfast and you can see what I mean."

"Well, alright. Do I need to…"

"Shh! This is the best part."

Jesse showed up about 4:30. Yeah, in the morning. Even the frogs were still asleep. She had two cups of strong coffee. Emily lapped up part of mine and then went searching under the front seat for either a tennis ball or some small rodent that was going to start its day by being maimed in a pretty ugly way. She produced a ball. I feigned sleep.

An hour or so later we arrived at the back gate. Jesse had a license, I had to sign all kinds of paperwork indicating that I wasn't there to drug a horse or kidnap Mickey Rooney's sister. I could have got into the Pentagon with less trouble. We parked and walked into the dark and secretive world that is the backstretch.

Jesse waved at random human shadows while I tried to keep from getting run over by horses that evidently owned night-vision goggles. Out in the blackened abyss, I could vaguely hear Spanish death threats, some serious horse spanking and what appeared to be about 10,000 rakes scraping off the surface of some remote planet. The smell wafting through the air was familiar: urine soaked straw, manure and...bacon frying?

Jesse escorted me to the backstretch kitchen, a little hole in the wall across from the racing secretary's office. Inside the racing office was a cantankerous troll, who I learned had got his job through nihilism, nepotism, cronyism, blackmailism, obscene forms of patronage and the ability to not only collect a lot of dirt on the racing commissioners, but to actually remember who's dirt was whose. Trainers spent many hours of their mornings groveling at the troll's feet to get a *number*, which allows a horse to enter a race it can't possibly win. It is a system based on cheap gratuities, mostly gifts of coffee and jelly donuts, and the ability to shamelessly lose at golf or poker almost continuously. The office is also the home to the *Stewards*, the guys (yeah, it is kind of sexist), who try to enforce the rules of racing. Mostly they confiscate batteries, conduct field sobriety tests on horses, oversee urine samples (horses can pee about a gallon, so that's a lot of overseeing) and admonish jockeys about road rage, illegal amphetamines and citizenship issues. They also make sure nobody has watered the bourbon in the Turf Club, parked in their private parking space or kidnapped

A Typical Race at a Typical Racetrack

However...The Steward's Notice that <u>Something</u> is Amiss

a trainer's pharmacist in order to get him to throw a race. Most stewards are retired racetrack types, who got the job because their tab at the backstretch kitchen was out of control. Racing people take care of their own.

The kitchen was a large open area with group seating and a long cafeteria-style counter wrapped around the cooking area. People shuffled along this counter ordering food at one end and getting a greasy plate at the other. The service was surly, the food recovered from a dumpster behind a Denny's and the clientele looked like someone had opened a homeless shelter in the lobby of a Hilton. Talk about societal enmeshment. I swore I saw Jack Benny talking to a couple of stall muckers from Brazil. And in perfect Portuguese!

The breakfast menu guaranteed a serious revenue shortage at the Ex-Lax factory. Even so, I went for the sausage and eggs, extra grease. Staring at my sausage drowning in its own juices, I pondered the future of ex-racehorses. Might explain the two guys that looked like Serbian butchers that had a shack behind the kitchen. Top Toad might want to think about that image the next time his legs get stuck in reverse.

Jesse and I took a seat next to a window. I just stared at the sausages. The way they floated on the grease reminded me of a compass. It was still dark outside so I couldn't really tell if they were pointing north.

"Remember, you can't talk about the horses." She had ordered a banana.

"You can't?"

"No." She was waving at somebody again.

"Well, what do you talk about? Can't be the food." I was carving legs and a head on my sausage. I'd make a saddle with the toast.

"Look, since people claim horses, everybody is trying to get some inside information, like if the horse is sore, or coming off an injury or if somebody is trying to steal a race or unload a dog. Nobody talks about a horse you know something about. You'll get booted off the track."

"Claim? Like the Gold Rush?" I'd read about this stuff, but then I had also read about abdominal surgery – didn't mean it made sense.

"All horses have a price, unless they're really good. Any trainer can claim a horse at the asking price, like Doc's $3200 herd. If he's in a $5000 race, nobody would touch him. Since Toad's at the bottom and hasn't won, nobody is likely to claim him. It keeps the whole system honest. If a $10,000 horse suddenly dropped to $6250, everybody would scratch their head a little. Could be trying to steal a race or the horse has got problems."

I almost had the saddle finished. Jesse hadn't noticed my artwork. "What if a person doesn't want to lose their horse?"

"Then you run it in allowance races, way over its head or you do what Elaine does."

"Elaine?"

"She claims them back. People around here know that. Somebody will claim Top Toad for $3200 and run him back in ten days for $4000. Elaine will tell Doc to get him back. The trainer makes $800 for boarding the horse a week. Goes on all the time. I wouldn't mention it though. Zyrtaki got claimed at least eight times. Eight times eight is, well, you get it."

Actually, I didn't, but that wasn't a new concept.

I turned in my second-grade art project to the busser and we headed back out the gate. I was introduced to a couple of trainers as Jesse's 'friend.' I guess that was more lateral progress. I talked about the weather and I think the wrong sports team. We stopped at the *Guinea stand* on the backside of the track and watched a few horses cruise by. Mornings were reserved for galloping horses or *breezing*, which is galloping above the posted speed limit. A guy on a bored Quarter horse with a Styrofoam cup enforces the speed limit. He is the *outrider*. If a horse runs away, dumps its rider or does some other stupid thing, then the outrider catches the horse, calls the rider a cab or writes somebody a ticket. Most appeals, like the case with the Stewards, can be mitigated with coffee and donuts, hence the Styrofoam cup – it's a hint. The stand is normally filled with trainers staring at stopwatches, overly dressed and hopelessly optimistic owners (the stand is where honesty gets a little skewed), or various deranged individuals mumbling about a Daily Double that got away. I'm not sure where the term *Guinea stand* came from, but the inhabitants did resemble a bunch of myopic chickens watching a tennis match.

I thought about stopping by to meet our trainer and check on Top Toad before we left, but with the spying thing ill-defined and my grasp on local major league teams still in the research phase, I'd be back to talking about the weather. The blonde on Channel 7 was much better equipped to handle cold fronts or barometric pressure.

We were almost back to the farm when a wild notion struck me. That was aside from Emily tearing off my shoelaces. That's what happens when you spill sausage grease on your shoe. What if relationships were based on the claiming system? Go down to the local watering hole, watch men race from the bar to the restroom and the women put in a claim with the bartender. "Hey Jess, what kind of a claimer would I be? I mean, what if women adopted the same sort of system for dating?"

"What?"

"Claiming. Women putting up a few bucks for the right guy. Like in old days when they'd bid on a cake or something. I think it was a fund raising thing."

"No. Men bid on the cake or pie. It was a courting thing."

"What would I be worth?"

"With or without the plaid flannel shirts?"

"Come on, I got rid of the sideburns."

"I don't think they write those kind of races."

"Theoretically, then."

"Donut holes."

"Cruel. I meant money. I was shooting for at least $3200.

"Maybe $1.59, but only if you buy some polo shirts."

She was smiling wickedly. I lifted my leg up with Emily once again attached to what was left of my shoelaces. "I'll take it. I need to make some repairs here."

Thursday morning I got dressed and headed for the track. I brought some extra money for the killing I was bound to make. I was going to convert $23.50 into a massive fortune. $21.50 after I paid for parking. I wandered down to the south end of the track where the Turf Club was said to be. I spotted the elevator and the doorman, a nicely dressed gentleman of about sixty. I wandered up, gave him my speech about a reservation and headed for the elevator.

"Sir."

There was something a little stern in his voice. I stopped and turned around. "Yes?"

"Sir, your tie."

"Don't own one."

"Obviously. A tie is required for entrance to the Turf Club."

"But I have a reservation! I have people, important people expecting me. I've got a really good horse in the fifth race. Mr. Weyerhaeuser will be really angry! You have to let me in!"

"Sir, Mr. Weyerhaeuser is in New York and the fifth race is a disgusting little affair to entertain the bettors."

I needed to regroup. The doorman was rocking back and forth on the balls of his feet and trying to look as impatient as possible. I pulled out two bucks and stuck the bills in his lapel pocket. "Let's overlook it this time," I stated with a wink.

His expression soured as he pulled out the crumpled bills. "Sir, I'd suggest you keep this for a tie. Something cheap, like your horse." With that he disappeared into the elevator.

I'm certain I mumbled a few things under my breath. Mostly about snobby cretins and getting even at some point to be announced. I finally decided to join the teeming masses in general seating. I rationalized the encounter as a good way to get down with the true denizens of the sport – retired Boeing engineers, chronic gamblers and guys who didn't own a tie. I bought a beer and wandered down to the rail. I sat next to a woman with an oxygen bottle. She was studying the *form* and aspirating like a broken sump pump. I picked another bench.

Fifth Race, $3200 Claiming, Maiden 3 YR. OLDS

Purse: $5000

1 1/8 Mile

SHIRLEY'S TEMPLE OF DOOM

1.	Rider: Dick Nixon	122lbs

WAYWARD WILLIE

2.	Rider: Willie Nelson	*116lbs

SEABUCKET

3.	Rider: Lloyd Bridges	126lb

PURPLEHEARTBART

4.	Rider: Ollie Stone	122lb

EARL THE WHIRL

5.	Rider: Earl Baaach	162lb

BUCKET OF MONEY

6.	Rider: D. Trump	*110lb

LOST IN SPACE

7.	Rider: Cap Kirk	122lb

WING NUT

8.	Rider: H. Thompson	126lb

DONUT HEAD

9.	Rider: D. Quixote	*116lb

PLUMBING PROBLEM

10.	Rider: Art Drano	Late Scratch

*Denotes Apprentice

The *program* contains all the basic information a bettor may need to pick a horse. Stuff like the horse's racing record, the weight it has to carry, the trainer, jockey and the approximate odds. The latter changes frequently since in the *pari-mutuel* system, all bettors bet against each other. The program also gives the horse's name, which is a prime source for wild premonitions. The fifth race had ten horses with one scratch. Evidently a case of cold feet. They were as follows:

The horse that scratched was named **PLUMBING PROBLEM**. Probably ate in the track kitchen.

Another source of information are the *Tout sheets*, little pamphlets put together by entrepreneurs who sell them for a couple of bucks under the guise of being in the 'loop,' so to speak. I think if they were really in the loop, they'd be on a beach in Bimini wondering what happened to their waiter. Since they are out in a parking lot getting sun burnt, I tend to discount them as a viable source of information. There is also the *Daily Racing Form*, which in my case is simply too scientific. We're talking horses, not cruise missiles. I went over the list of horses. Donut Head was the favorite at 5-2. I sort of liked Lost in Space because it described my overall condition. After two flat beers, Plumbing Problem seemed like the perfect hunch bet, but he was probably in the next stall using up all the toilet paper. I decided to wander down to the paddock and take a look at this bunch.

The *paddock* is a place where the horses parade around for the bettors. This is a chance to look the horses over, check their conformation and see what kind of accessories they'll be wearing. The owners all get to stand out in the middle on the lawn and look either very important or highly distraught. Pretty soon the trainer shows up to clarify which horse they actually own. With a lot of help, he or she somehow gets a saddle on the right horse and they parade around some more. The blankets all have numbers so that the announcer has a remote clue as to who's who. The owners have to take his word for it. Shortly thereafter, a small Hispanic guy in a funny shirt shows up. He's the pilot. The trainer then gives him his instructions. Something like, "If you don't win this race, I'm going to repossess your car." With that, the jockey gets tossed on board. Now comes the *parade to the post*, or really to the *starting gate*. It's a large metal thing that launches the horses down the track. NASA uses a similar approach with the Space Shuttle. This is a good time to ascertain how the horse moves, which in equine terms has something to do with a bad limp. All this *paddocking* and *parading* is simply a ploy. The more ludicrous delays the track can dream up, the more time to suck the bettors dry. The guy who operates the gate is actually the track's accountant. Nobody goes anywhere until he's done the math.

Certain things should be taken into consideration at this point. Beware of horses that have their tongues tied. If they can't keep track of one tongue, what are they going to do with four legs? Also, avoid horses that wear bar shoes. I once tried playing tennis in a pair of cowboy boots. I know how they feel. Same goes for horses that *wash out*, or basically suffer deodorant failure on the way to the gate. When I break out in a sweat it usually entails Jesse and a series of slight exaggerations that escalate into blatant lies somewhere in mid-sentence. *Blinkers* are another matter to consider. What is it that they are not supposed to see? Their own odds? Lastly, avoid a horse that supposedly likes the mud. They like to roll in it, not run on it.

With all that information stored away, one simply places his bet. The accountant springs the gate and off they go. I'm down by the rail hoping all those nights reading Dick Francis' novels are going to finally pay off. Oh, I went with Wing Nut. Thought about Earl the Whirl, but how can you bet on a horse named after a serial duck killer. Earl won, Wing Nut ran seventh and I was down to $19.50.

The sixth race was easy – all $18.00 on Top Toad. I waved to Doc and Elaine in the paddock but they were busy admiring the wrong horse. The preliminaries dragged on as usual and finally the horses thundered down the track. Since it was a mile-and-an-eighth race, they would pass my position at the finish line twice. As they roared down the lane, the announcer kept calling Top Toad in the lead. I was yelling and screaming, throwing beer around, waving my arms, calculating my winnings – attracting the attention of two security guards. Toad led all the way around. "And down the stretch they come!" And I was still screaming like a mad man, the guards were going for the handcuffs, the woman next to me was soaked in beer and then suddenly I didn't hear Toad's name anymore. The horse in the lead was the wrong color. As he crossed the finish line, I finally spotted Toad about ten lengths behind in a vicious duel with the last place horse. I looked at my tickets. No money for eleventh place. As the guards approached, I made a beeline for the parking lot. I gave the attendant my last fifty-cents and sped out the gate.

Later that night I pondered the highlights of my afternoon's adventure. I lied to Doc and said I wasn't able to make it to the track. He lied by saying that Toad ran a close fourth. Okay, two lies cancel each other out. I decided to regroup and tackle the lottery. This time I would use the firing order on the tractor, multiplied by Chet's weight. I would add in the $18 I lost, divide by the number of goats that escaped and subtract the number of dates Jesse and I had gone out on. If I didn't like the number, I'd just shoot for more dates.

Later that night the phone rang. It was her. "How'd you do?"

"Good, real good. Won quite a bit. This stuff is easy."

"How did Toad do?"

"Close fourth." Hell, it was Doc's lie.

A long silence. "He ran ninth."

"I thought it was fourth."

"Ninth. I can read a paper. How about we take your big winnings and get some dinner. I know a great Italian place in Bellevue. Might even wear a new dress I got. Had a friend bet on a horse named Earl the Whirl in the fifth race for me. We sold them the horse a couple of years ago."

"Hello? Hello? Jesse? Something's wrong with the connection. I can't hear you. I'll call you back." Click. The cat gave me a dirty look.

24.

<u>THAT STUFF</u>

THE PHONE MADE a remarkable recovery by morning. Getting caught is always just a matter of time. Around midnight of the previous night, I made a resolution. I always figure that they are better done on any day other than New Year's Eve. Mine? No more fibbing. I think I might be in *like* with this woman. Can't say the other word. The other word means you really need to remember birthdays. Plus, *like* + fibbing = permanent celibacy. Or, a really long stint in a single's bar, which as we all know, rarely ends in anything either productive or gratifying. Most $40 beer bills end in either a DUI or another night in an empty bed. When somebody makes you itch, I think you should start scratchin' around for the cause. As little time as we have on this pretty rock, it doesn't pay to go shopping for what you think may be better, prettier, richer, funnier or sexier. Work with the itch. There is probably more to it than you realize – like, maybe the truth. All you have to give up is a couple of sideburns and most of your wardrobe.

The word 'prolific' has been applied to many things. Famous stallions, congressional spending, the federal deficit and of course, rabbits. Around a farm, a lot of things get prolific. The hay bill, the grain bill, the vet bill – yeah, the shoeing bill, if Doc ever really had to pay it. But the thing that really gets prolific is the stuff that nobody can ever think of anything to do with on a regular basis. You know: manure.

It's a socially unacceptable subject. How many cocktail parties launch into a spirited dialogue about septic tanks? Sewage systems? The litter box? Uncle Ebineezer's outhouse? Unless you happen to have animals, which always brings the subject to the forefront. No more flushing the toilet and assuming that nothing really happened. Sure, that chicken pot pie you had for lunch is now somewhere in the Atlantic Ocean, at least theoretically, but most people try not to dwell on it. Farm managers as a general rule don't dwell on it either, mostly because with horses the stuff doesn't dwell quietly – instead it grows exponentially, so most of the dwelling is confined to finding something to do with it before it actually is a dwelling.

You might be able to train a cat to use a toilet (Silly wasn't goin' for this deal), but a horse? I'm thinking here about toilet engineering. A horse weighs about a thousand pounds. Horses rarely sit, so the device may need to be connected to a large vacuum-type device. Then the floor would have to be reinforced, the water bill would increase astronomically, a sewer back-up would require ten or twelve sticks of dynamite, and instead of a spot for *The New York Times*, I'd need to install a hay manger over the vanity. Then again, with thirty horses, the lines would go on for blocks. I'd need the police to control the crowds, the National Guard to truck in toilet paper and at least fourteen-hundred permits from the county. I could put on a Rock Festival for less money. Might even be able to afford The Stones. All right, bad idea.

I have found that the best way to ascertain the true meaning of 'prolific' is to clean a loafing shed. Shovel in hand, truck at the ready, I find the task to be non-rewarding, tedious, odorous and ultimately redundant in a round-about way. Part of the equation lies in the nature of *herbivores*. Horses as a rule tend to poop once an hour. Most lay people do not know this. That should explain the horrendous water bill and the need for traffic control around the bathroom if they ever were completely potty trained. Since that idea is both absurd and highly improbable, we're back to the shovel thing. A common wheelbarrow can hold the typical one-day deposit of a single, unmarried horse. Add in a child, and it increases to one and a half wheel-barrows. Multiply by thirty and change and you might be able to appreci-ate a New York City garbage strike. It is definitely not a glamorous pursuit, yet still, it seems to be the only thing deemed relevant on my resume. If you can solve the worldwide manure glut, then you can name your own salary. The key advantage is that nobody will actively compete for your job. They might want the shovel, but not the job.

All loafing sheds can be cleaned with one pick-up load. That is because I have found that one pick-up load of anything is enough. Any more than that and the high priest of agricultural etiquette will slap you with a fifteen-yard penalty. Besides, in an hour, the horses will have it full again, because they only leave such deposits where they know you will have to pick them up. It's their revenge for letting you ride them.

Stalls are a lot like loafing sheds, only smaller. My horses are all trained to the one-wheelbarrow load system. And it is an important rule, as I have a late model wheelbarrow that needs to rest between loads. If the horses produce more than the old barrow can handle, then they are demoted back to the loafing sheds where they can spend their day trying to fill up the truck, which unfortunately also needs to rest between missions.

The fascinating part about stalls is what horses tend to do with them. Some of our horses are quite tidy with a stall. Others treat the place like rental property. One mare will strategically place each and every pile (key word: 'pile,' as in substantial), right where my pitchfork is going to land, while the next mare will hit the feed manger, the water bucket and my shoes if I am stupid enough to stand next to her. And if I happen to sleep-in one morning, nothing short of a backhoe will get me in the door. This type of mare also views her deposits as some sort of poisonous reptile, because she spends most of the night stomping, twirling and gyrating on the piles until I have to chip the stuff off the floor with a jackhammer.

Over the years, horsemen have attacked the manure problem with all the zeal of a young Einstein. The first revolution came in the scientific pitchforks of the 1970's, the so-called *pooper-scoopers*. They were like giant plastic salad forks. Evidently the engineers measured countless horse turds to determine the proper distance between the tines. If the handle ever broke, you simply converted the fork to a pasta strainer or an Afro tamer. I used mine to hard boil eggs. The spacing was perfect.

Next came the Stall-Vac, which was little more than a 707 engine with a hose. It not only vacuumed up the soiled bedding, but it also sucked up the barn cats, foals under two months of age and any loose shoes the horses happened to be wearing. The worst part was the noise it generated. Most sounded like a B-52 on a bombing run, which left most horses hanging from the rafters, dazed and confused. After a while, even the sound of a small plane was capable of multiplying bowel movements by 129%. If power plants worked that efficiently, the electric moguls would be paying us. However, if the machine ever managed to get loose on its own, it could probably suck the plumbing right out of the ground.

Once all the class action suits were resolved and the Stall-Vac victims identified, an inventor with a recycling obsession invented the rubber stall mat. They tended to save a lot on bedding, but they looked terrible and smelled even worse. Even the most majestic of horses looked like a hamster in an oversized cage. The big advantage to mats was that they naturally reduced the mileage on the old wheelbarrow while helping to find a home for the two-zillion odd used tires that have been piling up in Oklahoma for decades. Even so, actual manure production figures continued to rise.

I think the real solution may lie in genetic engineering. Take some manure DNA, inject it with a few chromosomes from say, a bottle of bubble bath. The horse discreetly passes a pile of manure, (well, 'discreetly' might be a bad choice of words) which immediately transforms itself into a bunch of fluffy brown bubbles. The bubbles pop one by one until no manure exists. Forget curing cancer. We're talking global proliferation of some really nasty stuff. Atlantis didn't sink into the ocean on its own volition. The Atlantians had a lot of horses and well, there's only so much stuff you can pile on an island.

The only solution currently available for dealing with manure is the construction of a *manure pile*, a macro version of the individual pile, i.e., a merger of many random, individual piles into one large and ugly one. Aptly named, it is a concentric heap of steaming life forms that occupies the one part of a farm that you can't think of anything to do with otherwise. Here it sits, rotting and decaying until it either gets up and leaves on its own, or three guys in suits from the EPA ask you to please move it, a task that can be easily accommodated by something as simple as an air strike.

I decided to try the recycling approach. Or actually re-recycling since I was dealing with stuff that had already been digested, thereby eliminating most of the profit motive contained in what was left. Doesn't work the same as a can of beer. You get a few cents for the empty can, but the stuff that overworked your kidneys is actually worthless – unless your boss or the US Army is checking it for additives. Actually it is worse than worthless since every time the toilet flushes it shows up on the water bill. That's because you have to mix it with clean drinking water in order to flush it into the ocean, which naturally brings us back to the migratory habits of re-recycled chicken pot pies. See, doing the right thing is damn complicated.

So first I piled the stuff up into something that resembled one of those hot tourist attractions in Egypt. That resulted in a few sleepless nights wondering if the mummy was searching for a suitable piece of real estate for the afterlife. Then again, if he was already a mummy, then he must have already crossed over to the afterlife. Or maybe it was like Christianity's notion of purgatory, whereas you go from the before-life to a warehouse in New Jersey where a bunch of deflowered nuns and a drunken priest start adding up your demerits. Like the SAT scores, where only the top 30% can get into Harvard or Yale, which according to early Egyptian mythology roughly equates to qualifying for either the afterlife or graduate school. As for the mummy, I wasn't taking any chances. I converted the pyramid into what looked like the Pentagon with a few serious engineering problems. I slept much better.

Once I finished my monument, I let it sit and steam for a bit. Some sort of macrobiotic, biological thing I heard about at the feed store from a guy that thought I should save the world by getting rid of the horses and planting the farm with fava beans. At least I think it was fava beans. He had a lisp, so it was hard to tell. He was pretty adamant about the whole thing and forced me to take one of his pamphlets. It said something about "Save the Whales." So, I wondered, which is it? Can't save everything in one afternoon. Besides, I sort of favored growing chocolate-chip mint ice cream. I could make points with Jesse that way.

Once the 'pentagon' got to the volcanic stage (yeah, it was in all the papers), I relocated it to the new garden plot, which was really another useless part of the farm. All this steaming stuff was mixed with a few tons of dirt until it resembled, well, organized dirt. Sparing no expense, I raced down to the nearest nursery and bought 47 tomato plants and a book on Italian cooking. Now, in the first week of August, I had 46 dead tomato plants, the same old manure and the best crop of oats ever seen, which I could have probably grown just as easily without running them through the intestines of a horse. Maybe the fava guy was right after all, but I still had a question about whether you ate them or smoked them. Saving the world could just be a process of improving everybody's mood a little bit.

I took a survey of other farm managers around the state and they were kind enough to provide me with a few suggestions:

- Throw it over the fence into the neighbor's field. They'll think the birds did it. (Evidently this contributor didn't know about the razor-wire.)

- Ship it to China. They have centuries of experience dealing with impossible problems.

- Leave it at a shopping mall and report it stolen.

- Find someone with a garden the size of Cuba.

- Save the real round specimens, pop them in the freezer and hit the driving range. They're cheaper than golf balls.

- Store it in retired aircraft carriers.

- Import four million dung beetles from Africa. (I better check with Elaine on this one.)

- Find a bottomless pit and fill it.

- Disguise the stuff to look like fruitcake and mail it to your relatives. Nobody eats fruitcake anyway.

- And if all else fails, pack it in with the registration paperwork and send it to *The Jockey Club* in New York. Nobody will ever find it there.

Or, see what the 1930 *Annual Report of the American Scatology Society* has to offer. Found this little-known work in a box along with the warranty for a 1973 Cadillac and a whole year's worth of *National Geographic*. On page 28, Dr. Rubin Navosky went to great length describing coprophagia as practiced by the Naked Mole rat. Seems this particular rat survives by eating other rat's feces. Not sure if that's how he ended up naked, but the article went on to explain how many species, particularly herbivores, practice this rather unsavory pastime. I had witnessed our own foals eating their mother's droppings not realizing that it was a necessary action designed to inoculate their own system with the bacteria responsible for breaking down plant fiber in the digestive tract. Here I had nailed sheets over the windows so nobody could see what kind of weird horses we were producing when the whole thing actually served a purpose. The knowledge was so exciting that I wanted to share it with everybody. "I know why animals eat shit!"

Never found any takers. Seemed there is 'knowledge' and then there is…what, shocked silence. Well, I did learn that aside from Naked Mole rats, the habit is also practiced by hippos (knew where I could get one) and apes. In fact, apes preferred horse manure though it wasn't clear how the scientists determined this preference. That's the trouble with scientific journals – nothing but pie charts when you really need a good photograph or two. In any event, finding a few dozen hungry apes could be a problem. Introducing them to Elaine as 'staff,' probably a larger one

None of these plans seemed feasible as a long-term solution. I finally came up with a viable, if slightly dishonest solution. Every so often manure piles cross that thin line between biological interaction and spontaneous combustion. One afternoon while the cat was gassing up the tractor, he inadvertently spilled about thirty gallons of fuel next to my manure pile. God knows, I'd been trying to get the cat to quit smoking. I immediately called the fire department and gave them a bad address in another town. By the time they finally arrived and put out my smoldering inferno, most of the pile was wandering around the Ozone layer mingling with sheep gas and automobile exhaust. The Fire Chief was chagrined, but lacked any credible evidence since I had super-glued a Marlboro to the cat's whiskers.

Later that night I gave Mr. Fava Bean a call. "Burned up all the horses. So what about those fava beans?"

"Wow man, you're like a rathical dude! Tshaw the smoke. Really bad man. Hard on the ozhone broher."

I suppose that ruined my chances of joining Greenpeace, though they would have probably taken my money anyway, what with all those whales that needed saving from…you know, the pamphlet really didn't say from what. Us? Sounded more like a behavioral problem than something with the environment. I did figure out that you smoked the fava beans. I'd heard that kind of lisp before.

The hippopotamus? Seems the construction *magnate was awarded a baby hippo by some Kikuyu tribal king in Kenya for building a bridge to the new water purification plant that was never finished. It was a nice bridge though. Once the hippopotamus turned two years of age, it seemed that no*

type of fence could keep him on the property. The local fence dealer was quoted as saying, "Just keep him happy."

Since the old king had died rather suddenly, most tribal curses were called off. The hippo was sent to the San Diego Zoo in lieu of a $150,000 charitable tax deduction. Clean water continues to be a problem in Kenya.

25.

<u>SELLING THE KIDS</u>

THE DEPARTURE OF the fire department marked the end of my brief vacation of sorts. August had another distraction not connected to the fava bean crisis or global warming, not that anybody would coin that term for at least another decade. Nobody figured it was serious until a bunch of Eskimos washed up on a beach in Florida and Greenland was demoted as the world's largest island. And Iceland? Sent the tourism board into an emergency session.

Bjork Veédaâttkil: "Come to Iceland and see the…what? Ice?! We look like Seattle and you know the problems they have with tourists!"

Veédaâttkil Bjork: (Inbreeding is a problem in Iceland. Happens a lot on small islands.) "We'll call it something else. Hawaii East. Big Kahuna of the east. We'll have surfing contests."

Bjork Veédaâttkil: "We don't have beaches, we have rocks! Besides, we're part of Europe – we're west, not east."

Ŧhé Øťħeř Ģũy: "No, no, we go for American survival TV. We'll call it 'Rock Surfing with Hungry Sharks!'"

While Iceland was dealing with credibility issues, I had the somewhat select summer yearling sale on the calendar. All the planning, hoping, waiting, and the long hours trying to get a mare in foal are supposed to culminate in the classic confrontation between buyer and seller. Fortunes made and fortunes lost over the ficklest of commodities: a horse.

Horse racing operates on a business model roughly associated with piracy, laughing gas, used car sales, the giddier aspects of a lobotomy, tunnel vision, (or hysterical blindness), absurd but credible theories on ship construction, marginal luck (not dumb, just questionable), air-borne viral dyslexia and bourbon-induced hallucinations. Experience is not required to enter the business and behavioral problems are always encouraged. Just think of the fable of "Jack and the Beanstalk" and substitute any character with a horse.

Thoroughbred breeding revolves around these late August venues. For two-hundred years, the Secretariats, the Northern Dancers and the Nijinskys have walked up the runway and into the sales ring to be flatly and unequivocally judged on their potential worth. Not by some easily recognizable standard like the *Kelley Blue Book*, but by a couple of guys in the back row who had too many double Scotches and a blinding flash of inspiration. Or just the pre-death flash part. Oddly, the most expensive yearlings quite often don't pan out. They have the body, the pedigree and even the wide respect of some of the most astute buyers in the world. But sports are most often a matter of mind *and* heart, an esoteric equation few humans either experience or completely understand.

More often than not, a buyer's premonition is like a foul ball. Close, but not enough to wake up the umpire. But every so often, way down in the corner of the sports page will be a familiar headline: "Bargain Purchase Wins Kentucky Derby." The story, normally written by a junior reporter for the *Omaha Guardian*, relates how Elmer Fustus of Grand Rapids, Michigan, bought a yearling Thoroughbred for $12 at a sale, "Cause me and Ethyl always wanted to own a racehorse." Never mind that their children are trying to have them committed. Elmer's long held dream somehow wins the big one and the following year the sales company has to add a wing to the pavilion to seat the entire population of Omaha and Grand Rapids. Forget the other fifteen hundred people that bought 18,000 other Thoroughbred yearlings for close to $25 million and never won a dime, because Elmer Fustus did and that's all that matters.

The prospect is like jet fuel coursing through the veins. The imagination soars off into the land of sin-free greed…a new Cadillac for each day of the week, eating dinner in stuffy restaurants without making a reservation, throwing away left-over lobster, owning a rare dog from Armenia, and best of all, getting rid of your old friends and finding some new, incredibly rich ones!

Few other animals are capable of creating such a euphoric state of mind, or really, creating a whole section of the economy on their own. And remarkably, in chronological comparison, they are still teenagers – large in stature, small in mind and thoroughly engaged in the finer points of equine puberty, interested more in chasing the affairs of the heart than in where they might end up on the *Fortune 500*. It's great! Animals don't care!

No need to worry about that around here. Our job is to keep the trainer out of the unemployment line. For this August's rendezvous, I had three yearlings on the menu, including my friend Tubby. I was looking forward to getting my bathroom back. The others had been sent off with my new friend, the van driver. So, this August I asked the remaining yearlings to take a short break from their after-school activities and succumb to my silly little structured plans. One hitch: yearlings must be *prepared* for a sale.

My first introduction to *sales preparation* occurred in the fall of 1968. After my futile summer of searching for just the right job, September and the first day of my senior year in high school arrived on the same day. Needing a new wardrobe for the upcoming year (things like bleached jeans, Mexican sandals and tie-dyed underwear), I was faced with the divestiture of my primary asset – a 1957 Chevrolet with a problem I couldn't quite afford to remedy. Talk about a tough call. It was a coupe, sort of salmon colored with lots of chrome – mags on the front and chrome-reverse wheels and oversized tires on the back. Plus, it was raked – which means that I stuck short pieces of pipe in the spring shackles, giving the rear-end a nice lift and me bladder problems. The thing bounced so much that I could have worn my kidneys as earrings. It also had this incredible stain in the back seat where my friend Rusty flunked his first keg party. He must have had canned beets for dinner that night.

I priced the car at $500. The first two buyers thought that was pretty funny. The third guy couldn't speak English, so I was never quite sure what he thought. The fourth looker though, knew a good car when he saw one. We bickered back and forth for about fifteen minutes, finally settling on $435, mostly because of Rusty's misfortune in the back seat. As he drove off, I slowly recounted the fifty and twenty-dollar bills, musing to myself about what an awesome outfit I was going to buy. (Musing? No, more like Pauletting – she was also doing her senior year – for the second time.) In the distance, I could hear the old 283 V-8 accelerate. "Vvroooooom, knock, knock, knock…vroooooom…knock." It made me wonder just a bit about the difference in value between an engine that knocks and a seat stain created by your best friend.

Unfortunately, most yearlings can't be prepared for a sale on a Saturday morning. In fact, if the sale is scheduled for August, then the preparation needs to begin in May and it always begins with the *capture*, a really sneaky endeavor involving cod nets, harpoons and stun grenades. Yearlings are a lot bigger than weanlings so the notion of Doc and I gang-tackling one has about as much success written into it as eleven or twelve peace plans designed to encourage the Palestinians and Israelis to shop at the same Safeway. Maybe the same gun store, but not a grocer's. Since May was back about Chapter 15, then we can all assume that the initial process went just as badly as the first go-around and now we're ready for Step 2, which is a lot like Step 1 because the average memory span of a yearling is 4.5 seconds.

Our kids were shed-raised, mostly because of the manure crisis, my reluctance to be a slum lord and Silly the cat's need for a pheasant process-ing plant. Hence, they lived like Yaks in Outer Mongolia. They were smart, quick and well-versed on all the escape routes. If I went into a pasture at an inappropriate time of day, most of them would be well on their way to the nearest airport. Since hijacking was a big deal in the 80's, horses were rarely searched for handguns since they didn't have any hands anyway. Sure, the x-ray technicians had a little trouble with the carry-on baggage, (a bale of hay and 200lbs of sugar cubes) but most yearlings didn't really resemble anything even remotely connected to whomever the United States government happened to be a little chagrined with. Which of course, included most of the known world.

The thought of capturing the yearlings at birth and not releasing them until the end of a sale was highly appealing. I also considered just holding a sale out in one of the pastures. Doc and I would collect the money, make a round of insincere introductions and run like hell. Some farms avoided the *capture* problem by raising what the industry referred to as *hot-house* babies, where the young horses are incarcerated from birth and managed like potted plants. The idea had a certain appeal to me, but I wondered about a yearling's ability to adjust to the real world. They wouldn't know how to eat grass, how to get dirty, or God forbid, how to knock down a fence. It boiled down to a 50/50 maintenance debate between the joys of fencing and the thrill of shoveling more *stuff*. It was no contest. Doc's horses were going to live like free-range chickens.

As in the case of the weanlings, the yearlings got captured around June, or sometimes July if they happened to be a pretty speedy bunch. The pur-pose was the same: a little remedial education. Sometimes Doc would offer to help in this process, which was little more than water-skiing with-out the water or the skis. Jesse was naturally unavailable. Something about back-to-back sessions with a relationship counselor or a death in the family. She must have come from a big, sickly family with lousy doctors. Her grandmother had at least three funerals in one month. She still managed to call her occasionally.

The objective of the June hunt was to get a rope on the yearling and then have it drag us around the pasture for a few hours until it finally fell over from exhaustion. With two of us, the process could be completed in about half the time, much to the disappointment of the neighbors who are normally camped next to one of the fences with lawn chairs and cold beer. If the show is too short, they demand a refund. Seems the cat has been making a few extra bucks selling tickets and Milk Duds.

Once caged in their stalls – caged being the appropriate word – *processing* begins. Yeah, the same sort of thing that went on with the weanlings, only this time the patients weigh about 800lbs and have developed certain well thought out ideas on how the world should work. A philosophy that doesn't include human interaction on any level. I tended to look at these get-togethers as encounter sessions designed to impress upon the yearlings my overwhelming intellectual advantage. Most of them viewed the engagement as an opportunity to suck out my spleen, with or without my permission. Neither side is willing to give an inch, so after a week we compromise: I give up completely and they promise not to rub it in. Naturally, we're both lying. They run off bucking and farting (this is how a horse does the 'F you' thing to you) and I break out the tranquilizer gun. Modern farming through chemical intervention. Hell, in ten years they'll train kids this way.

For a Thoroughbred yearling, August preparation begins with a brush. Now, anyone who has ever watched a Gene Autry or Roy Rogers movie automatically assumes that horses like to be brushed. Wrong. That was typical Hollywood trick photography. Horses hate to be brushed and Thoroughbred yearlings even hate the brush itself. The conflict really intensifies when they finally conclude that the brush is attached to a human, reinforcing their belief that our sole purpose in life is to irritate the hell out of their skin. But still, they have to be clean. It's like motel etiquette. Who's going to pay $50 a night if three bikers are asleep in the bathtub and the maid is passed-out on the bed? It might make up for a lack of cable-TV, but personally I'd ask for more than the standard AAA discount. Maybe toss in a stale donut and a towel slightly thicker than fax paper. I'll keep the maid, as long as she doesn't snore. The bikers? Hopefully, they'll stay asleep until I can get checked out.

Other horse matters in need of attention include pulling the mane, trimming the feet and combing out the tail. The first task is tedious, the other two, just plain dangerous. The tail is located in the general vicinity of the hind legs, the two main appendages a horse uses to say, "No!" And the feet…well, after two hours of severe struggle I make the executive decision that they look just fine the way they are. That's what's great about being the boss – I can chicken-out whenever I feel like it.

Yearlings also require a certain degree of *panache*, which means good food, no bright sun to bleach out their coats and a minimum of bug bites or any other form of juvenile acne. This is a presentation issue, very much like the difference between organic lettuce and lettuce that has developed a relationship with the chemical industry: one looks perfect, while the other appears to have somehow survived an artillery barrage. However, as I was to painfully learn, *panache* has its drawbacks, especially if a certain veterinarian begins to lose sight of the real meaning behind sales preparation: that being to sell the damn thing!

It starts with an off-hand remark like, "Gosh, I never noticed what nice muscles Tubby has." Which are really parts of his body still swollen from running into the shed.

"Yeah, he's not badly built," I offer, and then quickly change the subject. "Boy, don't those Mariners really stink, I mean, they couldn't get a touchdown if their life depended on it." (Never mind that I got baseball mixed up with football – it's all about hot dogs, beer, jocks, a rich guy in a private box and a coach with more ulcers than an asteroid. Hell, the only difference is the shape of the ball.)

Doc though, is off and running. "Gosh, his knees are nice and flat and he has a good high croup. Hmm, what do ya suppose he'll bring?"

"Grief, if you don't sell him."

It is a farm manager's nightmare: slave away day and night to make an ugly yearling look like a swan and the only person who falls in love with him is the person who already owns him. And in the background lurks Elaine with her solar-powered calculator and a strong desire to get back to Palm Springs. Talk about a lose/lose proposition.

I guess there is an upside even if I don't want to watch the outcome. Tubby did look pretty good for my efforts, though most prospective buyers are not totally fooled by a pretty face. That basically means that the whole system doesn't work like a three-beer buzz in a dark bar. Well actually it does, but that's sale's night. Pre-sale is when buyers like to see the resume, next of kin, a recent CT-scan and what I call the *runway shot*, where a yearling trots back and forth showing off his rotten conformation. This is a human process – definitely – which turns a week at a sale into an escalating series of condemning remarks, blatant tire-kicking and outrageous claims, leaving most of us sellers wondering what bus ran over us. By the third day of the sale, most of us quasi-agents were thinking about becoming Yugo dealers in Bulgaria. Really, I didn't sire this damn thing, I just got stuck trying to peddle him. People with Rolex watches would look at me accusingly, snort and sniffle, blame *me* for double-digit inflation and waste precious minutes insulting an animal with a brain the size of a walnut. Sure, they still might be willing to plunk down $50,000 on what they considered to be a defective pile of bones, but was it my fault? Maybe I just have an overdeveloped sense of guilt – some kind of mental health thing that could be solved with a cheap revolver. Life demands a thick skin, but how thick?

Finally our happy little group of campers makes it to the sale grounds. You already know how they got there, though all the missing beer convinced Jesse that I had a serious alcohol problem. I finally broke down and confessed that the cat had agreed to go into treatment as soon as the pheasant season was over. Detecting her skepticism, I turned in the van driver. She responded by telling me that if she'd known that beer was involved, Earl would have come right over. I tried to mull over the pros and cons of choosing either a drunken cat, a drunken duck killer or a drunk piloting 80,000 pounds of Kenworth with my future inside. All I could visualize was an AA meeting held the night before a hanging. "One day at a time..." Yeah, that's about the time-frame here.

Elaine was busy on another front, that being damage control. She had been through this 'sales' thing before. Doc had a chronic problem about allowing his animals to go off to college. Elaine combated this by putting sleeping pills in his coffee and booking him on a one-way flight to Ecuador. I was sure he would find a way back, even if he had to hitch a ride on a banana freighter.

One of the biggest causes for consternation at a yearling sale is centered around a young horse's knees. They invoke the most poking and prying, for like the ball joints on your aging car or Joe Namath's hairy landing gear, they are the first part of the anatomy to falter. Why? Well, the front

legs carry about 60% of the horse's weight. The hind legs work like a propeller on a ship. Additionally, anatomy tends to cross-dress between
species. Knees aren't knees – they are actually wrists. Hooves are fingernails, everything below the knee is actually a digit – or, a finger, really. The
real knees are actually stifles, the hocks are ankles and racing pounds these
misguided joints at about 2000psi. I know it is confusing, but if you stand
up a horse on its hind legs and connect the dots, it will probably make
sense. Or, maybe it won't:

The Shin Bone is Connected to...it's in There...Somewhere

Buyers approach the knees like madcap melon buyers. They thump and maul the joint mercilessly. Others get back at a distance and ponder the shape and contour of the joint, stopping occasionally to scratch their heads or write a comment in their sales catalog. Normally, something like, "This horse sucks." The astute buyers pretend to be looking at a gaskin, while stealing a quick glance at a knee. Others put their money on the ankles (which are really hands), or the eye (which is really an eye), or that certain *look*, though I'm still working out the connection between a horse and a bald-headed bird that cavorts with vultures and hyenas. But that is our dilemma. We parade our yearlings, corrupt the truth and hope that three drunken buyers try to prove a point when our horse is in the ring.

Buyers engage in a form of subterfuge of their own and for a very good reason, or quite frankly, a whole collection of personality disorders. Some trainers, owners or agents have a reputation for picking out winners on a somewhat regular basis. Regular is a subjective term. Irregular is an industry standard. Either way, the divine chosen are subject to counter-intelligence operations of epic proportions. People peek at them from under the shed-row, behind corners, near Sani-Kans, or try to get them drunk at a cheap bar and swipe their catalog. The object of all these mental manipulations is two-fold: the first is to find out if one's own judgment is hopelessly corrupt, or at the least, shared by one other human on the planet. The second depends on the first, because two people can't possibly own the same secret. Then, the strategy is to either undermine the other potential buyer's confidence in a particular horse or undermine your own. The latter is complicated. It is like buying a used car from yourself. You know the damn thing has a hopeless stain in the backseat, but the price is…well, you get it.

Before yearlings can actually sell though, they have to be *identified*, which is the same thing a bank does when it has no intention of cashing your check anyway. Part of the problem is that horses really don't care who they are. This is a distinct advantage over humans, who spend an inordinate amount of time and money groping with a question God promised to answer, but was forced to defer to the nearest Lexus dealer. Horses also do not appear to know *who* they are. This can be substantiated by analyzing what is known as the *pecking order*, a corporate management tool that IBM introduced in the 70's. They got the idea from zebras. It seems that if everybody has the same stripes, or for that matter, the same dull suit and tie, identity is no longer a visual concept, but a reinforcement tool. Every morning, zebras, horses and middle managers meet in a parking lot to re-establish who parks where and who gets to have sex with Shirley, who doesn't know she's Shirley until Betty gets turned down. Meanwhile Frank, who really likes Betty, finds out that he has to have sex with Shirley, who looks like Betty, but somehow smells different. Frank attempts to solve this dilemma by asking George, who doesn't know who Frank is and is unsure of who George might be. Eventually, IBM resolves the impasse by tattooing most of middle management. Horseracing officials eventually adopt the tattoo as a viable form of identification, but horses can't read, so every morning they repeat the ritual: "Bob?"

"No, Frank."

"Ah, hell."

The ultimate problem for identifiers is that the world produces far too many brown horses and *The Jockey Club* insists on mitigating the mess. Before they order a tattoo to be placed under Bob's lip, they need to make sure that Bob isn't Frank, or worse, Shirley. If horses were yellow or green or had dots and stripes, the ritual could proceed with relative ease, but they are brown, and for some breeders even that color doesn't stay the same. Foals start out bay, turn chestnut, roan out into a gray and develop funny white spots in the middle of their foreheads that look like a golf ball, then suddenly develop into a Rorschach test. Sex changes too: colts become fillies, fillies get gelded, and the sale identifier is left with a pile of paperwork that might match a litter of puppies, but it doesn't match your yearling, or the one in the next stall, and it won't get you twenty-bucks at the bank. What it does get you is two hours with an official of *The Jockey Club* who takes your word for everything, believes your excuses, thanks God for His divine guidance and moves on to the next impossible mess, knowing full well that in six months he is going to have to repeat the whole insane inquiry again anyway.

Finally, sale night arrives. By this point, the yearlings find humanity a little overwhelming, or maybe just disgusting. The scenery has become boring, the routine abysmal and the thought of one more probing hand intolerable. Most want to go home, watch a little TV and go to bed. So do I. But I've got more than the yearlings to worry about. I've got this guy in dark glasses and a funny hat skulking around my stalls. I think the banana boat landed.

Buyers on the other hand, have either found a seat in the pavilion, ordered an intoxicating drink or are thrashing around in the dark forest of second thoughts. Those of us with the task of selling are getting into the first phase of total anxiety, face to face with the unpleasant notion that our yearlings may not be as cute, or as economically viable as we hoped. Coffee pots steam, cigarettes stay lit, the clock slows down – optimism creeps out of the room like a surprised lover. By seven o'clock, the pavilion is full. The yearlings are gaining their second wind. With speakers blaring and people bustling about, it doesn't require a lot of telepathy to know that something is up. Tails arch to the air, nostrils take in the wind and handlers shorten their grip. It's sale time.

In the darkness, you contemplate the formidable questions. The mind spins a wicked weave. Should I bid this yearling up, put in a reserve, or let fate take its fickle course? Maybe I should throw them all in a trailer and make a run for it. Doc wouldn't mind…no, Elaine would kill me…maybe she wouldn't notice. Boy, they are good looking yearlings, aren't they? I'll let 'em go at five-thousand. Yeah, but where could I get this good-looking of a yearling for five-thousand? I'll let them go at eight. Eight, huh? That's a lot; maybe I should do six like I thought before. That one does toe-out a bit, but it's not so bad. Lots of horses toe-out. Maybe five. God, what if no one bids?! What if one goes in the ring and everybody gets a bladder attack?! What if the bidding gets screwed up?!!! That's it! I'll let 'em go at five! I'm not going to worry about it, it's final, five-thousand…maybe four.

Maybe de-caf.

By eleven o'clock in the evening, it was over. I sold two yearlings, one for $4500 and the other for $6200. I did quite well, I told myself. The third yearling was Tubby. He sold too, to a guy in the back row with a funny hat. It seemed that a rather roundish Italian guy who just happened to own that 'San Francisco treat,' approached Doc with the intention of buying Tubby. "I'm gonna buy that colt and name him 'Kiss My Roni!'" Well, that pretty much snapped Doc's brain. He would have outbid Malcolm Forbes to re-own what he already owned. The sales company wasn't impressed. If they could have, they would have ruled us off for life, but they didn't have an insanity clause in their contract. I'm pretty sure they closed that loophole later.

Doc and I agreed to tell Elaine that Tubby fell down before the sale and skinned his knee, so we couldn't sell him. In exchange for that conspiratorial bit of cooperation, Doc promised to relocate the goats by Christmas. An equitable exchange. At least I think it was. Elaine was probably already handing a retainer to a private eye who would expose our clandestine enterprise. My only hope was that Tubby would go on to win $100,000. Fat chance. I hadn't seen the mummy in months.

Around eleven-thirty, I bumped into Jesse. She had worked the sale for Earl. Her yearlings brought eleven-thousand a piece. I acted unimpressed. Besides, I had consumed far too many cups of cold coffee, endured too many vague insults and smoked at least a carton of cigarettes. I needed a Laundromat, a tranquilizer and two weeks in a coma. Instead, I got a really sincere hug and a kiss. Why do women want to kiss you when your mouth tastes like a dead salamander? Probably a safety thing.

Summer was drawing to its fitful close. The nights were becoming crisp and cool, the horses shivering in the early morning air. Soon, their coats would grow long and thick to insulate them from the fall rains. At this time of year, everyone and everything turns inward, giving a collective sigh of relief that the madness of summer is slipping over the horizon. Leaves were falling, geese were getting the hell out of town and Silly the cat was no longer willing to sleep outside. Unmistakable signs.

Bjork Veédaâttkil: "We do Rock Surfing with Hungry Sharks and Women in Bikinis!"

26.

THE VICE SQUAD

I, FOR ONE was thankful to see all the yearlings leave. Out of sight and thankfully out of my life. Except of course, for Tubby, who was again home and following me around like a tranquilized Labrador. The bathroom window was still on his rounds, so me and the *Times* were rarely without help on the crossword puzzle. The worst part was that I had to go to the local drugstore and buy 'Midnight Black' mascara and some red lipstick called 'Mad for Magenta.' The sale's clerk smiled knowingly, figuring I was headed for the panty-hose section next. Little did she know that I needed to decorate Tubby's knee every morning just in case Elaine made a pilgrimage to the barn. The latter was unlikely, but given Doc's and my own track record, nothing could be left to chance. It was like dealing with the Israeli secret police. One slip-up and you had an *Uzi* up your nose. The sad part was that the sale's clerk was kinda cute. Big deal – I was buying eyeliner, not a six-pack of beer. My masculinity was down aisle three, next to a funny looking pencil called 'Blue Lagoon.'

I guess I'm not too different from most people when it comes to either having certain expectations of others, or having them limit their expectations of me. I honestly believe this to be a gender-specific anomaly and once the Human Genome Project is finished the male scientists are going to bury the evidence. It's the only way we're going to get to keep power tools and flannel shirts and prevent a world-wide plague of color coordination. What does this have to do with the previous paragraph? Nothing. Look, after two-hundred odd pages, you must be aware that the literary rulebook has flown out the window. If I had all my mental faculties I'd be delivering pizzas. Writing a book is a two-way street – I write, you try to pay attention. I confess – I'm unemployable! Be thankful I'm not re-wiring your house.

Males, like new cars, fall into the 'expectation' category. Everything has to work perfectly, there absolutely cannot be even a single smudge on the paint and just like the dealer said, it has to do 0-60mph in one second – about the time needed to get the toilet seat down. Otherwise, the whole damn thing is flawed. Now, the dealer would look at this from his own standpoint, probably saying something like. "Gosh, no big deal, it's going to get dinged the first time you park it at Safeway anyway." Meanwhile, you're screaming at the top of your lungs, "I don't even shop at Safeway!!"

Horses and children rarely meet expectations. You may love them, even like them, but sometimes it's a blessing when they get in a trailer and leave – well, maybe go off to college, which is really about the same whether you're human or equine. The bottom line runs about $80 a day at either Penn State or Santa Anita. To mimic Greenspan at the Federal Reserve, those figures are in 1989 terms. Add in inflation, the cost of living index, a severe increase in the price of beer and a certain degree of fiscal irre-sponsibility by every agency we've ever dealt with – well, just send the kids to camp and quietly move. The average cost of a college education is $150,000. That amorous honeymoon resulted in little more than twenty years of confusion and a non-refundable deposit. A racehorse is actually a lot cheaper. Within six months you know he's a dud and then it's off for a conversation with those Serbian butchers behind the track kitchen. Pup-pies? Even better. Six weeks, a little new carpeting, then off to the beach with the profits.

Expectations are a direct spin-off of human interaction, whether you believe that we got sick of Africa 200,000 years ago or that little miscom-munication in the orchard. Either way, all relationships start out basically the same: first comes biological electricity. Edison was working on a human surge protector, but his wife objected. The premise was that a man and woman (no, I'm not going to explore alternative options – I'm having enough trouble with my own options), would start firing protons, muons, quarks and other junk at each other causing watches to stop, VCR's to record Czechoslovakian folk songs and the re-emergence of really bad poetry. Everything about the other person is beautiful, sexy, gorgeous, sen-sual – she smelled good – all the time! Your heart thumps like an out-of-control fuel pump! Your car starts ten minutes before you're ready to leave the house! You invent lies about can openers! Oh.

Co-workers figure you have had a stroke, developed a drug habit, or have somehow connected your exhaust pipe to your asthma inhaler. You bump into walls, wander into the wrong restroom, experience night sweats *and* day sweats, bore people to death by recounting the object of your delirium to bank tellers, traffic cops, produce managers, tattoo artists (yes, you want her name on your forehead — backwards), even your boss, who is already on the phone to the HR department looking for severance options. If I was an insurance agent, I'd be writing policies for people who died twenty-years ago:

"Jim Morrison? Sure. Teddy Roosevelt? Why not. Imelda Marcos? Sure, we insure shoes." I'd take policies that even Lloyds of London wouldn't touch. "The Iraqi Army? Sure. $500 deductible. Yeah, we do tanks, chemical factories, presidential palaces. No sweat. You get hit with a smart bomb and we give a ten-percent discount on renewal. Kuwait? Never heard of it, but if you can spell it, we'll insure it. Is it a V-8 or a six-cylinder?"

But then…slowly…imperceptibly…things begin to creep into the room, things that dim the luster and corrode the sunrise. You notice that <u>his</u> nose hair is mingling with <u>his</u> moustache! <u>She</u> belches after every meal! <u>He</u> wears the same underwear three days in a row! <u>She</u> thinks Ed McMahon is really going to give her the money! <u>He</u> smokes cigarettes! <u>She</u> owns an ugly dog that sleeps in the bed! <u>He</u> leaves hair on the shower floor – the guy, not the dog! It is not just a pimple on the landscape, it's full-blown acne. IMPERFECTIONS!

But what happens when all this judgmental thinking gets thrown at a horse? When suddenly we demand a degree of perfection from a creature that has about one-fourth of our mental capacity? We assume the horse reasons in the same calculated manner as ourselves and are immediately frustrated when it fails to respond to our directives. So we stand back, arms folded in disgust, and make numerous unflattering accusations about its nearest relative. Yet, on the other hand, we view our own lives as some sort of divinity convention, incorporating the rest of the animal kingdom into a broad classification of four-letter words last used at the Stanley Cup.

However, contradictory evidence is abundant *and definitive: humans started World War II.*

Consider what horses do. (We have newspapers to explain most kinds of human activity.) A yearling sticks its head through a sixteen foot panel gate, pulls it off the hinges and stands there like Orville Wright, the gate swaying back and forth on the yearling's neck as if it were about to take flight. The farm manager walks out of his mobile home, spies something out of the norm, which by this point *is* the norm, only the wrong norm for a Tuesday and decides that somebody's Piper Cub is either taking off or crash-landing in a paddock. Further examination reveals that it is actually a young horse taking its first flight lesson, which is unusual only in the sense that Doc did own a boat, but not an airplane. Two options exist: one, shove a propeller in its ass and pretend you are the other Wright brother, or two, call a different airport and book your own flight out of Kitty Hawk. Extradition treaties normally do not cover animals, flying gates or derivatives thereof. 911? My calls are still blocked.

Another young mind suffers an attack of vertigo and flips over backward into a feed bunker and lies there like an upside down partially metamorphised tadpole. I'd rather swim in the Love Canal than figure out this kind of mess. A feed bunker can best be described as a wooden catafalque that gently cradles a cheap casket, which in turn holds a salad bar with an upside down horse as a garnish. Adding to the list of complications is the sad fact that this one is still breathing – not to mention complaining rather loudly to three or four other horses, who are in turn a little chagrined over finding a half-dead sibling mixed in with dinner. Oh, that's the only *real* problem for them. Horses don't react to another horse's plight quite like humans. No calling the police or the White House – not even the *maître d'*. They'll just eat around the upside down one and hope the farm manager will put the food on top next time. You could say they are selfish and uncaring animals. Actually they are and the best part is that they also don't care if you happen to notice that they don't care.

This situation actually marks the first time that the literary theory known as 'deconstruction' seemed to have any practical purpose. Instead of insulting a long dead author with footnotes and questionable sources, one was forced to dismantle the shed to extricate the horse, rather than the opposite of the initial job which was to build a shed and *intricate* the horse inside. [That's funny, I didn't think *'intricate'* with a hard 'a' was really a word. My editor holds two MA's from Stanford. I'm dedicating this paragraph to her.] In any event, the horse is saved, Chet is sworn to a marginally secret oath consummated with a fifth of Jack Daniels and both the salad bar and literary criticism are once again safely clutched in the outstretched arms (or legs) of the anarchists, (or English majors), those revolutionary people who put salt in a pepper shaker to make a point – (no, I don't know what point) – not realizing that the holes are different sizes.

Which goes a long way to prove something that will be outlined somewhere in Chapter 33, or immediately after the federal government ferrets through my will in a vain search for that student loan money. They'll only get the funeral bill. Can't bury a marginal writer on the $255.00 death benefit from Social Security, though you could have a pretty good party with the part they keep. Strange kind of poker the Fed plays when the other gambler is already dead. Makes you want to eat healthy just to get even.

For now it is enough to know that 'we' are all perfect, dead or alive evidently. Most of us have never procrastinated, never sucked our thumbs under the covers when we were young, never chewed our fingernails, or God forbid, sucked nicotine into our lungs. 'We' never 'did' drugs, drank beer when we were 20 1/2 (17 1/2 in Idaho), lied to the police, our parents, the principal, both girlfriends simultaneously, the boss, or anyone in the same room at the same time, facing the same awkward predicament. Especially our future children who are chastised continually about telling the truth by the two biggest liars they have ever met, forcing them to question the value of some virtue they will certainly have to discard later. Instead, we have always told the truth, avoided excesses of any kind and never put a thumb in our mouths (not going there!) unless it belonged to someone else. Right? Yeah, right. That's why we smile with our teeth and not our eyes.

So along comes this horse into our perfect world that really isn't perfect. Instead of our simply noticing the horse has a few questionable habits, we immediately accuse the poor beggar of having *vices*. According to federal law, a *vice* is a Class B felony, normally resolved by the perpetrator doing a five-to ten-year stint at a penitentiary, which is not a real productive way to get a horse to the races. Most racing secretaries don't write races for fifteen-year old maidens that never won one and are ridden by a jockey *and* a parole officer. Besides, the prisons are already overcrowded with perfect human beings as it is.

I like to refer to vices as aberrations, minor deviations on the equine path of life. Most are relatively harmless and only irritate people because of that perfection thing. I try to impart that philosophy on Jesse whenever she starts exploring my emotional closet. It's that chromosomal obsession women have to fix something – usually a man. Why more women don't go into the remodeling business puzzles me. I guess fixing a patio just doesn't rank up there with 200,000 years of defective genes and the chance to turn *Homo defectus* into a Cocker spaniel.

Cribbing is a good example of an equine bad habit. Derived from the Queen's English, the term attempts to explain how some horses grab the 'corn crib' (which is basically a food repository), in their teeth and belch in reverse. A corn crib is nothing more than a feed manger – horses don't do formal dining, so it's just a box where you throw in the food and clean up the slobber later. That of course demotes most farm managers to something like a busboy at a pie-eating contest. Blame it on the *Brits* – they always come up with terms that if pronounced with enough nasal discharge some-how sound terribly important, if not totally inaccurate. Horses don't eat much corn. In England, oats are called corn, probably because England is too cold to grow corn, which brings up the issue of the Boston Tea Party. You see, the British also couldn't grow tea either because of the cold, so they traded opium for tea with the Chinese figuring that once the habit got going, negotiations would be a lot more one-sided than they already were, allowing for a more aggressive approach for the third leg of their commerce – kidnapping Africans to sell to white people. England sort of specialized in the import and export of bad habits. Boston had to dump the tea since most kidnapped Africans couldn't swim and well, Chinese dope fiends were in short supply. We actually preferred the French more than the English because mostly they just shopped for clothes. Of course I'm still not sure what the English call corn. Probably wheat. Maybe Canada. I don't have a clue. However, once independence was assured, we decided to race our horses in the opposite direction – counter-clockwise. You know, don't slam the gate on your way home.

Horses normally eat hay, oats (corn), barley and grass. Every so often they go for farm manager's shirts, small BMWs, a farrier's favorite baseball cap, dirt, rocks and the careless cat. For special treats, they prefer apples, carrots, bananas, grapes and a pint of Guinness. And as I addressed earlier, the appetizer menu includes fence posts, expensive trees and plywood. They prefer interior plywood – something about the glue. Definitely an eclectic diet. And here I thought Guido was the only culinary school dropout.

I don't think *cribbers* get enough credit for thinking up the habit. I have never met a *cribber* who wasn't smarter than the average horse. After all, most racehorses sit around all day in a stall waiting for something to happen. Usually, nothing does. Maybe a rat runs by, or somebody stops by to sit on their backs, but otherwise it is pretty dull. Some horses get regu-lar visits by rather attractive grooms (girls) with a manure fetish, or more likely, Manuel from Barcelona who gave up maiming bulls in favor of per-forating horses with a pitchfork. So, they lock their teeth on the stall door, make a really obnoxious sound and swallow some air. Compared to compulsive vacuum cleaning or getting arrested in a Reno hotel room with your 'niece,' the habit seems pretty harmless. But it definitely isn't perfect. And there's always the problem of where all that air ends up.

Weaving is another one of those aberrations, except that it's a lot more complicated than *cribbing* because it requires a certain degree of coordination. Not every horse can be a weaver. They either become a *faller* (which probably *is* a vice), or they switch to something they can handle, like *cribbing*. Really, it is nothing more than a field sobriety test for an animal that A) couldn't fit on a bar stool, or B) drive a stick shift. However, they can fall off their own legs, which is a problem in itself since it's about an eight-foot free-fall to the ground. Think if giraffes took on this hobby, or worse yet, if the track's jockeys got wind of this odd habit. The truth is that w*eaving* is little more than a real-estate hunt, whereby the horse rocks back and forth in some vain attempt to change the scenery either by suffering a stroke or knocking itself unconscious on a wall. Human comparisons are rare, unless you consider professional wrestling or NASCAR, though I'm not sure the two are really much different.

Some other habits seem to have questionable value, at least as far as cause and effect goes. Biting is one of them. It's perfectly understandable in stud colts, as I can clearly remember being fourteen and wanting to plant an incisor into Paulette. However, other forms of biting seem to have a certain masochistic bent to them. A good example is biting an owner. A typical owner shovels money into a racehorse at the speed of sound, buying the best food, a warm bed, trainers, veterinarians, blacksmiths, etc. – all without the advantage of depreciation, which the IRS reserves for people who appear to be in control of their faculties.

A typical owner stops by the track on a Sunday morning to say, "Hi," and gets bitten in the arm. Women have it even worse – an appendage problem. Wander up to a stall door and suddenly they're missing half a bra and nothing – cash, jewels, self-disemboweling – zero, zip, nothing will mitigate the assault. I can only imagine the pain. Then again, I can compare it to…nope. I just don't care to be within 5000 miles of it.

Horses do not bite like dogs or even humans. Carnivores like to punch holes and then remove bite-sized chunks suitable for the *hors d'oeuvre* tray. Sharks do main courses and are not fussy about including surf boards, Zodiacs (with or without the motor), oars, rubber suits, other sharks or anyone dumb enough to swim to the rescue. A little like Guido's bunch, only with fewer witnesses. Actually, goats are in a category all their own. They don't bite people, they just eat their accessories.

Since horses are herbivores, their teeth are designed for shearing. When a horse bites a human or another horse, it grabs a large mouthful of flesh, clamping it securely with its front teeth. Since it can't actually cut off the flesh like a knife would, it just squeezes it like a wad of bubble gum until it hears either a horrible scream or certain key words, which I can't disclose here due to the obscenity clause in my publishing contract. As the horse releases its grip, the flesh gives off a distinctive 'pop,' which is actually a bunch of capillaries exploding into the surrounding flesh. The end result is an industrial size hickey that goes from hepatitis yellow to plum purple in about 27 seconds or less. Most humans retaliate with a left hook, a baseball bat or a stone-faced lawyer with no sense of chivalry *or* humor.

How many dogs would get away with such behavior? "No, I'm not going to fetch that damn ball again, I'm going to chew off your scrotum!" So what if it's a Jack Russell terrier talking. Even a twelve-inch tall habitual killer deserves a degree of respect, especially when it's half way up your pants leg.

I really think biting owners is an environmentally induced phenomenon, similar to the wild hand gestures people exhibit when trying to merge onto a busy freeway. It is not that they want to kill the guy in the blue Toyota, they want to really kill everybody so that merging doesn't require any sort of thought process. Maybe it's a reality check of sorts, kind of like shooting your mouth off in a bar full of tattooed women. Everything in a horse's life has been orchestrated to make it feel like a star – thereby allowing it to lose track of its Biblical origins as a humble farm animal. I've seen this happen to young women like Paris Hilton, who, in a vain search for honest parental affection, make a porn flick instead. Psychologists refer to this as...well, they'd have to see the movie first. The sensible thing for the horse to do in these cases is to bite the owner, (the horse, not Paris) get popped in the mouth and feel so much better afterward. As if to say, "Whew, I needed that!"

The last bad habit involves the feet, and the horse happens to have four of them. Occasionally they use them to kick people, but since that action is normally fatal, retaliation is a moot issue. Surviving members of the kickee's family normally sell the horse, continue to race it under an alias or use the insurance money to pick up a few promising yearlings. This of course, after a suitable period of mourning, the time frame adjusted according to Keeneland's fall sales schedule.

A double standard does exist here in that most cases of animal homicide are resolved in the racing secretary's office and not the county jail. A dead owner produces a lot less paperwork than a dead horse, and if, say, the owner had the horse entered in the seventh race on Thursday, but got the skull fracture on a Tuesday, the next of kin needs to know the penalties for scratching on race day. Plus, the trainer needs a new signature or two since he can't pick up his 10% commission from a dead guy. Complicated stuff, but all you really need is a fax machine.

Horses enjoy this immunity from prosecution based on a ruling from the Supreme Court (2-1 with six abstentions) that basically stated that whoever had a larger brain had 'primary responsibility for getting the hell out of the way.' This point of jurisprudence was argued on that Biblical definition of horses as "dumb beasts," and since the court was stacked with Reagan appointees, nobody wanted to cross-examine God. As such, most punishment handed down was limited to frowning, finger-pointing and banishment to another stable. Repeat offenders just move more often.

What horses really enjoy doing with their feet is stepping on people. Since a lot of horse maintenance needs to take place, a close proximity to the animal is a requisite of the job. Horses have little radar devices in their feet that detect the presence of a dirty tennis shoe. Highly subtle in application, the horse merely looks the other way while one of its feet crushes the human appendage into a bloody pulp. This tactic was quite popular in old Tarzan movies, where the local natives would try to dispatch white social workers and missionaries by having elephants step on their heads. The elephants were kind of ambivalent about the whole thing, but as soon as they tried to squash a woman, Tarzan would show up. The sight of this naked white guy was so terrifying that the entire tribe would be forced to look the other way, thus allowing most of the white people to escape. Any bad white guys got left with the elephants. Back then, movies had race-specific moral values that were ambiguous at best. However, the crunching sound was pretty similar to what a horse does to a human foot.

Screaming and yanking on the horse's leg only increases the pressure. Once the toe-nails pop off, the horse releases its grip and says, "What? What?!" You know the look. Total disbelief wrapped in a snicker. Yes, horses do have a sense of humor.

In the long run, I tend to think that most equine bad habits are rooted in the fact that horses spend too much time in the proximity of perfect people. In the wild, it was undoubtedly a very uncommon sight so see some mares off by themselves having a good crib – or even a beer. Weaving was definitely a bad idea considering all the cacti lying around the desert southwest. No, I think it's our perception of things. When you're perfect, everything else just seems a little bit flawed.

27.

HAY ETIQUETTE

WITH FALL JUST around the corner, it was time to behave like a squirrel and stock up on some nuts for the winter – hay actually. This is an annual tradition whereby you hoard fifteen tons of dried grass so the horses don't have to drink mud through a straw or try to live off plywood or hibernating frogs. Grass doesn't grow in the winter and it normally doesn't grow under-water. Without some alternative source of fiber, most of the buildings would be gone by spring.

Fifteen tons of hay won't fit in the spare bedroom, so over the summer I constructed a rather large loafing shed combined with an area to accom-modate the 300 or so bales of hay. This was strategic thinking on my part, (it does happen occasionally), as the hay would then be in the proximity of the dining room, saving me from the usual twice-daily drowning as I tried to traverse the mud flats with 100 lbs. of gourmet grass on my back. The mud flats were also the scene of numerous muggings and purse snatchings, particularly when the clocks changed back to Standard Time. Horses can't tell time but they do know the definition of 'late' and how to prevent it from becoming habitual.

Construction was not really my *forte*, though I was a disciple of the 'bigger is better' school of architecture. Doc nicknamed the building *the hangar* and warned me not to let Elaine see it. Hell, I'd already gotten another letter from the FAA. Something about having to divert air traffic. Plus, the lone remaining neighbors were a little upset since it blocked their view of my escapades. A week later, they broke down and installed a satel-lite dish.

It *was* rather large. I had designed it to house the seven (or nine, depending on whose paperwork you believed) broodmares who spent most of their days working out territorial issues. This is a dominance game horses play, roughly based on a sorority initiation rite combined with a really aggressive game of Musical Chairs. Horse A is dominant over horse B, but C is dominant over A. D hates A, but can't do anything about it, so she attacks E who takes it out on B. Remove E and she throws a fit because she likes being beat up by D. I tried giving them all rubber masks, but the issue didn't seem to be visual in origin. Added to that disappointment, all the eye slits were in the wrong place, so the mares kept colliding with the building or each other. I honestly thought a really large shed would remove the territory issues, but I guess the Nazis had already dispelled that theory in the 1940's. Seems every country they snatched was already full of people and we know how they took care of that 'problem.' Me, I'd need a shed the size of Algeria. At least I had enough room for the hay. The rest of the issues fell under the heading of 'anger management,' which is something I normally reserve for tractors and power tools. A direct confrontation with the broodmares would certainly end my career as a human being. That would make me an F on the current societal scale and we all know what an F means. Ask any cop who wanders into a domestic dispute with exactly one ounce of optimism. That's why they carry guns – if things really deteriorate, at least they can shoot themselves.

The hay business is complicated. The best hay is grown in eastern Washington, on the other side of Chet's infamous Cascade Mountains. Western Washington can grow hay, but it is considered quite inferior to the good stuff. A little like the marketing strategy of pot growers or coffee salesmen. "These beans were cultivated by Mayan kings who used sacrificed women for fertilizer. They were very happy to die for Starbucks." Or, "Hey man, this pot was grown in southern Sudan by Romanian gypsies expelled by the United States for simply selling aluminum siding. Man, this is heavy stuff. Blow your head clean off. Only $2000 a kilo. I'll throw in the rolling papers."

This hay snobbery was created by a bunch of defrocked scientists on the hay payroll who circulated a lot of rumors to the press. Stuff about dead frogs, baled up slugs, recycled newsprint, etc. The truth was that they were actually right, but like the White House, they needed to justify being wrong by dreaming up absurd research to prove they were right. After your migraine subsides, this will somehow make sense, though in a very convoluted manner. I'd just focus on the price of a *latte*, inject the same economic principles and apply for permanent mental disability benefits. Just tell them you tried to buy some hay. They'll understand.

Racehorses naturally require the best possible feed available, being the high-strung, fickle animals they're known to be. Owners embraced this notion completely, figuring it was a hedge against losing for a third week in a row. The PR folks invented all sorts of wild claims about nutritional value, digestibility, protein levels, Secretariat's favorite brand – nothing was out of bounds. Even people started eating alfalfa for their health, not realizing that a bale of hay is 20% bugs. And since it sort of grows on the ground, where everything else on the planet ends up, it also contains (aside from the bugs, both living and dead), leftover pesticides, herbicides, tractor exhaust, satellite parts, dead rats, marijuana plants, snakes, gophers, pheasants, diesel fuel, beer cans and probably Jimmy Hoffa's car keys and wallet. And those fields are a long way from the nearest outhouse.

Greed really ran the business though. Over in eastern Washington, in places like Yakima and Ellensburg, hay farmers knew the game well. Since it didn't rain much in the east, farmers could harvest their hay and simply stockpile it in their fields like stacks of green gold. They knew that hay prices would stay high until they were faced with bad weather on the horizon, which would force them to either sell it immediately or store it under cover. Under cover is expensive and in short supply. Those of us in the west knew it too. So when fall approached, the great poker game would begin. With clear skies, the hay ran about $120 a ton. Shifting clouds could drop it to $85. Better to sell than have it turn into a mountain of mold. It was a battle of nerves and weather reports.

Between the farmer and the buyer is the hay dealer. He is actually an expediter of sorts, in that somebody has to transport the fifteen tons of assorted legumes to my *hangar*. Our dealer was a second-generation grass facilitator. Like his father, he was named Ben, which tended to get a little confusing since hay dealers never seem to retire. Most hay dealers are a morose lot, overly sensitive and prone to fits of melancholy. It seems to be the nature of the business. They deal with a commodity, while their customers tend to personalize the whole thing. Women with one or two horses are probably responsible for most of the mental health problems that plague hay dealers.

"Ben! This is Susan. Susan Fescue!"

"Yes, ma'am."

"That hay you brought over. It's simply unacceptable. It smells funny and it's too stemmy. Bunky won't eat it. He's lost at least twenty pounds and has diarrhea! You have to come right over with something better."

"Ma'am, you asked for alfalfa and well, when it's fresh, they get the shi…er, it makes them a *little* loose."

"What about the stems?"

"Well ma'am, something has to connect the roots with the leaves. It's kind of necessary with plants."

"I want you to replace this!"

"But it's only one bale."

My other problem is that Doc is kind of cheap. Actually, he really isn't cheap unless Elaine tells him to be cheap, which is pretty much all the time. Anniversaries, birthdays, and post-tax time the obvious exceptions. So instead of following the stock market, he's glued to Channel 3 digesting the latest weather inaccuracies, which in turn control the price of hay. I watch Channel 7 because I'm kind of infatuated with the blonde weather girl who thinks a low front has something to do with her blouse. Meanwhile, I command control-central, which is really a phone in the kitchen, connected to a hot-line to one of the Bens. My immediate concern involves the road to the hangar, which is not really a road, but a potential swamp. While the price of a ton of hay waves in the financial breeze of indecision, I'm staring at the skies or seeking out a Navajo soothsayer. Ever try to find a Navajo this close to the Canadian border?

"Doc, I heard a storm's coming in on Thursday. We'll probably lose the road."

"Channel 3 says it's only a 20% chance of rain."

"Channel 7 said a downpour."

"Hay's still $105. It'll drop. Let's see what they say on the 11:00 tonight."

Meanwhile, Ben calls. He's got a load at his place that he wants me to look at. Ben junior, not senior. At least I think so. Without a breathalyzer it's hard to tell. Panic attacks tend to make things a little confusing.

Ben's waiting at his yard, a semi parked out front. "This is a good load. Should work out great for you. It's from that farmer I told you about, you know, the guy that does missionary work in Africa? Great guy. He wanted $105, but I talked him down to $100 even. Told him you were a great guy. It's about 80/20 alfalfa to Timothy grass. Good mix."

I looked over the load carefully, pulling little sticks out of the bales with a hay hook and sniffing the results. I once saw a guy do that. It smelled like hay. I decided to play hard to get. "I don't know, it looks a little heavy on the Timothy. 80/20 huh?"

Ben's head drooped and his shoulders kind of sagged. His eyes were hidden under a well-worn baseball cap. I thought I heard sobbing and his worn old boot was moving a little dirt around. He reached into his overall pocket and pulled out a piece of crinkled paper. "Gosh, I'm sorry," he stammered as he unfolded the paper. "It's 70/30. I forgot. Look, I'm kinda tired and the truck broke down and well, you heard about my dad and the liver transplant and I wasn't thinkin' real clear. I'll get ya another load and make sure it's 80/20...gosh, I'm sorry about..."

I just cut the guy's heart out. "No, no, it's great! God Ben, I didn't mean that. It's perfect, really! I was just teasin.' Get a grip man, it's okay. Can you deliver it tomorrow? I'll help you unload."

Ben kind of scuffed his feet a little more in the dirt, his eyes still hidden under his cap. "Well, okay. Thank you, really, thank you."

I jumped in my truck and sped out the driveway. All I could think was that I probably saved his life. The man was suicidal and I was to blame. One innocent crack and I got a dead hay guy! What was I thinking? A half-mile later, I knew what I should have been thinking. The damn news! I just spent $1500 without a weather report!

The afternoon went slowly, way too slowly. I needed the six o' clock news. Finally, it was on. The blonde on 7 stuck by her guns – downpour. I switched to Channel 3. Nothing. I forgot. I don't get Channel 3. I'm on the rabbit-ear system. I tried tin foil, a coat hanger and stuck empty beer cans on the antenna. No Channel 3. I called Doc. "Hey, Ben called and he's got a really nice load. I got him down to $100 a ton. Weather says rain tomorrow."

"Channel 3 still says 20%. I think it'll drop to $95. Why don't we wait a couple of days?"

I heard Elaine in the background. Evidently, she heard something about money. I hung up the phone. "AAAHHHHH!!!" The cat was sleeping in the microwave again. He slammed the door shut.

Okay, I thought, I'll go for the 11:00 news. Jesse gets Channel 3. *National Geographic* was on Channel 3. I'll just lie. Doc is normally in bed by ten anyway.

At 11:15 I was in Jesse's driveway. I had a house and a truck. No dog and no Jesse. Peeking through the drapes I could see the TV playing. It looked like Channel 3, but it was hard to tell. I thought I saw a grim looking Dan Rather describing some disaster that looked worse than my own crisis. The next day he'd be reporting the bizarre death of a farm manager that was run over sixteen times by the same Cadillac, the death ruled a suicide by a coroner who moonlights as a diamond peddler. You can fill in the rest. Or just maybe, he was worried about the weather. No, he was in New York. Sports was next. I was running out of time. I scanned the roadway for signs of Dorothy and Toto. Screwing around in Kansas again. Maybe shopping for tennis balls or live rats. No sign. A TV? Where could I find a damn TV!?

I raced into town, frantically trying to think of who might have a TV. I spotted an appliance store. The guy was just getting ready to lock up. I nearly ran him over as I plowed through the door. "TV's? Where are the TV's?!"

"What type were you interested in, sir? We've got a great sale going on the 27" Zenith's. It's a good deal. We even finance. This is one right here."

"What channel is this? I need Channel 3! Does it get Channel 3?"

"Why certainly. Let me show you the features…"

"Hurry, turn it to Channel 3!"

"Well, I can't really. These are demos. They're all set to Channel 7. It's the satellite dish on the roof. Now about this model…"

Too late. I was gone. I hit the street to the tune of "no payments until…" I desperately scanned the street. About a block away I spotted a sports bar with a few motorcycles out front. In 30 seconds I was through the front door. "Quick," I yelled. "Channel 3! Ty Cobb just died!"

The bartender automatically switched the channel, Dan Rather, still looking rather grim, pronouncing, "and that's the news."

He flipped the remote again. "Wow! Do you believe that! A quadruple play in overtime! Never in the history of baseball. Hope you caught it folks, because we're way out of time!"

The three bikers sitting at the bar began to slowly turn in their seats. It was kind of a slow and menacing turn. "Well, geez, we missed it," I stammered as I backed out the door. I ran the block back to my truck, but it seemed to be missing. However, the TV guy was still there. "What happened to my truck?" I asked him.

"Oh, the red one? Seemed you left it running and it rolled away and fell in the slough. I called you a tow truck. Now, about that Zenith."

It took me an hour to hike back to Jesse's. Fortunately, she was still up. I begged a ride home, skipping most of the details. I didn't lie, I just neglected the more troublesome answers. For once she didn't push it. She kissed me goodnight and left me in front of Doc's house. Oddly, the lights were still on. Figuring that I might as well get it over with, I rang the bell. Doc's face peered out a few seconds later. He looked a little green.

"Sorry it's so late…about the hay, I…"

"I'm really sick…food poisoning or something. Elaine made some kind of chicken liver, God knows what, probably got them from the damn dogs…just go ahead with the hay, I don't care." Doc paused a second, went from green to blue and abruptly threw-up on my shoes. "Sorry, I gotta go."

The door slammed shut and I was once again standing in the dark. I trudged back to my trailer, each step making a strange sucking sound. The cat thought I brought the shoes home for him.

Around 9:00 the next morning, Ben arrived. So did the rain storm. Seemed Channel 7 and the blonde were right. It was a deluge. We got the truck to the hangar and started unloading. Within an hour the tires began their slow journey to the center of the Earth.

28.

<u>THE BIG SEPARATION</u>

SECRETLY I HAD hoped that Channel 3 would win the forecasting competition. It didn't stop pouring, turning my makeshift road to the hangar into a mud wrestling contest, the only real difference being that none of the participants looked good in a bikini. The loaded hay truck made it to the shed, but by the time it was unloaded it looked like an aircraft carrier that got stuck in the Suez Canal. A lot of head scratching and wheel spinning produced nothing more than a trench suitable for the German army. I had to face the inevitable choice: calling Chet.

"Hi Chet, this is Andy. Got a slight problem. The hay truck driver got himself stuck in…"

"Who is this?"

"Uh, Andy. You know, next door."

"#$%!&?!"

"Excuse me?"

"Somehow I figured you were dead by now."

"Well, no, not really. But anyway, I need to get this truck pulled out."

"#$%!&?!"

"That third word? I've never heard that one before. Can you try using it in a different sentence?"

"God damned useless idiots!"

"Uh, so, you can come right over?"

A couple of hours later the hay truck was happily tooling down the driveway and Chet was collecting his usual fee: $50 and five-square yards of my thinning skin. Plus, I got to review his newest adaptation of the 'oil tanker over the Cascade Mountains' thing. This time though, he was evidently killed in a fiery crash – or at least somebody appeared to have perished. No, I didn't ask for any further details.

His wife came along for the occasion though for the most part she just sat in the cab of his truck smoking a cigar. She had on a robe, orange fuzzy slippers and her hair was in curlers. Hadn't seen curlers in about ten years. Forgot how frightening they looked on a fifty-year-old woman. Never mind the toothless grin and the cigar. She just sat there with the wipers going back and forth, back and forth across her face like an old one-reel silent movie from the '20's. Maybe she was pretty once – maybe we're all pretty once. Before the machinery wears us out. For a moment I felt a strange cold pass over me.

Now that I had a whole bunch of hay, it was time to tackle the most monumental of all fall traditions: weaning — whereby the *breaster* is separated from the *breastee*. Simply put, a group of six-month old foals are bluntly given the 'get a life' speech. No more free meals, free laundry, or television after eight o'clock. Brutal stuff, really.

Mothers always seem to take pity on their migrating children. Mine would open the door, smile benevolently, throw my dirty socks in the washing machine and go cook a pot roast or something. I think she understood these things far better than I thought at the time, for it was over five years before she finally took down my Led Zeppelin posters and converted my old room into a sewing center. Which was probably a sign of her enduring grace, as it would have been much easier to simply sell the house and move out of town.

Oh. That's right. You see, every so often the allure of a fantasy is simply too irresistible for the brain to pass up. We all like those 'what if' stories, especially right after we close our eyes at night. We then have eight, maybe nine hours to be blissfully lost in that borderless realm of deep sleep. We alter the landscape, change a few faces – maybe paint over the rough spots. Then the sun creeps over the horizon, birds start making all kinds of racket and our tired eyes open – and we notice, quite reluctantly – that the book on the nightstand has turned another page without us.

Sis left one night to baby-sit for a 35-year-old woman with a questionable reputation who lived about a mile away. She was about sixteen or so at the time. It must have been a pretty good job since she never came back. There seemed to be some sort of understanding involved – silence really, concerning her departure. I was out of the loop, or more accurately, a little busy in my own loop. 'It' was gone, but the presence seemed to loiter in the air. I did know that in the time it takes to cook a pot roast, one can either get to the emergency room and back...or simply look the other way for what seems like a long time.

I never had any normal, paternal sort of dealings with my real father, though we did meet briefly in a sugar beet field. My mother evidently dealt with him before he had the opportunity to deal with me. My 'loop' was his existence. Seems I had two last names, no birth certificate and my new school was requesting a clarification. So was I, but at thirteen I had no leverage and little money for a lawyer. And Mom – the cement was beginning to crack.

Imagination is very important in these situations. Other words are used to define the process, but if one reality is not working too well, then sometimes it is better to create one to your liking. You can't live in it forever – more like a short-term rental, but it offers you a little time to decide which last name you want. So far I had the initials AAKGJ. Put together they sounded like someone trying to dislodge phlegm.

With a little unforeseen help, I was able to cut my initials down to four. I also managed to eliminate the Korean War as a point of reference for anything other than the Korean War. Well, there was the assumption that I was born the same year MacArthur was getting sacked, but the rest was simply a matter of trading one disappointment for another of equal dissatisfaction. My real father was somewhere in California. California! I imagined water skiing and oranges. Imagine, oranges growing in your backyard! And sun. Sun everywhere.

Hollywood re-wrote my movie. I got the sun, but not much else. I found this man in a thousand acres of sugar beets. We spent the day weeding those sugar beets with a west coast shorty – a four foot hoe in the 100 degree heat. Nightfall found us in a labor camp somewhere out in the San Joaquin Valley. We had oil smokers for the bugs, beans in a pot and whiskey for the soul. Seemed the soul was always in need when you've got sugar beets to tend.

My sister had the right idea. I couldn't find a 35-year-old divorcee with a bad reputation, so a couple years later I hopped a crab boat and went to Alaska. Forgot to leave a note, though like my sister's case it didn't appear to really matter. A ship is like an ocean-going horse. A little slower, but it covers a greater distance. I told the skipper I was eighteen. He just nodded and said, "Ya, ya, get below."

I met a young woman named Sarah on one of the remote islands of the Aleutian chain. Her last name was Russian, common in that part of the world. She was pretty, shy and thoroughly forewarned about wandering fishermen. It was her last year on the island. In the fall she would be sent to Anchorage where the children of the Aleuts attend high school. It's a one-way trip. Ill-prepared, they are quickly consumed in the urban furnaces of cities like Anchorage and Juneau.

Many of her friends showed the contorted faces and the empty eyes – the dead lights, worn by those wounded by the horror of Fetal Alcohol Syndrome. They too, would make the trip. I was a witness to the process that is extinction.

I often wondered if a *real father would have followed the more conventional, though slightly clichéd pattern of logic in trying to motivate a young jobless nester. I mean some kid that actually wanted to stick around.*

"He doesn't need college, he needs a job!"

"He's just a baby."

"A job, that's all he needs. Something to teach him responsibility. Like coal mining. When I was his age, I worked seventeen hours a day in the mine. Tended bar at night."

"He's just a baby."

"Maybe send him out west. A cattle ranch or something. Knock some sense into that young head."

"Out west? If we were any further out west, we'd speak Japanese! Besides, he's just a..."

"Yeah, I know, a baby. Geez."

Perhaps that is why I hate the weaning process. All these poor young adolescent foals, trudging back and forth, despair etched across their tiny brows. Nickering mournfully, they pause briefly at the gate, their eyes burning a question into my soul: "What did you do with my mother?" Being the coward that I am, I immediately look away, knowing that they will make me pay for *their* misery by acting like yearlings for the next two and half years – a concept that any mother can surely understand.

There are many different methods of weaning. Unlike the gradual separation of human bondage between parents and children, horses usually need a quick, clean break. Toss mom in a van and speed down the driveway. Weanlings always react to this method by screaming wildly, tearing down the stall, running through a fence or developing some sort of milk-starved colic. It's kind of like holding your breath 'till you turn blue, only more expensive.

Most new weanlings follow the same routine. I call it the *weanie shuffle*. The weanlings all run around crazy for the first hour. Then they congregate in a corner to choose a leader. The guy that gets the long straw picks out a path and head to tail, they march around the paddock like soldiers on a scavenger hunt. Every so often, a voice from the wilderness will cause the formation to break up into small, noisy groups that think they heard something important. After a few minutes, they all decide it was a wrong number and return to their treks, only stopping occasionally to see if one of the group happened to sprout a *bag*. A *bag* being an unattached mammary gland, preferably one that was both available and full of something close to 2% milk fat. Colts are the worst, as they assume, quite illogically, that another colt's penis has a mystical power to convert urine into milk, leading to all sorts of crotch snatching and less than sincere apologies. Fillies join in of course, but they categorically fail to reciprocate the favor. Instead, they just kick the offender senseless.

I can only stand about an hour of this nonsense before I retreat into the house. Sure I feel guilty, but the best thing I can do is to watch the "Wheel of Fortune" and let the boys and girls process the mess. Besides, this is going to go on for at least a week, which is about the length of time it takes for me to lose my hearing and them to lose their voices. Now if I could just lose my vision.

UPS Guy: "Sign here, sir…ah, what's that horse doing…is he…?"

Me: "Nothing, nothing."

UPS Guy: "Well, I just took over this route…Geez! Look what he's doin'! Can I get a picture of this?"

Weanlings tend to transfer their emotional distress to the nearest handler; aka, the human running the place. Instead of coming up to the gate to get scratched, they wander up nonchalantly and fracture one of your kneecaps. They also savage feed buckets, knock over the water trough and dig large, cavernous holes throughout their paddock, either in some vain attempt to tunnel out, or mimicking one of those African spiders that builds a conical sand trap to snare the stupidest ant in the neighborhood. An ant that has an uncanny resemblance to the farm manager hiding in the house with a bowl of popcorn and Vanna White.

In nature (that euphemism for somebody else's house), weaning doesn't seem to be a big deal. Out in the Nevada scrub, mares probably sent their older foals over to the stallion for a bit of worldly advice. He explains to them politely that mom needs to get on with her life, which really means that he's looking for a clandestine rendezvous behind the nearest Juniper tree – milk-sucking interlopers not part of the equation. Basically, he boots them out of the herd, a notion that sends most human parents into hysterical bouts of manic glee. The weanlings then form into gangs, head into Palm Springs and terrorize a bunch of retired Republicans, creating the antithesis to the John Birch Society: peeing in swimming pools, trashing the best restaurants (the salad bar was the first to go), and creating large divots in most of the major golf courses. Next, they would attack the power grids and the cable-shopping network, rendering air conditioning and Ginsu knives a feeble reminder of some ancient, blissful past. They'd also eat most of the landscaping. Lurking on back streets and darkened alleys in well-worn leather jackets, they'd prey on anything stupid enough to wear polyester. They weren't after money, they just wanted to chew on synthetic fibers.

After a few weeks in the urban jungle, the weanlings experience a thorough trashing by a group of yearlings, misfits from some previous herd that went native: citified sophisticates with money, power, quick fists (hooves?) and a network of hydroponic wheat grass dealers on every street corner. Al Capone at twenty-two, James Cagney slapping around some dame, "West Side Story" with four legs and a tail, curry combs flashing in the street lamps of some distant *barrio*.

Visual imagery aside, a few of the smarter ones decide to take a sabbatical at Hollywood Park, leather jackets traded in for something known as a saddle and an *overnight book*. They earn their GED, which is synonymous with making a credible finish in a race orchestrated to promote mediocrity, that in turn designed to create vague interest at the remote outskirts of potential: like tripping over a diamond mine in a K-Mart parking lot.

After a couple of months earning money the old-fashioned way, they write home to mom, send a few bucks for groceries and confess to extreme homesickness – dad not confrontational since most of his sexual conquests are six-months pregnant and not exactly in the mood for anything more demanding than limp grass. The kids are invited back to the herd, albeit with a number of restrictions, most notably a ban on anything even remotely connected to nickering in an amorous manner. Most of the repatriates agree, since it is a much better option than being pummeled to death by a guy who hasn't had a viable date in six months. It has a lot to do with why bars hire bouncers.

Humans though, always manage to goof up this somewhat imperfect system. People want to be 'nice' to the young foals, choosing optional systems like *interval weaning*. This is a process whereby you wean for ten minutes the first day, fifteen the next and after eighteen months of careful attention, the foal, now a two-year old, only requires a gulp or two of milk in the paddock before its first race. Of course, if there is a delay at the start, then mom better be willing to either travel up the lane or leave a deposit with the starter.

Doc seemed to like this new-age approach to ripping a breast out of a milk-freak's mouth. "Well, according to this article in *The Thoroughbred Times*, we separate them for ten minutes the first day, fifteen the next...it's supposed to be foolproof, kinda accident-free." Doc showed me a picture of what was supposed to be a well-adjusted foal. It looked like any other smart-ass juvenile.

"How long does this go on?" I asked.

"Hmmm. Let's see, turn to page 59." Doc kept flipping pages. "Oh, it's a two-part article. Continued next month."

"Next month?"

On this farm, I decided to wean the old-fashioned way. The first thing I do is check for the *sign*. The *sign* is an off-shoot of some long forgotten secret society of Kentucky horse breeders who were expelled from The Odd Fellows Society for hanging around seedy places like racetracks, which in itself probably wasn't that odd – though what they did with the winnings evidently qualified. However, they could keep a secret it seems. All people can remember is that it has something to do with astrology, Bourbon, black mysticism, animal bones and an albino buffalo. Nancy Reagan could explain it better than I can though I am willing to try. Here goes:

Now according to "The Farmer's Almanac," that frightfully right-wing manual for potato cultivators, each part of the body (Apparently this also applies to humans, including children. More on those possibilities later.) corresponds with a particular constellation – the 12 signs of the Zodiac. This occurs when the moon wanders into say, Capricorn's neighborhood. However, since the moon's orbital cycle is about 28 days and somebody just randomly decided to add a day or two to some of the months of the year, the system is kind of sloppy. That leads to all that rising and falling stuff you read about in your daily *horrorscope.*

This system was formulated about 2000 years ago, though the 'Almanac' didn't say by whom. Plus, there is the small matter of the origin of Thoroughbreds, which only dates back to the 1700's and was not only contentious, but pretty arbitrary as well. Thoroughbreds were derived from Arabian horses (well, one Turkish horse too, but nobody likes to talk about that one) and given British colonial policy, probably stolen on top of it. The British actually liked the Arabian horse overall, but wanted something with longer legs. Once they achieved their goal, they changed its name and pretended the whole thing was their idea. That's really why oil is so expensive.

12 Signs of the Zodiac

Aires: Head

Taurus: Neck

Gemini: Arms

Cancer: Breast

Leo: Heart

Virgo: Bowels

Libra: Kidneys

Scorpio: Loins

Sagittarius: Thighs

Capricorn: Knees

Aquarius: Legs

Pisces: Feet

Same as Human Astrology...Though this Guy Either Got Censored
by the Moral Majority

Or

He Didn't Read the Instructions on Using Rogaine

But who decided on the birthday presents? Obviously it was Aires. He got the head. Virgo – poor buggar, he got the bowels. And Libra? A kidney. Aquarius got the legs, but Aqua is the root word for aquarium so he should have gotten something like fins or a good facemask. Ah, but there is Scorpio. Nothing like having your loins rising or falling every 28 days or so. Everybody else got appendages. Thighs, arms or a foot.

So according to our 2000-year old anonymous astrologer, young horses should be weaned when the *sign* is below the body. Why? Because we're weaning the 'body.' No, I don't know what good a body is without some legs attached, but who am I to argue with twelve constellations, the moon, Nancy Reagan or Aunt Bea's favorite moonshine recipe. This is tradition talking. Oh, children should always be weaned in December. You have at least six good days and they all fall before Christmas. That'll save a few bucks. And guys, be careful about May. The 'Almanac' says it's a good month for castrations.

Once I've figured that out, (I accept any sign below the mouth – I get more sleep that way.) I move the victims and their mothers into a small paddock by the house. I get a good night's sleep and bright and early the next morning I tie sixteen inflatable pink flamingos to the fence at the far end of the field. While the foals are all freaking out about this assault on their sensibilities, I quickly capture the mares and escort them to the opposite end of the farm. After that, I head to the phone and promptly call the vet, the insurance agent and 911. Then I jump into the truck, head for Tacoma and check into a sleazy motel for a couple of days. When I return home, the fences are usually a little bent, there is a vet bill tacked to my front door and all the noise has made the paint peel on the house. But the foals are weaned, the mares are once again alone, and hey, I didn't have to watch. Cowardice is a lot more work, but overall pretty painless.

Nobody asks too many questions *in Alaska. Some kind of local custom. It also seems that you never need to look over your shoulder like in the rest of the United States. It seemed to be that place — like Colorado, where kids* <u>are</u> *free. I liked the ocean. Sometimes at dawn, it appeared that an approaching wave was like the future racing to the present, only to escape to the past. Of course the 'present' part was a little tricky since it normally tried to wash you overboard. But I liked the sequence better.*

At some point the boat has a belly full of crustaceans. That means you have to go home. That means the waves race the other way. You still get wet, but you don't see it coming because your back is turned.

Yes, extinction. In real time. An island left with no seeds to greet the coming spring. To this day I wonder about the girl Sarah and those children bound to a different kind of voyage, one that had no clear destination. I didn't realize it at the time, but it marked an end to 'self' for me, that odd little protective badge we wear that tells the world that, "I got a shitty deal." Well, some deals are a lot shittier than others. I looked outside my private circle for once. I was merely a product of circumstances – these children the victims of a different kind of dissolution. That of hope, or perhaps that small light of love that covers any distance, overcomes any obstacle, to deliver its subtle message.

Horses have it better. They simply don't remember.

29.

THE RISE OF FALL

FALL. PICTURES OF the Vermont countryside splashed on the cover of an LL Bean catalog. Hills ablaze in the amber cloak of vanishing youth, wind rustling the tattered edges of an orange and violet kaleidoscope, caught, perhaps trapped, by the passing of an omnipotent God bent on delivering warmth and renewal to a more deserving hemisphere, one that has sickened from the cold and withered in the twilight of an ambivalent season. The sun feebly threatens warmth for the northern latitudes, but only delivers winter.

Cold beer is shelved in favor of Irish whisky. Everyone you know wears a turtleneck from Eddie Bauer. Hornets leave their nests to gorge on the fermented nectar of rotting pears, once a fragile flower given a mission to bear future life — its only mission — severed from the root, cast to the cold ground by a branch grown weak by the migration of a planet on a time-less, predetermined path.

Still, this small venomous creature of the same oval prison rejoices. A hated little beast, yellow and black with a painful sting and the arrogance, or perhaps the detachment of a prehistoric shark — creatures frozen by an evolutionary system that, contrary to human ambivalence, sought and somehow achieved perfection. No, we don't necessarily agree that the final product is one of God's better efforts. After 200,000 years of flexing our gray matter, losing an abundance of body hair and turning in our rocks, clubs, and swords for nuclear triggers, we still sit scared and alone – genetic anomalies that admire the hornet for its undeniable tenacity, yet try to kill the bastard because it represents what we cannot comprehend, control, or perhaps ever be. It acts, we think. The hornet eats the fermented fruit, flies upside down, attacks the occasional interloper and after two weeks of drunken fury, dies a sudden, rather insignificant death. A few guts on the pavement, nothing more.

Death comes in winter, but the illness shows up in the fall. Leaves rot and decay, salmon enter the streams to quickly reproduce, their century's old clock stubborn in its need to meet the next hour. Lifeless bodies, once the great ocean-going Coho, gentle in their passing, are carried headlong into the deep and silent cradle of the Pacific Ocean. Yet the seed, hibernating quietly in a shallow, nameless estuary awaits the warmth of spring, a million-to-one risk that begins with life and culminates in death. And we worry about the gas bill.

This man is not immune to the voice of the season. It begins with the uneven cadence of water striking the aluminum roof of a mobile home. At first, the isolated drop; then a few more, and more, until it finally erupts into a fast moving cavalry, rolling over the vast reaches of the aluminum prairie. Just as suddenly, the thundering hooves fade, again beating their distant, solitary drum: thump, thump, thump.

Instantly, I am awake. Sitting up in bed, I wipe the water from my forehead. Fall has arrived, and yeah, the roof still leaks.

September in Washington is rarely less than an Indian summer. Warm days, creeping toward cold nights and the random storm. The leaves do turn yellow and red, but unlike Vermont, the incessant showers hurl them to the ground where they become a great slippery mass ready for consumption by slugs and snails, those grandstand janitors that show up for dying summers or the last out of the last game of the final series. Walking is treacherous, sweeping endless.

Fall marks the end of many things. Chores become less critical, less practical in the declining weather. The days are shorter and darker, ambition less fired, sights more defined, as if the northerly wind causes the eyes to squint for more than protection – as if they speak quietly to a distant, vague, unknown, but critically important vagary. We came, we conquered; the cat tortured and ate another wrong-way pheasant. Feathers. Like leaves falling, I guess. We're only cold in the fall if we've lost our protective cover, if we have surrendered to a pending winter storm. In the half-light of early evening you can almost hear the earth repossessing the gifts of life. A band of noisy gravediggers that mark your every step with their distinctive sigh. A private apocalypse in a fog shrouded forest that is both bed and crypt. Grief and renewal. The salmon know.

Okay. People also pass at dusk. Their dusk. It is why we sit on the beach and witness the sun surrendering to water and time. It is reassuring in that it offers continuity as a defense against our personal confusion – sanctuary dismantling intelligence, swallowing our grief and uncertainty in the fond embrace of memory. A rare time to honestly choose the nature of our forgiveness, or to simply cry in peace.

Every year, in the last gasps of a summer gone south, the newspapers around the country disclose America's most livable city. Based on a statistical survey of fifty major metropolises in the United States, the statisticians weigh such important issues as air quality, crime, education, employment, recreation and weather, with *espresso* machines *per capita*, being high on the list. Combined, the elements dictate the degree and chosen lifestyle of two adults, 2.3 children and an ugly dog. As an example, San Diego would probably rate a 7 on a scale of 10, while Ulan Bator, the capitol of Outer Mongolia, would be about a -1, depending upon whether or not the reporter made it out alive.

Over the last few years, the Seattle area has managed to top the list of most livable cities, leading to a mass migration by middle-class people from places like Kansas, who actually believe what they have seen in the newspapers: images of blue skies, magnificent mountain peaks, roaring rivers, random oceans, green forests, Ivar the Clam Guy and invariably, someone water-skiing across Lake Washington. They see these wonderful sights in the August 12th edition of the *Topeka Times* and by November 1st, they have sold the old farm, got the station wagon packed with pots, pans and kids, and they are winging it over the Cascade mountains ready to see the *Wizard*, ever watchful for the errant oil tanker. Chet was born in Kansas.

Just east of the promised land, along an isolated stretch of I-90, a lone hitchhiker stands guard over the shoulder of the road. Yes, it's Rod Serling and he is slowly telling fifty-million television viewers the sad fate of another happy family from Kansas, unwittingly duped into a quest for America's most livable city. They don't have a map. Instead, they clutch an image of a water-skier, bathed in blue purity, eyes lifted toward Ra, tanned, smiling, height-weight-proportional. As the station wagon disappears into the gray dusk and drizzle of early evening, the camera pans back to the graven outskirts of that lonely chunk of roadway. We hear those dark, familiar words: "Tonight, this family is about to enter *The Twilight Zone*," followed by a Geritol commercial.

As long as I have lived here, I have never understood the outsider's sagacity. That combination of denial, disappointment with the past, the quest for a perfect future, decent weather reports – things the cat rarely bothers with. Sure, the summers can be rather pleasant every few decades, but even on the warm days there is still the problem of slug migration, chaining up the lawn mower and scraping the moss off the barbecue – or par-boiler, or steamer or whatever role it was playing. Or, in agricultural terms, trying to resuscitate a hypothermic tomato plant purchased for big bucks from the A & P. Important things the 'most livable committee' casually overlooked. But then, most of them live in Miami anyway.

October is the month that convinces most of us veterans that Washington can only be loved by someone who had the misfortune of spending 42 years in the Sahara Desert. It is cold, it is damp and the wind cuts through goose down faster than a rat caught in a feed bin. The horses huddle in tight masses, tails tucked between their legs, counting each dismal minute of the day in well-measured volumes of disgust. Yes, a horse invented the 'sigh.' Every few hours they reluctantly leave the sanctity of their sheds, following an ancient compulsion to seek food. They rummage here and there, ransack dumpsters or mug old ladies outside of Safeway. Some emaciated individuals take to the streets with paper cups and crude cardboard signs proclaiming that they "Will work for grass." Wait a minute. I just unloaded fifteen tons of hay and the farm has enough rolled oats and vitamins to feed the entire Chicago Bears' defensive line. The horses are just trying to get a head start on November and all those crank calls to the Humane Society.

They'll have to get in line. By November 1st, I'll be speed-dialing Starbucks. I bought one of those 'coffee-of-the-month plans.' I joined the 55-gallon drum-of-the-month club. I ordered XXX French Roast with an I.V. kit, fourteen gallons of Half & Half and a defibrillator. The salesman was a moonlighting cardiac surgeon working on commission. He threw in a couple of house calls as a bonus if I paid cash.

Most of us know what to expect in November: a thirty-day siege that is not unlike having a total eclipse in the middle of a nuclear winter. Life mimics the not so distant past, turning the landscape into the fuzzy, black and white image of an old TV program. Cars refuse to start, joints ache mercilessly and those small families from Kansas wander the empty streets in search of kerosene heaters. Winter lurks like a heartless landlord, intent on evicting the weak and fragile, those marginalized by fate or skill. Hmm. Maybe that explains the guy wandering around the loafing sheds with a briefcase taking depositions. I was stupid to trust those mares.

Maybe I'm suffering from 'weather redundancy,' an affliction born of recurrent nightmares associated with the annual migration of that unidentifiable ooze. Last January, I fought the invasion to a one-sided armistice of sorts. It ended up like the *Versailles Treaty* – a fine bunch of trenches, but a lot of unhappy Germans. That's the trouble with losing while you're winning. You're just going to end up fighting to the death all over again when you could have just kept driving a school bus...er, stayed out of Belgium, Holland, France, Poland, Luxemburg, Norway, Denmark...

Then there's the situation with the cat's diet and those by-products that naturally result from the process of digestion. Both issues involve flotation. One I had no plans on rectifying, the other seemed to involve the fall Chinook run – now spawning in the creek instead of the main aisle of the barn. You see, come fall the pheasants trek to higher ground, which is generally in short supply on this farm. They get replaced by ducks who happen to know how to swim and haven't ended up on Silly's menu board because he doesn't know how to swim. Come fall, the house specialty is salmon. Trust me, this was hard on the cat: broiled salmon, sautéed salmon, barbecued salmon, salmon mousse, salmon milkshakes – look, it's a cat. Even fish eyeballs were subject to an addendum on the contract. He actually made a smoker out of the trash barrel behind the house. He preferred a garlic rub with a little olive...hell, I thought about building a fish ladder up to the barn, but the best I could do was to put a plastic kiddie pool by the garage and every couple of weeks I'd catch one and leave it for him. Made for a hell of a wrestling match. The only trouble was I had bought an inflatable pool – forgot the manicurist part. Jesse thought it was cruel.

"I think that's pretty cruel."

See, I told you so. "The salmon is going to die anyway. He's just missing the sex part. Besides, ya think it's less cruel than being ripped to shreds by a bear?" Her nose was starting to crinkle.

"How do you know it's not a girl fish?"

"I checked." Actually I did. Not nearly as complicated as a cat. "See the hump thing. That's a male part."

"What's it doing *there*?"

"Ah…" I was still stuck on why you couldn't eat a girl fish. But then I wasn't eating it, the cat was. "It's to make it look mean or something."

"To the girl fish?"

"Ah no, to the other guy fish."

"Thought so."

Decided to go back to pondering why anybody would want to invade Holland – another place that was always on the brink of having salmon spawn downtown. Seemed I had the fall jitters, like maybe I was over pre-pared, under prepared – probably overly under prepared. Cold fronts were lurking offshore, thirsty dirt onshore. All the actors in the wings. Made for a great Hollywood saga – Charlton Heston and Kirk Douglas battling the ooze, Marlon Brando playing the part of the mud. Kevin Costner convert-ing the whole mess into a three-hour epic replete with numerous flash-backs, (they recycle pretty fast around here) historical *non sequiturs* and the usual disclaimers: "No animals were hurt in the production of this film. However…" I especially hated that last part.

When I first took this position last winter, I never thought that I would be learning the intricacies of goo management. Sort of like first-grade art class combined with a stint in the Army Corp of Engineers. My overabun-dant ego got confused with a spine that once belonged to *Acclimates*. Okay, so I invented a couple of cheap gods especially suited to the peculiar needs of Seattle and maybe myself. Women and weather are really not that dif-ferent. *Acclimates* is the God of Adjustment. He figured out that men and women had a lot more to argue about than opposing plumbing and that it was better for him to just throw in the towel than argue the points of law, god hierarchy or the Earth Mother, the latter one of those "Nah, nah, nah, I've got a womb and you don't" speeches meant to reinforce what you already figured out in a bath-tub-sharing ceremony when you were about five years old. And here you felt sorry for little sis cause she obviously was born with some kind of birth defect. Hah! Why do you suppose they name hurricanes after women? Because it has a nice ring to it?

Fail to honor the god's rules and you end up like *Prometheus*, chained to a rock with an eagle (disguised as a cat or…) shredding your liver. The problem with Greek mythology is that it seems to deal with both absolutes and contradictions. You have the 'guy gods' like Zeus and Neptune who seem all full of wrath and acrimony, ordering toadies around, yet they were always getting a haircut or something because they fooled around with girl goddesses or worse yet, mortals. Not much has changed, but I still managed to flunk Greek mythology because I believed something *had* changed, but failed to notice that nothing really did, other than the outfits – a breezy toga versus a flannel shirt. The only guy in all of this ancient mortal bashing I could really figure out was *Dionysus*, who had a thing about red wine and promiscuous sex. Most of the guys remembered that part because it sounded like the perfect Saturday night. It rarely worked out, but it was a hell of a fantasy. And with fall's angry footstep getting louder by the day, musing over *muses* was a far more optimistic pursuit than following the weather girl on Channel 7. She'd already switched to turtlenecks.

All things considered, my previous years' experience had left me feeling on the optimistic side of plucky – post-plucked sort of. I had developed a technique for making water run uphill (without divine intervention), the hay was stored above the high tide marker and it was safe to use electricity in the barn. So far the work was holding, but October showers were merely the enemy probing the defenses for weak spots. The cat was once again struggling with hygiene issues. On the rainy days, his offerings would float away again and he'd scurry after them, though he didn't exhibit the same level of enthusiasm he showed the previous season. Once his offerings hit one of the new ditches, he couldn't outrun them without falling in himself. I couldn't tell if he was just depressed or merely working out the details of retribution. He was pretty good at masking his emotions. I'd watch my back just the same.

I had bought at least a dozen litter trays and boxes of stuff that cats supposedly find 'defecating-friendly.' I spread them around the barn area, but he never bothered with them. Mostly the rats used them as a cheap flophouse, since they knew that the cat preferred poultry anyway. I even went to the library to see if there was a book on kitty potty training. Rubbing a cat's nose in its own urine would require the use of about six Vikings and a tranquilizer gun. A contaminated sock drawer was a lot easier to deal with than a really pissed-off cat. Particularly one that had picked up on that uniquely human desire for revenge.

Even with the opening salvo of fall's bitter campaign, I was not willing to give up on farming, which I still insist is what I actually do. I broke out the rubber boots and set off for the hinterland. There was always a tree to maim, a fence to rebuild or some manure to kick around. Daytime television would drive you outdoors anyway. Erica Kane gets married, Erica Kane has an affair, she divorces, she has amnesia, she's hit by a train – the latter a cheap ploy aimed at sucking in an audience from the chronically depressed folks that believe Johnny Cash is a motivational speaker who just happens to play a guitar. Flip the channel and its three people from Arkansas with bad teeth fighting to the death over a spinning wheel, somehow deluded into the notion that Pat Sajak is going to give them a Chevrolet that GM couldn't sell anyway.

In the pre-cable years, daytime television boasted three network channels and the occasional outlier that always got stuck with either Channel 11 or 13. No, I don't know what was wrong with Channels 8-10. They were probably reserved for those early Conelrad Bulletins that announced the ten-minute warning five minutes after the first A-bomb landed in your backyard. (Conelrad meant: **C**ontrol of **E**lectromagnetic **R**adiation – that's an oxymoron in case you were wondering.) I doubt anyone was fiddling with the rabbit ears by then anyway. Yeah, we were under our desks at school doing the math on the 12-mile radius. Most of our equations indicated that summer vacation would be early that year.

The network channels offered three choices according to what decade you happened to be stuck in: soap operas, game shows or re-runs. So you got "Gilligan's Island," "The Mod Squad," "The Six Million-Dollar Man," Erica Kane, or somebody trying to figure out the price of a can opener. Farming shows included "Little House on the Prairie" and "Green Acres," though it really didn't appear that agriculture was an integral element of the storyline – well, wait a minute. "Green Acres" had a blond who knew how to shop, a guy who fixed things with baling twine and a pig with a high IQ. No wonder I liked that show.

Channel 11 or 13 were the most fascinating though, but only if you had the patience to watch and hold the horizontal stabilizer at the same time. Believe me, this takes some concentration, especially if Red Skelton is on. These channels were so financially strapped that they had to buy shows from the 1950's and '60's. The only commercials they ever showed were for Metrical or Ex-Lax, products that seemed to be a little co-dependent…or maybe counterproductive. The bonus was that sometimes you could catch the best show ever: "The Many Loves of Dobie Gillis." Forget Dobie though. He spent most of the show narrating his own miserable existence and never could get to first base with anyone except Zelda, who didn't really look hot, but probably was. How could he score anyway with Warren Beatty in the cast? Yeah, play around with that image for a minute or two. The real star was Maynard G. Krebs. (The 'G' stood for Walter – sorry, never found out why.)

Maynard was the first hippie televised in real time. Actually he was a beatnik, but he nonetheless managed to create the stereotype that middle-America loved to scorn for the next couple of decades. Even so, he eventually sold out and got a job on a better channel, though I'm not sure that Maynard *or* Gilligan really approached life much differently. We all know the damn boat never did get fixed. Which naturally (if somewhat slowly) brings us back to some vague and possibly fascinating metaphor surrounding "Gilligan's Island" a pig with a high IQ, and perhaps the real subject of this chapter – a bad case of PMS – **P**re-**M**onsoon **PS**ychosis.

Technically though, it wasn't really winter, just fall in a bad mood, and I did have a few new weapons at my disposal. Topping the list was the John Deere, though I tried to keep it out of sight a great deal of the time. Whenever Elaine spotted it, she would get a funny look on her face and do one of those one step forward, followed by two steps back – one finger raised like a question in progress, then the eyes drooping in resignation, and finally, the 'I-don't-want-to-know' vertical drop of the shoulders signifying a dignified capitulation. You see, the <u>lack</u> of truth also frees you. But evidence was hard to find anyway. Doc and I didn't bury the bodies, we just covered them up with a lot of paperwork. The best kept secrets were secured in the barbecue next to a box of matches.

Since there was nothing "this little baby couldn't do" (dealer slang), the invitation was always open to test that theory. One thing it couldn't do was outrun a motorcycle cop or negotiate a hair-pin turn with a manure spreader attached. Since it only had one seat, necking on Inspiration Point was out of the question and using the drive-thru at the bank sent the tellers scrambling for air fresheners. I figured with a spreader full of manure they'd cash my check just to get rid of me. They just got rid of me.

I tried digging a few fence postholes, field harrowing and moving dirt from one bad location to another – I even used it to 'bond' with Chet. Seems he got *his* truck stuck. What an opportunity! We talked about brain lesions, Detroit diesels and how much gasoline it takes to melt a glacier! He recanted the part about being killed in that fiery crash in the mountains, claiming a memory relapse brought on by an old wound from the Normandy invasion. Or, his time in the French resistance. It was hard to tell. He didn't look French, but he did have an uncanny resemblance to Ernest

Hemingway, though with a lot less hair. I should have had my jaw wired shut. I grinned so much I pulled a muscle. I thought about charging *him* fifty bucks, but I'd had enough fun.

The coming winter would also include another sale. This sale is different though. It is a form of industry-wide recycling. By December, everybody in the Thoroughbred business is either broke, depressed, or both. It's a giant swap meet where everybody trades in their failures for somebody else's misfortune in order to fail with some new junk. It doesn't make any sense, but it keeps the sales staff off food stamps. Preparation is a little different since beauty and finesse don't fly here. I had already developed a plan for the pre-Christmas venue. I'd don my hip boots, wade into the pastures and look for large alluvial mounds about 16 hands high. Then I scan the lump with a stethoscope to see if it is alive. Confirming that basic requirement, I attach a rope to what I assume to be the head and drag it to the barn, trying not to lose my boots in the process. From there, I simply slide the lump into a horse trailer, whiz down to the local car wash and fill the trailer with soap and water. After the blow-dry, I hit the freeway, turn up the defrosters and drive like mad, arriving at the sale grounds with a couple of newly discovered movie actresses. When I step out of the truck, I absorb envy like a giant sponge and share my secrets with no one.

Even though the sale is in December and this is October, I can pretty much figure how it goes: Doc's natural indecision and a double Gin & tonic means I sell two and buy three. Once again, we'll have to find a witness protection program. I figure this time that my two will bring $1400 and Jesse's only $14.99. I like that idea. I sit around after the sale and needle her incessantly over my sale prowess. She listens to my runaway arrogance for about twenty minutes, finally agreeing that I'm absolutely brilliant. I know that, but I'm suspicious just the same.

"Oh, by the way," she says casually. "You did know that Doc bought Devil's Delight from us?"

"Ah, no, not really."

"Oh gee, that's too bad," she continues. "Want to call it a night?"

Hmm. Who wrote this chapter?

30.

A BUNCH OF TURKEYS
BITE THE DUST

AS THE HOLIDAYS approach, I tend to get a little retrospective. Or maybe introspective, or even overly inspected by potential in-laws who figure they can avoid a messy divorce by killing one of the potential nuptials. A few cold nights spent staring into the hypnotic flames of a fireplace converts quiet solitude into a stupid quest for the meaning of life. The cat's already figured it out anyway: eat, drink and shred things. Me, I think it's carbon-monoxide poisoning precipitated by a wood stove left over by the Pilgrims. Either way, the two of us sit and gawk at the flames, enamored by the warmth and all those unanswered questions the millennia have produced. Eventually, he lays a claw into my thigh clarifying the whole situation. This cat has connections that I don't even want to think about.

Fall is tough because it launches itself midway between summer's last exhale and the cryogenic handshake of Ol' Man Winter, so successful in this state that he was able to take early retirement. Some genius also fooled around with the clocks and I have it on good authority that it was a cartel of Candy Corn producers in Georgia and the American Dental Association. It's no accident that the meddling starts the day before Halloween. An extra hour of sugar extortion is worth about $14 billion in annual profits, a third of which is funneled to the cavity industry.

On a farm, molesting a clock causes dinner to be late. Horses respond by immediately forming a revolutionary council, donning berets and storming the nearest radio station. Since nobody knows what the hell they are talking about, the government remains secure. Peace is restored by reverting back to Daylight Saving Time, which, unbeknownst to my gang of outlaws, means that I get to sleep in while they wonder what happened to their waiter. One more piece of evidence as to why we're at the top of the food chain. We control time.

We don't get many trick-or-treaters visiting the farm. The driveway is about a half mile long and runs through a primordial forest. It is full of all kinds of lurking creatures and strange shadows, most created by our gang of wolves on a chicken hunt. The dogs don't normally collect children, but they might go for the Hershey bars. Since Doc was a veterinarian, post-assault stomach pumping is readily available if their natural tendency toward bulimia fails them. Still, only the bravest pirate, ghost or ballerina-bat-girl would ever make it to the front door. Those that overcame the forest and the boogey man earned a cab ride back to the street.

In spite of the clock, projectile hairballs, and carbon monoxide poisoning, I do dwell on esoteric principles when they pop to the surface right before I finish my second beer. Yeah, I'm kind of a lightweight so the beer buzz arrives before the first bathroom trip. Reincarnation is one of my favorites. It's the perfect compromise. Golf every Sunday morning, prime rib instead of tofu and those trips to the beach that have more to do with blood pressure than a good tan. Well, someone else's tan. It's the perfect arrangement: no guilt! You don't get it quite right in this life, then you get to come back and screw it up all over again! No fifteen-yard penalties, no stern lectures from the big guy and no vacationing in purgatory. Most importantly, no regrets about going to heaven and finding out that most of your friends took the second option.

I've given reincarnation a lot of thought lately. Two reasons really. The first is that with my kind of résumé, a future career of any kind seems unlikely. The second is how this job has aged me over the past year. I'm pretty sure it is a mid-life crisis even though my doctor insists I'm only 24 years old. Wait until they invent HMO's. He'll be more than happy to explore my neurosis for a couple of hours rather than face the avalanche of paperwork on his desk. He might even get in some practice with his stethoscope.

Meanwhile, I'm deluged with television commercials for calcium tablets and oat bran while the salesman from *Modern Maturity* camps out at my mailbox. Suddenly I see a crinkled old man, humped over one of those aluminum four-legged walkers, trapped in the middle of a crosswalk while the LA riot police battle with a horde of *latte*-crazed commuters with no air-conditioning. I'm trapped there with an artificial hip, nitro tablets in the left shirt pocket and a few bored paramedics taking bets on when the old fart will drop. Just the other day, while shaving, I was positive I saw one of those age spots – right next to a gray hair. It turned out to be leftover gravy, but the image in the mirror didn't lie. The big thirty was just around the corner, another old stallion about to be driven from the herd and I hadn't even decided on burial or cremation. Old, flatulent, decrepit – forced to eat day-old bread and cat food. Cat food? Next thing would be that dreaded magazine subscription. Ever thought about that title? It's the life-support-system-of-the-month club. With each subscription, you get an oxygen tent, 50% off on colostomy bags and a video on four-way bypasses. Never mind the special on sex toys. Nobody ever orders them because dementia has set in – we've heard the word 'sex' somewhere, but can't remember why or if we had that for dinner last night. Hell, we can't even find our teeth because we can't see without our glasses and if help arrives we can't hear the door-bell because we can't find our glasses in order to locate our hearing aid which we're pretty sure is sitting next to our teeth. The closest thing to sex is the Pekingese down the hall that humps an orderly's leg, or maybe it's just a large rat eating Mrs. Eddington's left foot. Hard to tell with cataracts in both eyes. A doctor finally shows up. "Good news Mr. Reynolds, it's not Alzheimer's, just senility! Mr. Reynolds? I'm over here, Mr. Reynolds."

I skipped the third beer and got on the phone. "Hey Jess. Got a question for you."

"No."

"It doesn't involve horses, just a quick question."

"It better be quick. I'm in bed."

"Are you sick...you need something? It's like 6:30."

"I've got horrible cramps. You know..."

Great!! There is hope! It's not menopause! "Geez, I'm sorry, anything I can get you?"

"No. My doctor said I should go on the pill. She said it would reduce the severity of them."

"Really?" I was suddenly somewhere between heaven and a transmission problem. "Listen, do you think I look older, or like getting decrepit or something?" I didn't dare explore the ramifications of birth control. I'd write Ann Landers in the morning. Wow, her doctor was a *her*. Every doc-tor I had ever seen was an old fat dude that always said, "Cough." I knew it was a hernia test, but shit? Even if I had pneumonia...?

"What?"

"I found some gray hair. I was starting to think that life is kinda skipping away. Maybe it's the job, I don't know."

"You're twenty-four…sometimes going on twelve. You look fine. You could even look cute if you wanted to…I mean…never mind. And it's *slipping* away, not skipping. What's this about?"

"I could look…cute?"

"I want to take a nap…please?"

"Cute?"

"Polo shirts. Good-bye!"

Back to reincarnation. Most days, I'd like to come back as a rock. Sort of sit around the Himalayas and watch mountain climbers run out of oxygen. Other times I have a certain desire to be an opossum. It's such a simple existence – you are born, make a beeline for a busy highway and boom! Off to life number three. Not even enough time to develop a bad habit or two. But, given my experience, I think the best option is to come back as a broodmare: a fat, expensive one. Oh, you were thinking maybe Nijinsky?

Some folks might question such a choice, opting for something like Julia Robert's mirror or Tom Cruise's lips – maybe the obvious, a stallion, but just maybe they are missing the point. Most broodmares live a pretty corrupt life. They start by being born a female, which I guess is a prerequisite for the job. Once that part is finalized, they go through the usual pre-puberty junk; make-up, frustrating boys, getting their ears pierced or some other part of their anatomy. Then, it is off to college, the equivalent of two semesters at Vassar, only sweatier. You know, twice around the track and then fall back on your upscale family connections. Or, in the odd case, actually win a big race named after a governor that managed to die before the grand jury got hold of him. That really seals the deal. Five minutes after the photo shoot, the mare develops a walk like Matt Dillon's sidekick – and no, not Miss Kitty, but off to the farm just the same. Either way, that forces everybody in upper management to do the sensible thing: they pack her bags, cancel the Mint Julep party and try to get the broad married off before American Express figures out why the payment is late. Miss Potential has a brief and fiery romance (not the kind the Surgeon-General had in mind), and is plopped, with somewhat glowing hormones, into a forty-acre field with her name on it. And she doesn't even have to come up with a damage deposit. There she sits for eleven months, *sigma delta whoopee* as a graduate of the Peter Principle – the severance package already tucked safely in the bank. If I could sprout an ovary, I'd get in line, but I think I'm stuck with the rock request.

Oh, the stallion choice? Two problems. First, you spend most of your life being led around with a stud chain under your upper lip by a guy holding a baseball bat designed to curb your enthusiasm. Secondly, if your first crop of foals are duds, then you get demoted to a 'teaser.' I'm already in that kind of a relationship so turning it into a career doesn't seem like a smart choice.

Now I know that Shirley MacLaine has her own ideas on reincarnation. Working out past conflicts, traveling up and down the existential ladder, really complicated stuff. She could be right, but then again, she could be wrong. And as much as I'd like to come back as General Patton's favorite jeep, it might be a lot safer in that forty-acre field. I'll get back to you on the labor pain thing.

November concludes with something called Thanksgiving. It's a holiday that supposedly focuses on positive thoughts, copious amounts of cardiac-flawed food and the death of 280,000-odd birds that as a group, are far too stupid to figure out that an oven is a bad place to hide. "Hi, this is Foster Farms, wondering if you guys could drop by for cocktails? Great! Hey, could you pick up some stuffing?" The snickering comes later, not to mention the cranberry sauce.

We all have this image of the Pilgrims – overdressed, somewhat plump people that seemed to get their clothes at K-Mart. They always had a few Indians standing around looking passive, but intent on butchering the whole bunch after dessert. The Indians weren't stupid. Quaint perhaps, but they had already met the Vikings so they had a fair idea of what to expect from tourists. They also knew that this bunch of idiots didn't seem to know the difference between an ear of corn and a parakeet. Sadly, the Pilgrims persevered through that first winter, quite contrary to what the Indians had hoped. Next thing they knew, the place had been renamed Manhattan and sold to Donald Trump. The Indians never could fathom the real estate business. It was like selling the sky. The land had no intention of going anywhere, so why would someone need to own it? Or build a fence around it. Was the land going to escape? Run away perhaps?

* **Chief Joseph of Idaho's Nez** Perce described it best: "The white man comes to my house and wants to buy my horses. I say, 'No, I need my horses.' So he goes to my neighbor and buys __my__ horses from him."*

Dynasties do come and go. Most don't go quietly. The quiet departures are those accomplished through population transfers. They get less media attention than outright genocide and manage to accomplish about the same thing. It is how a majority becomes a minority without ever leaving home. Goes a long way to explain why Tibet has a 54% Han Chinese majority. Beijing's response? "Oh, they're just migratory labor."

So, the problem is not enough buses.

One day the great American dynasty will join the ashes of the long dead pharaohs of Egypt's great kingdoms. Archeologists and anthropologists will be left to pick through the rubble, noting with astonishment that this civilization had 187 different kinds of cars. Nothing else, just the cars. And nobody knew where they drove off to.

The only bright spot in American expansionism was when Custer scratched his head and said, "I think we have a problem here." Well, it was probably more like using the 'F' word as a noun, verb and adjective in the same sentence, but I'm trying to keep my ratings intact. "Holy something!" is quite likely a more accurate declaration of the situation at hand. I'm pretty sure a lot of turkeys can relate to that image especially if they hang around Safeway the week before the big day. But that's the bewildering part about American culture – we seem to be always celebrating somebody's bad luck, even our own. What's the difference between Thanksgiving and Pearl Harbor Day? And who honestly believes that George Armstrong Custer got a bad deal?

Jesse was still working at shotgun Earl's down the road, no doubt plotting my embarrassment at some future sale. That in itself was almost a given, since the owners of her place of employment didn't have to invest large sums of money preventing a divorce that had no likelihood of happening anyway. Doc was into preventative medicine: a few Cadillac's, the revolving account at an upscale jewelers and gassing up the old 727. Cheaper than three guys with briefcases. Ah, but there was more. An affirmation that odd couples seem to make the best couples. Depending of course on just what kind of odd you find appealing. So given that…

…I decided to ask Jesse over for Thanksgiving dinner. By phone. They're safer.

"You're going to actually cook something?"

"Yeah, four or five rats, those green beans in the freezer, maybe pheasant if the cat comes through. I'm thinkin' of something traditional, you know, forage around the old farm and see what I can catch."

"The green beans? They were in the freezer when I met you. What's this foraging stuff? Safeway's right down the road."

"Well, I thought Thanksgiving should be about giving thanks, enjoying the bounty of the land…"

"You've been watching the *Discovery Channel* again."

"Actually, *Walt Disney World*. You know, I only get a couple of channels. What about that turkey farm over the hill? We could pick out a bird, whap its head off – like the old days. Sounds kinda like something people do on a farm."

"Sounds kind of sick. Besides, who's going to eat the thing? And you've got way too much of this *farm* thing going. 'Ol' MacDonald' raises racehorses. We're in the entertainment business in case you haven't noticed. Is *your* family coming?"

"No, I'm saving them for Christmas. 'Sides, I don't do family stuff. We'll eat it."

"I'm a vegetarian. What about your sister? Seems I heard somewhere you had a sister. And that trip to eastern Oregon? The old lady in the shoe?"

"Since when? And I might point out that honesty and Oregon aren't mutually inclusive." Only good comeback I'd had in months.

"Which *when*? And I don't want to rehash that."

"The vegetarian *when*." First signs of crinkling here. The nose. I can actually hear it over the phone. It's a male skill – one of the few.

"Since my cramps got so bad. The doctor said too much protein might be a problem."

Oh God, the cramp thing again. Why couldn't it be a bicep? She uses this menstrual process like a turn signal. "Okay, so Emily and I'll eat it."

"She's on a diet!"

"She's a shark for God's sake! She eats bugs! What about Diet-Coke Sue's Pit bull?"

"Shot by the Humane Society last month."

"Oh yeah. Sad deal. What about your mother?" Damn. I hate it when anger and enthusiasm get together. Makes the line go dead.

"Let's not go there. You want to murder a turkey, be my guest. I'm going to cook some eggplant. You can come over if you want." Click.

Eggplant? One of those purple footballs with a bunch of Kleenex inside? No giblet gravy, no wishbone to break, no quart of Pepto-Bismol afterwards? That's not a holiday, it's sacrilege! Besides, what's the turkey going to think? Last rites, halfway to the gallows, at peace with the world – then boom, the rug gets pulled out! The poor bugger will be in therapy until next November. It's not fair!

Over the years, I have gathered up a lot of stuff to be thankful about. Skipping the eggplant has just been added to the list. Most have involved physical carnage and a severe lack of personal discretion. Okay, so it's a 50/50 split between women, power tools and horses, but I'm still pretty relieved about the results, just a bit confused about who's grading the exams. I've been hit by a train, fallen off a motorcycle a few times, out of a car at 45mph (that was in the 'woman' category – a 70/30 split of opinion on whether I got to stay), a minor thing with a roll-over accident involving a '57 Chevy, a console TV (first one that had color) and an Irish Setter. The dog was driving. Then there were the 'tree falling' episodes, a couple of minor drowning's and a small problem with plugging my transistor radio into the dryer outlet. Still a little confused about drowning twice. Not sure if it's legal since drowning is normally a fatal activity. I think the confusion lies in the fact that they invented CPR and didn't bother to check with the English department at Yale for a new adjective. Something like, 'nigh upon drowning,' but saved.

I also discussed Paulette, so the only remaining question is why I am sharing this. I guess it's Jesse. She has a way of dragging confessions out of people. She missed her calling. She should have gotten a job as either Father O'Malley, or lead fingernail puller on a federal interrogation team. Or, maybe both – get to the truth and then confirm the confession with a pair of pliers. I guess that explains the look in her eye sometimes. I'm dating a mercenary who eats eggplant.

A lot of my recent near-death experiences have naturally been associated with horses. Or caffeine. Most are well documented by the hospital up the road. A few went unreported since they would have led to prolonged incarceration. Like the yearling with its head caught in the gate. He was the one with the motorcycle gang attributes. I first pictured him as the 'Flying Nun,' racing toward heaven with me in tow, but he merely backed up, depositing the gate on *my* head. I could picture the headlines the next day: "Horse Kills Man with Gate, Then Itself." Pictures at eleven.

I guess, given the state of the world, I should be thankful. War, famine, genocide, dislocation. The very fiber of life ripped away whether it happens to be a holiday or not. And here I'm having a conflict over turkey versus eggplant. I guess I could try the purple stuff, but I'm going to keep some Tabasco sauce handy. Or maybe hide a ham sandwich in the truck. And the turkey? Okay, I'll get him a bus ticket to Canada. Maybe he can ask for asylum.

'Tree falling episodes?' When I was pretty young, I tended to fall out of trees a lot. Usually around nine or ten o'clock at night. We were pretty lucky in that there were at least seven different emergency rooms around the area to deal with tree fallers. Mother liked to share our business I guess, since we never went to the same one twice. Usually it was minor stuff – a broken arm, maybe a rib, a few stitches or something. I was a sleepwalker, she told them. Fooled her. I was awake the whole time.

Eggplant? God.

31.

A DAY OF INFAMY

ROOSEVELT DIDN'T SHOW up at the farm to tell Congress that he was a bit chagrined with the Japanese government. The historical cliché may survive, (along with the resentment) but our personal experiences dictate the real meaning contained in the phrase. War was fortunately something I did not have to personally endure. However, my mother spent her teen years in a bomb shelter in Germany, my grandfather in the Luftwaffe, and my father trying to patch up fallen friends in France. A stepfather who was a belly gunner in a B-25, a brother-in-law who sprayed Agent Orange over the jungles of Vietnam – war kills them at some later, less convenient time. Numerous friends that were door gunners, medics and fighter pilots. Some of them remembered in the past tense, and some, sadly – not remembered at all.

The irony about war is that for all its absolute horror, its unspeakable atrocities and human suffering, when the rifles are finally laid down, a man on one side of the fence finds something in common with a woman on the other side of the fence and eventually produce a child. It is a thread that has somehow failed to break completely in 200,000 years of human misery. I often think about the ancient path that we've all walked and ponder the probability, the incredible impracticality, the absurd mathematical odds that can produce such an inconceivable equation: one that presupposes somehow that I'll be here and that you'll actually read this! And all of this absurd, unbelievable and completely queer human madness is attributable to one bullet, missing one person, at some unlikely crossroads marking the surface of this planet. Mere thoughts, put to paper and not consumed by the fires of 10,000 wars. Kind of figure that everybody should get a medal for just showing up tomorrow.

My personal day of infamy was December 3ʳᵈ. No, the Japanese didn't show up for breakfast. Instead, Doc caught up to me in the process of trying to catch some fence posts that floated away. He seemed pretty happy for a guy who knew he had to buy a new Cadillac in about a month. Way too happy.

"I was thinking," he started out. (Always a bad sign.) "Those stud fees are starting to add up, what with board and shipping and everything. I was talking to Woody, you know, the bloodstock agent, and he was saying why not get your own stallion? Something with good breeding that maybe had a little bad luck on the track. Look, he sent me this photo of this horse in California; he's out of a good Nashua mare and by that half-brother to that horse that would have won the Kentucky Derby." Doc's face was a little red and sweaty. First trip to the brothel, that sort of thing.

"Here Doc, grab this rope." Now if I could find a way to tie the other end to an orbiting satellite. "I don't know Doc, stallions are a lot of trouble and we're really not set up…"

"The agent said he was a cupcake, a real gentleman."

The only thing an agent knows is how to calculate his commission. "A what?"

"You know what I mean. What the hell am I holding on to?"

"My intestines, I think," I mumbled. About that time the fence posts came our way, kind of fast. "About time to let go!"

The posts sailed safely past us. I forgot to mention that the other end of the rope was attached to the power take-off on the tractor. A few seconds later, a crunching noise confirmed their arrival at some destination I hadn't planned on. "Doc, I don't want to fool around with a stallion – they're dangerous, you need help with the breeding, you know, it takes a few people to do that."

"I'll help."

"Help?" He had tried that once or twice before with pretty uneven results. Plus, breeding season coincided with tee-time in Palm Springs.

"It'll work out. Oh, the van will be here tomorrow."

"What!?"

"Gotta go. I think the phone's ringing."

I spent the rest of the afternoon on my resignation speech. Lots of verbs. Even invented a few new ones. The cat had heard all this before. He spent the morning sitting on the classifieds. Looked like the real estate section. Jesse's phone only produced voice mail – not much good in a crisis. I wondered if the Hot Line had voice mail? 872 kilotons mistakenly shipped to Vladivostok and the message, "I'm sorry, but we're currently unavailable. Please leave a…" I thought about giving my mother a ring, but hung up, figuring that was a little childish. I could already hear the response. "Oh, you got a stallion. How nice. Honey, what's a stallion?" Besides, her number in Idaho was unlisted. Already checked.

Actually, that is a pretty fair question. Male, big, prone to fighting to the death with other stallions. A lot of literature has been devoted to the male gender. Most of it was written by males preparing a good defense argument. The rest, by women who had the foresight to take the bar exam. All possible manifestations have been explored: the sensitive man, the insensitive man, man as woman, man as lizard, man as Earl…man as Earl? F. Lee Bailey couldn't win that case.

Out of that incredible pile of analytical nonsense, two facts emerged: the vast majority of males are terminally confused because every time they think they know what they are supposed to be, women change their minds. They (women) have fifteen different magazines (more like training manuals) devoted to house training us. What have we got? Hugh Hefner, *TV Guide* and *Sports Illustrated*! The 'Playboy Advisor?' A woman! Well, she did clarify the size question…I was a little confused on her research methods…so that means that some men and all stallions will always be nothing more than a small car with a big engine in need of a gas station. Now that I think about it, just whose ego was she really boosting?

The non-winning half-brother to the almost Kentucky Derby winner arrived the following afternoon. The van driver dropped the ramp, handed me the shank and said, "Here, take this miserable son-of-a-bitch! He's been kicking the hell out of the van for 1400 miles! I should have shot the bastard back in Oregon. I need a drink, maybe five!"

Well, there went the beer again. I was going to say thanks (a bloody lie), but the horse was bellowing like a moose and dragging me in the direction of anything that had the slightest chance of being female. I finally got him locked in a stall and went to the house for some oxygen. Not content with destroying a semi, he started in on the barn. I thought the cat was going to inhale its own tongue. He lit off across the creek and I know full well that he hates both strenuous exercise *and* water. Meanwhile, the mares heard this new guy and started screaming back, which was as if the entire population of China was rehearsing for the opera. I checked the phone book for cheap motels.

Doc finally got the guts to wander over. He thought the van driver had smashed into the house. "I guess he's pretty excited to be here. God, would you look at the build on that horse."

Excited? He was peeling the plywood off the walls. It was only a matter of time before he sacked Paris.

"Well, Elaine and I are going out to dinner, maybe a movie. He'll be fine."

I went back to the phone book. I figured there must be a listing for the National Guard. A little circular red paint on his chest, call in the fighters and it would be all over in ten minutes. Damn! They only worked on weekends and two weeks in the summer. I buzzed Jesse again. She was home. "Hi Jess. Say listen…" I heard a bunch of gurgling sounds.

"I'm trying to brush my teeth. Emily, stop that! What?"

"Maybe it's a bad time." Maybe the wrong decade.

"Look, you only call this time of day when you want something."

"I called the other night." That was the three-beer buzz call. No, I don't share everything in this book.

"Right, and you wanted something else then."

"I just wanted to show you what I bought. Come on."

"Three pairs of silk boxers at a quarter to midnight?" She was working her way toward sarcasm. Disgust was just around the corner.

"Well, they were on sale. You told me I needed some new clothes."

"What'd you get me? A wet T-shirt?"

Hadn't thought about that. Maybe I should have been a little more subtle. I guess the pair with the detachable ribbon and the printing about "Guess what's inside?" was a little too direct. The sales woman assured me that they were the most popular. She didn't explain why they were 75% off. "Okay, okay. Bad idea. I was just thinking…"

"Don't. What *do you* want?"

"Well, er, might, maybe need some, well, I was wondering if…"

"God, now what?"

"Doc bought a stallion." That had the immediate impact of making me feel that my call had been re-routed to Pakistan. "Hello? Jesse, hello?"

"He bought a stallion?"

I never knew that sarcasm was visceral. "Yeah, that explains the boxer shorts. They were for him." Humor wasn't working.

"And let me guess, you want *my* help to breed *his* mares?" I think I felt a little toothpaste in my left ear.

"Sure, Doc says he's a cupcake. Just need somebody to hold the mare. Thought we'd see what he was like with Boo Boo tomorrow. You know Boo, she likes everything."

"*We?* As in you and me? And the cupcake thing? What's that about? And Boo liking everything? That's a cereal commercial, not a horse. And what the hell is that noise?!"

"Just a little remodeling, no big deal"

"Look, I don't think so. Why can't Doc help…oh yeah, I remember. Palm Springs. Okay, maybe. I'll stop by in the morning, but no promises. Understand?"

"Sure, it'll be no big deal. Bye." Panic attacks are like hurricanes. They have that moment of calm right before your house disappears.

I had some planning to do. Elephant tranquilizer, I needed some elephant tranquilizers! Maybe I could break one of his legs, stick an ice pick in one ear, maybe drain out five or six gallons of blood. What would James Bond do? Nah, Jesse wouldn't go for that. I snuck down to the barn to see what was going on. He'd moved from plywood directly to the studs. (Okay, that's another pun – construction based.) Doesn't he ever sleep? I went out and caught Boo and threw her into the next stall. Figured the best way to appease a cannibal was to find him a meal. Instead, he cocked a hind leg and went to sleep. Where's Freud when you need him?

Bright and early the next morning, Jesse rapped on my front door. We had a silent cup of coffee together. Finally, the woman spoke. "Let's have a look at him."

The barn was eerily quiet. The stallion was in about the same position as I'd left him the night before. I downplayed all the shredded wood. "Okay, let's get 'em ready and see how things go."

The thing about horse sex, at least from the domestication standpoint, is a little different from the norm. People tend to get undressed, horses dressed. Nobody is quite sure who made up these rules, but they seem to exist just the same. Probably had something to do with the Catholic Church. First, the mare has to get her tail knotted and wrapped. Something about paper cuts. Boy and girl get their…well, parts washed. A little hygiene never hurts, but swapping disinfectant for perfume doesn't do much for me. The mare also gets to wear a neck cover since a lot of stallions are disposed to biting their dates. Some mares also get hobbled to cut back on that desire for pay back. The stallion wears a heavy halter and quite often ends up with a chain under his lip or a baseball bat waving near his head. (See, I warned you earlier about that part.) Call this stuff *industrial strength lingerie*. Oh, and Jesse and I wear hard hats. The whole entourage looks like the Roman Coliseum on gladiator Sunday. The only things we're missing are a few lions and a dozen road cones.

"Go ahead and take Boo out to the bull pen. I want to see what he's like first."

Jesse left with Boo and all her appendages. She walked like one of those chain gang convicts going out to chop weeds on the interstate. (Boo, not Jesse.) The stallion, upon taking notice of that, reared straight up in the air and split a roof rafter in half. "Be right with you!" I yelled. That was a bit of an understatement – we shot out of the barn, a little smoke rising off my boots. We skipped the gate and just plowed through a six-panel section of the bull pen. I yelled something that sounded like Japanese.

Jesse's mouth was down around her knees, her eyes expressing what a prisoner's might when he finds out the execution *wasn't* a practical joke. She chose to screech in French, the lower class variety, threw the rope in the air and jumped over the railing. I was busy trying to get the dirt out of my mouth. The stallion made a lunge toward Boo, who suddenly had a very strange look on her face. An angry sort of serenity. With one kick, she broke the hobbles, with the second, she caught the stallion square in the forehead, knocking him to his knees. She turned and faced him. He sort of stumbled to his feet and just backed up a few steps before he fell over again. The third attempt at the sobriety test seemed to work, but his eyes were focused on the outskirts of Neptune. Jesse was flat on her back, the French now fully translated to badly broken English and I was digging out from a pile of splintered lumber, smoke still rising off my boots.

"Ah, say mister, could you please sign for this?" It was the UPS driver, holding his clipboard and looking a little sick. "Can ya just sign this damn thing!"

"We were just trying to breed a…" I started.

"Look man, I don't want to know what you two were doing. Just sign it!"

I was gonna have to see if Elaine could switch to Fed-Ex. I needed a new audience.

32.

<u>STEVEN SPIELBERG ARRIVES</u>

IT WAS TWO days before the stallion and Boo Boo consummated the marriage. Didn't matter really, Boo had been infertile for five years anyway. She just liked the action. Turned out the big guy was what they refer to as a 'shy breeder.' Most of the time, he'd lick her hocks, sensually push on her side, nicker those sweet words that are in some other language, but no action. Even I could get bored with foreplay after 48 hours. Well, maybe not, but…oh, never mind. Maybe it is a reflection on men in general. A lot of bravado, but then, in the privacy of the bedroom, a woman takes all your sexual insecurities and turns them into root beer with too much foam in it. I think a lot of it is a lack of trust. Not in them, but in ourselves. The façade makes the mirror more palatable.

Doc wandered over the following morning, no doubt ready to return to Palm Springs. He seemed genuinely pleased that my self-perception about instant death turned out to be somewhat inflated, though I did spend two hours pulling splinters out of my forehead. He didn't mention the hole in the bull pen, most likely because another brilliant idea had surfaced: "The magazine called, seems the agent gave them a jingle. Something about the stallion directory? They think I ought to get a picture of him, something professional looking. The editor says I should advertise him."

Yeah, on Interpol. $50,000 – dead or…well, dead preferably.

"Maybe Jesse knows somebody. Give her a call, would ya? We're going to take the 7:15 flight. Got a spot at a new golf course tomorrow morning. Oh, can you keep this kind of quiet? I want to tell Elaine after the Cadillac shows up and the taxes are finally out of the way. Say, some van driver called me last night. All pissed-off. Wanted bail money. You know anything about that?"

"Naw, I think the guy's in the middle of a divorce. Wife caught him cheating or something. Think he drinks a lot." Wish I'd thought of that.

"Anyway, keep it quiet for now would ya?"

"The horse or the van driver?" So much for analogies.

I was hoping he'd connect horse + dishonesty = jail, and or, excessive drinking. No such luck. Something wrong with his wiring. "Sure, why not." Most of the noise was over anyway. "Look, have a good flight, I'll let you know." What I really wanted to know was if the coroner moonlighted. It wasn't the stallion, he was still busy licking a hock. Calling Jesse was the real challenge. Right now, even touching the phone produced a cold sweat.

God, I hate cowardice. Some people enjoy confrontation. Professional wrestlers are a good example and they probably get paid pretty well to demean some other guy dressed up like a half-naked biker at a gay bar. I mean, I'm okay if a nuclear reactor explodes and I need to rescue the kids from the day-care center next door – unplanned stuff. When you sit at the desk tapping your fingers, waiting to call the Kremlin to explain those fourteen missiles headed for St. Petersburg; that drives me nuts. If a woman calls…a woman? Here I was hoping I was terrified of snakes, or maybe being forced to walk naked through a Starbucks at 7:00 in the morning. "Triple mocha please…uh, extra napkins?"

Okay, gird up the courage. The woman hasn't gotten a restraining order yet. Look her in the eye, or the phone in the receiver and tell her the truth. A great statesman once said that "the truth will free you." Who was that? God, I hope it wasn't Richard Nixon.

"Hi Jessica. How are you?" 'Jessica' is a precautionary anticipatory formality. It's how you duck with words.

"I've got a big bruise on my butt. What about you?"

"Still flossing the gravel out of my teeth." I wasn't prepared for civility.

"Did they like…did they ever like do it?"

"Do what?"

"The thing. You know, the thing!"

Where's a color commentator when you need one. "Yeah, they did it and it was pretty. Took a while though...seems he is a little..."

"Look, I don't need the details."

"I need a photographer."

"What?! I mean the boxers were one thing...what in the world?"

"Whoa! For the magazine! Advertising! What the hell did..." So, she did have an imagination.

"Okay, okay. Give Stevie Spiller a call. But try not to get me involved."

"Okay, thanks. Got any plans tonight?"

"I'm soaking my butt."

"Who the hell is Stevie? Or what?"

Stevie showed up the next day. Turned out she (second half of my question) was also a friend of Diet-Coke Sue, part of a bigger conspiracy that was cloaked in secrecy and other stuff that only concerned women.

"Hi. I heard you were a friend of Sue's. How's that dog of hers, you know that Pit bull?" I was trying to break the ice. She looked a little stern. She kept looking through this little device she had around her neck. First at the ground, then up in the sky, then...at me. She also had on one of those green British thorn-proof field jackets, the same kind as Jesse's trainer. *Comfortable* wasn't running around in my brain just now.

"He wasn't a Pit bull and he's dead."

"Oh, where's your camera?"

"I need to look around first, see what I've got to work with. You know, this is a bad time of year. The weather's terrible. Is that the horse?"

"Yes."

"Well, you're going to have to get him cleaned up, pull his mane, clip his legs and put some polish on him. He looks like hell."

"Okay." Now I had to figure out how to get him to a beauty parlor.

"And look, we'll have to do the 'shoot' over there. You need to mow that pasture and cut down that tree over there," she continued. "Oh, and work with him on the proper way to stand. Here's a picture. Call me when everything is ready and we'll schedule a day."

She wasn't a photographer, she was an interior decorator with a landscaping fetish. The tree in question was a thirty-five foot fir, not exactly like digging up a shrub. I did get the pasture mowed, two days of freezing weather negating the drowning issue. I finally got brave and cut down the tree, the end result a potential lawsuit from the neighbor. Something about his new cable TV and a favorite cow. Jesse came over and cleaned the stallion up, who was extremely docile if Boo was in the next stall. However, putting his feet in the right places was like parking an aircraft carrier. Left becomes right, one goes this way, the other somewhere else. My idea was to dig some holes, stick his legs in them and pour concrete. Jesse told me to keep trying. The short version is that Thoroughbreds have to stand a certain way, like the 'Fonz' making a statement that, "Hey, I'm cool." The stallion hadn't been to acting school and I didn't hold a PhD in patience. The anatomical manipulations were driving me crazy. I couldn't believe it! The horse was incompetent at standing! I even showed him the damn pictures! Get the legs right and the dates are endless!

The big day came. Stevie showed up fully bedecked with cameras, lenses and sacks of God knows what. She stomped around checking the lighting, inspecting the dead tree, giving the horse a Marine Corp glove test, pointing here and there, measuring the length of the grass and sending me scurrying for things like olive oil and an umbrella. She shook her head side to side a lot, one of those condescending gestures that leads to most homicides.

We practiced a little leg placement in front of the lights. Bogart was off-camera smoking a cigarette. The make-up gal was powdering my face. No, I wasn't paying attention. The legs were still in the wrong places.

"His left," Stevie would yell, pointing at a foot.

I'd move his right, since it looked left to me.

Lots of Dates

No Dates – Beginning to Understand What <u>My</u> Problem Is

Same old stuff. Stevie's brow kept furrowing deeper and deeper, the canals of Mars sprouting up all over her head. After the tenth deep sigh, she called a halt to the proceedings. She suggested I change his head gear. I tried to explain that restraint wasn't big on his list and that we might have a problem. She said he looked as if he had swallowed a chainsaw. Interesting idea.

We started over. It was beginning to feel like the bad part of a dentist's appointment, the part with the drill. If Stevie wanted him pointing north, he would want to stare at some inanimate object to the south. The legs also had to match the ears, which were supposed to be cocked. As the session progressed, the stallion wandered through the various stages of frustration. The first was rabid excitement associated with the fact a mare grunted somewhere in a five-mile radius of the farm. That was followed by fifteen minutes of uncontrollable fidgeting which sent everybody scrambling in search of the mystery fly, even though it was about -10 degrees in the sun. Once that was over, he put his transmission in park, dozed off and looked no more exciting than a rock covered with lichens. Marsha suggested that we try to re-establish contact with the missing space ship. Jesse tried poodle squeak toys, tossing baseball caps in the air (mine), and even jumping up and down in the air like a manic frog. The horse continued to snore.

Stevie had one more idea. Placing Jesse just out of camera range, she waited until the horse's legs were perfect and then had her open a big beach umbrella about three feet in front the stallion's nose. That worked! I heard the shutter of the camera snap about four times before we exited the immediate area at a dead run. As he drug me across the pasture, I could vaguely hear Stevie in the background yelling, "Good! Good!" as the camera kept snapping photographs.

When the proofs came back, I was quite amazed at just how talented Stevie was as a photographer. In eight by ten elegance was a stallion at full stride racing across a green field. She had airbrushed out the lead shank, the fence in the background and a certain farm manager that had a lot of grass stains on the seat of his pants. She wouldn't show me the originals. She said she sold them to a woman that might let me have a look at them at a later date. A much later date.

33.

SANTA COMES TO
TOWN...INCOGNITO

"Twas the night before Christmas
And all through the house
Not a creature was stirring
Not even a mouse."

That's because the cat killed them. He's over in the corner gift-wrapping the bodies. I'll try to act surprised in the morning. However, the thirteen assorted creatures in the barn were stirring. In fact, most were busy ripping water buckets off the walls, digging holes in the floor and generally messing up the place. Which supports a long-standing theory of mine that most horses don't believe in Santa Claus. If they did, they wouldn't treat the place like a rental house.

Each year in December, the *Christian world stops for a few days to celebrate Christmas. Not necessarily the birth of Christ, or the gradual close of another year or even a sale at Nordstrom's. All cultures and all groups need a party, a celebration of a tangible belief that is unique to a single community, an entire nation, a religion or a family. The importance is not the date, as all calendars are a myth, an organizational necessity of a world that Copernicus, Galileo, Newton, Einstein and perhaps Sagan tried to put in some kind of rational order, without considering the needs, concerns and ramifications of a world that coveted security in religion and culture, power and defense. In some ways, physics was the devil incarnate, no matter what form it was wrapped in, no matter what cultural interpretation embraced its undeniable presence. Just ask Newton. He made the Church of England pretty nervous. He devoted five years in the pursuit of explaining God as a tangible phenomenon – and failed. And yet the physical world and metaphysical world remained married, far too dependent to separate themselves from a common need for logic* <u>and</u> *faith. A divorce was* *impossible: the answer, unobtainable in the physical world. We believe in something because we simply can't understand the rest. All religions are little more than a need to believe that our existence means something. The gift of intelligence is perhaps the curse of our uncertainty. Or maybe the salvation.*

In the Western world, we try to throw avarice and greed out the window in respect of this holiday. A great many of us are not certain why, or simply incapable of temperance. Still, we try to remember our turn signals, respect the rights of pedestrians and adhere to the speed limit wherever possible. We don't want to be killed in a car during a period of our naked uncertainty. Everybody also gets to eat all the foods we have been warned about and to finally witness the Post Office doing some real work. And the very best: a little reinforcement on a universal dislike for fruitcake.

Most of my early Christmases were not really fun. Life could get complicated when adults had too much time off from work. The best one I remember was one year when one of the 'Its' had a little too much eggnog and fell over on the Christmas tree. I guess he decided to take a nap. My sister and I weren't sure what to do, so we decorated him. Of course, when he woke up, we needed to run away. Since it was 28 degrees and snowing, we couldn't get far. At least, not far enough.

I've always loved the idea of Christmas on a farm. Not that I ever tried it before, what with my urban upbringing and all, but there was always an image of a snow-covered cabin where grandma tended a still and we dashed through the snow in a four-wheel drive truck with a false gas tank. Smoke would be filtering out from distant chimneys, lights would twinkle along icicled eves while some fool chopped firewood out by a shed for no apparent reason. All round, trees limp and heavy with a fresh batch of the white stuff. A *Hallmark* card.

This farm is a little different. The best I can hope for is mud that's less gummy, a self-dashing wheelbarrow and a crackling fire that isn't in the microwave again. I'll also include pipes that don't freeze and yearlings enrolled in anger management classes. A little help untangling last year's tree lights wouldn't hurt either. I retracted the part about the stallion and heart disease. Seemed a little callous considering it was Christmas.

Besides, there were more important things to worry about, like wrapping Jesse's Christmas presents: a freeze-dried buffalo leg for Emily the terrier, a few books on men, naturally written by sympathetic, though somewhat severe women (PhD's do that to women), something kind of personal and black (we'll see if I muster up the guts for a proper presentation), and some new hinges for the canopy on her truck. Plus, I still had to figure out how to get a 22lb turkey into an oven that I had never personally used or inspected and to prepare for a herd of incoming quasi-relatives – a minor detail that I didn't include in Jesse's dinner invitation.

The rest of my impending doom could wait until January. That's when both Elaine and the IRS would escort me to federal prison for evading Doc's taxes as well as my own. That's about a ten on the Richter scale of impending doom, but why worry? Toss a little extra butter on the mashed potatoes and hope the cholesterol works faster than a bunch of hostile accountants. If my dinner scheme goes badly, I'll be buried in the backyard anyway. Captains should go down with their…farm.

I decided to try to get the horses to join in the Christmas spirit, which was a little like calling a truce in Beirut (please feel free to substitute Baghdad, Kabul or Oakland for Beirut) right after everybody got a new load of ammunition. Even so, I began handing out a few presents. The cat got a can of salmon mousse, which is one of the few things I can watch him eat. He could throw it up later in my truck as kind of a year-end bonus. Next, it was off to the loading sheds to feed the broodmares. This time I take one buggy whip in lieu of two, and instead of calling Sybil, #$%&!%?!! Sybil, I just say, "Hi there." I give them extra grain, sing the shortened version of "Silent Night," toss a few carrots around and run like hell before they smother me with affection, which horses accomplish by pinning you against a wall until your mouth stops moving.

Next on the list is decorating the yearlings. Usually this can be accomplished with spray glue, a bag of tinsel and some angel hair. At the same time I string a few lights around their shed and hang up the inflatable Santa. The yearlings are so happy about the decorations that I won't have to clean the place until next June, which is my kind of present.

Then comes the really fun stuff – hanging candy canes on the weanling's tails. That went pretty well until I ran into a couple that held a grudge. The rest appreciated the opportunity to chew on something other than my skin and the whole escapade was actually a good way to ascertain if I'd had too much eggnog. Just don't use a stapler.

Most farm chores go on 'emergency schedule.' That means that the only thing that changes is the speed at which things <u>don't</u> happen. Given the current circumstances, I bite my tongue and go to the barn to wish the stallion a happy holiday. Since I didn't have a mare with me the conversation quickly deteriorated into a '<u>who</u> is going to do what to <u>whom</u>, <u>when</u>.' Kind of like eating a cheeseburger in front of a lion. It's a little hard to hand over carrots when both arms are in the digestive tract of a large carnivore.

Jesse finally shows up with a salad, eggplant surprise, a bottle of wine and a question: "Why so much food? I told you I don't eat turkey."

"Ah, well I mentioned something about some guests…'round Thanksgiving. You remember? Thought you'd like to meet them instead of just hearing about 'em, not that there's much to hear. It *is* Christmas."

"Meet them? I get it. You wanted them to meet me! This is like a set up or something! Like, take the girl home to meet mom, but without buying any gas. This is just another…"

"Jesse, just shut up and listen!" My voice, but not my brain. "Look, you would've never come over if I'd told you, which I sort of did a while back, but you always want to draw some damn line and I don't get it…really don't. You think I'm doing this because I'm trying to…I don't know what! Just get in your pants or somethin,' tell you to sell your horse, go to college…be a cheerleader or something! Christ, have I ever wanted you to be more than…this,this…what I'm lookin' at! What is it about men and you? I don't want anything you're not willing to give, but shit…get on or off the fence! I sort of…no, not sort of…dammit, okay here! I think I might, maybe, sort of…love you… or have a brain tumor or something. You do things to me…I mean what in the hell is wrong with that? And you just shove back like my thoughts don't count, don't matter, like…I don't know…I could be wrong, but I thought somethin' mutual was going on. I'm gettin' mixed messages, no messages…I'm tired of being your *friend*…sort of."

If it was any quieter, you could hear a frog fart. I was completely out of air. She kept glancing side to side like she was looking for the defense team, somebody else to take up the fight. Nobody was available. After an eternity, she broke the silence. "You never said that you…that I thought it was a thing to get me in…you know, typical crap."

"Yeah, and it really worked, didn't it?"

"No, but...look, you better check the turkey. They'll be here soon, whoever they are."

"It's not what you think. It's not *family*, family...I don't really have much there. Never did really. It's kinda like a bad joke, which really isn't funny anymore. You know, I'd be happier if you just walked out of here. I see something good and it's worse than something bad because it's not supposed to happen that way. You can't really understand this. There's things that I don't do, just don't.'"

"Oh? You talk in your sleep you know. The motel? The Bainbridge show? You were having a nightmare of some kind. You said some things that..."

"Probably about the cat." Fine time to find out I can't keep a secret awake or asleep. "Well, I hope the information was useful." Ouch, I heard sarcasm, which never sounds good in my own voice.

"It was actually. But listen for a minute and don't be so sarcastic. You notice I don't go home unless I absolutely have to. Did you know my brother tried to hang himself in the...shit! That's why I had to take off this summer." A spoon flew across the kitchen, missing the sink in favor of the floor. "This is...why I don't...whatever! I thought he was the tougher one. He walked away from this...this stuff, my father and his crap and well, look...*he* couldn't do it! How can I? I'm not...strong...I just hide, keep a distance. Sometimes I just lie. I lied about tonight. And I can't just sleep next to an open window like it solves something."

"You could've fooled me. You scare me shitless." I took my gaze off her. She looked hurt...and puzzled. Badly. But no tears. "You lied to come over here?" Never thought she'd figure out the window thing. So much for the asthma story.

"Uh, huh."

"And what about your dog, I mean Emily...that night? You left her sleeping on my stomach. Pretty weird if you ask me. That one I couldn't figure at all." I wasn't supposed to call Emily a dog even though she was a dog.

"She was listening to you. So was I. You were scaring me. Emily was like...I don't know, like...well...sounds stupid, but she was like listening." She turned to face the window.

Five minutes of silence can seem like an eternity or maybe just a weird breathing exercise. We both stared out the window – different views of the same dark sky. Where do you walk a conversation to when each step seems to take you further from the destination? And how much information is too much? I was used to running from the bad and yet running from the good seemed the same. I bent over and picked up the spoon. "Nice shot. Sorry…I'm kinda lost here…I thought…you really lied to come over here? When I was in high school most people lied to get away from me. I got ditched so often…finally got another dog." I touched her on the shoulder. Saw that in a movie once and it seemed to work.

"Don't. Don't do that…touch thing. I don't like being touched. Look, you don't want to meet my family, especially my father. You'd probably kill each other. He measures the grass before he mows it, draws diagrams of the cupboards and straightens all the cans so the labels all match…corn here, beans there, crap like that. Right now he's throwin' a fit because I'm here and not there. I made a choice and I…I don't really know why. It's not easy. I don't let people in anymore. Ever! A horse, a dog, that stupid cat, not this. Everybody just takes and what they want I haven't got." She finally uncrossed her arms and walked over to the oven. "You need to look at this thing. It's smoking."

I peered over at the cat. He didn't look insulted particularly. "Yeah, the turkey." It wasn't the only thing smoldering. "Listen, it's just my sister, an uncle and this old lady that insists she's related. Watch her though, she steals things. They might bring a friend or two or three…I don't know. That's all. My sister's a little weird so don't be too surprised." I was thinking that it was the first time I heard Jesse swear on purpose. Well maybe the second. But this was in English. "And watch your mouth, they're a pretty dignified bunch."

"Yeah, right. I suppose *they* introduced you to flannel shirts." Jesse kind of smiled in a pissed-off sort of fashion. "Go to hell by the way."

"What did I say that night?" The curiosity was killing me. Or maybe the outright dread.

"I don't know. That's the problem. It was scary. I was going to leave…Emily just kept looking at you and like…she wasn't worried at all…and you finally went back to sleep. So I left her out there."

Jesse went to puttering with things. Seems women putter when they want to discuss something with themselves in private. Men either drum their fingers on the hood of a tractor, chop wood or ruin a bartender's quiet evening. Puttering is like a scavenger hunt without a list or a winner, as everything is merely moved an inch or two and then moved back to its original site. A good putterer makes all this activity seem incredibly important and the expert accomplishes all this activity with their back to you. Which is okay if she's wearing the right jeans. Yeah, as putterers go, she was pretty good. I stayed in the kitchen and fiddled with the turkey. Couldn't drum my fingers on the hood of the tractor since it was down by the barn. Turkey fiddling didn't manage to clarify things. Mostly it just pissed-off the cat.

Around six o'clock the smoke detector went off. I use it like an oven timer. An eclectic collection of quasi-relatives showed up at about the same time. This collection included a couple of friends of friends who were under the illusion (or delusion) that I knew how to operate a stove. The group also brought one uncle of mine (we think) who got a day-pass from the senility board and of course, my sister. Leading the pack was my grandmother, twice-removed, not necessarily by choice. She always brought her passport along in case anybody had doubts. They proceeded to work their way through the liquor cabinet, only pausing briefly to meddle with the food or tell Jesse what a nice person she was. Jesse held up pretty well considering this strange entourage. It was more like inviting over a theme park than people. Twice she asked me 'who is that?' only to get my best shrug. She sat next to my sister, the two of them talking through most of dinner. Sister smiled once or twice which created a face I barely recognized. Maybe she had managed to turn a corner or something. I tried to lip-read, but you know how it goes with a mouth full of mashed potatoes.

Uncle Bert was the self-anointed *horse expert. Which means that every horse gets a bale of hay for dinner, 200lbs of grain and a lecture dealing vaguely with a plow, two mules, 50 acres in west Texas and something about Aunt Ellen's favorite hat. Bert actually was an uncle, my father's youngest brother. He and my grandmother were the co-conspirators in clearing up the details of my inflated initials. In the world of questionable family values, they seemed to be the outliers. If there is a genetic connection for the ability to get out a window in a hurry, I probably inherited it from these two. They escaped decades ago. Still, it always seems odd to have ghosts over for dinner.*

Bert loved the eggplant. Told him it was armadillo. He wanted the recipe. Bert had polio when he was young. My father stole penicillin from the Army to treat his bone infections. Bert lived, the thief went to the stockade for a long time. All things considered, it was just another chapter in what was to become a life sentence.

Around 7:00, we all sat down to dinner. According to farm tradition at 7:15 a number of things are destined to occur: either A), the horses knock down a fence and head up the freeway, or B), one horse decides to get an incredible case of indigestion, which can only be cured by either a $300 vet bill or the collected sympathy of fifteen or so well-oiled relatives, or, C), a very expensive mare decides to cut her gestation period by two weeks because no one ever taught her how to read a calendar. D) and E) are the unmentionable disasters that invariably involve either the septic tank or what one of the relatives happened to step in on the way to the house. Either way, dinner gets served.

Jesse's a little nervous, but sister only talks about how nice it is that I found some new animals. I'm pretty sure that some of that secret feminine conversation was going on, but I'm too busy passing around mashed potatoes and eggplant, casting the occasional glance to see if anybody looks suicidal. Jesse just smiles back. No not that 'I'm going to kill you after dessert smile,' but soft. Approachable maybe, if I actually knew what that kind of smile looked like. That makes matters worse. I'm pretty sure she's harvesting dirt for some later use. The cat's trying to imitate a cute dog, but it's not working.

Around 9:00, it is time to do the nightly barn check. Since most of the turkey is acting like a bowling ball in everyone's intestines, the whole entourage decides to pitch-in and see what mischief the horses are creating. The cat chooses to stay, as a carcass is just too much to pass up.

Uncle Bert leads the procession, once again launching into the tale of Aunt Ellen's hat. The rest of the folks break into small groups, stopping by each stall to tell the occupant how cute they appear to be. The horses respond by either blowing their noses on someone's clean shirt or removing whatever part of a relative's anatomy that happens to be handy. After twenty minutes of this carnage, the whole troupe heads back to their cars and drives safely home.

Jesse and I collapse on the couch. Family things are hard work even when most of this family was adopted anonymously. I put my arm around her and for once it's okay. A Bing Crosby tape is playing in the background – something about a muddy Christmas.

"It wasn't so bad," Jesse said.

"Even Uncle Bert?"

"Funny man. I liked it when he tried to feed Boo a drumstick. I hope your sister's boob is okay. I told her not to get too close to that colt."

"Yeah, I'll mail back her bra. I'll go to 'Cups Are Us' and get it fixed."

"Don't. I can't stand you sometimes."

"I always figured that. You still mad?

"Yes. Well, maybe not. You just won't give up and I still don't know why I'm here or what you want from me. I was doing just fine before…" She suddenly stopped talking, went a little blank and left the sentence hanging in midair.

I waited politely for the dangling conclusion, but it wasn't going to materialize any time soon. "What's your father going to say?

"A lot."

"Sorry." Well, only slightly. Curious was still pretty high on the list, what with this image of a guy surveying his front lawn. "He a gardener?"

"No. Engineer. Listen, I don't want to go…enough, okay?"

"How can I know you without knowing a little something about him?" God, I sounded like a guy pretending to be some other guy.

"I'm nothing like him. Are you like *your* father, which seems to me like a much better question?" She was blowing hair out of her eyes again. Another eye contact session had started.

This time I locked on. "Ya know, I don't know the answer to that."

"And you can live with that?"

"Well…I guess. I have to. I met him once and it wasn't the best kind of situation."

"Why?"

"That's not fair. You don't reciprocate…play fair really."

"Where did you get *that* word? *Reciprocate!* Earl would call that a $3.00 word. And no, I don't play fair, not always. *Okay?* What was it like? I mean him…like?"

"Look, it was disappointing, that's all. He can't live in this world, not like other people. Seeing me sent him off on a six-month binge. I was looking for some answers and all I got was…guilt I guess. He finally blew a blood vessel out in his brain. All that from just seeing me. It doesn't go anywhere from there."

"Did you like him?"

"Like? I don't know. He was smart though. Probably where I got *that* word from. Other people liked him it seemed. He always seemed to be helping other people. It was weird, I mean he didn't have any-thing…nothing, and it didn't seem to matter. Look, I roll it around in my head and the only thing I come up with is that it's safer for everybody to leave it the hell alone."

At that she broke her gaze and closed her eyes. I felt a little hot around the edges and not sure if anybody's question really got answered. Probably because the questions were like 'Who killed Kennedy?' and the answer would probably never be found even if you read all 912 books written on the subject. So what then? A truce? We just look at each other and not our-selves? Or we could just get an Ouija Board and magic-finger all the important stuff.

"You're mumbling again."

"I'm thinking."

"Whatever."

We fell asleep on the couch, not because of Bing, but because of what turkey (or eggplant) does to a person. I had the strangest dream. Or, I re-wrote a Stephen King novel. I'm not sure which. It went something like this...

Fast Rudy

 nce upon a time, in a faraway land, a young lad named Young Jack was sent on an important family matter. Wearily trudging through the countryside, Jack hoped to trade his last bag of magic beans for a $5000 claimer. Jack's mother, who trained some runners at a local track, was having a terrible season. In fact, she was down to her last horse, a sad looking gelding named Fast Rudy, who had never been able to get in a race because of a red spot on his butt. It really wouldn't have mattered in most cases, except that it had been overlooked on his registration papers, a discrepancy that the evil Sheriff of Nothinghappening happened to notice, who coincidentally moonlighted as a racetrack identifier, duly appointed by the governor to rob the poor and stop those 5-2 favorites from walking away with a race. He also had a 'thing' for Mrs. Jack, who was widowed after her husband stepped on a land mine in Cambodia. There was also this bony appendage on Fast Rudy's head, but so far everybody accepted the notion that it was simply a training device – like a run-out bit, only bigger and uglier.

Fast Rudy had been a tremendous disappointment for Mrs. Jack. The best he could do was run for a $2500 tag, but even so, he couldn't pick up a check if he couldn't run. Plus, he was coming back from a training injury, had coughed all summer and was on the steward's list for erratic running. By now, it was December and Fast Rudy's prospects for picking up any kind of check were almost as good as his chance for getting a meal. Zero. But for some reason, Mrs. Jack still believed in him.

Meanwhile, Young Jack was having his own problems. The search for a $5000 claimer ended at a small shack. The owner, a wizard named Obi Wan something-or-other, gave him the grievous news. Voice crackling like a broken welder, the old fellow spoke: "Yes son, all of them have gone. Gone away to run for big money at a place called Santa Anita. Can I interest you in a *Millennium Falcon*? Low mileage, recently overhauled. Your girlfriend would really like the color.

"Santa? And I don't have a girlfriend."

"Just a coincidence," the old wart answered. "What about the *Falcon*? This thing'll get you lots of girlfriends."

Depressed, Jack moved on. Someone was following him, though. After a few miles, the stranger caught up with him. "Hey, pilgrim," the tall man said. "John Ford is shooting a movie around here, and well, I can't find him anywhere. Ya happen to know where the Rio Bravo El Dorado Big Valley is?"

"Well, no. I'm trying to find a race horse."

"Ah, hell, give Mickey Rooney a call. He's done a lot of those pictures; little guy, lives in LA. "

"Okay. Say, where's LA?"

"Waaaaal, over thar pilgrim. Say, have you got a spare cigarette?"

"I'm sorry sir, but they haven't been invented yet."

A few miles down the road, Young Jack came upon the Scrooge Hay Company. That's it, he reasoned. *I'll trade these magic beans for a ton of hay and a bottle of liniment. That'll at least get Fast Rudy through the winter. Maybe by then...*

Young Jack's thoughts were immediately interrupted by the appearance of old man Scrooge himself. Bundled against the cold by an oversized down jacket, only his lips peered out at Jack. "So, you want John Gotti burned, huh? You must be Lucky Lasagna from Jersey."

"No sir, I need some hay. I have to feed my horse. A ton in exchange for these magic beans. Oh, and I need some liniment." Young Jack held out his hand, showing the six multi-colored beans.

"Magic?" old Scrooge inquired, his face creeping out of his coat. "Just what kind of magic, dear boy?"

"With these beans," Young Jack whispered. "You can meet Julia Roberts."

"Really? She your girlfriend?" Scrooge said. His smile gave away the value of the trade. "All right young man, I'll give you nineteen bales of hay and a half bottle of liniment."

"Nineteen?!"

"They're heavy bales, my boy," Scrooge countered. "Take it or leave it. If you don't buy it, I'll sell it to the Russians. They'll buy anything."

"But sir, Russians haven't been invented yet."

In the meantime, Mrs. Jack was trying to figure out what to do next. The race meet was scheduled to close on December 24th, a mere five days away. The final race of the card, *The Last Gasp Handicap*, run at 22 furlongs, looked to be the spot that Rudy had always needed. With a purse of five golden rings, three French hens and a bird in a pear tree, a victory would save Mrs. Jack from the poor house. Eat the birds, hock the rings. Real simple.

But there was still the problem with the red spot on Rudy's *derriere*. Once again, she confronted the assistant identifier, a one-legged hunchback related to the wicked Sheriff by marriage. His name was Quasi-Forget It. And boy, did he smell bad.

"Forget it!" he said bluntly. "No, no, no, never! Not in a million, zillion years!"

"Is that your final word?"

"No, this is. Forget it!"

Crushed, Mrs. Jack led Fast Rudy back to his stall. There were no oats for his dinner, no hay and hardly enough straw for his bed. Knowing how hungry he must be, she went to the adjoining tack room and searched vainly for something to feed to him. In her haste, she dislodged something from a shelf that fell into Rudy's stall. Soon, she heard the horse thrashing about his stall, a sure sign of colic. Rushing to his door, she arrived just in time to see him fall to the floor.

"Oh, my gosh! Rudy's sick!" she wailed. Glancing around the stall, she finally found the source of Fast Rudy's distress. Lying in his feed tub was a half-eaten fruitcake. And was it ever hard.

Summoning Dr. Gauze, the kindly veterinarian, the prognosis seemed grim. "When you eat fruitcake, you pay the price," he said. "It doesn't look good." He left Mrs. Jack with three cases of *bute*, a gallon of *Banamine*, electrolytes, a flu shot and a can of hoof dressing. He promised to stop by later. Fast Rudy only groaned. "Say, did your boy ever find a girlfriend. You know, he's gettin' on 25 years now...should have a girlfriend! Looks kinda' funny otherwise."

Tears rolling down her cheeks, she slowly walked back toward the tack room. Her progress was stopped by the sight of Jack pulling up with a cart of what appeared to be blue hair. Young Jack looked miserable as a toad.

"Fast Rudy's terribly ill," she said softly. "It really looks bad."

Young Jack's face drooped even further.

"What's in the cart, son?"

"Hay, or at least it used to be. It got rained on. I'm afraid that's all I have to show for the magic beans. I thought we could at least feed Rudy, but now...where is he?"

As Jack jumped off the cart and ran to the stall, Mrs. Jack was interrupted by her favorite jockette, one S. White and her seven agents. While the group of bickering agents surrounded Mrs. Jack, S. White slipped into the stall where Young Jack was sitting, Fast Rudy's head cradled gently in his lap.

"Poor Rudy," she said, her eyes beaming down at Young Jack. "Maybe this will help." Leaning down, she kissed Fast Rudy on the forehead. As Young Jack's eyes met S. White's, the world seemed to come to a stop. For a brief second, they were in Paris, sitting at an outdoor café, drinking red wine and eating *escargot*, not realizing that they were snails.

Outside the stall, Mrs. Jack had finally beaten off the seven agents with her broom. S. White wished Mrs. Jack well, slipped Young Jack a card for a motel in Fresno and disappeared into the darkness, leaving Jack with some throbbing things and a very sick horse. He kinda' liked S. White. Then again, he kinda' liked blueberry pancakes too.

But things change fast in a fairy tale. Four days later, Rudy was able to pass the fruitcake, and while one stall cleaner ended up hospitalized, the horse was on his feet, the fire once again dancing in his eyes. And to everyone's astonishment, the red spot on his butt was gone – vanished!

"Quick!" Mrs. Jack shouted. "Let's get him to the identifier before it changes. We only have an hour till race time!"

Arriving at the test barn, they were once again confronted by the wicked little assistant identifier. "You again!" Forget-It yelled.

"But the spot is gone!" Young Jack countered. "Ask Frosty."

Forget-It spun around, not knowing that Frosty, the overweight, albino steward had been standing there the whole time.

"Well?" Forget-It inquired sarcastically.

Frosty, sweating profusely, looked closely at Rudy's butt. No red spot could be seen. "Boy, it's warm," he said. "Don't you guys think it's warm? I think it's warm. Whew, it's almost hot..."

"What about the damn spot?!" Forget-It yelled.

"Oh, that thing. Anybody got any ice. Ah hell, it looks fine to me. The horse can run. I gotta get out of here. It's too hot to stand around and worry about it."

With that, Frosty wandered off, leaving Young Jack and Mrs. Jack to watch as Forget-It applied the official tattoo. As he quickly worked, the numbers and letters formed into an eerie XMAS 0 HOUR.

"Just a coincidence," Forget-It sniffed.

"Waaaal, pilgrim, I reckon you got a race. I could sure use a cigarette, but I guess they don't have any in this movie. How come you don't have a girlfriend? Most of my movies had one, but...shoot, I always ended up with a noisy sidekick and my horse...he was a goodn' though..."

Young Jack spun around, but all he saw was a tall guy who walked like he had something wrong with his hips.

Finally, it was time to run *The Last Gasp Handicap*. Fast Rudy drew the number one hole. Around the racetrack, a thick and menacing fog had settled on the course. In the distance, lightning flashed. The horses nervously pawed the ground. S. White coaxed Rudy into the starting gate, an immense steel and wood structure that stretched across the entire track, quickly removed once the horses were released. S. White shot Young Jack a quick little smile and mouthed the words, "Last chance." Jack just nodded. He already knew the name of the race was Last something or other. He was going to be First in the Last..."What?!" he shouted. She just shrugged.

The starter, one Claus Krinkle watched patiently while each horse settled in, waiting for a fair start. "There they go!" the announcer yelled as Krinkle sprung the gate.

Fast Rudy broke on top and quickly took command of the lead, Donner was second with Cheese Blintzes a close third. As the horses disappeared into the fog shrouded backstretch turn, the race-track suddenly went dark. Out in the middle of the track sat the starting gate, its electric motors frozen in the fog and pitch-black night.

"They're going to hit it!" the announcer yelled, his voice unheard due to the sudden loss of power. The crowd gasped as the horses rounded the final turn. Fast Rudy, at the head of the pack, could see the impending disaster. Somehow, someway, the red spot re-appeared on his butt, like the trailing light of a caboose, shining brighter than ever before. Illuminated in the ghostly red light, the horses followed Rudy safely around the crippled starting gate and once again vanished into the fog. As the crowd roared its approval at the outcome of the race, the fog began to lift, the lights returned to brightness and the sound of pounding hooves gently faded away. To everyone's astonishment, the horses were gone, somehow lifted into the night on the wings of the fog. As the crowd peered over-head, a small red glow emerged briefly from the clouds, only to vanish once again into the dark sky. On the ground, the tote board flashed its message: IT'S OFFICIAL!

Around 7:00 in the morning I was awakened by the phone ringing. Jesse was still curled up next to me on the couch. Extricating myself from her sleepy embrace, I caught the phone on the fourth ring. It was my sister. "Hi Andy. I hope I didn't wake you. Look, I found a bunch of bird bones and a cat in the car. He seems like a really nice cat. What should I do with him?"

I thought about it for a few minutes and decided that all things probably change. I glanced over at Jesse, dead to the world and figured that just maybe I should keep her and dump the cat. "Keep him," I said.

A few minutes later Jesse woke up, yawned and stretched. Cats stretch like that when they have something on their mind. "Why don't we go to bed?"

"We just got up. It's morning and…" Geez.

How many times had I *gotten close to a woman…too close, only to go to the store for a pack of cigarettes and never come back? It wasn't that I didn't know the way back as much as I didn't know the way forward. Sometimes the best directions are given by someone that is also lost.*

The cat was returned a few days later. Something about a missing canary.

THE END

AFTERWORD...OR AFTER THOUGHTS?

CONFESSIONS
OF A CARELESS LIAR

CONTRARY TO MOST fairytales, Young Jack and S. White did not marry. With the winner's share of the golden rings, Young Jack was able to start up his own training stable at Belmont Park. Mrs. Jack and Forget-It did, however, marry, retiring to a mobile home park in Florida, just a few miles from Gulfstream Park. Fast Rudy never did win another race, most likely because he was never found. Oh, Jack checked the motel in Fresno, just in case she...no such luck. Note on the door said, 'Gone out for cigarettes.'

Fairy Tales are like that though. Wishful thinking wrapped in a somewhat bemusing contradiction. Yeah, I'm bemused, confused and befuddled. I got caught in my own trap and I'm not that unhappy with *my* ending – or beginning.

Christmas rapidly gives way to the New Year. And it seems with *every* new year that is fortunate enough to pass our way, the opportunity to clear the slate and start fresh somehow falls victim to the peculiarities of being human. God knows, we try, but somewhere between the necessity for a little old-fashioned self-esteem and our credit card balance, the world gets a little fuzzy. I sometimes think that it is little more than a profound responsibility to the rest of the human race to not look too good, too often.

This year, as always, I will probably sit down at 11:58pm and go over my list of dirty laundry. A discarded sock here, a favorite shirt there and somewhere in the pile, the remnants of last year's vows. I will bundle up the mess, look toward heaven and tell whoever that happens to be listening, that next year will be different. Then, as usual, I will gather up the clothes, march to the bedroom and hide them in the closet. That's the great part about resolutions. No one seems to be keeping score.

Invariably, I tackle the big three: smoking, procrastinating and pro-crastinating about smoking. Smoking is always a tough one. Quitting seems so easy when you have just finished your *last* cigarette. The broken one you fished out of the garbage can. I usually puff up my chest, cross my arms and tell myself that an army of wombats can't shake my resolve. Then somehow I find myself listening to Dan Rather on the evening news as he recounts the mayhem of the day. Holes in the ozone, nuclear winter, silicon recalls and most importantly, the average down at Keeneland.

Before I know it, my eyebrows begin to sweat, my pulse pounds in my throat and that great wall of resistance crumbles to the floor. And since I fear that my very life is at stake, I convince my inner mind that just one more cigarette will be enough. Then I'll quit. Of course, we all know the rest: midnight runs to the 7-11, only smoking *other* people's cigarettes, experimenting with chewing tobacco (already tried that — hard to chew and vomit simultaneously), maybe a pipe – no, keeps falling out of my mouth. Life Savers, gum, a No. 2 pencil…and resentment. The addict's best friend.

Perhaps the primary problem with resolutions lies in the redundancy of the themes. Why pick the tough ones or those that really piss you off? What's wrong with simple, easy resolutions? Ones that are easy to execute, fulfilling to the ego and possible to handle in one afternoon. Something like: "I resolve never to lay naked under the tractor during a full moon." Accomplishing that simple act could furnish the impetus to finally break every ashtray in the house.

Around a farm there are always a lot of things that need to be resolved. In fact, there are so many of them that they could easily be spread out over six or seven years. Sort of like depreciating a truck. Thirty-percent the first year, ten-percent each year afterward and in five years the problem is com-pletely gone. Not only is it gone, but it generated a refund from the IRS in the process. Naturally, that was before tax reform. Nowadays, they would disallow the problem, penalize you an additional bad habit and insist that you only declare resolutions under five-acres in size. I suppose that they could also conclude that any person with that many problems has little time to run a business.

I don't think it is totally hopeless. Tragic maybe. But after a long year or so of trying to raise horses in the rainforest, managing an urban renewal project financed by subterfuge and counterfeit paperwork while dealing with the vagaries of humanity and the heart in general, I still believe that some resolutions can be met. I am going to start with these:

1) I am not going to let Doc breed a mare that is worth less than his lawnmower. She is going to have to find her own date.

2) The next time a horse knocks down a fence, I'm going to declare it 'environmental revisionist thinking ' and leave it that way. I have no idea what that means and nobody else will either.

3) I am never going to lose my temper with a yearling again. (Well, maybe.)

4) The stallion will learn some manners. I'm sure I can hire somebody mean (or terminally ill) to deal with that one.

5) Maybe consider moving my bed a little further from the window. Just a foot or so.

6) I will live to see a vet bill under $500.

7) I'm going to find a cat with some degree of loyalty <u>and</u> table manners.

8) I will deal with the manure pile before it decides to deal with me.

9) All halter breaking will take place in-utero.

10) I'll hear a trainer say, "You know, you could be right."

11) I am going to check my rubber boots for slugs before I put them on.

12) I am not going to get my thumb caught in the manure spreader... again.

13) I will confess the whole sordid story of farm finances to Elaine. Actually, I'll send her an anonymous telegram from Mexico.

14) I'm never going to try to look smart in front of Jesse again. Boy, that's an easy one. Wonder why it's so far down the list?

15) And, if it happens to work and she's willing, I am going to ask that woman to marry me. Or go steady, or…still, I'll have to quit smoking. And maybe reconsider the advantages of a college education. Who knows? Might write a book or something.

THE CONFESSION PART

The trouble with writers is that we're notoriously dishonest. We don't start out that way on purpose. The whole reason we do fiction is that nonfiction can be pretty boring, especially if you were raised in the 50's. That goes a long way to explain why "Dick and Jane" was never made into a movie. "See Dick run. Run Dick, run! Faster Dick! See the cops run after Dick. Run Dick, run!" Well, maybe it was, actually.

I also tend to believe in the notion that true fiction is a myth rather than a classification. All stories, whether verbal or written, contain elements of fact, bits and pieces of personal experience, wild bourbon-induced hallucinations, dates and times, history, sociology, psychology, bad parenting, art and theatre, music, war, and an assortment of cultural norms and aberrations. Since we are born with an empty brain, it obviously has to be filled with something. A story is little more than the contents of a sponge in the hand of a small child. Squeeze it, and part of a real life drips to the floor. The Library of Congress, that vault of immortality, will probably demand that I pick a classification for this book. I chose fiction since a few of the witnesses probably know where I live. If I do manage to libel, defame or simply hurt a few feelings, then fear not. I have already retained counsel and immediately after publication I plan to sue *myself* for incompetency – maybe malfeasance, or dereliction of some duty that a judge will be happy to point out. We can make it a class action if you like, though that will probably reduce everybody's share of the settlement to about 34 cents.

This book began as a series of columns penned for *The Washington Thoroughbred*, most written in the middle to late 1980's. Two gentlemen, Mr. Joe Laduca (Editor) and Mr. Ralph Vacca (General Manager, Washington Thoroughbred Breeders Association) decided to let a marginally witty farm manager pen some columns about life on the farm. Little did they know what they unleashed on the literate world. It took another two decades to convert an unmanageable pile of paperwork into a book. Most authors know why. It's a disease called 'life.' It gets in the way. The title piece originally appeared in the July 22, 1988 issue of *The Chronicle of the Horse*.

The title of this book is based on that short story. It was actually a true event, or maybe I believed it to be, or just wanted it to be. It occurred during the Hombre-horseshoeing school/Nancy Arbuckle's hair period of my life. During this short period, I was presented with a unique opportunity to own a Thoroughbred mare. Unique? Maybe that's a stretch. Given the rather embarrassing circumstances surrounding this purchase, I offer the *Dragnet* defense: the names and dates have been changed to protect the stupid: me.

This unhappy saga occurred during that portion of a young man's life known as the 'female relationship development period,' whereby all normal realms of decency are sacrificed in order to get laid by the woman of your dreams. It is the point in every young male's existence when the brain ceases to operate like a responsible organ and your underwear starts running the show. Mine was looking to make a corporate merger of major proportions. I couldn't think, responsibly drive a car, buy a can of soup or change a light bulb. Jimmy Carter once mentioned something about lusting with the heart. Okay, maybe it starts there, but some kind of arterial travel agent books it on a flight to your underwear. It's inevitable.

MARES, FOALS & FERRARIS

I was desperately trying to impress a certain newly arrived blonde from California. I think she was trying desperately to find something to be impressed about in me. Or, maybe she was just simply desperate for conversation. That's a lot of desperation when the only reward seemed to be a couple of incoherent sentences. You'd have thought we were both in Ethiopia searching for a can opener. Since I didn't have much money, or a red sports car, or even a decent haircut, the sum total of my available attributes could fit into a coffee cup. Finally, she mentioned that 'Daddy' kept a few horses at Santa Anita. I leapt at the opening.

"I've got a few Thoroughbreds myself," I blurted out, suddenly aware that my spine had curled into a knot. I knew what was next.

"Ooooh, I'd love to see them!"

Two hours and $500 later I was showing Daddy's girl a dirty gray Thoroughbred mare. She was very impressed, but kept looking around for the rest of the herd. That lasted for about a week. As it turned out, a Thoroughbred mare only ranks about a five on the social significance scale, while a Ferrari, particularly somebody else's Ferrari, adds up to a ten. So while romance headed up the freeway, the mare stayed.

'Old Gray Legs,' as I called her, really wasn't much of a mare. She was gray (obviously), short-legged, short-backed and when about to foal looked similar to a moldy watermelon with legs. But she was a Thoroughbred and regardless of her poor looks, I felt a far wider degree of acceptance as a Thoroughbred breeder than just your average short-fat horse breeder. Which added a certain elitist flair to morning press conferences held at the local feed store, conversations that allowed me to throw around names like *Mahmoud*.

"Can't find that kind of breeding anymore," I would announce, aristocracy flowing off my tongue in that nasally way only the British have perfected.

"Nope," the oat man would respond, sipping coffee from a Styrofoam cup. "*Moomud*, huh?"

"Won the Irish *St. Leger*."

"No kidding. What da ya have to pay for a horse like that?"

"Ah…" What could I say? I was into the guy for $150 worth of hay and *Mahmoud* had died in 1928.

When I purchased this great-great-great granddaughter of the Irish *St. Leger* winner, I was told that she was eight months pregnant. I assumed the termination of her pregnancy would be quite similar to events I had witnessed with cats. She would build a nest composed of old newspapers and dirty socks, disappear for a short time, followed by a parental explanation that skipped basic reproductive terms in favor of the stork story.

As her time came and went, I faithfully checked her pasture each day hoping to see a new foal. After about two months of this daily vigil, I was summoned to the front door by an eleven-year-old set of pigtails. Pigtails informed that she was with the 4-H (obviously a government agency of some kind), and that my mare was in full *estrus* and assaulting her pony in some fashion. The pony occupied the neighboring paddock. From the look on Pigtail's face, the situation was serious.

Not wanting to look like an idiot, or for that matter mess around with anything fully *estrusized*, I immediately called the local veterinarian. 'Doc' arrived later that afternoon. (All veterinarians are called 'Doc.' They hate being confused with dentists.) This Doc was quite thorough, but evidently born without a sense of humor. I told him how worried I was about this *estrus* stuff, especially since Old Gray Legs was due to foal any day now. With the look of an insulted waiter, he examined my mare.

"Yep, it's full *estrus* all right," he declared flatly. "Only one cure." Somehow I saw a $500 look in his eye. "Son," he went on. "There's a rule about this. You have to get pregnant to be pregnant! She's in heat!"

I guess that explained the rather extended gestation period. In Doc's mind, stupidity did have rewards. I paid him $100 for the visit and turned a very indignant mare loose. Like a homing pigeon, she made for the pony.

Fearing Pigtail would get the pony a lawyer, I hauled Gray Legs off to the stallion owner who had supposedly left her glowing in pregnancy the year before. He was apologetic, yet firm.

"You didn't own her when she was bred. Read your contract." He spit tobacco juice in the general direction of my big toe.

"Contract?" The only paperwork Gray Legs had was a tattered *Jockey Club* certificate and a hay bill. Outgunned, I handed her over.

Over the next ten months, I occupied myself with shoveling hay in one end of her and removing what came out the other. Not desiring to come out short in the animal husbandry department again, I hit the books. Foaling literature though, seemed for the most part to be written by relatives of Edgar Allen Poe. After three chapters on aneurysms, mastitis and breached deliveries, I was terrified. If women read these books, they wouldn't let a man within fifty-feet of them.

According to leading experts on equine birthing, my small barn needed rebuilding. I would have to camp in it day and night until the big event and I would need enough drugs and paraphernalia to open a pharmacy. It made me wonder: in the vast American west, which mustang boiled the water?

Once the carpenters were finished and my large overstuffed chair strategically located near her stall, I settled down and waited for the *signs*. I religiously checked her *bag* and poked her croup for signs of muscle softness, whatever the hell that was. Her bag, a horsey term for an udder, was always confusing as it would sort of expand and contract from morning to night like a tire with a slow leak in it. My expectations soared and fell with it.

Gray Legs seemed to enjoy the stall immensely, stretching out for long sessions of heavy breathing. I, in turn, had become a crazed insomniac.

Finally a milestone was reached. *Wax*! At least I thought it was *wax*. (Oh, here we go again.) *Wax* is like the ear variety only it forms on the milk faucets. It's a plumbing thing, maybe like running Drano down the sink to unclog the pipes. I moved into the barn in full battle gear. I had my rubber gloves, my towels and my two-volume set of "Equine Reproduction." The iodine and the scissors were placed within easy reach. The coffee machine and television were turned on and I brought the microwave just in case I needed it. I took to sneaking around the barn with the stealth of an Indian, not wanting to disturb what the books referred to as her *mental processes*.

About 3:00 am, Gray Legs got a really serious look in her eye and began pacing the stall. Suddenly, her water broke! I knew that because I was looking under her tail at the time. Down she went! I panicked. All my training turned into VCR instructions. Quickly phoning the vet, the only words I could find were, "She's foaling, Doc!" after which I hung up the phone and ran back to the stall. It would be a full two hours before I would realize that I hadn't told him who I was.

Back in the stall, this shiny, wriggly mass was halfway into the new world. My heart pounding, I reached down and touched it. It yelled at me! Suddenly, my courage returned. Pulling off the thin white amniotic sac from its body, I proceeded with all the midwifely chores I had so patiently studied. I toweled it dry, iodined anything that looked like it needed it, and did the boy/girl inspection thing. In about an hour, it had struggled to its feet, pitching and bobbing around the stall like a drunken sailor. Gray Legs was the perfect chaperone, nuzzling the foal into position to have its first meal. After tanking up on high-octane white stuff, it plopped into the straw and promptly fell asleep. By now, Gray Legs had donned an expression only mothers get to wear.

Collapsing into my chair, I drifted off to sleep, vaguely wondering what happened to the vet. Some hours later, I was awakened by a tapping on my shoulder. It was Pigtails from the 4-H.

"Well, you missed it," she proclaimed sarcastically. "But they're okay," she reassured me. "I checked 'em."

Later that spring, I gave the mare and foal to Pigtails. I just wasn't cut out for parenthood. If I wanted that much stress, I'd….well, I'd drive a school bus or something.

I still muse from time to time about where the blonde and the guy with the Ferrari ended up. Maybe they got married and had a kid. Talk about revenge. Ferrari doesn't make a station wagon.

Oh, the foal was a boy. At least I think it was.

EPILOGUE

THE ROAD TO forgiveness is not a straight one. Lot of turns, some lanes composed of loose gravel, sudden dead-ends and terrifying merges onto an interstate where the speed limit is far beyond your skill level. At the beginning of this book I alluded to the notion that "My Friend Flicka" doesn't live here. The implication, or perhaps indictment, is that life rarely mimics the screen.

Children are an extremely precious commodity. They are also annoying, frustrating and pretty messy. They live in a world of giants, with little understanding of the ways of this formidable tribe. Far too many of them perish along the path to enlightenment, victims of a rare but deadly enmity that slowly and imperceptibly corrodes that great armor of the spirit. Few children are immune to this assault and fewer still know the way back to the gentle light of trust.

As I approach my sixth decade, I find forgiveness to be a much less troublesome master. Time, and perhaps the mind itself tends to dim the screen that endlessly plays our past like some trailer for a movie we don't quite recognize. The highlights seem to get brighter, the lows fainter, while the overall picture loses focus. Quite often, forgiveness is simply a matter of exhaustion defeating anger.

And that in itself is a sad compromise. When I look back at my own family I tend to be startled by the sharp contrasts — how memory attempts to both deceive *and* clarify in a single swipe of the artist's brush. Yes, I am forced to condemn the actions and decisions of the warring parties, for they have broken the one unforgivable covenant of both nature and humanity: protecting the young. Apparently even that basic instinct has somehow been dismantled by the greater ambitions of what we have created: a society that incessantly seeks to apologize for the same failed lessons of the past while rushing headlong into what has always been an uncertain and dangerous future. And it is on those very coattails that all children travel.

I haven't been very kind to my parents in this book, particularly my mother, a woman who managed to make a career out of bad decisions. But I have also come to realize that a *Mother* is simply one role of many that winds its way through a single life. And perhaps that view, my view of her, is corrupted by that extremely narrow focus. She was also a 35 year-old woman with three children, three jobs, three destructive relationships and wants, needs and desires of her own; and somewhere above the relentless demand of surviving another day, a small bit of anything she could selfishly claim for herself alone. Perhaps her yearning for that moment was stronger than most. She was raised in Nazi Germany, in the very vortex of a world war, where the vulgar intentions of ordinary people carried the plague of uncertainty, depravity and annihilation to the front steps of your house. If you had a house. And perhaps that is where the truth really haunts the facade, for war is an erratic and disturbing canvas, and all that is supposedly real or deemed sacred or held closest to the heart is declared false or capricious, and violently swept away. What intangibles are offered for sacrifice when one person has nothing left to lose and the maelstrom asks for more? Perhaps it is here, at just such a point, that the soul tries to stand alone, and for once, falters at the task. It is by chance the crossroads where God and humanity no longer have anything in common.

As for the world, it seems that perhaps the generation plagued with the purest form of idealism in a troublesome century ultimately built a palace for the cynics. We lived long enough to witness the return of an errant boomerang and stand watch over a society devolving into violence, social dismemberment and tribal justice – the vivid evisceration of a once compassionate horizon. No, we never used the bomb again after Nagasaki, but we didn't throw it away either. You see, the last thing humans trust is another human being. It is the predator's code.

I tend to believe that the conclusions drawn from the first round of the Nuremberg trials had more to do with condemning civilization than with sending a few degenerate Nazis off to the gallows. Hitler may have been on trial, albeit in absentia, but Hitler was merely a symptom of a far greater disease, one that infects the very strands of DNA that make us what we are. Take away the good manners, the full stomach and the Sunday sermon and the shaking fists will take to the streets.

Hitler was no anomaly. Put together the same social and historical circumstances – the same fear and uncertainty – the us becomes them – and little Hitlers will sprout out of the ground like spring daffodils. For you see, the real shock to mankind's system was the perpetrator of the crime: Ger-

many. *White, educated, Christian, acculturated – and situated in the very heart of western Europe. This wasn't a bad month in the outback of Rwanda, and that is both the frightening and perhaps pathetic truth about the ambitions of man – any man. These were not crimes of passion committed in the heat of conflict, but rather a well-orchestrated genocide put forth in the footnotes of a business plan. A plan that excluded at least 10 million people. And we want to simply say that Hitler was an aberration? Hmm.*

We have an odd conflict, we humans. God, science and technology have created a triad in which we scamper about trying to suppress our ambition through moral boundaries. Most predators don't bother with such niceties and therein lies the conflict, and perhaps our path of continuity as a viable species. We make war in God's name and let science and technology not only pick up the pieces, but construct the means to break them in the first place. It is a battle between our conscience and our toys. And in the vast emptiness of all that may or may not exist beyond our very limited view, mankind may indeed be little more than a tree falling in the forest. The only witness to what might have been, or perhaps never mattered in the first place. Shakespeare without an audience.

As for horses? I hate to say it, but they still make more sense than people. The more complicated <u>we</u> get, the purer they become. There is an old horsemen's adage, one that has been around racing for as long as people have cherished the sport. It goes something like this: "A man can never die when he has a promising two-year-old in the barn." I don't imagine it to be exactly true, or for that matter, politically correct, but then it speaks universally to a couple of mankind's loftier and perhaps more useful inventions: hope and a uniquely human creation: laughter. Somehow we never completely exhaust the supply.

They Might Be Alive

Of distant fields and triumphs
An aging eye believes
That fading accolades upon
Such things we might deceive
As ghosts go rushing by the gate
And pastures fade to brown
This horse upon the edge does fall
Go round and round and round

Spirits leave to live in wood
Electric lights they dance
Carousels by night do haunt
These horses of romance
In children's hearts where horses dwell
Forever to survive
Touch such wood with gentle hands
They just might be alive.

1987

THE OTHER END